Hardly Working

Betsy Burke

RED
DRESS
INK
™

First U.S. edition November 2005

HARDLY WORKING

A Red Dress Ink novel

ISBN 0-373-89542-9

© 2005 by Elizabeth Burke.

www.RedDressInk.com

Printed in U.S.A.

Hardly Working

ACKNOWLEDGMENTS

My heartfelt thanks to Yule Heibel and her family,
my Canadian and Italian families, Elizabeth Jennings,
Jean Fanelli Grundy, Marie Silvietti, Helen Holobov
and Kathryn Lye.

For Brock Tebbutt and Joe Average

November

Chapter One

"So…Dinah. The big THREE OH," said Jake.

My mind hurtled back from the dreamy place where I'd been idling. I slammed my hand down on the mouse. The Ian Trutch page closed and up came the brochure I was supposed to be working on for the important December fund-raiser. The event would also be an opportunity to award the year's most generous donors and present the pilot project we'd been trying to push through for the last two years, the ecological aquatic waste treatment system, affectionately nicknamed "Mudpuddle" by those of us at Green World International.

"Hi, Jake." I swiveled around to look at him.

Jake Ramsey, my boss and the office's token male, hovered, filling up the doorway to my tiny office. He hid a nervous laugh with a nervous cough. "So…you've got your great big thirtieth coming up in a couple of days. How are you going to celebrate?"

"Shhh, keep it down, Jake."

"What? What's the problem?"

"That three oh number. I didn't expect it so soon."

"Life's like that. You just turn around and there you are. Older."

"Terrific, Jake. So who finked about my birthday?"

"Ida."

"I should've known." As small, sweet and wrinkled as a hundred-year-old fig, Ida worked the switchboard at the front desk. She was the employee nobody had been able to force into retirement. Well past the average employee's spontaneous combustion age, she was very good at her job. Irreplaceable really. She took half her pay under the table in the form of gossip. It was, she said, excellent collateral.

"Well, don't tell anybody else," I whispered. "I was planning on staying twenty-nine for another couple of years."

Probably too late. If Ida knew then everybody knew.

Jake looked expectant. "Big party planned, eh? You have to have a big party." His reformed alcoholic's eyes brightened with longing.

His own thirtieth birthday had sailed by a couple of decades ago, leaving him with a pear-shaped torso and an ex-wife who blamed him for everything from her lost youth to the hole in the ozone layer.

He often let us know that his only passion these days was his La-Z-Boy recliner positioned in front of the sports network. He was immune to women, he said, and no woman would ever trick him again. But Green World International was an office full of women. We weren't fooled.

"I don't know about a party. The trouble is," I said, "my birthday falls on the Sunday, and we've got Mr. Important

CEO from the East coming in on Monday morning, haven't we?"

"We sure do. Ian Trutch," sighed Jake, his features clouding over.

Ian Trutch was higher management. In our office, all higher management was referred to as The Dark Side.

The sudden announcement from the main branch about Ian Trutch had come just the week before and everybody was on edge. Trutch would be arriving in Vancouver to do a little monitoring and streamlining around our office. In other words, there might be a massacre.

As soon as Jake had let the Trutch bomb drop, I'd gone into a state of panic. I wanted to keep my job. The downside of working here was the pitiful wages, cramped ugly offices, weird volunteers, and all that unpaid overtime. The upside was the altruistic goals and the great gang of fellow party anima…uh…employees.

So I immediately Googled Ian Trutch, then called the scene of his last slaughter to try to get information on him. When I finally got Moira, my connection in Ottawa, on the phone, she nearly had to whisper. "Listen Dinah, he's ruthless…last month there were four more empty desks…lower-level employees. You think they're gonna touch The Dark Side? No way. I don't even know if I should be talking to you…Big Brother might be watching…and he has cronies… I've gotta tell you what happened to a woman here…uh-oh…one of his cronies has just come sleazing in…gotta go." The phone slammed down. I sat there a little stunned. I knew Moira was overworked and probably needed a vacation—bad. But four empty desks were still four empty desks.

So maybe he was ruthless. And if his Web-site picture was any indication, he was also first-class material.

Ian Trutch was beautiful.

The beautiful enemy.

Green World International's in-house magazine had run

a long article on him. It stated that Ian Trutch had been hired by GWI to bring the organization into the twenty-first century, that his aim was to make GWI into a smooth-running and profitable machine.

Profitable and *machine* were two words that did not fit Green World's profile at all. We were an *environmental agency,* for crying out loud.

GWI's current interest was biomimicry, which studies the way nature provides the model for a cradle-to-cradle, rather than cradle-to-grave, use of natural capital, or the planet's natural resources. Our mission was to redefine "sustainable development," make it less of an oxymoron, promote bio-diversity as a business model, and the idea that a certain kind of agriculture was killing the planet, and that the flora and fauna of a forest or an ocean did not need human intervention or human witnesses to be a success as a forest or an ocean. We were trying to talk world leaders and policy makers into letting the planet's last few resources teach us all how to live.

Simple, really.

If you happened to be God.

My job was in PR and the creative department, finding as many ways as possible to pry donations out of tight corporate fists. And I was good. My degree in environmental studies enabled me to scare the wits and then the money out of people, because the world picture I painted for the future was scientifically backed up and not pretty. Not pretty at all. And let's face it. Having a world-famous scientist for a mother may have helped a little. The biggest problem was making that first contact with the right people.

And now there was the whole water business. In the last year since Jake had been promoting the Mudpuddle model to our international counterparts, the office had gone crazy. We'd moved to bigger premises. They were still shabby as hell but bigger. Communications with the other Green

World offices, in Moscow, Barcelona, Rome and Tokyo, had been flying back and forth.

And the best part of all? We'd finally found Tod Villiers, the superdonor we'd been seeking. The government was going to match his donation one hundred per cent and it was a sum that ran close to half a million.

Tod was a venture capitalist in his late forties. He was fat, sleek, bald, olive-skinned, and had the most unfortunate acne-scarred skin and bulging pale-brown eyes. But the bottom line was that he loved the project, recognized its worth, and wanted to invest. He'd written a check that amounted to a teaser. So lately, I had to keep his interest inflated until the second and largest part of his donation was processed and his contribution awarded at the fund-raiser in the spring. Because although we'd also received the final check, it was post-dated. I wasn't worried though.

It did mean that all of a sudden, the spotlight was on us in a way it never had been before. We had begun paying fanatically close attention to anything that had to do with H_2O. National Bog Days and World Water Forums were suddenly big on our agenda. Never again would we take a long deep bath, use the dishwasher, jump into a swimming pool, or run the water too long while brushing our teeth, without feeling horribly guilty.

Green World was experiencing a huge growth spurt and this, according to head office, was why Trutch was being sent in. To do a little strategic pruning before the branches went wild.

"Listen, Jake," I said, "when this Trutch guy arrives on Monday morning, send somebody else out to get the coffee and donuts. Weren't we going to be democratic about the Joe jobs? Send Penelope."

Jake perked up and asked, "How are things working out with Penelope anyway?"

A deep, languid female voice broke into our conversation.

"Jake, darling, the next time you decide to hire someone who's good at languages, make sure they're old enough to drink alcohol and get legally laid first."

It was Cleo Jardine, GWI's Eco-Links Officer, and social co-conspirator to yours truly. Cleo is part Barbadian and part Montrealer, a wild-haired woman with coloring that makes you think of a maraschino cherry dipped in bitter chocolate.

She draped a slim dark arm around Jake's neck and half whispered in his ear, "Little Penelope has a trunk full of brand-new pretty little white things for her wedding night, Jake. She's got it all figured out. The perfect pristine little life. In any other situation I might find it charming."

"Huh?" Jake looked slightly startled. Then he laughed. "I know she's young, but she's very talented."

It wasn't the young and talented part that bothered us.

Well.

Maybe it did.

Just a tiny bit.

"The kind of talent we need in this office," said Cleo, "pees standing up. And if you had to hire another *female,* Jake, why couldn't you have hired somebody with a face like a pit bull but a nice disposition?"

"I couldn't find a pit bull with her qualifications," said Jake.

The new talent, Penelope Longhurst, was a very smart twenty-two-year-old. She'd graduated from Bennington College, summa cum laude, at the age of twenty. She was very pretty, too. She had big green eyes and shiny honey-blond hair. But if her necklines got any higher they were going to choke her. She was a self-proclaimed virgin and proponent of the New Modesty and Moralism Movement.

Every office should have one.

Since Penelope had come to work at GWI three months ago, we could sense her getting more superior by the minute, filling up with smugness. Any day, she was going to burst, and purity and self-righteousness would fly all over the office.

"It's fear," Cleo observed. "Penelope's just afraid. She's sensitive. You can tell she is. She just needs to get over that hump. No pun intended."

So it was sheer synchronicity that when I left Jake and Cleo and went down the hall to the ladies' room to splash cold water on my face and fix my makeup in the mirror, that Penelope, Miss Virgin Islands herself, happened to burst out of one of the cubicles in that moment.

She moved with maniacally nervous energy. I couldn't help thinking that a few orgasm-induced endorphins would have done her good.

For crying out loud.

They would have done all of us good.

She planted herself in front of the mirror next to me and fiddled with her buttons and hair and the lace at the top of her collar. Her fingers wouldn't stay still. They skittered all over her clothes like policeman's hands performing a search.

"Hey, Penny. Something wrong?"

She shook her head and huffed.

"So how's it going?" Bathroom mirror etiquette requires that one must at least make an attempt at friendly chitchat with fellow colleagues. I popped the cap off my new tube of cinnamon burgundy lipstick.

Penelope's expression was strange. She looked at me as if I were applying cyanide to my lips.

"Like this color?" I asked.

She stared at my mirror image and remained motionless.

I kept it up. "I figure you never know when some gorgeous specimen might come into the office, right?"

Her mouth became small and brittle.

I'm not a person who gives up easily. "Have to be prepared for any eventuality, I always say."

Now you would think, with Penelope being younger

than everyone else, and new to the job, that she might try to get along?

Be nice?

Speak when spoken to?

Even suck up a little?

But do you know what she said? She fixed me, one superior eyebrow still raised, and said, "You know what you are, Dinah? You're a man-eater."

I stared at her.

A man-eater?

A man-eater was something out of a forties movie.

An extinct animal.

And furthermore, Penelope knew nothing about me.

There was nothing to know.

Well, almost nothing.

In some ways my life was so narrow you could have shoved it through a mail slot. I was just plain old Dinah Nichols who three years ago had left her ex-fiancé, Mike, over on Vancouver Island, and exchanged her cozy and familiar little homespun angst for the big cold new angst in the city of Vancouver. I had been badly in love with Mike. Sloppily, sweetly, desperately, wetly, thrillingly, forever in love with Mike. And then I had one of those revelations about him. It came as a lightning flash from the overworked heavens. In twenty-four hours I had my bags packed and was ready to leave for Vancouver. I didn't even give Mike the satisfaction of a fight.

During my last three years in the city, I'd been operating on a tight budget, both financially and emotionally. I had a pared-down existence of work, home, home, work, apart from my occasional clubbing forays with Cleo and my next-door neighbor, Joey Sessna. Joey was the only man in my life. I'd spotted him at one of the GWI fund-raisers a few weeks after I started working there. He was the one guest who didn't fit the profile for that occasion (millionaire and over ninety). Joey was in his late twenties and remorselessly gay (he's quite appetizing in the smoldering Eastern European overgrown schoolboy sort of way, with his straight dirty-blond hair, his pale blue eyes, and his pearly but crooked teeth). The day I first set eyes on him, he had snuck into the event through a side door and was shoveling hors d'oeuvres onto his plate with the kind of style and abandon you only see in starving actors. I managed to wind my way over to him before anybody else could kick him out, and by the time the fund-raiser was over, Joey had performed his entire repertoire of imitations and given me a lead on the apartment I have now.

I tried to play things up. If I wasn't always having as much fun as I'd planned to, I at least tried to give the impression of somebody who was having more than her share of good times.

Whereas Penelope, as far as I could tell, had everything, and could have been having an authentic blast. She was fully financed by her wealthy parents, owned an Audi, credit cards, and could book airplane tickets whenever she felt like it. There were rumors of a nerdy, virginal boyfriend back East, and more rumors that he would pay a visit in the near future, no doubt to indulge in some heavy petting and assure himself that his Penelope hadn't been accidentally ravished by one of the office Alphas.

Through my lunchroom eavesdropping I knew that Penelope, before university, had been to a Swiss finishing school and it was there that one of the worst moments of her life occurred.

Penelope confided to Lisa that in the school's elegant dining hall, she was served rabbit on Crown Derbyshire plates. Nobody had been aware that those same rabbits had been her best friends, her furry confidantes, and that every night she'd gone down to the rabbit hutches to tell them all her woes (until they became dinner, of course).

She'd had no other friends at school. Penelope wasn't like

the other girls, that bunch of hoydens who slid down the drainpipe to hitch a ride into town to meet boys and neck and grope and have unprotected sex in the back of a car.

To hear Penelope going on about it, the Swiss finishing school had been torture to a soundtrack of cuckoo clocks. She'd watched from the sidelines as the other girls acted out their fantasies all around her, experimented with their commandment-busting sexuality, destroyed their best years through carelessness.

How tempted I was to cut in and challenge Penelope. I wanted to ask, "When in history have the teenage years ever been the best years for anybody? The teenage years suck."

And then there was her mortification with the results of her schoolmates' adventures. At first it was the smaller things, the broken hearts and first disillusionments, and then came the bigger things, the STDs, the pregnancies and designer drugs.

But Penelope had kept her head above water while the other girls had been drowning. She'd kept her corner of the room tidy and her virginity intact. She was able to replace her furry friends with books in other languages. They hadn't been hard to tackle at all. Everybody in Switzerland spoke at least four languages. And she had a taste for music, poetry and literature. In the lunchroom, I'd overheard her droning on endlessly to Lisa about her favorite books, *Le Grand Meaulnes* for its hopelessness and romanticism, and *Remembrance of Things Past* for the lost world she would have preferred to this modern one.

I had the impression that Penelope was like a new-age geisha, cultivated in arts and languages and femininity, putting everything on offer except the sex.

As for me, well, perhaps I'd overdone the whole business of single girl fending for herself. Because there *had* been offers of help from my mother but I didn't take them up. Our family's wealth had been dwindling for quite a while.

I stared back at Penelope's reflection in the mirror. Man-eater. It was a silly, outdated thing to say. I had to think about it for a second. Was it a backhanded compliment? Penelope must have made a mistake. She'd mixed me up with Cleo. Fearless Cleo Jardine, who saw the entire masculine population as her own private buffet.

I said to Penelope's reflection, "You've got the wrong person."

Penelope replied, "No I haven't. I know about you."

"I have a Green World question for you, Penelope. How do you say home, work, work, home in Russian?"

"Dom, robotya, robotya, dom."

"As in robot?"

"Yes."

"Thank you, Penelope, for that depressing bit of information. Now I'm going to say this to you once, and you better believe me. My life is dom, robotya, robotya, dom."

"I meant what I said. I know about you. You're a man-eater."

I didn't know how to defend myself. I'd grown up on the edge of a boreal rain forest and been homeschooled with a small motley crew of children, the progeny of artists, scientists, and freethinkers seeking an alternative existence. Now that Penelope was standing in front of me, I regretted never having been involved in a schoolyard scrap.

How could I tell her that it had been ages since I'd devoured a man, that I'd barely nibbled on one in over a year? Sure, I was hungry enough, but since breaking up with Mike, men had been getting harder and harder to digest.

Okay, I admit I may have given her the wrong impression. Accidentally on purpose. It had been *my* idea to get Ida at the switchboard downstairs to give the Code Blue signal any time a hot guy entered the building. And perhaps that could seem a little predatory to the uninitiated. Or the undesperate. But every woman in the Green World International office except Penelope put their shoes back on, slabbed on the cover stick, fumigated themselves with their favorite perfume and got ready to scope when Ida gave the Code Blue.

And I confess that it had been my idea to provoke Penelope a little once we understood her position regarding the opposite sex. She had *no* position. Not in bed, anyway.

Maybe she was still thinking of the day I got Joey to pick me up for lunch. I stayed away for two hours, then came back to the office with a rose in my hand, a little chardonnay dabbed behind my ears, and my dress on inside out. I stood in front of Penelope's desk for at least five minutes, so that she couldn't possibly have missed those great seam bindings.

She'd avoided me for the rest of the day. She hadn't understood that it was just one of our little office tests.

To see if she had a funny bone.

But the test had resulted negative.

And really, one ersatz male morsel during the lunch hour doesn't qualify a woman as a man-eater.

Sunday

Here it was, two hours and twenty-five minutes to the official end of my thirtieth birthday and I was still brooding on Penelope's words, wishing they were a bit true. I was still having trouble imagining me, Dinah Nichols, as a man-eater. Penelope clearly needed to get a life.

Cleo and Joey were late. We were supposed to be having a birthday drink together at my place. I'd even dusted.

Thirty was so big, so critical, so depressing now that I was minus a boyfriend, that I decided maybe it was something I would just brush off lightly.

Okay.

Deny completely.

It didn't matter, I told myself, that my closest friends had better things to do on my birthday. I'd just stay at home, holed up by myself and meditate on my singleness.

Okay, to be fair, both of them were very busy.

The office had sent Cleo down to the Urban Waste Congress in Seattle. Joey had gone down with her to do an agent audition there and they'd be driving back together.

Joey's film and TV roles were mostly very, very small and nonspeaking. He'd been lucky. He'd worked a lot over the last few years in sci-fi and police drama series. In the course of his career, he'd been slimed to death, machine-gunned in the street, set on fire, pushed off the side of a building, had his eyeballs drilled by Triassic creepers, had himself disintegrated into fine white talcum powder, and been sucked violently up a tube.

Ever the perfectionist, trying to improve himself in his craft, Joey often begged me to critique his performances. What can you say to a guy who has basically been fodder for extra-terrestrials? "Excellent leg work. Fantastic squirming, Joey. You really look like you're being mashed to a pulp."

I made some popcorn to stave off the gloom and settled back into the couch to wait for my friends. Some irrational part of me expected a sign that I'd reached that scary thirty benchmark, like an earthquake or a total eclipse of the sun. But it had been a very quiet Sunday, filled with vital activities like scouring the rough skin off my feet and giving my hair a hot oil treatment. By evening, I'd slumped onto the couch to wait for Joey's immortal three seconds in an ancient *X-Files* rerun. I was going to have to resign myself to a life of solitude and strawberry mousse.

Then the phone rang.

I jumped up from the couch too fast and tripped over the plastic bowl on the floor, scattering salty buttered popcorn all over the Persian carpet. It wasn't too late to hope. Someone had remembered after all.

Some ex-boyfriend from my past?

Or Mike—my ex-true love?

Or an ex-boyfriend-to-be from my future? Some guy I'd met at a fund-raiser then forgotten about, who might be a friend of a friend of a friend and had gone to a lot of trouble to get my number?

Or Thomas? My therapist? For all the money I was paying him, he was supposed to be making me feel better, wasn't he? And a little birthday call would make me feel better.

And then I remembered.

The Tsadziki Pervert.

He'd been phoning me up and, in an eerie hissing voice, proposing to cover my whole body in tsadziki. You know that Greek dip made of yogurt and cucumbers? Then he was going to scoop it all up with pita bread until my skin showed through. It had to be some guy who had seen me around. Probably with Mediterranean looks and visible panty line, knowing my luck. He knew who I was because he was able to describe some of my physical features. If it was him again, this would be his third and last call.

I skidded into the hallway and found the shiny silver whistle, the kind that crazed PE teachers use. It was supposed to be dangling from a string next to the phone for any kind of Telephone Pervert Emergency that might come up, but I'd forgotten to do it. I'd made a mental note to avoid all of Vancouver's tavernas and Greek restaurants but I'd forgotten to tie on the secret weapon. I held the whistle near my lips and got ready to pierce the Pervert's eardrum.

I know what you're thinking. Why didn't I have a call-checking phone or an answering machine? And you're right. I should have. But that would have taken such a big chunk of mystery out of my life. Not knowing who was on the other end, and anticipating something good, or something evil involving sloppy exotic foods, burned up at least fifty stress calories. And there was always that got-to-have Gap shirt to spend the money on instead.

My buttery hand grappled with the receiver. "Hello?"

"Happy birthday, Di Di."

"Mom." I was relieved and let down at the same time. If my own mother hadn't called, it would have meant that things were grimmer than I thought. "I didn't expect to hear from you. Aren't you supposed to be out in the field up there in the Charlottes?"

"Cancelled that, poppy. Off to Alaska in a couple of days. They want me to go up and take a look at the Stellar's sea lion situation there. Been following a project on dispersal and we've got quite a few rather far from natal rookeries. Shouldn't you be celebrating with friends, Di Di?"

"I am." I turned *The X-Files* up higher.

"Sound a little odd. Not on drugs, are they? By the way, a couple of things. Now…what would you like for your birthday? I think it should be something very special. Thirty. You're on your way to becoming a mature person."

As if I needed to be reminded.

"I'll give it some thought, Mom."

"Righto, Di Di. We'll be seeing each other soon anyway. I'll be popping in and out of Vancouver. Have several guest lectures to give up at the university. Migration of the orcinus orca is first on the schedule. They've organized an entire cetacea series this year. I told them I was quite happy to do the odd one as it would give me a chance to see my daughter. Oh, and another thing I keep forgetting to mention. Mike and his little wife came around several weeks ago."

"His little WHAT?"

"Tiny limp thing, Dinah dear. Believe they've been married for about three months. I should think she might just blow away with the first strong wind. Don't think she'll be helping old Mike much with the hauling."

"What hauling?"

"She and Mike were just about to move to Vancouver

when I talked to them. I gave them your address and phone number. He seemed very eager to see you again."

I could feel the popcorn backing up into my throat.

I liked to blame my mother for the fact that I was cruising into the end of my thirtieth birthday and flying solo. And even if it wasn't her fault, I needed to blame my manlessness on someone. She was the logical choice.

I'd often whined to Thomas, my therapist, "How am I supposed to deal with a proper relationship? I've had no role models. My mother thinks that men are beasts of burden who are useful for mending your fences, mucking out your stables, feeding your seals and whales, and worshipping at your feet, but should definitely be fired if they can't be made to heel."

My mother is a zoologist. Marine mammals are her specialty.

And Thomas would reply, "No life is accompanied by a blueprint."

As for a father, well, that was the main reason I was paying Thomas. There was just a terrible lonely rejected feeling where a flesh-and-blood father should have been.

Thomas was very attractive. I'd shopped around to find him. I went to him twice a month. He wasn't your full-fledged Freudian—I couldn't have afforded that. He was a bargain-basement therapist with just the right amount of salt-and-pepper beard and elbow patch on corduroy. He cost about as much as a meal at a decent restaurant but wasn't nearly so fattening. His silences were filled with wisdom. And he had a real leather couch. This probably worried his girlfriend upstairs. I could picture her creeping around, but then having to give in to her suspicions and stick her ear to the central heating grates, just to be sure that nobody was pushing the therapeutic envelope down in the basement studio.

I talked and Thomas listened wisely. Then he'd pull on his pipe, expel a plume of smoke, and sprinkle his opinions, suggestions and bromides over me.

All through my childhood, I'd fantasized about this father of mine. When I was six, and asked my mother who my father was, she gazed coldly and directly at me and explained that he was out of her life, and therefore out of mine, and that I was not to ask about him again.

My mother is tall, lean, white-skinned, rosy-cheeked and blond with the beginnings of gray. She looks like a Celtic princess and is considered beautiful by almost every man she meets. I'm medium height, black-eyed, dark-haired, and on the good side of chubby. Genetically speaking, I had to wonder if that made my father a short, dark stranger.

My mother had been orphaned young, and my great-grandparents, whom I vaguely remember as a couple of gnarled, complaining, whisky-drinking bridge players, had left her a trust fund. My mother is the triumphant product of an elite private school in Victoria where she and other rich girls bashed each other's shins with grass hockey sticks and studied harder than the rest of the city. There, she acquired her slightly English accent and a heartiness that plagued me all through my childhood. There was no ailment that chopping wood, cleaning fish or a good hike along the West Coast Trail couldn't cure. I was fit against my will.

From the day I hit puberty, I couldn't wait to get somewhere where the fish, feed, and manure smell didn't linger on my clothes.

I'm convinced that if my mother had grown up without a trust fund, and had been forced to have a man support her through a pregnancy, things would have been different. I would be a well-adjusted girl with a steady permanent boyfriend. Studying marine mammals is not exactly a lucrative profession. Only somebody with an independent income could carry out the kind of field work or maintain the kind of hobby menagerie my mother had over on Vancouver Island. The animals; the seals, raccoons, hawks, dogs, cats, sheep and ponies required extra hands and lots of feed.

When I was little, I was convinced that I too was a member of the animal kingdom and that all those pets were my brothers and sisters. To get my mother's attention, I would get down on all fours and eat out of the dog's dish. My mother didn't even blink. Maybe I really was just another vertebrate in all her *animalia,* an experiment, a scientific accident. But whenever I brought this up with Thomas, he'd tell me that I probably wasn't seeing the whole picture. Maybe he was right. And maybe not.

I knew what I wanted for my thirtieth birthday.

At twenty-five minutes to midnight, there was a knocking at my door. When I opened up, Joey barged past me brandishing a bottle of Asti Spumante. Cleo followed, holding a bottle of chardonnay. Both of them looked as though they'd run a marathon.

I followed them both to the living room, then Joey did an about-face, said, "Glasses," and went straight back into the kitchen to look for some.

Cleo flapped her long burgundy fingernails at me. "I know, Dinah, I know, we're so late and you're going to kill us."

"I don't turn into a pumpkin until midnight," I said. "That gives us twenty-two minutes to get toxic and sing 'Happy Birthday' to me. How was the conference?"

"Shitty, Dinah."

"Really?"

"No, literally. It was all about what we're going to do or not going to do with the planet's crap. Excrement. I feel like I need a bath. You know who the biggest culprits are?"

I shook my head.

"Cattle. The methane emissions from all the cow flop on

this planet are going to blow us from here to kingdom come."

"Imagine it, Dinah," shouted Joey from the kitchen, "all the way home in the car, I get to listen to a lecture about cow farts."

"It must have been a gas," I said.

"Har, har," he bellowed. I could hear him crashing around in my kitchen cupboards. "Dinah. You've got no glasses. Where are all your Waterford crystal wineglasses?"

"They were Wal-Mart, not Waterford and they got broken," I said.

It was a little embarrassing.

"All of them? Should I guess? Accidentally on purpose?" asked Joey.

"Thomas said it was okay to break things as long as nobody got hurt. Mike bought them years ago and I finally got around to breaking every last one. It felt great."

"Okey-dokey. We'll drink out of the Nutella jars. Who wants Minnie Mouse and who wants Donald Duck? I get Dumbo."

We poured the drinks and toasted my thirtieth.

Cleo sauntered over to my west-facing side window and gazed out. "Ooo. Your neighbor's awake. Very, very awake."

I panicked. "Close the curtains, Cleo. If you're going to be a peeping Tom, try to be subtle about it."

She whipped the curtains back across the glass and continued to spy through the crack in the middle. "God, what's that he's got with him? A black cat? Ooo. Hey. He's taking off his shirt. Look at that bod. Fantastic. So toned. That man is so buff. This is better than *Survivor*. Take off the rest of it, honey, we're waiting." Cleo's hot breath steamed up the window glass.

Joey raced over to the window and tried to elbow Cleo out of the way. "Shove over. Let me see."

"You gu-uuys," I protested.

Cleo's face was flushed. "I don't see how you can stay away from this window, Dinah? Does he always leave his blinds open? He is one hot hunk of man."

"How would I know? He just moved in. And I try not to spend all my time glued to the window spying on my neighbors."

It was a lie.

The new neighbor had moved in that summer. From the side window in my living room, I could look straight down into my neighbor's ground-floor living room. His was a nineties house with floor-to-ceiling sliding doors that filled the lower north and east side of the house. A tiny L-shaped patio had been created outside the sliding doors, and beyond that, a row of bamboo had been planted to shield the windows from the street. Except that from my second-story side window, I could see everything. It was like looking into a fishbowl, perfectly situated for anonymous viewing of his living room as long as I kept the lights turned off and the curtains closed. It was an exercise in futility though because my neighbor was gay.

The neighbor's partner would show up sporadically, sometimes for the weekend, sometimes for a couple of days during midweek, and there would be small moments, never anything overt, but a hand on a hand, an occasional woeful hug, long intense talks in the living room, wild uncontrolled laughter bubbling up, the both of them so easy with each other, so completely relaxed, that there was no doubting how well matched they were. They were perfect soul mates. I envied and admired them. From my window, their relationship appeared to have everything. Then the partner, who was small and dark in contrast to my heavier brown-haired neighbor, would disappear for a week or more, and my neighbor, obviously at a loss, would pull out his home gym and work out.

During those hot evenings in late August, I was behind

that curtain watching him move his half-naked sweat-shined body. And I swear, if Russell Crowe had come along and hip-checked my neighbor out of the way, and taken his place there at the bench press, and let the last shafts of light catch the muscular ripple of his arms and torso, you wouldn't have been able to tell the difference between the two of them.

August flowed into September and September into October and I still went to the window to catch a glimpse from time to time. My voyeurism told me that I'd been hanging on too long. How could I criticize the Tsadziki Pervert when I too was becoming an urban weirdo? I told myself that it was because I needed time before getting burned again. But now the years were beginning to speed up. I'd reached thirty without even realizing it.

"You can get your mind off his éclair, Cleo. It's not ear-marked for you. Take my word for it," said Joey, "Dinah and I have been surveying him for a while and we are happy to inform you that he is of the religion Pas de Femme. Where information gathering is concerned, we make the CIA look like a bunch of wussies." Joey's expression was triumphant.

"He's not gay," wailed Cleo. "He can't be, can't be, can't be."

"He is, he is, he is," said Joey, stamping his foot in imitation.

She clumped over to the table to pour herself another larger slug of wine. "The best ones. Always the best ones. And anyway, Joey, how do you know?"

Joey said, "I've seen him around. In the clubs."

"Which clubs?"

"Well. I've seen him at Luce and Numbers and Lotus Sound Lounge. And he always has his arm around the same guy. The guy that comes over sometimes. Small, dark French-looking man with zero pecs. I'm telling you, he's so monogamous he's dreary."

I took one last peep. The neighbor stood motionless now,

looking out at the sky and the luminous gray clouds that threatened to burst. It was odd that we'd never met, never crossed paths. Just bad timing, I supposed. He only lived next door, but his world and mine could have been a million light years apart.

"Oh shit," said Joey, "he's turned the light off."

"Probably tired of his voyeur neighbors," I said.

Cleo had turned away from the side window to face my big front French doors. She shrieked and pointed. Outside the windowpane, hanging in midair above the little balcony, dangling from a cord, was a shadowy man.

Chapter Two

The man-shaped silhouette waved.

I ran over and opened up the French doors, then stepped out on the balcony to help the guy down.

"Simon. You're back. Come inside before somebody calls the police."

With expert rock-climber's maneuvers, Simon lowered himself down to the balcony, then began to haul his cords down after himself and wind them up. He was grinning the whole time. I stepped aside to let him into the apartment, then I picked up his equipment and passed it through to him. He stood in the middle of the living room, straightened up and brushed himself off. He was dressed in black, and very lithe, thinner than when I'd last seen him, two years before.

"Hey, Di. Happy birthday. Figured I'd drop in on you. Hey, so cool to see you."

Joey muttered, "Now that's what I call an entrance."

I smiled at Cleo and Joey. "This is the Simon Larkin I'm

always telling you about. The one I grew up with. The one who shared my dog biscuits."

"Yeah," said Simon. "You could say that Di's my honorary sister."

Joey batted his eyelids and leapt forward to offer his hand. "Hi, great to meet you, Simon. I'm the famous actor, Joey Sessna. You may have seen me in—"

I punched Joey's upper arm.

He yowled. "Ouch. Jeez, Dinah. Wha'd you do that for?"

"Simon doesn't know who you are, Joey. He doesn't watch TV. He doesn't have to. He has real-life entertainment. When he isn't scaling some terrifying rock face, he's infiltrating some interesting urban landmark. Right, Simon?"

"Hey, babe. That's me." He grabbed me and squeezed me in one of his death lock hugs. Cleo and Joey were practically drooling. Simon was tall and toned with messy strawberry-blond curls and navy-blue eyes. He looked like a Renaissance angel in Lululemon sportswear.

Cleo grabbed my glass out of my hand, poured some wine into it, and handed it to Simon. "I'm Cleo Jardine."

He said, "Thanks, Beauty," and downed it in one gulp.

Joey began to jabber at Simon and I started to whisper to Cleo, "Before you get any ideas, there's something I've got to tell you about Simon…." But she and Joey were so involved in ogling him that they couldn't hear me.

"Hey Di," said Simon, "got any growlies in the house? I'm perishing with hunger."

I knew what was in my fridge. The Empty Fridge Diet was the most successful one I'd tried so far. We quibbled for a few minutes, then decided to call out for Chinese food when Cleo offered to pay.

When the food arrived, we all attacked it like starving refugees. But after a minute or two, I noticed Cleo and Joey making way for Simon as he helped himself two and three and four times. Simon had that effect on people.

Joey's chatter turned into a runaway train as he tried to impress Simon with his TV and movie credits. Simon just grinned and nodded but I doubted he knew what Joey was talking about.

I said quietly to Cleo, "Simon is a bottomless pit. You don't ever want to invite him over for dinner."

A sly look came over her face. "I was thinking I could take him to one of those all-you-can-eat smorgasbords."

Finally, when all the little cardboard cartons were empty, Simon rubbed his stomach and beamed angelically. "That was a nice little snack. We can get a proper meal a little later, huh, Dinah? After we've been out for your surprise birthday treat."

"A proper meal? What were we stuffing into our faces just now? And a surprise? It's after midnight, Simon. I've got a big day at the office tomorrow. The CEO's coming in from the national headquarters…"

"Dinah, I'm bitterly disappointed. When was midnight ever late for you? Better face it. You're only thirty and you're so far over the hill you might as well just lie down and roll the last little bit of the way into your grave." He fatefully shook his head.

I took the bait. I leapt up and began to run around, clearing up, snatching glasses out of hands and throwing away balled-up paper napkins and empty takeout boxes. "Okay, so where are we going?"

"Like I said, it's a surprise. And I should add that I actually put some research into this." I was very familiar with Simon's brand of surprise. I both dreaded and longed for it.

Cleo and Joey looked at each other, then at Simon and me, and said in chorus, like two schoolchildren, "Can we come, too?"

"You don't know what you're getting yourselves in for. This is my whale rub friend," I said.

"Oh my God," said Cleo melodramatically, "not your

whale rub friend? Now would that have something to do with massage?"

"Whale rub?" chirped Joey. "It sounds obscene."

"I'll tell you about it sometime," I said, "when I'm really, really drunk."

Simon nodded and chuckled. "Yeah. I'd forgotten about the whale rub."

"Please, Simon, can we come too, wherever it is you're taking her?" schmoozed Cleo. "I hate to be left out of the party."

"Can we, Simon, can we?" asked Joey.

Simon moved into his inimitable and rare business mode. "I don't know. You're going to have to be fast. Comfortable clothes. Dark stuff. No high-heeled shoes, eh, babe?" He directed this at Cleo. "No tail ends that could hang out or get caught in or on something. We should get going, Di. We've got a bit of a tight and squeaky time frame here."

I said, "What he means, is that if we don't have the timing perfect, we'll be like mice in a trap, squeaking our heads off. Simon doesn't have much respect for legalities."

"Aw, c'mon now, Di. I've got a most excellent lawyer. So let's breeze on outa here," said Simon.

Joey went back to his place to change and I lent Cleo something in black. I had a closetful. Nothing hides the fat better than black. While we were getting ready, Simon was going through my kitchen cupboards. He managed to find an old bag of sultana raisins, some chocolate chips, half a box of muesli, and a joke tin of escargot that I'd won at a New Year's raffle. He inhaled all my remaining food supplies and announced that it was time to leave.

Simon guided us up to the roof of the Hotel Vancouver in *Mission Impossible* style, dodging porters and chambermaids, coaxing us through poorly-lit, forlorn hotel arteries that gave off stale and slightly greasy-smelling odors, corridors and dark places that had a vague presence of skittering creatures nearby—rats, mice, pigeons. All the way up the endless flights of stairs, he whispered, "Don't fall behind."

I managed to keep up with Simon. Joey, who was skinny and hyperactive, was just behind me. I sprinted along but my legs felt it around the tenth floor. Cleo, who was only interested in physical activity if there was a man dangled like a carrot at the end of her efforts, lagged about a floor behind us all, complaining that she wished she'd made her last will and testament before we'd left. We went up and up and up until we reached a door. We followed Simon out into a long musty narrow corridor lined with tiny gabled windows that looked out onto the city, a zone where chambermaids must have slept once, country girls who cried into their pillows night after night until the city was finally able to distract them.

Once he had coaxed us all out onto the roof, Simon explained. "The idea behind a good urban infiltration is to take the road less traveled, find those forgotten back routes and rooms. For example, I've got a friend who did an infiltration in a part of the University of Toronto. He kind of lost his way and ended up taking a tunnel to another wing that had all these more or less abandoned barrels stored there. They were full of slime. No kidding. Later he found out the barrels were used to store eyeballs. Hundreds of thousands of eyeballs. Must have been part of the ophthalmology department. That's the fun of it. Discovering things. He said it was a pretty freaky place. Could have been a hiding place for all kinds of crazies."

We were seated precariously on the green copper roofing looking out over the myriad of city lights under the cloudy night sky. The gray stone of the hotel plunged downward just a few feet from where we sat. We could see between the glass high-rises to the North Shore and Grouse Mountain high up in the distance. Beyond the dense bright core of downtown in the other direction I could see the Burrard and Granville Bridges, the beads of car lights in constant motion.

Simon opened his small backpack and pulled out a bottle of Brut. "For you, Di. Happy birthday, eh?"

"Jeez, Simon, if somebody had told me that I was going to toast my thirtieth birthday on the rooftop of the Hotel Vancouver, quite a different picture would have come to mind."

"It's exciting," shivered Cleo, paler and stiller than usual.

Joey nodded in agreement, looking no less terrified.

Simon could have been telling Cleo and Joey that the earth was flat and the moon was made of blue cheese and they would have had the same expressions on their faces. Simon was so decorative, so distractingly gorgeous. I should have, I really should have told them what else he was. And wasn't.

"Fascinating," oozed Cleo.

"Absolutely," agreed Joey.

"Now I have something to say," I announced.

"Here, here," said Cleo.

"I have to inform you all that Penelope Longhurst…"

"Oh God, here we go," said Cleo.

"Penelope Longhurst has decided that I, Dinah Nichols, am a man-eater."

"A what?" squealed Cleo.

"How quaint," said Joey.

"You been up to tricks while I been away, Di?" asked Simon. He laughed, took the Brut bottle back, popped its cork, took a swig and handed it back to me.

"Not enough tricks," I said.

"Now let me see," said Cleo. "There are the Joan Crawford, Lana Turner, Sharon Stone, Madonna, Hollywood kinds of man-eaters. Then there are the literary kinds—the Iris Murdochs and the Sylvia Plaths who eat men like air."

Joey said, "Actually, the image that comes to my mind is more basic—a jungle animal, a lioness ravaging some poor male."

"If only I had it in me, Joey. I hate to say it, but that Penelope's starting to piss me off big-time," I said.

"We're pretty sure she was sexually traumatized at some point in her young life when she was at Swiss finishing school," said Cleo.

I muttered, "I wish somebody would sexually traumatize *me*. It's been nearly three years if you don't count that one stupid little mistake with Mike. Here's my point; if the shoe doesn't fit, cram your foot in a little harder until it does. Here's to me, Dinah Nichols, man-eater." I raised the bottle and drank.

Monday

I felt as though I had a hamster wheel in my head. And worse, the hamster was hungover. I made a list of all the no-brainers I could do that day to make myself look busier than I was. Penelope wafted past my open door with her The-Intact-Hymen-Shall-Inherit-the-Earth look on her face. Jake was right behind her and when I caught his eye, he pointed at her and mimed eating something. Yipeee. He was sending her on her way to do gopher errands.

I felt a bit better and was just contemplating how to continue avoiding any real work when the office intercom suddenly erupted with Ida's voice at top volume. "CODE BLUE, and I mean REALLY REALLY BLUE." I raced out of my office and into the main room.

What was left of breathable air was bombarded with fragrant powders and atomized scents. A frenzy of beautifying shook the office. Jake came out of his office, too, and looked on, shaking his head.

Ida's voice came over the intercom again. "Code Blue about to advance."

We all raced over to the window. On the street below, a black Ferrari with beige leather upholstery was inviting the local grunge merchants to either take it for a joy ride or just leave it where it was and vandalize it. But a second later, a svelte figure in a dark-gray glam Goth suit stepped out on the sidewalk.

Ida's voice broke in again. "Code Blue looking better than my dreams."

He had a full head of messy black hair with a hint of silver that stayed perfectly in place even though huge gusts of wind were making litter roil up the street. He gazed up at the facade of the GWI building. We all leapt back out of his view, except for Lisa Karlovsky, our big blond volunteer coordinator, who smiled and waved down at him. Then she turned her head upward and laughed. "Guess who else is hanging out the window upstairs?"

"Not Ash?" said Cleo.

We all shoved and jostled and pushed ourselves out through the window frame to get a look at Ash looking at Ian Trutch. She was leaning out above us, her glasses dangling from her hand, her dark eyes wide.

"That," said Lisa, "is the first time I have ever seen her without those bottle bottoms covering her face."

"We should hold a press conference," said Cleo.

Ash, otherwise known as Aishwarya Patel, was our entire accounting department. Thin and sallow, of undetermined age and wearing a dull black frump suit intended to be a power suit, Ash seemed to think she was the most important person in our organization because the donation money was processed by her. She was allergic to the human race and ate her daily lunch of sour grapes at her desk in her office. Her door was always closed. All communication from Ash came through e-mail directives, usually capital letters, which came across like cyber-screaming. Even though her office was upstairs, right next to the lunchroom, where all of us made at least ten stops a day at the fridge full of goodies, Ash found it too socially challenging to get up and walk those few feet into the lunchroom to tell us anything in person, to give us, for example, her last earth-shaking directive, TO ALL OFFICE STAFF: DO NOT STIR COFFEE THEN PUT WET SPOON BACK IN SUGAR BOWL. LUMPS FORM.

And I heard that Jake, in a rare moment of unprofessionalism, sent an e-mail back to Ash, "Well, hey, Ash, sweetheart, that's life. LUMPS FORM."

Ian Trutch frowned up at all of us, then walked toward the main entrance.

Ida's voice burst in. "Code Blue advancing. Code Blue advancing...oh baby..."

We all pulled ourselves back into the room.

"So that's the big mucky-muck, eh? The new CEO. Like them apples," said Lisa.

"It's him," said Cleo. "And thank goodness for that. Can't have a morning's makeup wasted."

Fran, the secretary, said, "He's had work. I'd put money on it." Since her husband had dumped her and her three children for Silicon Chick, Fran had been wearing her forty-nine years, crow's feet, double chin, limp gray hair and extra hip-padding with pride. Her favorite game these days was Spot The Cosmetic Surgery. "He's a careful piece of work, I'll bet. Expensive work."

"Fran." Cleo laughed. "He's only in his thirties. Why would he need work?"

"Wake up, sister. This is the Age of Perfection. And perfection can be bought," she snorted. "But I just want to add the footnote that I'd let this one warm my bed on a cold night, nose job and all, just as long as he's out of it by morning."

I was reserving judgment. I got myself a cup of coffee and went back into my office to think about what I'd just seen. Ian Trutch was everything we were not. He was trouble in a fancy package. And it was going to be very bad for our image to have a CEO who whizzed around town in a black Ferrari. But then the frisson of nervousness kicked in and for the next few minutes I fantasized about meeting the enemy halfway and riding around in a fast car with an even faster man. Something I'd never done.

The ringing phone interrupted my reverie. I picked it up and said, "Dinah Nichols."

The voice on the other end was incoherent. It took me a minute to realize it was Joey. He was crying and stuttering.

I said, "Joey, Joey, calm down. I can't understand a word you're saying."

All I could make out was "hoia…coy…hoia…glop… oodle" between the gasps and the tears.

I tried again. "What's happened? Get a grip on yourself."

"It's too horrible…." sobbed Joey.

"Just take a few deep breaths then tell me slowly."

There was a wet silence and then he started. "You know I walk dogs for Mrs. Pritchard-Wallace out near Point Grey?"

"Yeah?"

One of Joey's filler jobs.

"Not anymore."

"What happened?" I asked.

"Well, early this morning I was taking Jules and Pompadour, Mrs. PW's miniature poodles, for a walk along by the golf course, when this thing, this creature from Hell comes streaking out of nowhere, snatches Pompadour in its jaws then streaks away. Nothing left but Pompy's diamond collar. It was a wolf. I'm sure it was a wolf."

"It was probably a coyote."

"You're kidding me, Dinah."

"Was it sort of a yellowish color?"

"Yes, my God, it was. How did you know?"

"Don't you read the news?"

"*Variety.* I read *Variety.* You know that. I haven't got time for global disaster."

"Jeez, Joey. They figure there must be at least two thousand coyotes in and around town. They can't catch them because they're just too smart. I'd heard about them, I'd just never had a firsthand account. Wow."

"Wow is right. Mrs. PW's going to have hysterics. She doesn't know yet. She's out getting her facade renovated."

"Her what?"

"Getting her face stripped and varnished. A peeling and a facial, darling."

"Oh."

"And I'm shaking all over. I'm going to have a Scotch right now."

"Joey. At nine forty-five in the morning?"

"It's not every day somebody's thousand-dollar poochie gets to be part of the urban wildlife food chain."

"God, yeah. Listen, Joey, you don't want to get the coyotes used to a diet of expensive house pets. It might build their expectations. You know? Like potato chips? Once you've had one, you just can't stop. So don't encourage them…careful where you walk your dogs. Listen, speaking of predators and prey, the big boss from the East just blew in driving a Ferrari and I'm really worried, I've heard he's completely insensitive to people's feelings. He decimated the last office he was in and then some. And I'm told that there may be a total massacre in this office, too…"

It would have been better if I hadn't looked up at all.

"Ooops…gotta go." I slammed down the phone.

He, Mr. Silent Shoe Soles, was standing in my open doorway, staring at me. The CEO. He was so luscious-looking in real life that I could hardly swallow.

Chapter Three

Ian Trutch continued to stare at me. I tried to match his stare but I couldn't stop myself from taking inventory. My eyes went first to his face and then to the mahogany skin and black chest hair at the neck of his unbuttoned white shirt. I swallowed with difficulty. If I'd been another kind of girl, if I'd been Cleo, for example, I would have been tempted to climb down inside that crisp shirt and stay there. Maybe all day. Definitely all night. Little things, the length of his fingers, the way his cuffs circled his wrists, made me shiver.

He had eyes the color of swimming pool tile, surrounded by long, black, almost feminine lashes, and a little set of deep thinker creases between his eyebrows, reflecting his Harvard Business School prowess. His thick, silver-black, stylishly electro-shocked hair was just waiting for some girl's hands to give it a good running through, though I suspected he was the type who didn't like having his hair messed up. Everything else about him was immaculate. He had a know-ing, ever-so-slightly cruel mouth and a pirate's tan.

Sailing, sailing, sailing the bounding main...

It was a good thing I knew where the boundaries lay and wasn't the sort of girl who fell for that whole superficial gorgeous man thing. If I had been a real man-eater like Cleo, I would have considered pursuing him for his body alone. Like wanting a whole bottle of Grand Marnier for yourself, it would be a sweet, intoxicating blast, but ulti-mately bad for you.

I stopped staring at him. He definitely clashed with the office décor, the splodgy lemon custard walls, the burnt car-amel Naugahyde furniture, the mangy, pockmarked beige wall-to-wall carpet. The big question kept nagging at me. Why was a glossy high-rise type like Ian Trutch playing CEO to a low-rise walk-up organization like ours?

Jake appeared behind him. "Dinah, this is Ian Trutch. Ian, this is Dinah Nichols, our PR and communications associate."

He reached out his hand then clasped mine in both of his. They were warm and smooth. "Dinah. Very, very nice to meet you. I've heard a lot of good things about you."

I swallowed. "You have?"

"You're the girl who goes after the donors. Jake's been tell-ing me about you."

"He has?"

Ian Trutch still had my hand prisoner. I knew I shouldn't fraternize with the enemy in any way, but when he let go of it, my whole body screamed indignantly, "More, more."

He added, "Join us, won't you, Dinah? I'm just going to have a few words with the staff in the other room," and then he touched my shoulder. I stood up and like a zombie, fol-lowed the two men out into the main room.

As soon as Penelope saw Ian Trutch, she bounced to her feet and went up to him. "Welcome to our branch, Mr. Trutch. Can I get you a coffee?"

Ian Trutch's face became delectable again. He said, "Yes, thank you...and you are?"

"Penelope."

"Penelope. A classical name for a classical beauty. Don't wait too long for your Ulysses. I take my coffee black and steaming."

Every woman in the room was staring, breathless, vacillating between envy and lust.

"Sit down, Mr. Trutch. I'll bring it to you," said Penelope.

But Mr. Trutch didn't sit down. His tone became snappy. "There's going to be a meeting in the boardroom upstairs in exactly thirteen minutes. Ten o'clock sharp. Everyone should be present." He took one sip of the coffee Penelope had brought him, put down the mug and walked toward the back door. On his way out, he winked at me and said so softly that only I could hear, "Get ready for the massacre, Dinah."

A little laugh escaped me.

He'd recognized me for who I was.

The worthy adversary.

I was looking forward to the battle, to showing him that our branch of Green World International was a great team. Excluding Penelope, of course.

Jake looked slightly ill. He turned away and headed back into his office. I followed him in. He sat down heavily then looked up at me with his tired bloodhound eyes. His hand was already dipping into his bottom desk drawer. I had a microsecond of panic that he might have a bottle hidden in there but he pulled out a Bounty Bar, ripped it open, and finished it in two bites. Then, ignoring the little chocolate blob dangling from his moustache, he tore open an Oh Henry! and gestured to the drawer as if to say, "Help yourself."

"No thanks, Jake. I'll just sniff the wrappers. I'm counting calories." I was always counting calories. *Four thousand, five thousand, six thousand...*

He didn't come out and say, "Ian Trutch doesn't belong here," but I knew he wanted to.

"Jeeee-susss," sighed Jake, shaking his head. "I'm not sure I'm ready for this. I've got kind of a creepy feeling. A few years ago a feeling like this would have had me out of here and heading for the pub."

I couldn't stand to see Jake depressed. "Well, let's think positively about this."

He gave a sad little chuckle. "Ah…yeah, sure, Dinah. That would be the world's greatest female cynic talking to the world's greatest male cynic."

"Well…there are some donors out there who respond better to the kind of image that Ian Trutch has. Maybe a little polish could attract more of the kind of donors we're always trying to attract."

"Polish, Dinah? I don't know. I guess…"

I could see how troubled Jake was by all of it, by the suit that followed the lines of the perfect body perfectly, the chunky gold Rolex watch and sapphire signet ring, the aftershave that smelled like a leathery, wood-paneled library in an exclusive men's club.

I'd spent most of my dating life with Mike, who was gorgeous in a subtle downscale kind of way. But Mike was a man who had, maximum, three changes of clothes, the highlight of which were artfully faded jeans and a pair of expensive but battered Nikes. Formal for Mike was a clean T-shirt.

It was the first time I'd ever been monitored and streamlined by such chic management. When I stepped back out into the main part of the office, I realized that it was a first for all the other women, too. The female energy was radioactive, buzzing out of control. The other women in the office were primed, and when ten o'clock rolled around and we trooped up to the boardroom, they were all ready to convert to his religion, whatever it might be.

Ian Trutch strode into the room, stood at the end of the long table, looking around him as though he were checking out all the emergency exits, then he nailed each and every one of us with those blue eyes and said, "First of all, I know how you're feeling and I just want to reassure you all that my presence here does not represent what you think it represents."

The tense expressions relaxed only slightly.

"I don't know what you've heard from the main branch, but I want it to be understood immediately that this branch and the main branch represent two situations and methodologies that are in no way analogous. Main branch is the administrative headquarters so it follows that it was getting top-heavy with administrative personnel."

Top-heavy? According to Moira's version, it was the little guys who'd been axed back East. The people who did the legwork. The people like us.

"I've been told that this branch is known for its teamwork." He smiled. "But it needs to be stated that the individual player, for the sake of the team, will be rewarded for any private initiative taken in terms of information exchange. In the weeks that I'll be monitoring this office, I'll expect the maximum effort from everyone. It goes without saying that if there is deadwood here, then it will have to go. It's also possible that there will be no redundancies. I want it to be known that there will be no unnecessary suffering. So let me just finish by saying that I am looking forward to a fruitful collaboration." He smiled radiantly.

There was an audible group gulp. We weren't sure whether we were praiseworthy or being judged guilty before the crime had even been committed.

And then he launched into his strategy. It was all in code of course, full of very businessy-sounding words that had little to do with the way Green World International operated. Best practices, upstream, downstream, outsourcing.

Somewhere around the word *input* I looked sideways at Cleo. She had obviously fallen into a fantasy involving Ian Trutch and a round of input, output, input, output…

Lisa Karlovsky was sitting on the other side of me. She elbowed me and scribbled on a pad, "You following this?"

I scribbled back, "Sort of. Don't trust him."

She scribbled, "Don't care. Waiting for him to smile again. Catch those nice dimples."

Cleo, who was on the other side of me, grabbed Lisa's pad and wrote, "Like to see all dimples. Not just head office dimples but branch office dimples too."

For the rest of the meeting, I watched Lisa and Cleo watching him. The women were all working hard to understand as much as possible of Ian's talk, but also to keep a euphoric expression off their faces, their jaws from relaxing. Except for Penelope, the little priss. She was taking notes briskly.

When Ian had finally finished, Jake stood up and went over to corner him in private. Cleo, Lisa and I huddled together.

Lisa whispered to us, "So. What was it we were supposed to understand from all that razzmatazz business-speak?"

"Sorry, I drifted. I didn't follow it. He's so amazing to look at, to breathe in," said Cleo.

"I'm not sure," I offered. "It sounds good at first, like we're all supposed to be working together, but then you realize that what he's really saying is that we're all supposed to be spying on each other to see who the biggest slack-ass around here is and then go running to tell him about it."

Lisa said, "I totally lost track. I was imagining what he'd be like naked and horizontal."

"Don't do it to yourself, Lisa," I said. "He's a complete vampire and will suck up all your goodness. I know because I called up Moira in the East and got a bit of dirt. Four empty desks, she said. No higher management. Just little guys. She couldn't talk but I'm going to call her back and get more on him. We need to know the enemy."

Lisa looked woeful. "But main branch is much bigger, Dinah. He just said it himself. It's a whole different thing."

"I'm immune to his charms. If I have to go down, I'm going down kicking."

Cleo smiled. "You take men too seriously, Dinah."

Lisa nodded.

I shook my head. "He belongs to a win-lose world. You either have to be beneath him, or above him, and if you are above him, he'll take you down. I know the type. The animal kingdom is full of them. There is no win-win here."

But Cleo was not discouraged. She eyed him hungrily. If she continued at the rate she'd been going, her sexual odometer would soon be into the triple digits. She was a woman who was used to taking men at face value, but *taking* them.

"We're not the only ones lusting around here," said Lisa, nodding toward Ash.

We all looked over at Ash who was watching Ian. She had a soft glazed-over look, never seen before that day.

I said, "She's got him where she wants him all week. He's going to be in her office going over the books."

Cleo said. "She's going to have human contact? Somebody's actually going to talk to her *face-to-face?* It'll give her a nervous breakdown to have to look him in the eye."

After work that day, Jake, Ida, Lisa, Cleo and I got together at our usual, Notte's Bon Ton, a pastry and coffee shop on Broadway, just a few blocks from our office, to save the world.

"Energy crisis? What we do is we exploit people power," said Lisa. "Harness the energy of all those people who go to the gym to pump and cycle off all the fat the planet has labored so hard to supply to their necks and waistlines. We hook 'em up to generators. We don't tell 'em, though. So they're giving back some of the energy they stole from the grasslands when wheat was planted and the flour was ground up and baked into the donuts that they are right now stuffing into their mouths, right? Very cost efficient." She punctuated this by sticking a cream-filled pastry into her mouth and wiping it broadly.

"Sure, Lisa," I said.

"We go back to the horse and buggy," said Jake. "Best natural fertilizer in the world, horse poop. And you drink one too many, your horse knows the way home."

"Windmills," I said. "The old-fashioned Dutch kind. They could do something arty with the sails, paint them. Stick them out in Delta. People could live in them. Wouldn't that be cool?"

"Trampoline generated power," said Jake. "Kids love trampolines. You harness that bounce, you could light up the whole city. Or that thing they do when you're trying to drive across the country and they kick the back of your seat for thousands of miles. Man, if we could harness that…"

I shook my head. "We can't do that one, Jake, exploitation of minors."

"I'm just glad I won't be around when the big food shortage hits," said Ida. "And if I am, I'll be too tough and stringy for anybody's tastes."

"Ida," gasped Lisa, "you're not suggesting cannibalism, are you?"

Ida pontificated. "I figure it like this. With the agricultural society going at it with all those nitrogen fertilizers, it's going to be hard to return to being hunter/gatherers. What's going to be left for us to gather or to hunt? You can't even be a decent vegetarian anymore. I figure a nice roast brisket of fat arms dealer is a good place to start."

"Here, here," everybody agreed.

Cleo said, "Okay now, forget saving the world. I've got a headline."

Now that we'd all given up pretending we didn't fritter time away surfing the Net during working hours, we called our surfing Headline Research. At the end of the day we'd

throw them at each other and play True or False. Losers paid
for the pastries.

Cleo started with, "Delays In Sex Education, Education
Workers Request Training."

Jake's was "Girl Guide Helps Snake Bite Victim In
Kootneys."

Ida gave us, "President Urges Dying Soldiers To Do It For
Their Country."

Lisa's was "Cougar Terrorizes Burnaby Dress Shop,
Trashes Autumn Line."

I finished off the round with, "Scientists Say Oceans' Fish
Depleted By Ninety-Five Percent."

Everyone turned on me, protesting.

Cleo said, "Ah, Dinah, there you go again. You're being
an awful bore. I know you're an eco-depressive but couldn't
you just play it close to your chest for once."

Lisa said, "Don't focus on those negative things, Dinah, or
you'll draw them to you like a magnet. Life isn't as bad as you
think it is. Your glass could be half-full if you wanted it to be."

I thought this was good coming from a woman who had
been used all her life by professional navel-gazers and full-
time fresh air inspectors she called "lovers."

Ida sat back and contemplated her rum baba then said,
"Be as negative as you like, Dinah, because by the time they
really heat this planet up I'll either be six feet under or too
gaga to care."

"Idaaa…" said Jake.

"There are worse things," said Ida.

I held up my hands. "I come by it honestly, guys. I have
an illustriously cynical mother. Now you all have to vote.
Which is the fake?" I asked.

"Cougar," said Cleo.

"I agree. Cougar," said Ida.

"Girl Guide. Jake, you're a fake," said Lisa. "It's an old joke,
that one."

"You nailed me, Lisa," said Jake, his hands in the air.

"News for all you fish eaters, and that means you, too, Cleo," I said. "The ocean's fish stocks are only depleted by ninety percent and most of what you get these days is fish farm stuff. You should know that. That's the other fake."

"Oh friggin' great. Big consolation. But you and I win, Dinah," said Lisa, "which means the rest of you guys are paying for our cream puffs. The cougar headline was in the *Sun* this morning. I'm surprised you guys missed it. He's been roaming around Vancouver and they just can't seem to catch him."

"We're getting these cougar sightings around here from time to time," said Jake, "but it's been a while now. Then there's the coyote situation. Damned forestry practices. They cut down the damned forests, these big cats lose their damned habitat, have no damned place to go, so what does anybody expect? They come into town on the log booms, stir up trouble."

"If I didn't know better I'd say you were making it up," said Cleo.

"No way," said Lisa, "and these are not happy animals. They're feeling pretty crazy mad by the time they hit town. Look behind you when you're walking down the street."

"I knew about the coyotes. But cougars," said Cleo. "Who would have thought it?"

I said, "The only wildlife you've had your eye trained on lately, Cleo, is *homo sapiens,* the male of the species."

"True, true." She smiled.

"There hasn't been a cougar sighting since you've been here. Not in the last two years," I said.

"There's a whole variety of urban critters out there, believe me, Cleo. Our building was skunked last week," said Lisa. "Little stripey guy got into the basement bin under the garbage chute. Quite the distinctive odor is skunk."

"And speaking of distinctive odors," said Ida. "How come the new CEO, Mr. Ferrari, isn't here stuffing his face with butter cream bons bons like the rest of us? Boy, does he smell good."

Jake polished his bald spot nervously and gave his mustache a little good luck tug. "Time management thing."

"Yeah. The management ain't got no time for us, eh?" joked Lisa.

"And what about the new girl?" Ida went on. "What's her name again?"

"Penelope," said Jake, perking up.

"How come she isn't here either?" asked Ida.

Cleo said, "You have to make a choice, Ida. It's Penelope or Dinah. The office virgin has taken a disliking to poor Di."

"I thought Ash was the office virgin," piped up Ida.

"We don't really know anything about Ash," said Cleo, grinning and wiggling her eyebrows.

"Just to change the subject slightly, I wonder how Ian Trutch is going to go down with our Indian volunteers?" Lisa pondered.

"Lisa!" We all pounced. "You can't say that. It's so politically incorrect."

"Oh jeez, you guys. *Dots* not *feathers.*"

We all sat back. "Oh…okay then."

Dinah Nichols the eco-depressive. It was another one of the reasons I was seeing Thomas. And again, I liked to blame my mother for forcing me to absorb a lifetime of scientific data that promises nothing good.

At night when I closed my eyes, the vision came to me on schedule. I could see the whole planet from a distance, the way the astronauts must have first seen it. But I saw it with an eagle's eye, first hovering way off, out in infinity, and then honing in and zooming to all the trouble spots. The Chernobyls, the devastated rain forests, El Nino, the quakes and mudslides, the beached whales, the factories everywhere pumping and flushing out their toxins, cars, a gazillion cars studding the planet, and a brown sludge forming around the big blue ball like a sinister new stratosphere. It was only head-line overload, but sometimes it got me down so low, it was hard to get out of bed.

Tuesday

By 8:00 a.m., I had learned that Ian Trutch was damag-ing our grassroots image even further by staying in a plush suite on the Gold Floor of the Hotel Vancouver. After a bril-liant example of minor urban infiltration, I also found out very brusquely that nonguest people like me weren't allowed to wander its corridors, not even with the lame excuse of having to deliver business-related papers. No siree.

When I got back out to the street after the nasty run-in with the Gold Floor receptionist, there was a parking ticket shoved under the windshield wiper of my battered red an-tique Mini. I swear, even to this day, that they moved that fire hydrant next to the car while I was inside.

I drove fast back to Broadway and the Green World In-ternational office. I was twenty minutes late for work because I had to play musical parking spaces for half an hour and then run ten blocks to the office. Of course, Ian Trutch was there to see me arrive late and all sweaty and flustered. He gave me an inquisitive blue stare and tiny smile, then went off to monitor somebody else.

I went into my office and shut the door. It was opened again immediately by Lisa, who pretended to have impor-tant business with me but was really just hiding from one of the needy cases. Every so often, some loafer would shuffle in off the street and say, "Hey, man, I'm a charitable cause, you guys do stuff for charities, so waddya gonna do for me?" And Lisa, being Miss High Serotonin Levels, and "good with people," had been elected to handle them.

Lisa eyed my collection of office toys then picked up my Gumby doll and tied his legs in a knot. I looked up at her.

With her blond hair in braids, her lack of makeup, and loose pastel Indian cottons over woolen sweaters, she looked as though she'd stepped through a time warp directly from Haight-Ashbury, from a gathering of thirtysomething flower children.

I said, "Another passenger from Dreck Central, eh, Lisa?"

"Shhh. It's that bushy guy again. His name's Roly. You know the nutty one with the long gray hair and beard who always wears the full rain gear right down to the Sou'wester? He keeps coming around and asking for me. I guess I shouldn't have been so nice to him."

"Lisa. You don't know how *not* to be nice."

"Shhh. If he hears my voice he'll want to come in here. I mean, I feel really awful. It's not that I mind him really. He's quite polite. Quite a gentleman really. Not like some of the human wreckage that washes up here. But I just don't feel like dealing with him today. He's so darn persistent. He keeps asking me out for lunch. I mean, he's a street person. Don't get me wrong. He's clean for a street person but he wears that nutty rain gear all the time. You just have to look at him to know who'll be paying for the lunch. Yours truly. If it wasn't so sad it would be sweet."

"Hey, but Lise. It's cool. It's a date. That's more than I can say for myself."

"Sure. Right. And that Penelope's driving me nutty, too. You know what she said? She thinks we should clean up our image. She says our phone voices are no good, that my way of speaking when I deal with the public is too raunchy."

"Oh God, Lisa, for her to even use the word raunchy is sexual tourism. What could she possibly know about raunchy?"

My phone rang as if on cue. I picked it up with a voice as smooth as extra-virgin olive oil, and said, "Green World International. Dinah Nichols speaking."

"Halliwell's here," said the phone voice.

I put my hand over the mouthpiece and whispered to Lisa, "The pain-in-the-butt printer," took my hand off and said, "Hello, Mr. Halliwell."

Halliwell drawled, "Are we going to get that campaign material some time this decade, Miss Nichols, or should I give you up for dead?"

I watched as Lisa put down Gumby and picked up Mr. Potato Head. She ripped out all of his features and limbs then rearranged them in unlikely places.

I pulled my Magic Eight Ball out of my drawer, gave it a shake, and read the message into the phone, "Well, Mr. Halliwell, signs point to yes."

"Yes dead? Or yes this decade?" he growled.

"This decade," I said.

That seemed to satisfy him. He grunted and hung up.

Lisa said, "I guess I better go back and deal with the dreck. Hey Dinah, don't forget about the protest tomorrow, eh? We should be able to get out and back over lunchtime."

"Yeah, okay. Where did you say it was?"

But she had already gone.

After that, with Ian Trutch's nearby presence forcing me into uber-employee mode, I plunged myself into real work and finished all the campaign material for Halliwell that morning.

Around lunchtime, Jake knocked on my door. He looked like a kid on Christmas Eve. "There's somebody here for you, Dinah. Waiting by the coffeemaker."

I left my desk and went out to see who it was.

My mother was dressed in her favorite town outfit; hiking boots, anorak, and gold and diamond jewelry. Everyone in the main room was staring at her and groveling and calling her Dr. Nichols with awe in their voices. My mother is, after all, quite a famous scientist. She's been on TV countless times to talk about the destruction of the natural order and extinction of the planet's wildlife.

I said, "Mom. You're supposed to be in Alaska."

"Cancelled. Sent one of the masters students. Old enough to know what he's doing by now. Came over with the new undergrads. To break them in, you know."

She always came to Vancouver in her own boat, unless the weather was really rough. She made her students come along as crew because it was important to know if they were seaworthy or not. She moored in the marina under the Burrard Bridge.

"Thought we might have a bite of lunch then do a spot of shopping."

It was a good thing Ian Trutch was out of the room because then she got that tone in her voice. "Di Di. I thought we could make it a belated birthday lunch, poppy. Have a reservation at the Yacht Club. Then we can pick out a nice little birthday treat for you." It only took those few syllables, Di Di and poppy, to make me feel twelve years old again.

Half an hour later, I was inside the Yacht Club lunching with my mother. She plunged her knife into the thick steak and carved. A mountain of roast potatoes filled the rest of her plate, and on another plate, vegetable lasagna. And after that, she'd be ready for the dessert tray to roll by, perhaps even twice.

I stared bleakly at my chef's salad. It looked the way I felt; sad and a little limp.

It was unfair, so unfair that my mother should be statuesque and lean, with an aristocratic bone structure, and the appetite of ten men, and I should be like one of the scullery maids in her castle, of the shorter, stockier, full-thighed peasant variety. Not that I'm fat. I'm not fat. My thighs are simply my genetic inheritance. No amount of dieting would ever add the extra length I desired. As I'd often said to Thomas, my mother was Beluga caviar; I was Lumpfish.

"I thought perhaps a rather nice navy-blue duffel coat I saw down in that British import shop near Kerrisdale," she said, through her mouthful.

Oh great, I thought, then I can walk through the streets looking like an enormous navy-blue duffel bag.

She was the only woman I knew who could wear hiking gear and diamonds together, talk with her mouth full, and inspire the husbands lunching with their wives at other tables to sneak longing glances at her. Even though it was a deception really, my mother's entire look, her vibration, her persona, said, "Come and get me. We'll have hours of athletic no-strings-attached sex. After a brisk climb to the top of the Himalayas, of course." My mother demands a lot from her men, but never in the way that they hope or expect.

"I know what I want for my birthday, Mom."

"Do you? Oh, lovely. Tell me then."

I told her.

Her hands froze in midair. She didn't know whether to put her fork down or move it to her mouth. All the color had drained from her face. "Don't ask me that, Dinah. You simply can't ask me that," she said, quietly.

"Of course I can, Mom."

"But it would be like opening Pandora's Box. You've no idea."

"I know. That is the idea. I want to open Pandora's Box. I have to. It's *me* we're talking about. Not you. I can't wait forever. You've got to tell me. First of all, everyone needs to know about their parents even if it's only for genetic purposes, to eliminate the possibilities of transmitting diabetes, cystic fibrosis, hemophilia, porphyria…"

"Porphyria, Dinah? The disease of vampires? Good lord, dear, the only vampire in our family was Uncle Fred who worked for the Internal Revenue."

"Now, Mom. I need to know now. Before something happens to one or the other of us."

My mother flashed me a startled look. She sat very still for what seemed like an eternity. I'll always remember the moment, because it could have gone either way and I would be a different sort of person for it today, wouldn't I? White sails slid past the Yacht Club window and sliced through the glistening windy October ocean.

Slowly, my mother started to move. She reached down for her bag, pulled out a pen and piece of paper, wrote something down, then offered it to me. "This may be out of date but I don't think so, if what I've heard through the grapevine is true. I don't know if you ever met Rupert Doyle, rather a long time ago…"

I had a memory of a tall lanky ecstatic man, hair like tiny black bedsprings, bouncing me on his shoulders. I recalled storytelling after some big meals, and hearing from my room later the waves of hysterical adult laughter rising up to me until I drifted off to sleep. He told stories of exotic places where the landscape was in brighter warmer colors and people died suddenly and dramatically.

I said, "When I was little. He was often over at the house, I think."

"Yes. That's right. He might be able to help you. That's all I'm going to say on the subject. You do what you like. But after this moment, I don't want to hear another word about it for as long as I live. Do you understand, Dinah? Not one word."

Well, happy, happy birthday.

The words scribbled on the piece of paper were *Rupert Doyle, Eldorado Hotel.*

That night, at home, I Googled Rupert Doyle. The situation was looking good. Up came a number of Web sites listing documentaries that Rupert Doyle had produced, some of them award winners. War zones, famine zones, and sometimes, royal sex scandal zones. Where there was disaster, hunger en masse, or a violent uprising, Rupert Doyle was there getting it on videotape for posterity. There was even a photo. It looked like the man I remembered, but twenty-five years older.

At work I was puffed up with pride just thinking about Rupert Doyle. I was already a taller, smarter, longer-thighed person for having his name written on that little slip of paper. I couldn't wait to tell Thomas about it. Around the office, I managed to drop the name "Rupert Doyle" into at least three work-focused conversations that had nothing to do whatsoever with the kind of thing Rupert Doyle was involved with, like political documentaries about South America or Africa or the UK.

While Jake was talking about Shelter Recycling Project funds, I really pushed my luck and said, "You know, perhaps we could get Rupert Doyle, an old family friend of mine, to document the Shelter Recycling Project. I'm sure he'd do it if I asked him."

Everyone looked at me as if to say, "Enough with this Doyle guy already, Dinah."

Then Ian Trutch said, "Rupert Who?"

And I sort of stammered and said, "Rupert Doyle's a very important person, a film producer."

"Never heard of him," said Ian Trutch.

So I blathered on, "Well, he's an important person. He's like…ah…Michael Moore. Would you say no to Michael Moore if he offered to come along and do a short for your organization? No, you wouldn't. It's about the same thing." I was getting red in the face by then, and feeling quite small.

Wednesday

The portico of the Eldorado Hotel was framed in ceramic tile that must have once been white but was now stained yellow. The glass in its doorway was smudged with a month's worth of dirty handprints. Inside, the air smelled of smoke, stale beer and Lysol. The sound of peppery upbeat music shuddered through the whole hotel. Behind a cramped reception desk with an old bronze grate, at the start of the cor-

ridor, a man with a papery thin skin poked letters into num-
bered slots. I cleared my throat and said, "Excuse me, I'm
looking for Rupert Doyle. I was told he had a room here."
The man jerked his head toward the music and said, "You'll
find him in the lounge." Then he leaned forward, about to
become confidential. His face crinkled up like an accordion
and he added, "Drinking with the Cubans."

I hesitated then hurried down the corridor. When I
stepped into the lounge, I felt as though I were inside a large
streaky bell pepper. The walls were a wet dark red with the
old wooden siding painted green and yellow. A mud-colored
linoleum dance floor, stippled by a million stiletto heels, took
up the centre of the lounge. A chubby middle-aged couple
moved across it to a salsa rhythm, seeing only each other.

Up at the bar, a huge man was hunched in conversation
with a short fat dark man. The tall man had the Rupert
Doyle hair I remembered except that it was completely silver and he had a silver three-day growth of beard to match.
His tall powerful bearlike body was almost exactly the same
except for a slight thickening through the waist and chest.
Otherwise, he was the same.

I approached him uncertainly. "Rupert Doyle?"

He swung around, saw me and said, "Christ."

Now he was frowning.

"Mr. Doyle?"

"Do I know you?" He was cautious.

"Sort of," I replied.

He was handsome. One of what I call the electric men.
You can see ideas sparking in their eyes, the life force cours-
ing through their bodies. As if they'd been given a double
dose of energy right at the start. There was still a remnant
of that old ecstasy in his face, but it had been tested over the
years and now was worn down to vague contentment.

I didn't give him a chance to blow it.

I came right out with it.

I said, "I'm Marjory Nichol's daughter. My mother said I'd find you here."

He put his hand on his heart. "Oh Jesus." Then he put his hand to his head. "Christ. What a shock. That explains it. You scared the life out of me."

"I did?"

"Just give me a second. Now. Marjory Nichols. Hell. You're...? Goddamn. You're...uh...wait a minute...Diane."

"Dinah. You used to come round to our house years ago."

"Well, sure I did. Of course I did. Stand back and let me look at you. How about that. So, well... How about that? Goddamn. You're Marjory's daughter."

"Yes, I am."

"How is your mom, anyway? How's Marjory. I haven't seen her in ages. I keep meaning to get in touch but life has a way of conspiring against old friendships...."

"Fine. She's fine."

"I keep meaning to get in touch but I'm often on the move. You know, I caught her on TV, that interview she did on the dying oceans for the BBC, a couple of years back. She sure is something. I was about to pick up the phone but as usual was interrupted by a business call. I'm rarely in the country these days and when I am, it's all work."

"She's often on the move too so..."

"Yes, right, well, good, Marjory's daughter. Unbelievable how time flies. You were just a little kid the last time I saw you...."

Then I blurted it out. No formalities. "I made her tell me. How to find you. You know? She knew how badly I wanted to meet my father. And well, now, here we are."

Rupert Doyle's eyes opened a little wider and took on the shape of half-moons as he peered. He took a step backward and held up his hands as if he were pushing me away. "Nooo," he exhaled. "No, no. Just a minute now. You're making a big mistake."

Chapter Four

I was devastated. My first thought was, What's so horrendous about me that you don't want to admit that I'm your daughter? A minidepression was starting to form in me, like a tiny whirlwind building into a hurricane, with a pinch of pure rage tossed in for good measure.

I wanted to run crying to Thomas, make one of my emergency calls to him.

But Rupert Doyle read my expression right away. Total dejection edged with fury. He leapt in to correct himself. "No, no, please, don't misunderstand. It's not the way you think…you think I'm your father? Is that it?"

I nodded.

"I'm not your father…Dinah."

I shook my head.

"I may have a few kids scattered around the world for all I know, but you're certainly not one of them. Rest easy in the knowledge."

I couldn't bring myself to look him in the eye.

"That's not to say I wouldn't be proud to be your father. But I'm not him. You're too young to know about it but I can't tell you how many men, myself included, wanted your mother to be the mother of their children. That woman was something special. Imagine she still is. Marjory Nichols had us all hopping like fools for the love of her. Damn her anyway."

I started to frown and then to laugh. He laughed, too, and suddenly my mother's powers of attraction gave us common ground, something to grab on to, to make us old friends, as though he had been a constant visitor to the house for the last twenty-five years.

He rubbed his face vigorously with both hands, like someone waking from a long sleep. He seemed about to say something but his words were replaced with a frustrated sigh. Until he finally said, "Listen. I *do* know who your father is."

I gave my own huge sigh of relief.

He smiled. "Your mother probably didn't want to have anything to do with it. Am I right?"

"Yes."

"She can be a very stubborn woman." His expression was odd, his blue eyes luminous.

"You're telling *me.* I mean, we're talking about my own father and I'm not allowed to know anything about him. I'm only just realizing now how pissed off I've been with her for not telling me about him. Information is advancement, evolution. She's not being very scientific."

Rupert Doyle chuckled. "Here, Dinah. Sit down." He pointed to the scarred black bar stool. "Can I order you something? A beer?"

"A coffee…" But then I saw the glass pot on the hotplate behind the bar, untouched brew with a scummy encrusted high tide line, so I accepted a soda water.

Rupert Doyle said, "I can imagine how your mother

probably feels about this and I don't want to be responsible for starting a family war. They're the worst. So you need to go carefully with this one. Your father is what I'd call a...difficult character...apart from the fact that he's volatile...he has...he *had* the power to take people places where they didn't always want to go."

"Who is he? Tell me something about him."

He stroked his chin. "Yeah...well, now. Let me think about this. I can do better than tell you about him. I can introduce you to him."

"He's here? In Vancouver?"

"Sure is. I'm just trying to figure out the best way to go about this."

"Why? Is there a problem?"

"We really did not part as the best of friends." Rupert shook his head and let a small bitter laugh escape.

"Well, I'm not too secure about this whole thing myself. You're scaring me a bit."

"Oh, no...don't take this the wrong way..."

"Mr. Doyle..."

"Rupert."

"Rupert. I'd like to get a glimpse of him first. From a distance, you know? Not have to commit myself. Without him knowing anything about me."

"Sure. Of course, Dinah. In the interests of not prejudicing your opinion, I can see how you'd want to take your time before you decide whether or not you really want to get to know the man. You might take one look and decide it's better not to. He might not want to have anything to do with you. Or me." He laughed again.

"What's the problem?" I was picturing my mother with some impossible kind of man. A married politician? Another mad scientist? "Does he have a high-profile job or something? Would this create a scandal for him?"

"No, no."

"Or is he some kind of criminal?"

Rupert Doyle frowned then bit his lip. "There have been accusations, and he has felt like a criminal at times, but no. Or rather, it would all depend on who you asked. No, he's not a criminal although he has been accused of being one."

"I don't understand."

"Your father is a representative from a distinct moment in history. An icon in some ways. Not an easy history, not at all. I would say that the very fact he's alive implicates him. Or so he would see it. You may have the chance to find out about it as you get to know him. If you decided you want to get to know him. But I think the person to give you all this information is your father himself. You need to hear the story from the horse's mouth, as it were."

I shook my head.

What was he talking about? I was as unenlightened as ever with all his beating around the bush. "Okay. So. Now. What's his name and where do I find him?"

"You can find…just a second, Dinah."

The man with the collapsed face from the front desk was standing in the doorway signaling to Rupert.

Rupert held up an authoritative palm to him. "Yeah, yeah, I'm coming." He turned back to me. "Listen, Dinah. Let's do it this way, for the sake of Auld Lang Syne. And then we can catch up. I'd really like to catch up on your mother, too."

My face must have twisted a little. My expression made him add quickly, "And you, of course. Hell, I remember you when you were just a little—"

The front desk man pointed his thumb toward the street, and said loudly, "Cab's here."

Rupert said, "Look, we can…hell, I gotta go…got a production meeting at…" He looked at his watch and grimaced. "Christ. It started five minutes ago." He slapped some money on the counter and started toward the door. I hurried along after him. His last words before he was out the door were, "You meet me here at seven Friday night and I'll take you there myself. You have a car?"

I nodded.

"Great. Wouldn't mind seeing the old *picaro* again myself."

I idly sharpened pencils. Ian Trutch was locked up with Ash. There were fleeting glimpses of him and whiffs of his aftershave hanging on the air, but that was all. Ash was looking delirious behind her thick lenses. She'd taken the clips out of her hair and let it down.

Penelope was declaring all-out war on me. It's amazing what a total lack of carnal knowledge, of real sex, can do to a person. I mean, at least if the rest of us weren't actually *having* sex, we still had our experiences and memories to fall back on, but Penelope... Penelope was beginning to show the mental strain that comes with ITD—Incoming Testosterone Deficit.

She had the war drums going strong when we got on to the topic of funds for AIDS awareness and sex education. She had a litany of sexual terrorism tales, nasty little stories on hand to make her case for chastity. Poor Lisa, who was genetically predisposed to being nice to everyone, to her own detriment, got stuck in the middle.

Penelope smoothed down her calf-length black skirt and said, "Did you know, Lisa, that the introduction of sex education at too early an age has been known to cause trauma in adolescents? It's been documented."

I smoothed my red leather skirt and said, "Did you know, Lisa, that too much *pregnancy* at an early age has been known to cause trauma in adolescents?"

"Ah, jeez...ah, c'mon, you two. Cut this out." Lisa, on the edge of despair, looked back and forth between the two of us, imploring.

Penelope continued to inform Lisa. "Some schools have grade-schoolers practice putting condoms on the fingers of their classmates. What a disgusting thing to do to children. Now, in my opinion, that is exactly like telling a nine-year-old to go out and have sex."

I looked Penelope straight in the eye, "Yes, but the message here is *safe* sex, Penelope, safe sex."

"Well, I'm sure you'd know all about it, Dinah, given your long and varied experience in the field," said Penelope.

Cleo arrived just before I was about to grab Penelope by the hair and knock some sense into her. Cleo pulled me by the arm toward my office, calling out to the others, "We're going for lunch." And then she whispered to me, "I heard all that. It would be so much easier if we were at high school and Penelope had just called you a slut outright. You know? Then you could just corner her in the girls' bathroom, hold her head down in the toilet bowl and flush."

"And flush. And flush," I agreed.

Whenever Cleo dragged me to lunch like that, it meant two things.

Hunger.

And she was seeing somebody new.

When she wanted to talk about her private life she refused to go to a restaurant because she was afraid somebody would overhear. And for good reason. Cleo waded indiscriminately through the tides of men who washed up on her shores. Married, committed, or fit to be legally committed, the men that Cleo chose were safely designed for dumping when she grew tired of them, poor guys. But she had a special fondness for the high-profile married type, and she was right to be cautious. The thing about dating high-profile married men is that you never know when a low-profile wife in the know could pop out of the bushes or the woodwork, ready to reduce you to a pulp.

But this day was a little different.

Cleo gave me just enough time to grab a cup of dishwater

in a paper cup and a cardboard-and-pink-mush sandwich, and then drove us both up to Queen Elizabeth Park. We sat down on a bench and admired the autumn colors of the maples and alders for a second or two, then I said, "Okay. Tell me all about him. What's he like?"

"You know all about him," said Cleo.

"Somebody I know? Who?"

"Can't you guess?"

I didn't have to think very far back. I could feel a heaviness in my stomach and it wasn't just the bad sandwich. I shook my head. "Simon. It's Simon. Of course it's Simon. Oh, Cleo, you don't know what you're in for."

But she didn't give me a chance to go on. She told me how warm he was and how beautiful, and that she couldn't get enough of him, that she loved younger men and that she hadn't slept because he'd kept her up all that night. I should have ruined her fun, right then and there, but I just kept my mouth shut because…well…I did more talking about living than actually doing the living itself, and I admired Cleo for being a doer.

When we got back from our so-called lunch, Lisa said, "Hey you guys. You know there's been another cougar sighting?"

Cleo raised her eyebrows.

"Yeah, this time in the Spanish Banks area. Don't know how the poor kitty got from Burnaby to Spanish Banks but they haven't caught him yet. Careful when you're out jogging, Dinah. He's on your side of town now and those big cats move fast, especially when they're feeling hungry and tetchy."

The Tsadziki Pervert came on hot and heavy that week, too. I'd lost the whistle I was going to tie onto the phone. It had probably skidded under the furniture and I didn't feel like heaving around all those heavy Deco bureaus I'd inherited from my great-grandparents. Or facing all the other junk I'd find under there. Joey was always teasing me, saying, "Just because your furniture dates back to the nineteen-twenties doesn't mean the junk you find under it should date back to the twenties as well." The day I moved the furniture was going to be a revelation.

The Telephone Pervert Voice was now a regular feature of my evenings. "I want to come over," it hissed, "and cover your thighs in taramasalata (Tuesday), hummus (Wednesday), tsadziki (Thursday), then lick it all off." I mean, the guy was really hooked on Greek. And my social life was so not-happening that his propositions were almost tempting.

Almost.

I had better distractions though, more solid ones. My gay neighbor, for example, was performing a very fine sideshow in his fishbowl of a living room. Tuesday night he decided to go through his usual body-building routine. Whatever it was that weighed on his mind, it had him worked into such a state that I wanted to run over there and say, "C'mon now. Out with it. Stop bottling it all up. Let me give you the number of my therapist." Because he really seemed troubled and I guess the workout was a good way of keeping his mind off the problem. At times his expression seemed almost tortured it was so serious. While he hefted and pulled and pushed and sweated, I watched and tried to ignore the little thrum of longing in my solar plexus.

The next night, Wednesday, his partner was there for dinner. My neighbor had placed fat white candles around the room, and after dinner he and his friend took their drinks over to the brown leather couch, where they began to have an intense conversation.

I wondered if lip-reading courses were given anywhere in town.

And then the guest stopped talking and my neighbor grabbed the other man and gave him a long tight hug. He had such a tender expression on his face that watching them brought tears to my eyes.

The next night, strange things were going on. My neighbor had guests but they weren't human. I counted five black cats in his living room, skittering around, climbing up the curtains, scratching the furniture. My neighbor didn't seem too concerned about the damage. He picked each cat up in turn, stroked gently, rubbed their ears until they were calm, rolled them onto their backs and stroked their bellies, then held their paws and played with them. In that moment, I wanted to be a black cat, too.

Friday

At ten-thirty, Lisa, Cleo and I knocked on Jake's office door. "Come in."

We all entered, our faces plastered with the most business-like expressions we could muster. Ian Trutch was lounging in Jake's extra chair. He raised his hand. "Hello ladies."

We gave a chorus of hellos.

"I was just telling Jake that I was going to have to corner Dinah to go over the figures." Ian's smile made it clear that he wasn't just talking about numbers. Cleo nudged me hard and Lisa giggled.

I let out a long breath and said, "We just wanted to let you know that we're on our way out for the afternoon. Have a few office errands to run."

Lisa and Cleo piped up a little too quickly, "Field work."

"And I have to see Halliwell, the printer," I said.

Jake wasn't used to us justifying our actions. "Yeah, sure. No problem."

Our eyes were fixed on Ian. He looked at Jake as if to say, "Do they normally do this?"

We all nodded a little nervously then hurried out of the building.

"I think he bought it," whispered Cleo.

I said, "Well if he didn't, I'm sure we'll be hearing about it."

"And what's more, Dinah, he likes you. Milk it for all it's worth."

I laughed. "You mean I might still have a job while the rest of you are standing in the bread line if I let the CEO crunch my numbers?"

"Something like that."

We rushed out to Lisa's battered old rust-and-rhubarb colored VW van. She drove fast to my place. We tumbled out and raced up the stairs.

In my bedroom, Cleo said, "I hope I'm dressed okay. What does one wear to a tree-hugging anyway?" It didn't matter what *she* wore. A burlap sack would look good on her.

"Cleoooo," sang Lisa, "we do not call it a tree-hugging. And it's not a fashion event either. McClean and Snow Incorporated are about to knock down a stand of boreal forest that is millennia old, destroying the habitat of numerous species of wildlife with the runoff polluting I don't know how many streams and fixing it so the salmon won't be returning…"

Cleo examined the polish on her nails. "Lisa, we know you believe that plants have feelings…"

"And that if their feelings are hurt they should get therapy…" I added.

"You guys…." Lisa laughed.

"And animal rights?" said Cleo.

"If you swat a fly around Lisa, she's likely to try CPR on it…." I countered.

Lisa clarified herself. "Before giving it a dignified funeral."

We all grinned, then Cleo looked at me. "Uh, Dinah? Do you actually know what you're looking for?"

"Sure." I peered out from behind the high-rise of cardboard boxes that had inhabited the corner of my bedroom for ages. "My protest-against-the-big-money-grubbing-corporation wardrobe."

Lisa smiled. "We all go through it. You'll outgrow it."

"Outgrow what?"

"Dressing up for protests. You'll be wearing your worst rags at the next one. These kind can get messy."

"Lisa, when I left Vancouver Island, I promised myself I would try not to look like a shrubbie from the Island. If I can just figure out which box the damned clothes are in," I murmured.

Cleo said, "It's important to consider your wardrobe at all times. There could be some interesting men there. When they come to arrest us, there could be men in uniform. I love men in uniform."

Lisa said, "You love men… period."

"Ha. You're right." Cleo took in the varnished pine floorboards, oyster-white paint that was no longer fresh, and mountain of cardboard boxes. "You moved into this place…when, Dinah? Three years ago?"

"Two and a half." I tried not to sound defensive.

"When are you planning on unpacking them?" Lisa asked.

"Just these boxes I haven't unpacked. I had them sent over later but there isn't enough closet space. So they're staying there. This is my storage depot."

Cleo stopped flicking her Ray-Bans back and forth and parked them on her head. "Come on now, Lisa. Poor Dinah. Give her time. Moving is traumatic. It's number two after divorce."

"I wouldn't know anything about divorce," Lisa muttered. "Never having been married myself in the first place."

I had once caught a glimpse of the pile of *Bride* magazines stashed in Lisa's desk drawer at work. They definitely marred her free and easy earth-mother image.

"To hear Fran tell it, we're not missing a thing," said Cleo. "She's always saying there's nothing like marriage to cure you of wanting to be married."

This was one conversation I had no intention of getting

involved in. I set a carton precariously on top of another and was not quite in time to catch it as it tumbled to the floor. The three of us winced in unison as its contents tinkled dangerously.

"Not the Limoges, I hope," said Cleo.

I shifted the box gently out of the way. "I have no idea and I'm not going to open it to see. Then I'd have to deal with it. You know I'm cleaning-impaired."

Lisa smiled, revealing her big teeth. "Confession is the first step toward recovery." She glanced at her psychedelic Swatch. "Just grab something so we can go, will you, Dinah. We're late. The others will be there already."

I tore frantically at packing tape and box flaps. My eye lit on something charcoal black. "Aha." I held it up, triumphant.

Lisa made a face. "You cannot wear a Chanel suit to an environmental protest."

"Yes, she can," said Cleo. "She can wear whatever she likes."

I was already pulling off my office skirt and scrutinizing the little black suit with the red trim. "It's a demoted Chanel suit. I got it at a secondhand place. It was a steal. Secondhand means it's recycled so that makes it environmentally correct, right? Now where have those flats gotten to...?"

Lisa shrugged.

After a burst of haphazard ironing, elaborate squirming and a tiny intervention with a safety pin at bust level, I was dressed. I grabbed the deluxe knapsack I'd prepared and followed them out. As we ran down my stairs, I felt proud. We were a squad, ready to lay down our lives for a stand of ancient trees. Well...maybe not our lives, but part of a sunny October day. Or so I thought until we were standing in front of Lisa's van.

While Lisa was doing a last check of the heavy chains and padlocks in the back, Cleo leaned into me and whispered, "None of that stuff is touching my body. I agreed to be a presence but I'm not chaining myself to a damned thing.

You know how hard it is to get grease or pitch out of corduroy? This is my best Lands' End protest outfit. I'd planned on wearing it to the next No-Global."

"Get in, girls," ordered Lisa. "It's already going to be hell finding parking."

The van wheezed into gear and coughed and spat all the way up West Fourth. I was in the back, and Cleo, up in the passenger seat, turned back to face me. Over the sound of the engine, she said, "This apartment is definitely a step up from your last."

"Ten steps," I mumbled.

"I remember Dinah's last place well," said Lisa.

"It could have housed morgue overflow," said Cleo.

"It wasn't that cold," I protested.

"No? You didn't notice my fingers turning blue from hypothermia whenever I came to visit you? And those clog dancers living overhead were amazing."

"The upstairs tenants *were* a little noisy."

"Your landlord had a nerve. Calling it a basement suite," Cleo said. "It was a bunker. It was almost completely underground."

"It was a bit dark," I admitted. I didn't tell them that it had been so dark that once during a power failure, I thought I'd gone blind. My only consolation in that moment was the possibility of expanding my love life to include ugly men with beautiful voices.

"If you can just get those last few boxes unpacked, you'll be all set," said Lisa.

It was a very big if.

We rode along in silence for a while. Then I said what we'd all been thinking. "I sure hope nobody finks on us."

"It was a previous commitment," said Lisa. "If it gets back to Trutch we'll just tell him that protests like this are part of Green World's constitution." She made a fast turn and came to a screeching halt.

"Stanley Park?" Cleo raised her eyebrows.

"This is it," said Lisa. "This is our destination."

I was confused. I'd been expecting a long ride into an immense dark rain forest.

"Douglas firs. And not just one but four," said Lisa. "They're saying that they're diseased, but it's pure propaganda…."

I laughed.

"Okay. Let's go," sighed Cleo, and climbed down from the van.

Lisa bulldozed ahead of us. "It's not far from here."

I grabbed my knapsack and we followed, almost running to keep up.

When we reached the site, it was deserted.

Lisa stood immobile. "Oh my God."

"We obviously have the wrong day." Cleo looked a little relieved.

Lisa was close to tears. "We're too late."

The freshly cut naked stumps of four huge Douglas firs made us all feel cheated. A couple of minutes passed before we could hear a strange low hum coming from Lisa.

"What's she doing?" whispered Cleo.

"Singing, I think."

We decided it was better to leave Lisa alone with her grief. It was the first time I'd ever heard a hymn for a dead tree. When she was finished mourning, I held up my knapsack and said, "Now girls, come over here. I have something to show you. You have to know that I do not like to miss an opportunity. While my mother thinks that a field or a forest or a beach is a place where animals and insects regenerate the species, I happen to think that it's a nice place for a picnic." I unzipped my deluxe knapsack to reveal plates and glasses, bread and cheeses, and a bottle of chilled white wine. "I came prepared for any eventuality. It's a beautiful day. Let's make the most of it."

"Right on," said Lisa.

We chose a section of beach just beyond the seawall and were just polishing off the bottle of wine when a man's voice called across to us, "Dinah? Dinah Nichols?"

I hit the ground like an infantryman under attack. "Who is it?" I hissed to Cleo.

"Big-time corporate donor," she hissed back.

I eased up slowly, and when I saw who it was, uttered, "Tod."

He was dressed in jogging clothes and dripping with sweat. He looked less jaunty than usual. Unsmiling. "What a stroke of luck. I tried calling you at work but you weren't there."

"You did? Uh…"

"We have to talk. My place? Around four? It's important." Without waiting for my answer, he turned and jogged away.

Lisa dropped me off at my car and I drove to Halliwell the printer's. I pushed open the door. The shop seemed deserted. "Anybody here?"

Halliwell's voice came from a distance. "Downstairs."

I descended the narrow wooden steps and called out, "Mr. Halliwell?"

He was standing at a press, watching the paper pile up, and didn't bother to look up at me. He was tall and scrawny, more of a ghost than a man. Every word he spoke came out in a slow drawling taunt. "Well, I'll be damned. Miss Nichols in person. I feel privileged."

"Don't I always come in person?"

"When I called your office to let you know the brochures were ready, they told me you were out and didn't know when you'd be back. Tough job, eh?" He made the huge effort of looking at me from under one eyebrow.

"Fieldwork," I said.

He took a few leisurely steps toward me, plucked a piece

of dried seaweed from my hair and held it in front of my eyes. "Gives fieldwork a whole new definition."

"Well…uh…we are an ecological organization, Mr. Halliwell. We actually get out there and check up on the ecology."

"I can see you're really making…*head*way. Get it?"

"Can I see the brochures, please?"

"Over here." He oozed over to some shelves and picked up a pile of glossy green-and-white papers. "Still have to be folded."

"I thought your people were going to do that." I looked closer at the type on the page. "Er…Mr. Halliwell…there's a typo here."

He shrugged.

"It says 'Green World is worping for you.' *Worping,* Mr. Halliwell? It's supposed to be 'Green World is *working* for you'. Can you do them again? Correctly? I can't distribute these. This is a big event."

"You're the creative here. I'm just the manpower. You create it, I print it. Your people should have caught that. If you don't like our prices then change printers."

I couldn't argue. He'd been roped into donating his services by my predecessor, in exchange for his shop's name at the bottom of the brochure.

I looked at him imploringly. He shrugged again. "Sorry, Miss Nichols. No can do. I'm backed up here. Got four other jobs to do before tomorrow. But I'll tell you what. I'll throw in a bottle of White Over for ya."

As I left his shop, with the brochures and bottle of White Over, I vowed I would start my hunt for new volunteer printers that very afternoon.

I stood in the centre of Tod's magnificent white bedroom.

"Are you serious?" I gasped.

"Never been so serious in my life."

"But I…but we…"

Tod threw brand-new shirts into a Gucci suitcase. "It's a bitch but these things happen."

"Completely bankrupt?"

"If you're going to be in this game, you have to be ready to start over. It's only money, Dinah. That's what I always say. Money is an abstract concept anyway. Some of my investments turned out to be a not-so-abstract disappointment, however. These things happen."

"Only money," I echoed.

He placed his hand on his chest. "But I have my health. That's the important thing."

"Yes." My tone was halfhearted.

"I wanted you to be the first to know because I know how important Mudpuddle is to you."

I nodded absently.

"I'm off to the Caymans tonight but I wanted to tell you face-to-face that I'm not abandoning you. I told somebody else about the project and he wants to come on board."

"What's his name?" Now I was already following Tod at a run along the marble corridor.

"Hamish Robertson."

"*The* Hamish Robertson? The near-billionaire Hamish Robertson?"

"The same."

"But nobody can reach him. Nobody's ever seen him. Not in recent years. We've been trying to get in touch with him for ages but nobody knows where to find him. We thought he might be dead."

We were already outside. Tod put his key in the front door and locked it. "Oh no. He's fine. He's a neighbor of mine. Didn't you know that? Lives four houses down the road. And he wants in on Mudpuddle. Oh…and Dinah. You better tear up that check."

"But how do we…where do we…?"

He tossed the suitcase into the back of his Spider and got in. "Dinah, it's been great doing business with you, but I really have to make tracks."

As I was opening my mouth to say goodbye, he was already roaring down the driveway.

I raced back to Green World with the brochures. As I hurried along the corridor toward my office, I passed the Yellow Slicker Guy, Roly, who had taken to sitting all day near Lisa's cubbyhole like an office fixture. He had done a few menial volunteer jobs for Lisa so I checked out his hands. They were clean enough. I said, "Roly. How would you like something to do while you're waiting for Lisa to come back?"

He made a noise like the start of a distant thunderstorm. I took it for a yes.

"Now you can sit over here at Lisa's desk. All you have to do is take this White Over and cancel the *P,* then with this pen, draw in a *K.* There are five hundred of them. Think you can manage it?"

"You said you had a car, Dinah." Outside the Eldorado Hotel, Rupert Doyle was staring at my Mini as though it were a complex Chinese puzzle and he had to figure out which piece he was and where he fitted into it.

"It *is* a car, thank you very much. It's a classic Mini."

"It's a classic sardine tin. Okay, Dinah. Let's move on out." He threw up his hands in surrender, opened the passenger door and squeezed himself in. When he finally stopped squirming and shifting, his knees were practically touching his ears.

I suppressed a laugh.

He grinned and said, "It's not so bad. I've ridden in worse, I guess. Places like Guatemala. Nam. At least this isn't a pig or cattle truck."

"About tonight, Rupert. We're agreed on that one thing?"

"What's that?"

"That you won't say anything. You won't tell him I'm his daughter?"

"Yeah. Well, as I said, you might not want to claim him as father material at all. You're grown up. What difference is it going to make now? And it looks as though your mother did a very good job of being both parents."

I eyed Rupert with disappointment. What did he know? If my mother's parenting was so great then why did I feel the way I felt? Like half an orphan? And why was I seeing Thomas, I wanted to ask.

But I had to cut Rupert some slack. He spent most of his time among cultures whose social values were completely different, where female expectation was low, where girls became brides in arranged marriages at thirteen and were worn-out old women at thirty. It wasn't Rupert's fault that I was the neurotic product of a first-world country, thirty years old and still at the starting line.

Rupert watched the road and navigated for me. We were heading East into a no-man's land of factories and warehouses. Clouds had been looming all day and as we turned the corner into an unpromising street, the one he said was "the right one," the sky opened up and rain poured down. I drove at a crawl while torrents streamed over my windshield.

"There it is," said Rupert. "Down there. You are about to meet Hector Ferrer, your father."

"Hector Ferrer? God. What kind of name is that?"

Rupert laughed. "Argentinian."

Argentina. I had to think about it for a couple of seconds. That big country stuck down near the bottom of South America. Its best-known exports were beef and Eva Peron legends.

"Hector Ferrer." I tested the words on my tongue as I

pulled up where Rupert asked me to. He pointed to a huge old five-story brick building with rows of floor-to-ceiling windows set with small square panes. A set of narrow rusting iron stairs ran up the outside. It seemed more of a fire escape than a real stairway. At the second-floor level a single light illuminated a sign painted in black on white.

LOS TANGUEROS.

I shrugged and looked at Rupert bleakly. "And what kind of word is that?"

Rupert said, "Los Tangueros means tango dancers in the Argentine language, which is a kind of Italianate aberration of Spanish."

I had a sudden image of Rudolph Valentino as a sooty-eyed sheikh, gliding across the silent screen in the embrace of a woman with crimped hair and Kewpie-doll lips. I imagined ballrooms and moth-eaten gowns, geriatric hotshots, slick old hustlers, a room full of trussed-up cadavers lurching around a dance floor with roses between their teeth. Marlon Brando making animal noises and dragging Maria Schneider by her legs around a seedy tango salon in Paris.

Rupert unfolded himself from my Mini and pulled up the hood of his jacket. He was indifferent to the rain, like a man who was in and out of monsoons every day. He hurried toward the stairs. I pulled a fold-up umbrella out of my purse and followed him.

He looked back at me and said, "Steel yourself for this. It's a cult, and people in the tango cult take it very seriously. I don't know why, but those who start dancing the tango become obsessed. It has a unique allure—it might look easy to outsiders but I hear that it's actually quite hard."

When he pulled open the big iron door, I heard first the instruments tuning up and then a fragment of music.

It began as something staid and European, a string quartet, but then picked up and shot off onto a dark musical side street. There was an accordion, a violin, cello and piano. As the playing progressed, the sound struck me as stark and beautiful, driven and melancholy. Like something that was hurtling toward a dramatic ending, violent sex or death.

It was completely unexpected.

Just as unexpected as the name Hector Ferrer.

Rupert saw the expression on my face and said, "Some call it the Latin blues. There's a quote by Borges…let me see…something like, '*El infinito tango me lleva hacia todo…* The infinite tango takes me towards everything.' Something like that."

I nodded, still trying to take it all in. I followed him into the building and along a dim corridor. The music stopped, then there were more tuning-up sounds. From every part of the building, I could hear low voices, and strange outbursts, riffs of knocking or tapping, footsteps, little clusters of rhythm banged out on the floor that started and stopped.

"We're early," whispered Rupert. "They're just warming up."

The music started up again. It was coming from down the hall. We followed the sounds until we came to an open double doorway. There was a huge space before us. Circular shafts of pearlescent light were cast by antique bronze lamps attached to huge old Edwardian pillars, and above them, the ceiling was metal stamped with an intricate pattern and painted a dark green. Under several lamps, small groups of young couples in trim black dance studio clothes silently worked through steps, bends, turns. They talked and whispered, and occasionally broke the quiet with a burst of laughter.

There were at least a couple of dozen young people there with the bodies of classical dancers. Very serious about their moves, they executed them over and over, perfecting them, as if their careers depended on that dance. The cellist began to play again, a thin low grating wire of sound. With the streetlights beyond the huge filmy windows casting a silhouette of beating streaming rain on the worn wooden floor, the whole effect was exotic. Ghostly.

Against three walls were rows of small round tables and folding chairs. At one end of the room was the four-man orchestra.

We sat down at a table and Rupert whispered, "Hector first started getting himself in trouble by taking the basic tango and turning it into something of his own, something more artistic. That's what the younger dancers here are likely trying to pick up from him. Sort of taking it to a balletic extreme. They probably dance professionally around town. But the older dancers, the purists, maintain that you have more freedom if you learn the simple basics well. They say even getting the posture right is hard. The posture's very important."

"You seem to know an awful lot about it. Are you planning to do a tango documentary by any chance?"

He smiled and shook his head. "No, no. Wouldn't be a bad idea though. I spent a lot of time in Buenos Aires at one point in the seventies. You have to see a real *milonga* in Buenos Aires, Dinah. That's the place to see it. Crowded as hell and brimming to the eyeballs with all that Argentine pride, unhappiness, fierceness, hubris really. Simultaneously exhilarating and depressing.

"People in Buenos Aires, the *portenos,* feel themselves to be so depressed that they have more psychoanalysts than any other city in the world. There's actually a neighborhood in the city called Villa Freud. Fathom that. And *bronca.* There's a hell of a lot of that there too. When you meet Hector, you'll find out all about *bronca.*"

"*Bronca,*" I repeated. Another word to taste.

"The *milonga* is a place where a person can do something with all those feelings. See, it was a poor dance, maybe a street dance originally, according to the academics. All these immigrants, Spanish, Italian, Cuban, Creole, French, English even, who went to Buenos Aires looking for a fortune and found misery, had nothing to do and nowhere to go, being stranded at the end of a new and empty continent and surrounded by nothing but ocean and *pampas*. So they made up a new way to strut their macho, to pass the time and impress the whores. It was folk music at first. Then it got stolen by the upper classes, taken for a ride around Europe, and came back semirespectable in the forties and fifties. The earlier tango culture culminated in the movie star Gardel, but he died in a plane crash. Yet another tragedy. Argentina doesn't have very many happy endings. So here's this dance that expresses that tragic, violent nature of the place, a nailing down of all that loneliness and bad luck and passion and jealousy. It's definitely Argentina's theme music."

"Well, put like that, Rupert, you make it sound…I don't know. Important."

"As I said, it becomes very important for the people dancing it."

"It's not part of my world. I don't know anything about it. I mean, I like dancing a lot, but not in any organized way."

"You'll have good reason to learn all about it now," said Rupert, then winked.

And then the orchestra started up, the tune a simmering cocktail, smoky and slightly menacing, reminiscent of dark jazzy clubs and the last century's first glimpse of black net stockings.

The longer I watched, the more I came to sense that the older, less flashy couples were more intuitive dancers, moving in a unison, a subtle interplay of refusal and acceptance.

Rupert was smiling at me as I watched the people on the floor, which was now starting to turn as a whole in hypnotic motion. There were mysterious rules in force. Nobody came right out and asked the other to dance. It was all done with a look, a nod, a raised eyebrow, or a step toward that other person. And nobody smiled. Everyone was serious and intent. Each couple was their own little cosmos, each couple dancing a sad love affair in miniature, passionate and completely detached at the same time. The music was now urgent, now whining, clashing, dark, complete.

My mother had taught me music, but she'd done it coldly, scientifically, dissecting it and analyzing it until there was nothing left to enjoy instinctively. But I knew that once she'd had a real feeling for it. Or at least that was my impression. It seemed to me there had been a time when our house was filled with music of all kinds, and then a time when it had been unnaturally silent. Sometimes, I doubted myself though, unsure of whether it was an early memory or an invention of mine.

Later, my mother let me know subtly that music was a frivolous indulgence. She would disapprove if I spent too many hours in my room with the music channel or CDs, dancing with my reflection in the mirror and imagining myself somewhere else, being someone else. She would quietly humiliate me for being interested in it, and intimate that it took away from the real business; the sciences. When I was a teenager and turned the car radio onto a music station, she was always quick to turn it back to a talk program or the news. So in a mean-spirited way, I loved all kinds of music because I knew my mother would disapprove.

Sitting there at the edge of the *milonga* gave me a sensation of eating forbidden fruit.

And then all those fruits turned rotten and mushy.

Rupert touched my arm, looked toward the stage area, and in a low whisper said, "There he is. There's your father. That's Hector Ferrer over there."

I peered through the half-light, the whirl of bodies. A man stood apart from the others, on one side of the small stage platform, overlooking the scene with a proprietary air. He wore a hat, a gangster hat, a borsellino or coppola, and when he lifted it, I could see that his gray, thick, slightly too-long hair was greased back. His face was heavily grooved and he had an intelligent thin-lipped but cruel-looking mouth. He was slightly paunchy, with a posture that had been pressed down by time into an S curve, hunching shoulders, pelvis thrust forward. He wore a tight black shiny shirt, a brocade vest of red and black which only emphasized his paunchiness. His cream colored-tie was knotted tightly. And sticking out from the bottom of his black dress pants with the clean pleat down the front, was a pair of black-and-white two-toned shoes.

I buried my head in my hands. It was too funny and at the same time, horrible. I wanted to laugh out loud and then curl up and die. After all my fantasizing about a father, fantasizing about someone who would have had enough of the right stuff to trick my mother into getting pregnant, someone a bit scruffy but intellectual, someone with downscale clothes but brilliant upscale ideas, this was what I got, this joke of a father; a sleazy spiv tango dancer with a gangster hat and two-toned shoes.

"Watch him. Watch the way he moves," said Rupert.

But I didn't want to watch. I didn't want to know about it. I wanted to run out of there and forget the whole idea. Finally, I understood why my mother had never said a word. There was only one possible answer. She'd been cornered. She'd been duped. Drugged even.

I mustered a voice and said, "I can't imagine my mother having anything to do with that guy."

Rupert put back his head and looked at me, almost analytically. "She did so. Did she ever. She had plenty to do with him. Believe me, Dinah."

So I forced myself to watch. Hector Ferrer's partner was a small henna-headed woman in a tight cream satin fringed dress, vintage roaring twenties. Before Hector linked up with her, she had been standing close to the other side of the stage, smoking, a hawklike look on her face, a similar look of ownership. Then they stepped in and became part of the circular motion of the dance floor. I couldn't see it, whatever it was I was supposed to see, because I just couldn't get my eyes off those two-tone shoes. They continued to move until they were on our side of the room.

Then the redheaded woman spotted Rupert. An expression of astonishment rushed over her face. She broke out of Hector Ferrer's embrace and wove her way through the other dancers over to Rupert. He stood up and went to meet her, put a big hand on her small back and pulled her over to one side, out of my earshot.

But the prize moment was when Hector saw the two of them meet up. He blanched and froze, then turned red with anger. I half expected to see steam spouting out of his nostrils. Then he strutted off the dance floor and disappeared through a black door to one side of the stage. Rupert was still bent over this woman, talking intensely. Both of them briefly looked over at me and then turned back to each other again.

The woman was shaking her head. She was distressed. I stayed put, the sense of anticipation building as the music crescendoed. She nodded toward the door where Hector Ferrer had made his exit. Rupert nodded back then walked quickly around the edge of the floor and disappeared through the door.

The woman returned to the other side of the room to talk to groups of people at the tables. I anxiously stared at the door. The spare sound of the tango music wasn't enough to hide the shouting that had erupted from beyond the closed door. It must have been the two men. They were yelling in another language, Spanish, I guessed, and one of the voices was Rupert's.

I could see the people on the dance floor becoming distracted and edgy, worried that their tango might be interrupted by a real rough-and-tumble fight any minute. And then the shouting stopped as suddenly as it had started. There was only the music. The dancers went back to their dance. I waited for the sound of the voices to explode again but there was nothing.

The tango ended and a more upbeat version of the dance began. I stood up. I'd waited long enough.

I made my way toward the black door but the henna-headed woman must have seen me. She headed me off before I was able to open it.

"You can't go in there," she said, over the music. "It's private."

"But I'm with Rupert. I saw him go in there," I protested.

"You can't go in there. I told you. It's private."

But I pushed past her, shoved open the door and went through. I was in some kind of staff room. There was a desk with a computer and piles of paper beside it, and the smell of old whisky, stale and fresh cigarette smoke, and another closed fuggy smell. But there was no Rupert and no Hector Ferrer.

At the far end of the room was another closed door. I rushed up to it and opened it. It led to another corridor and at the end of that, an exit onto the street. I stood on the landing in the pouring rain. There wasn't a soul out on the street. Rupert Doyle and Hector Ferrer had gone.

Chapter Five

The woman stood in the center of the room. Her whole body was rigid.

"You must be Rupert's girlfriend," she said.

"No. No. I just wanted him to introduce me to Hector Ferrer. I know they're old acquaintances."

"That's a polite way of putting it." She laughed. "They're certainly not old friends. No. I would say that they're really just old rivals. Hector doesn't have many friends...."

"Do you know where they've gone? I gave Rupert a ride here. I wanted him to introduce me to Hector Ferrer and now they're both gone."

"Perhaps I can help you. What did you want to see Hector about?"

"It's complicated."

The woman shook her head as though trying to clear the slate and came over to me offering her hand. "I didn't mean to be rude. I'm Victoria. I'm Hector Ferrer's partner."

"Rupert didn't say anything about a partner."

How Thomas would have laughed at my reaction. I could just imagine him taking a long drag on his pipe, a cloud forming around his head like a halo, and then he'd study the ceiling with a wise philosopher's look on his face and say, "What did you expect, Dinah? That the world would be frozen in time? That you could be an infant again with your two immortal adoring parents adulating over your cradle? I understand your discomfort but people have to move on. The only thing you can expect in life is the unexpected."

I shook her hand. "I'm sorry. I didn't mean to be rude either. I'm Dinah. So Victoria…you're his partner in life or in art?"

"In life and art. We run this place together. We were a professional dance team some time ago but now we do more teaching than exhibition dancing. What did you want to see Hector about?"

I said, "All that shouting. What happened between the two of them? What were they arguing about? They sounded like they really hated each other."

"They had a falling out. Many years ago. Before Hector and I…before we got together. They may have gone to have a drink and talk about it. It's incredible that Rupert showed up here tonight…I always hoped that he and Hector could patch it up, but you don't know with Hector. You never know what he's going to do next. They must have gone for a drink." Then she did a strange thing. She put her hand on my shoulder and said, in the tone of a mother giving a daughter a lecture on the birds and the bees, "Hector can't talk about anything emotional without a drink. There are men in this world who have to choose between a woman and a bottle. It's like a love affair. Often he prefers the bottle to me."

It was obviously eating at her so much that she had to tell me, a total stranger, about it.

Her eyes, which were pale green, became glassy under fine

red worried eyebrows. "They could be away for days. He goes off on these bouts sometimes. They've probably gone off together. To lose themselves. Completely. And to fight with each other." She sighed with exasperation. "They used to enjoy doing it. Years ago. Before they fell out. You might as well give up for tonight. I know these men."

As we walked along the corridor toward the door, I was sure Victoria could sense the disappointment flowing from me. She asked again, "I'm sorry. I got sidetracked. Please. What was it you said you wanted from Hector?"

I struggled to think of something. "Uh…the…uh… tango. Tango lessons."

"Yes, of course. Well, Dinah, we always hold our *milongas* on…"

"Your *milongas*…yes…your dance night, right?"

"It's the big gathering, the important get-together in tango vocabulary. We hold our *milongas* on Friday and Saturday nights and Sunday afternoons. The rest of the time, during the week, we give group and private tango lessons and workshops. Come back next week. Monday, we're closed but Tuesday is the beginner's night. We'll see what we can do for you if you want to come then." She walked with me to the exit door. "Take care not to slip on those stairs. They're dangerous when they're wet. I keep telling Hector we need to do something about them, but he doesn't care about the practical things of life."

Reassuring.

"Can I ask you something?"

"Certainly," said Victoria.

"What does the word *bronca* mean?"

She laughed. "It's seething fury, badly contained, just on the edge of exploding." Then she added in a near whisper, "Hector's full of *bronca*."

Terrific.

I said goodbye to the gangster's moll, got in my car and

drove slowly home through the wet night. Hector Ferrer was putting that poor Victoria woman through hell and she was letting him do it. She had been so nice to me, really, that I sensed she probably did that often, tried to compensate for Hector's bad behavior by being nice to everybody and making excuses for him.

The *milonga* had been full though, so he had to have something special, some kind of drawing power, but for the life of me, I couldn't see what it was. If it was inner beauty it was well-buried. Usually, inner beauty sends at least one tiny periscope up to the surface.

By the time I had driven home and was towel-dried and in my bathrobe, my neighbor was in full swing. I pulled up a chair and parked myself beside the window with a glass of wine in my hand.

Along with the cats, he now had two goats frolicking around his living room. As soon as I realized what they were, I got up and went out through my French doors, along the balcony and in through Joey's French doors.

"Joey? Where are you?"

The living room door opened and Joey posed dramatically in his black satin bathrobe, his face covered in brown gunk. "Mud mask," he said, "It's supposed to cleanse and purify the skin."

"Joey, you have to come and have a peek through my curtains. Right now."

"But I'm cleansing. I'm on a schedule."

"Just a look. Go wash your face then come over. I'll see you in a minute."

Joey sighed, said, "That's a very expensive free sample going down the drain, I'll have you know," and went back into the bathroom.

A couple of minutes later, I ushered him into my darkened apartment. "Here, if you sit up on the arm of the chair, it's not too uncomfortable and you can see almost everything. Now, tell me what you think."

Joey perched and peered through the crack in the curtain. "Oh my God, what are those creatures?"

"Goats, Joey. He's got two goats in his living room."

Joey hummed the *Outer Limits* theme, then said, "Satan's beasts."

"What?"

"Satanic ritual."

"Naw. You think?"

"Are you kidding? This town is one of the hot spots for Satanic worship."

"Did you read that in *Variety,* too?"

"No. I read it in the *Demonic Daily.* Don't look at me like that, Dinah. Okay, maybe it was *Vancouver Magazine* or something like that. Other than Geneva, this is one of the Devil's capitals. So it's logical he'd have all those animals. Walpurgisnacht," he said, giving it his eeriest voice.

"Walpurgis what?"

"Halloween in the spring. It's like Christmas for the Satanists."

"Oh shit. Just what we need. Evil living next door."

"So that gives me an idea."

Most of Joey's ideas were extravagant, involving casts of thousands.

He went on, "What we need to do is get him out in the open on Halloween night." Joey smiled brightly. "Wanna have a party?"

Saturday

The next morning I didn't get to indulge in my usual weekend activities, such as lying around in bed reading real live dead tree newspapers, or watching *Magnum P.I.* reruns, or sipping my coffee so slowly it had to be heated up in the microwave at least twice. The phone call I'd been dreading came early.

"Hello?" said a man's voice. "Is that Dinah Nichols?"

That voice yanked me back to another time, when I'd been a different Dinah. A younger, more naive Dinah. Some would say a stupider Dinah. At any rate, a Dinah who had sex more than once a year.

So even though I knew exactly who it was, I said, "Yes. Who's this?"

"It's me, Di. It's Mike."

"Mike. I didn't recognize your voice. How are you?"

"I'm great. Fantastic. I got married."

"I know. My mother told me. Congratulations."

"Yeah. We're just getting our place organized. It's not far from yours. Close to Kits Beach. We were out in Burnaby for a couple of months but we finally got this great place in Kits. It was a real coup. Yeah, we're really happy about it."

"Oh, that's…uh…that's uh…really…"

Irritating. Afraid you might lose your important Nichols connection, are you, Mike?

"What did you say, Dinah?"

"Terrific, Mike. So, do you have some work over here?"

"I have some hours as research assistant up at the U. And there's a big field project I've applied for. Doing some pods of orca off Friday Harbour. I'm getting your mother to put in a good word for me."

I'll bet you are, I thought.

He said, "So how's it going with you? We haven't seen each other in…how long?"

"It's been nearly a year, Mike."

A year since that last strange accidental meeting at my mother's house after not seeing each other for months, and the afternoon of accidental farewell sex that followed while my mother was out chasing whales.

"Yeah, well, I thought you and me and Dawn…that's my

wife…I thought we could all get together. Dawn really wants to meet you."

"I'll bet she does," I said.

There was a knocking at my back door. I had a sudden moment of panic over the state of my place. Now that Mike was a couple, he would have expectations.

Since there was no point in prolonging the agony, I had invited them over right away. Dinner at my place that night. Just to get the whole miserable business over with.

Dribbles of moisture had made long lines on the steamed-up windows and my vision was obscured. I'd labored all afternoon and the cooking smells were gourmet and delicious.

I went to open the door.

Mike, the same as ever, downscale gorgeous in a ratty gray pullover, messy longish curly brown hair, permanent five-o'clock shadow, and worn jeans, was standing there with a tiny girl, a sort of miniature pale breed of female, tucked neatly into his armpit. She was at least a head and a half shorter than him and had ethereal looks, white-blond baby-fine hair, transparent white skin that showed blue veins throbbing at the temples, tiny slender hands, and feet so small that she probably had to buy her shoes in the children's department. She was wearing a long drippy dress that resembled a body-size white spiderweb and over that, an off-white crushed velvet coat.

Against my better judgment, I invited Mike and Tinkerbell in.

"This is Dawn," said Mike.

"I'm Dinah." I shook Dawn's hand, taking care not to break it right off.

"I know," said Dawn, in a child's voice. "Mikey's told me all about you."

But Mikey wouldn't have told Dawn all about me, the whole story about him and me, because he didn't really know it himself. He couldn't see what I could see. He was

too involved, too caught up in it all. At least that was what
I'd speculated to Thomas in one of my therapy sessions, and
he'd agreed that it was possible.

Mike handed me a bottle.

"Thanks," I said. "You brought some wine. Nice...
good...where's it from?" But then I had a closer look at the
label. "A great vintage...nonalcoholic wine."

"Dawn doesn't drink," said Mike.

In a voice that didn't sound old enough to use Tampax,
let alone alcohol, Dawn said, "I'm allergic to the histamines
in red wine and the antifreeze in white wine."

"That's okay," I said, holding up their bottle, "this will go
just fine with the goulash anyway."

Dawn and Mike exchanged a quick look of panic.

I winced. "Don't tell me. Dawn doesn't eat meat either?
I'm sorry. I should have asked about that. My fault."

Where did Mike, that flesh-eating, Scotch-swilling man,
find a girl like Dawn? Under a buttercup?

Now Mike was leading Dawn into my living room, and
sitting her carefully down in the biggest armchair, the armchair that had once been mine and Mike's, in another apartment, in another life.

He touched her the way one might touch an invalid. "She
doesn't buy any kind of animal products," he said, "and that
includes shoes, purses, belts, all of those things. She wears
leatherette or natural fiber shoes. It's amazing to be with
someone who lives by the strength of her convictions."

By the look of things, her convictions were her only
strengths. Those and her ability to get Mike behaving like
her private slave.

Mike jerked his head toward the kitchen. "Find something
she can eat, would you, Dinah?"

I excused myself, went into the kitchen and rummaged
around for some fairy feed, some celery and carrot sticks. She
wouldn't be able to touch the smoked oyster and bacon ap-

petizers that I'd set on the table. They were dead pig and dead mollusk in her books. Mike helped himself though, shoveling in the appetizers like there was no tomorrow, and when I brought out a bottle of real wine and poured myself a glass, he helped himself to that too.

Dawn nibbled on the carrots.

As I was setting the rest of the food on the table, I asked Dawn, "So what else can you eat, Dawn, if you can't eat goulash? What can I give you?"

"Well, tofu…"

"Sorry, no tofu. I can't stand tofu. It's like eating hand soap."

"Do you have some other kind of vegetable? Apart from carrots?"

"I've got some broccoli."

"I can eat that."

"I'll prepare it for you."

Five minutes later everything was on the table. Mike began to dig in, no formalities. He ate like a starving man. Dawn eyed the broccoli with suspicion. "How did you get this cooked so fast?"

"Microwave," I said.

She shook her head violently. "Oh, no, I can't eat this. Not if it's been microwaved."

I shrugged and went into the kitchen. I picked up the salad bowl, brought it out and held it under her nose. "You can eat this. This is star grass, red lettuce and rocket leaves. They were all cultivated in my mother's vegetable garden over on the island. No pesticides. My mother, as Mikey will tell you, is perfect at everything she does."

Mike nodded vehemently. "Absolutely, Dawn, you don't have to worry if it came from Marjory's garden."

Dawn plucked up a lettuce leaf and nibbled at it. "You're right. You can taste the difference. You can tell it was grown organically."

Sure. Grown organically for the big-city mass market by

my friends at Safeway up the street. What Dawn didn't know wouldn't hurt her. Well, only a little.

It went downhill from there. Over the goulash, I got to listen to an in-depth analysis of Dawn's health. It started with her headaches and degenerated into a complete rundown of her periods, the length and size of them, the measures that had to be taken to lessen her pain, and the fact that they'd have to hurry up if they wanted children because Dawn's uterus was a complex affair, more complex than any other woman's on this planet.

I kept a big stupid grin on my face the whole time and to numb what was left of my senses, I brought out the brandy bottle and poured myself huge slugs. Then I watched as Mike did the same. As they talked on, I drifted over to my window. My neighbor was exercising again, amidst the cats and goats. Soon I was drifting into a strange fantasy in which my well-toned neighbor had magically gone from gay to straight and given up Satan.

Sunday

The following morning was sunny and crisp. My hangover and I were going for a jog. I was just pulling on my Nikes when Joey appeared at my French doors. He had his mug of coffee in one hand and copy of *Variety* in the other. He pushed past me, marched along to my kitchen, back up into my living room, looked around and asked, "Did they catch them?"

"Who?"

"The people who broke into your apartment last night."

"I had a dinner party."

"Anybody I know?"

"Yes, but not very interesting. Except from an anthropological point of view. Ex-true love Mike and new wife Dawn. It was so awful, Joey. This woman he's married, I think she's been genetically modified. She's very small and wan. Like a pixie really. Did you know that pixies have very bad periods that last for at least five weeks? I'm not inviting them over ever, ever again. I don't know how he married somebody like that. Mike's completely lost it."

Joey shuddered. "Glad I couldn't come. It sounds fucking awful. Have you ever noticed that most married couples look as though they'd been lobotomized? Until they start having affairs, that is. Count yourself lucky to have gotten rid of Mike."

"Oh, I do," I said, wistfully.

Joey stretched himself out on my couch with his feet on the armrest. I went over and yanked them off. "I'll bet you don't put your feet up on your armrests. What's wrong with your apartment?" I said.

"I like yours better. I like the clutter. My place is too tidy. It doesn't feel lived in."

"That's because it isn't. You do all your living here. See you later. If anyone calls, tell them I'll be back in an hour. I'm going for a run."

On the back porch of my building, in the brisk gleaming fall air, I did a few warm-ups on the porch rail then forced my leaden legs to get moving. I sprinted sluggishly down the stairs, along the side path, turned the corner leading into a tight passageway, and ran straight into my neighbor. He was coming and I was going and it was a huge flub (Joey's and my word for running smack into someone you've gawked at from afar). The big body bump became a spontaneous embrace, because we had to grab each other to get our balance.

Then we dodged back and forth five or six times until he said, "Wanna dance?"

I grinned. He placed his hands on my shoulders and said, "Okay now. You go first and I won't move."

I had a little twinge of sadness. It was a pity that the best ones were taken, by other men, or other women. We passed each other slowly. But I forced myself to be optimistic. I turned around quickly and shouted, just as he had almost reached the end of the path, "Oh wait, we're having a block party on Halloween. I'm letting everyone on the street know. In case you happen to be around that night. And spread the word."

Over his shoulder, he said, "Block party, eh? Okay."

But he seemed apprehensive. Maybe he was worried it would cut into his Black Mass? Or his rendezvous with a goat?

I nodded and ran off in the direction of Kits Beach and the new address that Mike had written down for me the night before. I needed to check it out. My plan was to whizz past their place faster than the speed of light taking everything in from the corner of my eye but keeping my gaze straight ahead as if I couldn't possibly be running by there except by pure chance. Mike had been a jogger when I knew him so there was the risk of running into him, but I was willing to run it. I doubted that I would bump into Dawn jogging though. Her body was so smooth and tiny, with no muscular definition whatsoever. She probably didn't use her legs to get her around. She probably just opened up her transparent fairy wings and fluttered over to her destination.

Kits Beach was Pickup Heaven that day. A strip of deep blue ruffled ocean separated the green park with its russet trees from the glassy West End high-rises gleaming against distant blue mountains. The long stretch of beachside park was crowded, guys and girls out in full flirtation regalia, joggers in the skimpiest sportswear, dog-walkers using their animals as an excuse, even a few diehard topless sunbathers taking up the patches where there was shelter from the wind. I wanted to shout at them, "It's all a trick of nature. It's a trap. Autumn is the natural mating season for human beings. Don't fall for it."

I started to worry when I turned the corner onto Mike and Dawn's street. It was too nice, a small Yuppyville of big classy renovated houses the whole way along. As I approached Mike and Dawn's place, my plan of racing past fell to pieces. I just had to stop and gawk. In the past, Mike's accommodations had always been a little funky, in the grottiest sense of the word, two-story duplexes of scientific interest (fungi and silverfish), no balconies, no surrounding gardens, no fireplaces, no curlicues, no Bauhaus chic, no character. Because Mike was thinking of other things, of his studies in marine mammal science, of his career. My first night with Mike had been spent on a sheet spread out on the wall-to-wall carpet in an otherwise empty apartment.

Mike and Dawn had a whole three-story house to themselves. There was only one doorbell. I peeked at the name on the post box and there was only theirs. It was a huge old converted family home with lots of new cedar siding, three glassed-in balconies looking seaward, useful for tanning on winter days, brass fixtures and railings, and more southern exposure than I could dream of.

I wanted to hate him. He'd used my heart as one of the rungs in his ladder to success. But when I saw that house, it just wasn't possible to hate him properly. I knew something about his taste in women. He liked them well rounded. He'd married for money and now he'd have to live with the consequences of his actions, fairy wings and all. I turned around and jogged toward home, my legs still feeling like sticks of lead.

When I got back from my run, Joey was prone on my couch.

"There were two calls while you were out of the office, Miss Nichols."

"Oh, really? Tell. Tell."

"Yes, okay. The first was your Greek Food Pervert. He thought I was you when I answered. Okay, I confess I did a very good imitation of you."

"What did he say?"

"He said he wanted to come over and lick your thighs and I told him that it could take forever, given their size, but that if he wanted to come over and lick mine it would only take a quarter of the time."

"Thanks a lot, Joey. You're a *big* help. What was the second call?"

"Oh, some very boring-sounding straight macho type called Trutch. Said he wants you to come into the office."

Chapter Six

"Trutch," I nearly spat. "Ian Trutch?"

"Something like that."

"Ian Trutch phoned me at home on a Sunday?"

"Uh-oh. Trouble."

"What else did he say, Joey?"

Joey rolled his eyes. "Oh, God. She likes him. Dinah's got the hots for him. Get out the antidepressants, we're in for the big one, the World Expo special roller-coaster ride through emotional hell."

"Joey, c'mon. He's the enemy. He's come directly from The Dark Side to ruin our lives. So what did he say?"

"Now we're going to get the oh-so-boring daily descriptions of his every move, what he wore, the way he looked at her, *when* he bothered to look at her, the way he poured his cream into his coffee."

"He doesn't take cream. He takes his coffee black and steaming but I could care less."

"It's worse than I thought."

"But he does drive a Ferrari, black with beige upholstery. I've never been out with a guy who drives a Ferrari."

"Dinah, you've hardly ever been out with a guy. Period."

"How can you say that? What about Mike?"

"Oh, I don't mean the serious heartbreak kind of guy. I mean the fun kind. The use once and throw away disposable kind."

"I envy you, Joey, I wish I could but I can't."

"It takes practice, lots and lots of practice."

And then came an anxious hour, waiting for Ian Trutch to call me back. Much as I distrusted him, I still wanted to impress him. Show him how I absolutely, but absolutely stylishly, did not care. Joey gave a sports announcer's play-by-play of me showering and choosing my clothes.

And then the call came.

"And she scores," yelled Joey above the ringing telephone.

"Quiet," I blasted, then said sweetly into the mouthpiece, "Dinah Nichols here."

"Dinah, Ian Trutch."

"Hello… Mr. Trutch."

"Call me Ian."

"Ian."

"Sorry to ask you this on a Sunday, but I'm down at the office right now, and I can see that there are a few things that need a working over."

A working over?

"And you're the woman I need. Right now if you don't mind." His tone was playful. "I've got some of the campaign materials right here in front of me. Do you mind coming down and briefing me on them?" he asked.

I didn't want to sound eager. At the risk of being fired, I said, "It's Sunday, that famous day of rest. I had other plans," I lied.

"It won't take long at all. I'll pick you up. I need a break from all this paperwork. Where do you live?"

I told him. "Park at the front," I said, "The Pataran Café's on the ground floor. I'll come out to meet you."

I was ready for the enemy. I'd been ready ever since I first Googled his name, ever since I'd saved the Web page with his picture to my Images file. I was ready from my tight crimson sweater with the low neckline, my hipster jeans that shifted the focus from my thighs and showed off my trim waistline, my open and unbelted Burberry and its Sunday casual look, right down to my black lace underwear, which, I confess, was a case of my body, not my mind, choosing my clothes.

An hour later, even Joey was impressed that I was going to be picked up by a guy driving a Ferrari. "Now Dinah, I suggest that before he gets here, you go down to the corner and buy a can of gasoline, then take a cab down to Green World International, pour the stuff around your office and light a match, then hurry back here so he can pick you up. That way, you should be arriving just as the news team reaches the scene of the crime, and everyone watching local TV will be able to see you riding in that car."

"Thanks, Joey. I know I can always count on you for good practical advice."

When Ian pulled up in front of my building and honked, I took the stairs two at a time. I shot down the back path and around the corner and BLAM, almost ran into my neighbor again. He was carrying something live and off-white in his arms, and yelled, "Careful."

The thing started bleating and kicking.

"It's a…goat. Sorry. I'm really sorry," I said.

Sorry, Son of Satan.

"We're okay here. Just got to get a grip… calm ourselves down a little." The goat kicked in his arms.

Hmmm. He shared a Royal We with an animal. He identified with a goat. I have to say it piqued my curiosity, given that I'd been a sister to cats, dogs and ponies.

He went on, "We might need to put a traffic light on this path." Still gripping onto the goat tightly, he set it down on the ground and kept one arm around its neck. He kneeled down next to the animal, stroked it, looked up at me, gave my clothes some close scrutiny, and smiled.

I gave him a nervous little wave, said, "See you," and headed toward Ian's car.

My neighbor was still kneeling and watching, now with a look of awe on his face. It was either the Ferrari he was admiring, or its driver. Ian Trutch looked uber-gorgeous leaning against the car, in a vampiresque sort of way. He didn't fool me though.

Ian actually came around and opened the door for me. In my Mike days, it had always been my Mini with Mike in the driver's seat, and when we were out together in public, Mike running five paces ahead of me while I hurried to keep up. His legs were long. Mine were short. I had always put that rushing ahead of his down to childlike enthusiasm. Now I put it down to childishness.

As Ian helped me into the passenger seat, I knew it was an "on" day, one of those special days you can feel down to your heels. You know, even before you leave the house, that you're going to attract the right kind of attention. Because you just don't care about any of the men around you. You feel so great that it absolutely does not matter whether you have a boyfriend or not. In fact, you're beginning to think that you're much better off without one. Boyfriends can be so oppressive, especially when the world belongs to you and you're running free in it, when you're flying. And naturally, it's in the male's predatorial makeup to want to bring any free-flying bird to the ground. And the more he chases you, the further and higher you want to go.

It was a giddy feeling.

As we rode along in Ian's Ferrari, he put some old soul tunes on his stereo. The volume was so high it was impossible to talk. It made people on the street turn and look at us, which suited my mood nicely.

We roared toward the office, zooming and weaving dangerously between the other cars. As we careened through the streets, my heart was pounding with excitement, not because I thought Ian Trutch could ever be more to me than a higher management dictator who viewed me as a corporate lackey, but because for the first time since breaking up with Mike, I didn't look over wishing it were Mike in the driver's seat of the car.

When we arrived, Ian politely ushered me ahead of him and up to the boardroom, where he had papers arranged in various piles along the big table.

He picked up a printed sheet. "This. Your list of guests for the next fund-raiser, to be held at the…Space Centre?"

"Where did you get that? From my desk? That's my personal list," I accused. "I haven't finished working on it."

"It belongs to the company. When you're in the office, *you* belong to the company."

"You're joking."

"Only a little." He flashed a brief smile, then frowned again as he went over the list.

"Something wrong with it?" I ventured.

He pointed to the first name and said, "Come here and sit down, please." He patted the seat of the chair beside him. I sat.

"Okay, Dinah, who's this and how much is he worth?"

Ian wanted to know everything about each guest, who they were and most importantly, what kind of financial bracket they were in and how much we'd succeeded in getting them to donate in the past. The interrogation went on for more than half an hour.

And then he asked, "Is there anybody not on this list who should be?"

"What do you mean?"

"Who are the wealthiest people in the city?"

"We try to approach them all, names like Lui, Sosa, the Haljis, Wallis, Cohn, Patterson, and some of them make a donation occasionally. But the elusive one is Hamish Robertson. Nobody's seen him. Nobody even knows what he looks like. He's a recluse."

"We need to get him on the list."

I couldn't tell Ian Trutch how right he was.

He picked up another sheet of paper. "Maybe it's my Eastern mentality but can these really be viable? The recycling depot? Tree Canada? The Coalition for Alternative Renewable Energy."

"Viable?"

"We're supposed to be building business models here, Dinah, not throwing money directly into the ocean."

"But these are all pilot projects. Start-ups. Some are government funded. They all need time."

"Mudpuddle? What's that?"

"Aquatic waste-treatment ponds. Where natural organisms convert the toxic substances."

"Ah."

"Some of our cities are still dumping raw untreated sewage into the ocean, if you can believe it, and we're going to pay the price. Mudpuddle uses natural elements, zooplankton, phytoplankton, microbial communities, algae, snails, in other words—critters—that are naturally present in aquatic systems, lakes and wetlands, to break down waste. Instead of some of the present systems—sequential batch reactors, mixed oxidant disinfection, membrane systems. But the process still has to be further tested and refined. Biomimicry takes time."

He gave me a luxurious smile and said, "Biomimicry.

Batch reactors. I love the way you say those words." He laughed. "There's a bit of a learning curve for me here, Dinah. I hope you'll help me out and explain a few things. So you're saying the priority at this branch is water?"

"Water."

Ian's mouth turned upward into a little smirk.

"Without water we have nothing. It's the most precious thing on the planet."

"Yeeeees?" he said, as if waiting to hear the alphabet recited by a small child.

"Mudpuddle will be an important prototype." *If I could only find the replacement donor.*

He pondered it and I could almost hear the gears turning in his head. "Dinah, as you know, I am here to get things running smoothly and profitably. If I find that my crystal ball doesn't give me any figures to back up the feasibility of these projects, then changes will be made."

I stared at him, incredulous. My whole body tingled with shock symptoms. I was going to have to use all my energies, for the sake of our jobs and future, to try to bring him around.

In a quiet staccato voice, I said, "Science has the figures. Science is *bombarding* us with the figures. Every day. Pollution of every kind. Even the heads of the big oil companies are admitting that they're worried, that there's a problem. Even *their* people are saying we have to change our ways, cut emissions, start sequestering carbon dioxide, find alternative renewable fuels, replant, or it'll be big trouble for the planet. Can't you feel the way the sun burns your skin?"

He grinned. "Financial considerations will always rule the day. There's too much big business involved, too much money at stake. Nobody can afford to run at a loss," he replied.

"So we might as well lie down and let them screw us. Is that what you're saying?" I'd expected him to be difficult, but not *oblivious* to our mission.

He smiled and I almost had to shade my eyes. He said, fatalistically, "I think that Green World is going to have to re-examine its priorities. So far, all this Mudpuddle has produced is a deficit. And apparently will go on producing it for a while."

I felt a little queasy but I wasn't discouraged. I'd had a lot of success in the past at converting even the most hard-hearted and self-centered hedonists to our cause. I leapt back into the fray. "But Mudpuddle is going to be our big presentation at the Space Centre. We're inaugurating it, presenting the experiment results and plans to our foreign counterparts. We've moved offices because of it. We've hired more people. We hired Penelope. We hired…"

Ian sat up straighter. "Ah, yes. Now tell me more about Penelope."

My least favorite topic.

"Not much to know," I said. "She went to a Swiss boarding school, and after that, Bennington College where she studied Prudery 400. Her family's in Toronto and all of us here at GWI think that she's a bit of a pain in the ass. I mean, maybe under all that paranoia, there might be a nice girl, in fact, I sense there is. So I just don't understand why she's on this modesty crusade. If she weren't so good at languages, she probably wouldn't have been hired. Because she doesn't try to get along. Not with me, anyway."

Ian smiled then asked, "Well-to-do?"

"Does it matter?"

He didn't answer me. I had the feeling that Ian Trutch obsessed about money above and beyond the call of duty.

I said, "I'm pretty sure she is. I haven't actually hacked into her parents' bank account but she has all the trappings of wealth. We'll find out soon enough. We systematically hit up all employees for donations, Ian. We ruthlessly persecute people in our own offices all year long, hounding everyone to death, as well as the families of people who work here, and the people we buy coffee from and those who take out

our garbage and bring our mail and anybody else who is unfortunate enough to cross our paths or be the target of our
e-mails and phone calls and general harassing, so rest assured
that Penelope's parents, if they have a cent to toss our way,
will not get off lightly. All of us working here give to the
cause. I hope you'll do the same."

He laughed and tossed back his dark head. He was so
beautiful in that slightly evil way, and he was having an attack of charisma. It was all coming in my direction. My body
and mind wrestled, everything shifting and swaying. I could
feel my principles weakening, falling away in the face of his
gorgeousness. Maybe it was the fact that I'd turned thirty and
life's unpredictability was weighing on me. Maybe it was the
horrible dinner with Mike and Fairy Girl the night before.
Or maybe it was the fact that I could get hit by a bus tomorrow and all my great principles wouldn't be of the
slightest use then, would they?

Man-eater? Okay, Penelope, I thought, I'll show you a
man-eater.

Ian said, "It's well past lunchtime. Should we get a bite?"
He cocked his head to one side and added, "You know, I've
been meaning to tell you, you have the most striking eyes.
When I saw those black eyes of yours for the first time, I
wanted to see what you looked like when you got mad."

I do have striking eyes, if I do say so myself. Large and
dark, and set off nicely by my thick glossy black hair. It's almost enough to take the focus off my thighs.

He said, "If looks could kill I would have been a little pile
of ashes. You scorched me. I love it."

And then he laughed again and poured a few more gal-
lons of charisma over me.

So I let him take me out to lunch. It was a perfect opportunity to convert him to our cause.

We went to Diva at the Met. My choice. I liked its un-
derstated style, marble, wood, brass and glass, its open kitchen,

its unaffordable prices. Ian helped me off with my coat, pulled out my chair, stared at me, and smiled at me as though no one else in the world existed. I felt a little overwhelmed, like being under a spotlight, but I managed to hold my own.

Our conversation started off with Ian's opinion and rating of all the famous restaurants he'd tried in his lifetime. Not what you'd call a groundbreaking discussion but it didn't matter. He was mesmerizing to look at and if I timed my nods carefully, it seemed as though I was actually interested in what he was saying. And then when the moment was right, I would go in for the environmental kill.

I had the lobster risotto and chicken with truffles and Ian had the lamb shank and we shared a warm chocolate soufflé for dessert. The chilled Riesling went down too well.

The waiter wouldn't stop ogling Ian. He kept finding excuses to come over to our table, dropping things and taking forever to pick them up, and hovering and never once making eye contact with me. In an eyelash-batting marathon, he would have been a gold medalist. But Ian Trutch was watching me that day. Then I decided to turn the conversation in another direction.

"So…Ian. Now tell me all about yourself. I've been studying your dossier…"

"My dossier?"

"Okay, then. I've Googled you. More than once."

Flattery. According to Cleo, they love it. They can't get enough of it.

"Ah."

"Well, we have to know the enemy, don't we?"

He laughed. "Am I the enemy?"

"Of course you are. You're higher management. You want to axe a bunch of nice people who are trying to save the world. Now, according to your page on the company Web site, you're a Harvard Business School graduate."

He didn't flinch. "Graduated in the top five of the class."

He pressed his hands together, prayer fashion, and touched his forefingers to his lips.

"Modest, too, I see."

"I had a plan."

"I'll bet you did. Swoop into office like a higher management vampire ready to create a new army of undead."

"Undead? Sorry?"

"Unemployed, Ian. Only with slightly healthier complexions, but still undead if you leave them without a job. Sorry, should have said leave 'us.' I read the whole dossier. Including the gritty bits."

He tried to derail me. "Those Harvard days were good times."

"Uh-huh?"

"A lot of fun. Yeah. A lot of parties. Martha's Vineyard. Sailing into the Newport Festival. Me and Chaz Vanpfeffer."

"A friend of yours, this Chaz Vanpfeffer?"

"We were great buddies. The Vanpfeffers are an old Boston family. I'm surprised you haven't heard of them."

"Me, too." I would have remembered a name that sounded like a Dr. Seuss character.

The conversation turned into a monologue on all the society parties Ian had been to when he was at university. I had to fight to keep my eyes open. He finally paid the bill and we drove toward my place in wine-fuzzy silence.

He said, "Today was fun, Dinah."

Fun? You're about to nuke our workplace and you call it fun?

I needed to try a humanizing tactic. Maybe if he knew the office people better he might care about what happened to them.

I replied, "Ian, we're having a block party here on Halloween. I hope you'll come. Everybody from the office is coming too."

"I might. I'll think about it." He leaned slowly into me. In an ideal hard-to-get campaign I should have pulled away but I wanted to hang for a guilty second on his leathery fragrance. I was expecting a dry peck on the cheek but he startled me by kissing me on the mouth. I faked indifference, got out of the car and walked up the path to my apartment without looking back.

Monday

I was in the office early. Roly's yellow slicker outfit was hanging from the coat hook when I arrived and he was already installed at Lisa's desk folding brochures. We figured his sleeping quarters must be a hot air vent nearby.

"Morning, Roly."

He said a husky, barely-audible "Morning."

I found Lisa and Cleo alone at the coffee machine upstairs, and told them quietly, "Meeting at Notte's after work. Just us and Ida and Fran. It's important. I don't want Jake there."

Ian had been swallowed up by Ash's office again. There was no glimpse of him, but she kept coming out of her office to go into the bathroom and I have to say, she was a work-in-progress. She'd let down her long black hair and was wearing a hundred noisy silver bangles on her wrists. With her frump suit. Each time she emerged from the bathroom, her perfume brought tears to our eyes.

All morning, I made calls to the big businessmen I knew, trying to get information on the whereabouts of Hamish Robertson.

"Hamish Robertson? I thought he'd died," said one.

Another offered, "Oh, a friend of mine spotted him in the Bahamas last year."

Yet another said, "Didn't he move back to Scotland?"

The last person I talked to said, "I heard a rumor he'd been carted away to Riverview in a white dinner jacket. A total nutcase, apparently."

Terrific. They knew as much as I did. But I trusted

Tod's word. He'd never let me down. Well, almost never, that is.

After that I left several messages for Rupert Doyle at the Eldorado Hotel to call me when he got in. We needed to talk about Hector Ferrer.

At Notte's, Cleo bit into her éclair and said through her mouthful, "We are in deep shit. Bankrupt. Tod, of all people. I don't believe it. Do you think he has other people's money down there in the Caymans? What's this going to do to Mudpuddle? Are we screwed or what?"

"Gosh," said Lisa, "we'll have to cancel the whole thing. Two years of work."

"*Many* years of work," I corrected, "if you throw in all the university's effort."

"Cancel, shmancel," said Ida. "What's wrong with you girls? Where's your fighting spirit?"

"Do we tell Jake is the burning question," said Cleo.

"I want to hold off on telling Jake a little longer. And we're not canceling anything," I said. "We just need to find this Hamish Robertson and get his donation. Tod's word is as good as a signed check."

All the other women burst out laughing. "Like his last check, right?"

"What crappy timing," said Fran. "Just when we got Wonder Boy breathing down our necks. Mind you, I wouldn't mind a little of his hot and heavy on my neck, just as long as it's in the bedroom and not in the office."

Tuesday

I dragged Joey with me to Los Tangueros.

"Oh my God," he said. "It's a ballroom."

"Tango only."

"Dinah, you're trying to torture me. There isn't a gay man in the place. They're all metrosexuals."

"How can you tell? We only just arrived."

"I can tell. I can tell. I get my gay radar serviced every week."

The room was surprisingly full. There were couples of all kinds, all ages, learning the basic steps from Victoria, who went through the movements slowly at the front of the room. Then she stepped back while Hector Ferrer wandered through the couples correcting body positions and barking insults at them.

That night he'd left the gangster outfit at home and he looked a lot better. The dancing duds he'd been wearing the other night had significantly exaggerated his worst features. Tonight he wore jeans, a black T-shirt and running shoes. Apart from the thickness through his waist, he appeared to be handsomer, more muscular than the first night I'd seen him. Tonight, as opposed to looking thuggish, he looked like the craggy tragic antihero of an off-beat European existentialist art film, something involving a girl and smoking gun.

His face was more expressive tonight. His eyes were dark and sad, with heavy purplish circles around them. Sometimes, a wry little smile would dart across his mouth and his face would light up. Then it would disappear and everything darken again. An eternal cigarette hung off his lower lip. He must have had the full respect of his students. Nobody dared protest when he breathed clouds of smoke into their faces.

I wavered between vague disappointment and fascination. At one point, when he was actually shouting—no, raging—at a pair of students, I thought about quietly slipping away and forgetting about him. The problem was, I would have to answer to Thomas. He would accuse me of supreme cowardice, take it as a personal failure, if I ran away.

My fabulous father, the bad-tempered Hector Ferrer.

And then Joey, who can never resist being the class clown, said just a little too loudly, "So what the Hec, eh?"

Hector turned his head abruptly and glared at Joey then at me. "You two. Be quiet or get out."

I stammered, "We're here to look into lessons. I spoke to Victoria about it."

"Ah." He stared at me and blanched. He looked confused. Then he inspected me and nodded, his eyes brightening a little. "Talk to me at the end of this session. I am busy in this moment, as you can see," he said in a surprisingly eloquent growl, a strange clipped accent with a tinge of something British and a tinge of something foreign and unrecognizable.

Joey and I sat down at one of the little tables and watched the lesson.

I forced myself to shut down my emotions and try to see him in an objective light, ignoring what I'd seen the first night and concentrating on the moment. After observing him for half an hour, I had to admit that he had a special quality. There was a stealthy menacing grace in his movements. Whenever he made the class stop to watch him perform or demonstrate a dance sequence, the air around him seemed more vibrant.

"*Caminata. Paseo…paso, paso, paso…*no," he scolded a pretty young dancer. "It is just a walk. Do you remember how to walk or is this too difficult for you? Now, show me." Hector's tone was so intimidating that I'm sure he had all of us doubting whether or not we knew how to walk.

"Try again," he said.

One minute he was barking at one couple, the next, sinisterly crooning at another. He was a tyrant and I was dragged through every emotion by Hector during that lesson, even though I was only an observer. It was exhausting to watch the way he treated his students. Empathizing with them, I felt like a beaten dog one minute, and an elated professional dancer the next. Elated because Hector was suddenly kind and gentle to a student, just like that, for no reason, out of the blue.

After an hour and a half of teaching the steps in unaccompanied silence, Hector surprised us. He walked down to the little stage at the end of the room, sank onto the piano stool and began to play. It was a surging, exciting, modern snarl of tango rhythms and jazz combinations. The people in the room perked up. They were being given their reward. They began to dance. The whole room turned to his piano music and when he stopped playing, I realized that he'd been improvising. Then he switched on the recorded music and the people resumed their dancing.

After that, he came over to me, an odd expression on his face. I wondered if Rupert had said anything he shouldn't.

"So you want tango lessons," he asked, in a challenging tone.

"Yes."

Joey barged in. "She wants private lessons. With you and you only Mr. Ferrer. Just the two of you."

I glared at Joey. He was jamming out on me. "Well...you do, don't you?" he said between clenched teeth.

"My lessons are expensive," said Hector.

"That's... that's okay." I'd have to put Thomas on the back burner for a while.

Hector was looking at me with a softening faraway expression. "Do I know you? Have we met before?" He actually smiled and there it was. A glimmer of his mystique.

Hector snapped his fingers and called out, "Victoria, the agenda," as if addressing a servant. Victoria nodded and hurried off to get it. I loathed him again.

Wednesday

The next morning, Ian passed me in the hallway. His "Hello Dinah" was definitely distant and frosty. Maybe he'd somehow found out about Tod. I made a resolution to avoid him for the rest of the day.

A little later, two girls came into the office and asked for Lisa. They were volunteers, a pair of young, ditzy, annoying narcissistic girls, who had been sent by a big clothing company to donate their time to Green World.

Lisa left them in the main room and came back to consult with me. "What are we going to do with these two?"

"I don't know. I was hoping you'd have some ideas?"

Lisa said, "They're mentally and socially challenged. You remember our last event. Well, I had them filling up our basic GWI balloons and I'm telling you, there was no getting them away from the helium tank. They were breathing it in and squeaking and peeping like a couple of chipmunks on drugs. I couldn't keep them away from it. Just what I need. A pair of airheads with a helium dependency issue."

"Now that you mention it, I remember that. It was dire."

"Well, now. Let me think. The city just cleaned out the civic fountains and wanted to donate all the spare change to us. At first we were going to say no, but then we thought, heck, it's all money. Usually we wouldn't take coins, but there are heaps and heaps of them and they're all really slimy from being in the water so long. How about we get these babes here to wash and count them all for us?"

"Lisa, you are a genius."

"I figure they're allergic to work. Probably thought this would be a nice little holiday away from their regular job. So I thought I'd get Roly to oversee the Helium Sisters when he gets back. I sent him out to get some donuts for coffee break."

"Hope he doesn't run off with the petty cash."

"Oh, he would never do that. He's very…uh…nice…"

"Nice?"

"And reliable. It really surprised me. Phlegmatic."

"Well, just as long as the phlegm stays where it belongs."

"He's not like other street people," Lisa insisted. "Really, he's not. You should talk to him sometime, Dinah."

"Oh, I will." *Not.*

A few minutes later, Lisa had the two girls set up. Their arms were deep in basins of soapy water as they sloshed and complained. "This is so not hot…like…whatever. Can we go now?"

I was stretched out on the leather couch and Thomas, with his longish curly salt-and-pepper hair and beard, his patchy corduroys and pipe tobacco scents, was breathing and puffing smoke not far from my ear.

"I saw him, Thomas. I saw my father."

"Yes? This is great news, Dinah."

"I don't know. He's a tango teacher. He has a place. A dance studio, I guess you could call it… Los Tangueros. It's in the middle of nowhere. And he has a…companion. It's a bit…"

"Yes?"

"Awful. It's awful."

"Why?"

"It's just not what I expected. Who I expected my father to be."

"Have you spoken to him?"

"I told him I was interested in tango lessons. I had to say something."

"But you haven't told him you're his daughter?"

"I'm not ready."

"Fair enough."

"It was such a shock."

"Yes?"

"I was expecting somebody more…more…like us. Like

my mother. A scientist. An intellectual. And not foreign. And there's something else."

"What?"

"He wears two-toned shoes. I mean, I don't know if he wears them all the time, but he definitely wears them for the big dance nights."

Thomas laughed. "Dinah, sometimes you surprise me."

"Oops, sorry, Thomas. You wear two-tone shoes too. I might have known."

"People are often attracted to their opposites. And you don't know the man."

"I don't know if I want to."

"That would be a hasty judgment. You know, Dinah, the idea of tango lessons isn't such a bad one."

"For who? For me?"

"Who else are we talking about here?"

"You're joking. It was just something to say on the spur of the moment. I needed an excuse."

"You know, Dinah, there is something about tango lessons…."

"Yes?"

"Tango lessons might help you learn how to follow a man."

I turned and stared at Thomas. For the first time since the start of my sessions with him, I was speechless.

Saturday

The weather on Halloween night was warm and almost clear. There was a pumpkin-colored moon veiled over by a lacy scrim of milky cloud. We had lucked out because according to all the weather forecasts for that day, it should have been pouring rain.

Joey and I had canvassed the entire neighborhood, passing out information and invitations in English, French, Spanish, Chinese, Punjabi, Tagalog and Vietnam-

ese, Somali, Farsi, Kurdish, and Arabic. We had our per-
mits, barriers and tables and although the curfew was
supposed to be nine o'clock, we had been able to get an
extension to eleven. Joey and I did the rest with mild
doses of You-Scratch-My-Back-I'll-Scratch-Yours and
my GWI fund-raising connections. We even managed to
get some free food supplied by the Pataran Café on the
ground floor of our building. In a way, they owed me the
favor for constantly permeating my place with the smell
of curry.

That night, for my costume, I settled on the classic simple plastic hatchet through the head with plenty of dripping
blood, and Night of the Living Dead clothes. Joey had been
working on his costume all day and just before the party
started, emerged as Joseph Merrick, the Elephant Man.

Cleo and Simon, dressed as a pair of mummies, were at
the sound equipment that night, playing DJ, constantly
touching…well, as much as one could with all those ban-
dages in the way.

"So, Simon," I said to my old friend. "You're still around.
I thought you were off to that rock in Australia."

"Ayer's Rock?"

"Yeah."

"Thought I'd hang out a while longer."

"Where've you parked your stuff?"

"Cleo's, babe." His navy-blue eyes glittered. I needn't have
asked. I already knew. Simon took the road of least resistance
whenever he wasn't hitched to a rock face or the outside of
a high-rise.

The neighbors were arriving en masse. Witches, Jedi
knights, generic ghouls, Buffy-style vampires, and hobbits all
brought plates of cookies, snacks, drinks. Our permit didn't
allow for alcohol but people were drinking anyway.

There was no sign of my gay goat-loving Satanist neighbor and Joey kept reminding me of the fact. "Big night at

the cemetery," he whispered into my ear in his Elephant Mannish voice.

Then Jake, Lisa and Ida arrived, dressed as three of the Beatles from the cover of the Sergeant Pepper's Lonely Hearts album. Just after them came Ash. Her face was locked in a deep pout and her thick glasses made the whole effect worse. She was wearing a flame-orange sari embroidered with thousands of tiny white beads in flower and leaf shapes. A hundred silver bangles tinkled on her wrists.

"Aishwarya. That's quite the outfit," I said.

"It was my mother's idea," she said, looking completely peeved. "I made a big mistake and mentioned Ian Trutch to my mother…he is coming tonight, isn't he?"

"Don't know."

"Oh." Her whole being sagged.

"Come with me," I said. "This neighborhood might have a few 'suitable boys.'"

I grabbed her by the arm and together we made the rounds, introducing ourselves to all the neighbors who'd turned out so far. I left Ash chatting with a family from New Delhi and went to check on supplies.

Everything was in place. I just had one last trip to make to get the final box of plastic cups and plates. I hurried down the side path and around to the steps leading up to my apartment.

And then I spotted it.

At first it was just a creamy beige shadow, caught between the street and house light. It came to me as I stood, rigid, frozen with fear at the bottom of the path. Goat. It must have caught the scent of my neighbor's goat and now there it was, five houses away down the alley, watching me from between some shrubs when it made its first streaking steps in my direction. With the adrenaline smell of sheer terror in my nostrils, I instinctively recalled all those things that had been drilled into me as a child. I grabbed what was nearest to me, the lid of a garbage can, and a rock, and started to bang the lid with all my might, while talking to, no, screaming at, my predator.

I babbled and stammered and shouted and hooted, anything I could do to create a loud, constant stream of sound. "Go away, shoo, scat, get out of here, you big old cat. Vamoose, go back to where you came from. It's going to be trouble if you stay here in town. I ought to know. There's no cougar food around here so scat…and stop…stop looking at me like that…"

He was stalking me, slowly zigzagging back and forth across the alley with those gliding haunches, moving closer to me as I stumbled backward, banging and crashing and yelling to save my life. I reached my back steps and began to start up them banging faster and faster. By now the cougar was only a house away. I seemed to have developed telescopic vision because every whisker was visible, every tooth, the glint in the big hungry cat's eyes, as he glided closer on those haunches and prepared to sink those teeth into my thighs.

Now I was banging the garbage can lid against the support post at the top of the steps and with the other hand, digging into my pocket for my keys. I tried to push the keys into the lock with one hand behind my back, maintaining eye contact with the cougar, but it was impossible. Not being able to see what I was doing and with my hand trembling so hard, I kept scraping at the metal of the lock with no success. The cougar continued to make a wide slow zigzag all the way to the bottom of my stairs.

I bashed furiously with the garbage can lid at the post and porch rail, slamming the lid down with both hands to make as much noise as possible, and I probably would have tried to slam it over the cougar's head if he got close enough. He placed one paw on the bottom step, then the second step, then the third. My heart banged into my throat when the cat leapt up, snarled fiercely, and then whiplashed his big body backward into the air. My world veiled over as if someone had suddenly thrown icing sugar in my eyes and then everything went dark.

Chapter Seven

My gay goat-loving Satanist neighbor was kneeling over me. His face was knotted up with worry. As I opened my eyes, the frown fell away and he nodded very slowly, his mouth relaxing into a smile.

My first thought was to yell out, "Stop the sacrifice. You guys have it all wrong. Whoever told you I was a virgin was lying. Penelope. Get Penelope." But then I realized that my neighbor wasn't tricked out at all. No requisite black cowl and face mask. No upside-down crucifixes. No evil acolytes lurking and chanting in the background.

"You're a lucky girl," he said.

"I'm alive. I *am* alive, aren't I?"

"Sure you are."

Everything was aching. Slowly I said, "Am I all here? No parts missing? It hurts. I don't want to look. What if it's phantom limb pain?"

My neighbor was still grinning. "I got him before he

made dinner of you. You didn't lose your head. Good for you."

"Noise. You're supposed to make noise if a cougar stalks you. You're supposed to make yourself big and loud and mean if a cougar stalks you."

"Something you don't expect to happen in residential Vancouver," he said.

"Where is he? The cat, I mean?"

"Having a little nap."

I was about to pull myself into sitting position when my neighbor eased me down again, saying, "Take it slowly." He shifted positions so that now he was holding my head in his lap. Gently, he began to feel my head. "Just the cut but no other contusions."

"What?"

"You have a nasty cut along here." He traced the air above my cheekbone. I was about to touch it but he said, "No, don't. We'll disinfect. Might need a couple of stitches. Check you over properly. You must have hit the side of your face when you fell. You'll probably feel a bit achy in a few minutes."

"The cougar…"

"Down there. A fine specimen of felis concolor," said my neighbor.

He pointed to the pathway at the bottom of my back steps.

It was an impressive animal. Tawny and muscular, completely conked out but not looking so bad for all its big-city adventures. Then I looked at my neighbor again. Beside him on the porch floor was a big rifle. He picked it up. "Don't get much call to use this around here. Mostly for large animal sedatives. Rhino, lion, zoo animals usually. Good thing I heard you banging and shouting. Saw him just in time to grab the rifle and aim. If you'd run, there's a real possibility that he might have attacked you."

I felt woozy all over again. "Don't tell me. I don't feel so good." I lay back down and held my stomach.

My neighbor laughed and then stopped himself. I looked up at his face. He had the most amazing irises. They were grayish-green around the outer ring, giving way to pure amber at the center. I couldn't stop staring at them. Then I noticed how much he was smiling. I wanted him to cut it out. It was unnerving and totally seductive.

"My name's Jonathan, by the way. Jonathan Ballam. Everybody calls me Jon though. We've been dancing partners on the old path there for a few days now and we still don't know each other's name. That's not so good."

"Dinah," I said. "Dinah Nichols." I stuck up my hand for him to shake. He gave it a small squeeze. "What would you be doing with big animal tranquillizers anyway? You work at the zoo?"

"Sometimes. I'm a vet. Large animals. Though I often get called upon for small animal emergencies."

Cats. Goats.

I started to laugh the kind of laugh that rises up when your nerves are shot and you've lost all control. It must have seemed that his being a vet was the funniest thing in the world.

Jon said, "Well that was fast. They're already here."

Somebody had called all the forces they could think of. There were the city police, the fire department, the Feds, a wildlife officer, somebody from the Parks Board and a regular ambulance and all of them were arguing about who got to deal with the cougar.

The small crowd had now blossomed into a big gathering. Everyone had come around back to get a look at the cougar including Cleo, Simon, Joey and Lisa. And there I was, a near wild animal victim and I was guffawing my head off. While Lisa and Ida harangued and harassed the various forces telling them to be gentle with "poor kitty," Joey and Cleo rushed up the steps to me.

"Hey, you guys," I managed to say between howls, "this is our neighbor, Jonathan Ballam. He's a vet. A veterinarian." And that was all I could get out before a new bout of hysteria set me off again.

Jon ordered somebody to get him a handful of clean paper napkins. He pressed them to the cut on my cheekbone, then said, "Hold this and don't let go. I can't tell the real blood from the fake. Are you feeling well enough to walk to my place? We've really got to do something about that cut. You could go with the ambulance but you'd probably have to wait in Emergency all night. Halloween."

I shook my head.

"Can you stand up? Okay, let me just have a few words with these guys then we'll deal with it." Jonathan went to talk to them. He came back and said that in the end it was decided that the ambulance would transport the animal to a "holding facility" and the Parks Board would deal with getting it back to the wilds.

He asked me again, "Okay, feel like walking to my place, Dinah?"

I nodded. Although it must have looked as though I were walking myself, my knees felt like jelly and Jon took most of my weight as we made our way down the back steps toward his place. Everything hurt.

"We'll fix that cheek up and then Kevin has a few things that will help the ache."

"Kevin?"

"Kev's a sales rep for a company that makes homeopathic remedies."

The perfect names for a gay couple, I thought. Jonathan and Kevin.

I raised my eyebrows.

Jon laughed, "It's quite safe. You'll see."

"Ah…okay."

He opened the back door and called out into the beige kitchen, "Kev?"

"In here," came a voice.

The smaller darker man appeared in the doorway.

"Kev, this is our neighbor, Dinah. We have a little emergency. Think she'll need about three stitches." He quickly lifted the napkins to give Kevin a peek then put them back in place.

"Oh, ooo, yes, that's a real conversation piece. I'm envious. You don't often get to have a nice dramatic gash along your cheekbone. Here, come with me, Dinah." There was excitement in his tone as though a long-awaited guest had finally arrived. Perhaps I hadn't been the only person spying on my neighbors. Perhaps the spying was mutual.

"She's just taken on a cougar," said Jon.

"Good Lord." Kevin's eyes opened wide. "You're all in one piece. That's your only injury, I hope."

"I got to her just in time. Heard her yelling and screaming on her back porch. She was showing him up. He's got a dose of sedative that'll keep him snoozing into tomorrow. Now. We need some of your magic potions. What do you suggest?"

"Some Arnica to start with. I'll get it," said Kevin.

Jon led me into the wheat and wood-colored living room and eased me down onto his big brown leather couch, a couch I'd fantasized about so much that it was familiar, just like coming home. "I'll be back in a sec. Just gotta get my bag. Hold on to those napkins."

After a few minutes, Kevin came back into the room with some bottles and tubes in one hand, and a mug balanced in the other hand. He held it up under my nose. "Now drink some of this. I know it smells like stewed seaweed but it has all kinds of wonderful natural calming ingredients."

"Not too calming. I want to get back to the party."

"Go on. You'll feel wonderful afterward."

"It does smell like stewed seaweed." I took a sip. "It *tastes* like stewed seaweed, too."

Jon reappeared with an enormous old-fashioned black leather medical bag. Really handy if you happened to be delivering a calf or foal, I thought, but what about human beings? He grinned at me, then slopped a powerful-smelling disinfectant onto a piece of cotton and dabbed carefully at the cut. Then he prepared a syringe and held it up expectantly.

I howled, "Hey, that thing's big. I'm not an elephant."

"Sorry. I have nothing smaller. But don't worry. I've had lots of practice. On oranges." He grinned malevolently and waved the instrument of torture back and forth a few times.

I huddled away from him, deeper into the couch.

"Just kidding. Trust me."

Cleo would have said I was out of my mind, allowing a vet to sew up my face but I wasn't Cleo so I let him go to it. He was very delicate and precise and I barely felt a thing. When he'd finished stitching, he cut a piece of pristine white bandage from an industrial-size roll and applied it. I sank into the couch with relief.

"There. You see? That wasn't so bad, was it?"

"No. Thank you…thank you…for saving my life."

He laughed. "My pleasure. Usually when I save somebody's life, I ask that they become my personal slave, but I'm willing to lighten up with you, okay? No starch in the shirts."

"Yes, master." I put my palms together and bowed my head in his direction.

"You know," said Jon, touching the bandage on my cheekbone again, as if admiring his masterwork, "Treating a person makes a nice change from treating goats."

"Interesting house pets, your goats…" I said.

"They're not my goats. They were brought to me. Somebody found them on a boulevard in South Van along with a few black cats in cardboard boxes. Half-starved, dehydrated. We figure it's some kind of devil-worship cult that got cold feet and changed their minds about slaughtering animals. Idiots."

"Ah," I said. The seaweed was already starting to take effect. "That's pretty funny, I mean, it's interesting. What's in that stuff you gave me, Kevin?"

"Feeling relaxed, are you?" Kevin grinned.

I was feeling more than relaxed. I was feeling so good I wanted to attack all the men in the room regardless of the fact they only liked men.

"I threw in some eye of newt for good measure," said Kevin.

"Aha, I thought so," I said.

"So what were you saying, Dinah?" asked Jon.

"What was I saying? Oh, yeah. That it was sort of interesting about your being a veterinarian."

"You think so?"

"I grew up with…animals."

"Ah. Some people get a glazed-over look in their eye when I tell them what I do. But I don't mind being a social outcast. Really." He grinned.

I said, "I don't mean that our animals were pets. I mean that I was one of them. I was them and they were me. I thought I was a pony for a whole year. That was one of the best periods of my life."

He chuckled. "It's not unusual."

"It's not?"

"Nope."

"So tell me now, Jon. Where are you from?"

"Right here."

"So how come you have that little southern twang?"

"Did my training in the States, a while in Texas for cattle and horses and later on, in San Diego. I did some more training with the zoo there. Then Kevin was moving back up here from San Francisco and asked me to come back up here, too."

Kevin nodded. "I needed to come home."

Jon gave Kevin a compassionate look. "Things were getting pretty serious down there."

"In more ways than one." Kevin looked as though he were about to burst into tears.

I really had to wonder what was going on with the two of them, but I didn't want to ask.

Jon said, "And we figured it was time to breathe some of this northern air again."

"Are you glad now that you made the move?" I asked.

Jon leapt right in. "Oh yeah. I'm loving it here."

Kevin shrugged and said, "Me, too." He didn't sound at all convincing.

Jon put his hand on mine. "So. Now. How're you feeling, Dinah? Do you feel well enough to get back to the party?"

"Could you go ahead of me? Just in case there are any more cougars?"

"Will do," said Jon.

Going back outside, propped between Jon and Kevin, I was thrilled that the ice had finally been broken. Two more gay friends plus Joey meant triple the fun. I hoped Joey wouldn't be jealous now that I had these new friends. It would have been small of him. After all, Jonathan Ballam *had* just saved my life.

Although I was drinking wine, I couldn't get drunk. My life was suddenly a series of bright, wonderful colors and sensations. I'd never felt so alive. Then Cleo and Simon put on some music that sounded Turkish or Greek and I did this strange ring-around-the-rosy dance with Jonathan and Kevin, the three of us with our arms around each other's shoulders and kicking up our legs in unison, improvising a dance, and then everybody else joined in and I thought, Gee, I bet the Tsadziki Pervert would really enjoy this, it's sort of Greek. I even felt a kind of goodwill toward him, the poor bastard.

The night had turned into a celebration.

In the end, I think I must have danced with everyone, the entire block and all the extra friends and relatives there, every single man, woman, husband, wife and child. I was so happy to be alive, to be in the Big Now, because I swear, just as that cat was coming at me—and I could hear his breath, and see the shape of his teeth, the saliva glistening around his maw, just before I blacked out—my life, my thirty years of life, and all that I hadn't done with it, flashed before me like a promising but unfinished movie.

Sunday

Almost the entire morning was spent in bed, nursing my hangover and laughing out loud by myself, savoring the delicious sensation of just being on the earth. When I finally tore back the sheet, the sun was streaming through my windows, and the light dancing on my walls seemed like a gift especially designed for me. My coffee tasted intensely coffee-ish. I could feel myself attached, one well-connected cell in the greater organism of a perfect world, and it all worked the way it should. This was a new chapter. I could feel it.

My reflection in the mirror didn't say anything about a new chapter, however. It looked like the same old Dinah. So I took my credit cards out to get a little exercise. I did some major retail damage that Sunday, single-handedly giving the nation's economy a big boost.

Monday

At work, Lisa said, "There she is," as I came through the door. "Cougar Woman."

To oblige her, I clasped my hands and held them over my head.

Even Ash paused in my office, smiled quickly and nodded, then walked on. Any acknowledgment from Ash was a big deal, a bit like being awarded the Nobel prize.

Jake came by, hovered in my doorway and said, "Great going, Dinah. I'd have been shitting myself if I found a big cat like that in front of me. God, I remember when I was at high school, I had to do one of those outdoor camping survival courses, all that big man crap, cutting your own firewood, making a bed out of fir boughs, living off roots and berries, yecch, thought I would die before it was over. So when I finally got the diploma from the teacher, I told him, 'I'm strictly a hotel man.' You got guts, Dinah."

"I sort of grew up in the wilds. You could say it's my mother's doing. One of the few good things she has done."

"That's pretty uncharitable of you. You got a bone to pick, or something?"

"No," I said defensively. The picked-over bones were Thomas's department. But Jake didn't know about Thomas. Nobody knew about Thomas. He was my private Dumpster in human form. I didn't want to start the day with more nickel and dime psychology about my relationship with my mother, so I changed the subject. "Hey, Jake, what do you know about Hamish Robertson?"

"Lower mainland's third wealthiest man? That Hamish Robertson?"

"Yeah."

"Been trying to track him down for years but he's untraceable. These days all his mail goes to a box number. Sometimes I wonder if maybe he hasn't died."

An hour later, Ian Trutch came into my office. Now that I had a little experience in standing up to predators, I didn't feel so threatened by him. I even felt a kind of sympathy for him.

Poor man.

The life he led couldn't be easy.

Darting into strange new cities where he didn't know a soul, devastating companies and terrorizing all their employees, few of whom he'd had the pleasure of knowing before cold-bloodedly giving them the axe.

Surely his days were lonely and exhausting.

He sat down on my extra chair—I didn't get a chance to
tell him the dust would ruin his suit—and he said, "Well,
Dinah. I hear you took on a cougar." He was transfixed by
the bandage on my cheekbone.

"Jeez, the news travels fast around here. Yeah, I guess I did
in a way. Just me and him in eye-to-eye combat. I really had
to use my mouth to talk him off me. He never touched me
but he wasn't far from it. It was crazy. My life flashed before
my eyes. I think I had an epiphany or something."

His blue eyes shone. "You did? Tell me about it."

"Nothing new. Nothing you don't already know, I'm sure.
Just that now I really believe it. That your big exit could happen any time. That life is completely unpredictable so you
better live it as intensely as you can. Feed every sense."

Could I hear myself?

What are you doing, Dinah? part of me was thinking.

My mind was telling me to shut up, but my mouth was
telling him to come and get me. And as if that weren't bad
enough, I was wearing a new tight bubble-gum-pink sweater
that bared my shoulders in the most unprofessional way.

My mouth babbled on without me, "Now tell me, Ian,
have you ever had your life flash before your eyes?"

"Once, driving on a highway."

"Well, I'm not a danger freak but a little danger makes you
glad to be alive. It makes everything taste better. Delicious.
Sensual." I said the last two words very slowly.

"Perhaps I ought to take you out to lunch then, so you
have something to taste."

"Oh." I hadn't expected it. He was closing the circle again
with the old lunch routine. My mouth finally slowed down
and let my brain catch up. "I uh…I don't know. I have so
much to do today. It's starting to rain. You'll have a terrible

time finding parking. And I really have to work on the list of invitations for the Space Centre."

A dark butterfly of irritation crossed Ian's face. He whispered, "Just stop it, Dinah. I know you feel it, so stop pretending you don't. Stop denying the most natural thing in the world."

"I'm not denying anything."

"No? Well, then it's settled." He lifted the sheet of paper out of my hands and put it back on my desk. Then he gestured toward the hallway and said, "Come on. We need to hold a summit. A private one. You and I."

I knew it was a ruse. There are beautiful men who seduce less beautiful women to have a submissive handmaiden, or a favor, or just the thrill of adding another notch to their bedpost. But then my motives weren't so straightforward either. I wanted to do it if only for the sake of statistics. I just couldn't let another year go by and on the physical front, Ian was one of the better candidates around. And I had a brandnew man-eating reputation to live up to. Life was short. I knew that now.

I followed him along the narrow hallway like a prisoner walking Death Row for the last time, and although the only thing that was going to die was my long stretch of celibacy, the foreknowledge made it worse.

As we headed toward the exit, Jake popped his head out of his office. "Hey, Dinah, you leaving?"

I nodded weakly.

"Where can I find you if I need you?"

"Where? Uh…"

"We're going out to do some fieldwork," interjected Ian.

I wanted to say, Don't look for me, Jake. But if you care about me just a little, have my principles scraped up off the floor of my office, glued back together and sent to me c/o Mr. Hot and Cold Running Charm, Esquire, Higher Management Vampires Unlimited, Lower Circle, Hades.

Ian led me outside and down to his car. Perhaps he had genuinely intended to take me out to lunch first, but as soon as we were safely belted into our seats, he reached across the Ferrari's gearshift and beige leather divide and lightly rested his fingers on the back of my neck. I said nothing, looked out the window as if I hadn't seen all that scenery a hundred times before. He didn't drive us to a restaurant but straight to his hotel without a word. In the parking lot, he came around to let me out, then guided me ahead of him, pushing slightly, his fingers on the back of my neck again. In the hotel elevator, he grabbed me, but not so roughly that I needed to complain, and kissed me, explored me with his hands.

"I don't think I should be doing this," I said.

"Why not?"

"Because I think I hate you."

"I love the way you hate me," he whispered and grabbed me again. A body ache that was three years old (if you didn't count that pathetic accident with Mike) made me grab him back.

Once inside his suite, our clothes flew off as if they'd been caught in a hurricane and torn away, and an hour later, Ian and I lay naked across the scrambled bedding in his Gold Floor suite, amazed. A full unopened bottle of champagne sat in a bucket of melted ice. Outside, the November storm beat against the window glass, which was now steamy.

Ian whispered, "I love doing this in the rain."

I stared at the streaming window.

"You're awfully quiet," he said.

"I've got a lot to think about."

"Like what. Tell me."

Like how to keep you sweet until I find my donor.

"Oh, just all the things that have happened to me in the last few days."

He ran his finger across the bandage on my cheekbone.

"Well, now you have this great souvenir of your adventures with wild animals. That's always a good thing."

"Hey, city boy, what would you know about it?"

"Well, let me see. I recall lots of wildlife from my New York and Boston days. Albino alligators. Pink elephants. Pigs with wings. And…oh yeah…there was that tenant on the floor above me. The city can be a dangerous place."

I moved his finger off the bandage. "There probably won't be much of a scar. Nothing so exciting as claw or tooth marks. I banged my face when I fainted. So now I want to see all *your* scars. I'm sure they're much more interesting."

He kissed my fingertips. "Mine are strictly emotional."

"Uh-oh. Does that mean you're going to turn out to be a big needy mess?"

"I don't know." He wedged his knee between my legs. "Let me give you another sample of my neediness."

"Do you think it's a good idea?"

"A fantastic idea."

"If it's anything like what we were just doing, I'm afraid we might murder each other."

"But what a great way to die. I say we go for the double homicide."

Late into the afternoon, the enemy and I punished each other's bodies. I hated to admit it but the summit was a success. Although the Cold War of minds hadn't actually ended, a bilateral accord of bodies was reached. Twice.

Chapter Eight

When I woke up it was seven o'clock, dark and still drizzling outside. Ian's side of the bed was empty but on his pillow was a large glossy black box embossed in gold script with the name of an exclusive boutique. Written on a little tag were the words: Dear Dinah, Open the box and put on the contents.

I pried open the lid. Under a layer of black tissue was a slinky, silky, black knit dress with tiny rhinestoned shoulder straps that crossed over an otherwise bare back. Under the dress were a pair of low black sandals with similar rhinestone straps.

I gingerly picked up the dress and went over to the full-length mirror. I held it up to myself and paraded back and forth until the ringing of the phone interrupted me. I hesitated then picked it up, knowing it would be Ian.

"Have you opened the box?" he asked.

"Yes. They're gorgeous. I hope it's not for services rendered."

He laughed.

"Because if it is, Ian, you're the one who should be putting on the dress."

"I wanted to give you a little gift. To celebrate your newly awakened senses."

"It doesn't feel right. It's too much. I can't take it."

"Would it make you feel any better if I told you my motives weren't altruistic? There's a party I think we should both attend. At the Golf Club. One of the GWI board members gave me the invitation. Word has it that Hamish Robertson was invited as well. You don't want to add this to your list of missed opportunities, do you, Dinah? I want you to put on the dress and shoes and meet me at the main entrance in twenty minutes. Is that enough time for you?"

"But Ian, it's pouring outside. There are puddles and these are sandals. And it's cold. These are the skimpiest clothes I've ever been asked to wear."

"Your feet won't even touch the ground. And look in the closet, the garment bag. Twenty minutes." He hung up before I could protest again. I went to the closet and found the black-and-gold garment bag. I unzipped it. Inside was a soft black wool knee-length coat with an astrakhan collar. My stomach hollowed as if I were on a plane that had just dipped a hundred feet. Ian Trutch had just sunk to a lower circle of hell and was trying to drag me with him.

Twenty minutes later, showered, perfumed and freshly made-up, I was standing at the main entrance, shivering. I had obligingly put on the dress and sandals, but my clothes were stuffed into my purse for the moment of my getaway, and I wore my Burberry instead of the new wool coat over the elegant dress.

A Blue Top cab with Ian in the back pulled up to the entrance.

As I climbed in, I could see his irritation. "You're not wearing the coat."

"No, Ian. I'm not wearing the coat. Find someone else to wear it. Someone else who doesn't mind a collar made of slaughtered unborn lamb's skin, a lamb whose mother the ewe also died just to give us the pleasure of the astrakhan experience. Jesus, Ian. We don't come down on the shoe leather and the practical sheepskin for big winters, but really, astrakhan is definitely pushing it. It rates up there with clubbing baby seals. Beginners' stuff."

Ian put a hand to his forehead and shook his head. "Sorry, Dinah. I just didn't think about it. It just didn't occur to me."

"Don't worry, Ian. I'll help it occur to you whenever necessary. I'm proud to be the one who drives everybody crazy with animal rights."

"You see, Dinah? You see how much I need you? Especially tonight. You know these people. I don't. I'd hate to offend anybody's political and ethical sensibilities." But he grinned when he said it and it sounded as though he didn't mean it, as though he were just toying with me.

"And I need you in other ways, too." He slid an arm around me, lifted my hair and began to kiss my neck. I couldn't believe it. He was starting all over again, right there in the back seat of the taxi. And the worst part was that I didn't stop him. As his hands moved under my dress and he got ready to shift himself into me, I realized he was a man who wanted, who was *compelled,* to raise the stakes. One thing was certain. Given the weird smirk on the driver's face, I would never be able to ride with Blue Top cabs again.

When we got to the Golf Club, the party turned out to be a dinner dance. It was in full swing. Ian was right. I knew a lot of the people there.

"Now Dinah, any sign of our man?"

I shook my head. In my files back at the office, I had one photo portrait of Hamish Robertson and it wasn't recent. He'd been a younger man when the picture was taken.

Twenty years younger. It showed a slender good-looking type with a shock of curly black hair, bare knobbly knees below a red, blue and green kilt and dark eyes, winking at the camera. I'd found it in an old business magazine in my great-grandfather's basement treasure hoard. The elusive man had once been featured in an article on early success stories. I scanned the room all evening but there was no sign of him. When the orchestra struck up a tango later in the evening, the image of Hector Ferrer wouldn't leave me alone. As the roomful of some of Vancouver's wealthiest citizens bumbled around the dance floor I couldn't help but think that they could have benefited from a few lessons with Hector. He really was, in comparison to these people, a very good dancer.

Throughout the evening, Ian stood just behind my shoulder as I chatted with people and playfully extorted donation pledges. I had the feeling that he wasn't as comfortable with the Vanpfeffers of this world as he should be, but I was willing to cut him some slack because his bilateral accords were truly amazing.

Around eleven, I turned to Ian and said, "Please, can we leave? I'm exhausted. Tomorrow's another working day and it's always a good idea to have Ash process these pledges before people forget they've made them."

"I'll take you back to the hotel and we can…"

"No," I interrupted. "No, take me back to my car. I'm really beat. I just have to go home."

In the cab on the way back to my car, Ian's voice took on a strange pleading tone. "I wish you'd reconsider. Stay the night with me, please. Stay the night."

There was a long kiss in the cab, and I thought I better get out while the going was still good.

"I'll see you tomorrow, Ian. Listen, what about work?"

"What about it?"

I was half expecting him to give me a little speech about

not mixing business and personal lives but he said nothing except, "Tomorrow," and our hands slid apart as if we were a pair of figure skaters gliding away from each other.

When I reached my back door there was a note taped to it.

It read, Dinah, I'm at Jon and Kevin's for dinner. You were invited, too. Join us at theirs, even if it's late. Joey.

It seemed like a sane way to finish off a day of insanity. A nice chat with Joey, my Savior and his partner. I turned around and headed back down the stairs to their place. As I approached their front door, screeches of laughter came from within. I rang the bell and the noise stopped abruptly. The door was opened by Kevin, bright-eyed and flushed with high spirits. He sang out, "Dinah, we were just talking about you."

Now *that* was something to worry about.

He caught my expression. "No, no, just wondering when you'd get here. Not rewriting your bio for *People* magazine or anything like that. You're so elegant tonight. What's the occasion? Come in and show everyone how fabulous you look." I followed him inside.

The wreckage of a banquet filled the table. Joey and Jon were leaning back in their chairs one-upping each other with titles of B-rated science fiction classics.

"*Attack of the Killer Tomatoes,*" said Joey.

"*The Amazing Two-Headed Transplant,*" countered Jon.

"Dinah's here," announced Kevin, with a loaded voice.

My Savior came right over, boldly lifted the flaps of my Burberry to have a look at my dress, then held me at arm's length and said, "Well, wow. Look at you. Who do you think she looks like? She reminds me of one of those big movie stars of once upon a time but it won't come to me."

"Ava Gardner," said Kevin.

"That's it," he agreed.

I was flattered. It wasn't the first time somebody had compared me to Ava Gardner. But just between you and me, Ava Gardner had much longer, slimmer thighs.

Jon went on, "Where were you tonight? We wanted you to come to dinner. You look lovely. Looks like you've been out winning Oscars."

Joey held up a hand. "Whoa, whoa. Just a minute. Hands off. The Oscars are my department. God knows there are few enough of them to go around. We can't just start giving them out to any old bag in a fancy evening dress that happens to come along."

Kevin said, "Oooo, touchy," then ushered me over to the bar. "Now Dinah. What would you like? We're drinking Avocat. Dutch egg liqueur. You must have some. The pale yellow would look so very classy against that black dress."

"Convincing enough argument for me." I took the glass that was offered and joined the communal toast to good health and good sex. Joey's words.

And then I added, "But you have to be careful that good sex doesn't take a toll on good health."

Joey was suddenly alert. "Good sex…what? Okay, Dinah. What's going on here? Where have you been? Is there something you want to tell us?"

"Uh…" I could feel the blood rushing to my head and it wasn't just the liqueur.

"Oh, go on. You're among friends," coaxed Joey.

Jon and Kevin nodded.

"As long as it doesn't leave this room," I instructed them.

"I'm a tomb," said Joey. Jon and Kevin nodded in unison.

"That's what they all say, until it gets exhumed," I said.

"Talk or I'll be forced to blackmail you. The dirt," squealed Joey. "I want to hear it all."

I hesitated, then let it spill. "The dirt is the new CEO."

"No," exclaimed Joey.

"Yes." I was emphatic.

"The new CEO and who else?" asked Joey.

"Who do you think?" I did a little curtsey.

"I can't believe it. You didn't."

"I did."

"Nah, really? You and your highly comestible boss?"

I nodded.

He turned to Jon and Kevin. "You both have to know that she has this new boss, straight out of the pages of *GQ*. How did you do it, Dinah? I mean, not to say that you're as ugly as a fistful of squid bits or anything like that, but as soon as I saw him, I thought, this guy does not dally with the plebes, this guy goes out with models."

Jon had crossed his arms and had that concentrated serious expression on his face again. Everything seemed to be an enormous riddle for him.

"I'm a plebe?" I protested.

Joey went on, "I've been trying for ages to get Dinah back out there and grab some guy, any guy, the first guy who can tie his own shoelaces and pronounce his own name, then throw him down on the spot and have plenty of sex therapy with him, then fling him aside and find somebody else and repeat the procedure over and over until she gets it right."

I took off my Burberry and hung it over the back of a chair. "It's part of my new plan. I'm supposed to be a man-eater, according to somebody I work with."

"You are?" asked Jon, smiling faintly.

"Yeah. It was news to me." I laughed like a true skeptic. "This guy, the new CEO, Ian Trutch, well, he's very smooth. Smoother than anybody I've ever known. I'm wondering if I shouldn't be worrying about not being as perfect as he is. I'm not really sure where all this is going to lead."

"Just be yourself. That always takes things where they need to go," said Jon.

Joey tossed back his lank blond hair. "If it flops you just tell yourself that it doesn't matter because he was only a man to practice on, Dinah, not the real thing. But then if it *does* work out, then good. You can lie and say it's the real thing. Then you'll be an official couple, complete with that lobotomized look and I can invite the two of you over and then lock you in a closet and have my way with Mr. Ian Trutch. Right?"

I raised my glass to him. "That'll be the day. But how do you know when it's the real thing?"

"It's all the real thing and none of it's the real thing. It is what you make it." Then he said to Kevin and Jon, "You should have seen the way she used to moon around over that grubby fiancé of hers when she first came over here from the backwoods, after breaking up with him. Really, it was enough to put you off your food. I had to get a forklift over to her place to pry her off the couch before I could get her to come out clubbing. She was starting to resemble The Blob. And her clothes didn't help. Would Mexican field worker's widow describe her look? I don't think so. She was wearing these black drapery things that people hang over mirrors at funerals. I started to think maybe she was just hiding some hideous skin disease...."

Jon frowned. "Some people just need more time than others."

"Well, I hope if I ever take three years to get over a man, that somebody will shoot me, because it'll mean that I've become senile and a burden on society."

I made a face at Joey.

"Come and sit down, Dinah," said Jon, nodding to the empty place on the brown couch. "Over here, next to me." A strange look was exchanged between Kevin and Jon, and Jon gave a little flick of his head in Kevin's direction. Was I detecting jealousy?

I sat down.

"So now that you have this new person in your life, does

it mean there won't be any more Greek dancing with your neighbors?" asked Jon. His voice had a little edge of regret.

Was there trouble in paradise between him and Kev?

"There can never be enough Greek dancing with my neighbors."

He stared at my cheekbone. "While I've got you here, let me take a look at those stitches and put on a new dressing."

"Okay."

He got up, left the room and came back with his bag. Then he sat facing me and carefully pulled off the bandage. I felt my insides slide into my shoes. Maybe it was just an aftereffect of being with Ian Trutch but I was like hot melting candle wax as he touched my face.

"It's doing well. I don't think you'll have much of a scar."

"Too bad, Dinah. Scars are the big word this year," said Kevin.

After that, Joey told us all about his latest job as an extra on the set of a new environmental disaster film in which the Pacific Northwest was supposed to heat up into a seething jungly swamp where giant flying cockroaches ruled supreme. It sounded extremely gooey and uncomfortable. We all grimaced.

I stood. "I've gotta get home, guys. Thanks for the drinks."

"I'll come with you," said Joey. "I have a big day in the swamp tomorrow."

"Please, drop round whenever you feel like it," said Jon. Kevin nodded vigorously in agreement.

On the way back to our place, Joey said, "You missed a great dinner. They were both counting on you to come. But then, you have more interesting things between your teeth now, don't you. Or do you?"

"Good night, Joey."

He made a clownish sad face and I shut my door.

It was really late but I decided to take a bath anyway, just to meditate on everything that had happened. I was in the middle of a reverie, replaying Ian's every move, when I was interrupted by the phone ringing. I dragged myself out of the tub, pulled a towel from the rack and ran to pick it up.

The voice at the other end hissed, "I'm going to dip you in yogurt and honey and have you for dessert."

I was shivering and dripping all over the floorboards. White marks were appearing in the varnish.

"Get a life, you moron," I yelled back, and slammed down the phone. Then I thought again and took it off the hook.

Tuesday

My first job was finding creative ways to make yawns look like livelier things, like exclamations and expressions of amazement. Ian, I learned, was out in the field with Cleo. Just as well. Maybe she'd seduce him and all my worrying would be over. But then just before lunch, he appeared in my doorway, as silent as a ghost.

I looked up and my heart leapt. "You scared me, Ian. Don't do that."

He held a finger up to his lips and stepped inside, pulling the door closed behind him.

"Somebody's going to hear us," I said, as he took my hand and pulled me to my feet.

"I'm just saying hello." He pinned me against the wall and kissed me. His agile fingers were inside my clothes and running along my skin in seconds.

"If this is hello," I gasped, "I don't need the rest of the conversation."

"Are you sure? You feel tense."

"But I'm *not* tense," I said, through clenched teeth.

"I wanted to persuade you to come out with me later."

"Persuade me? Ian. You could just ask me, you know. With words?"

"You have to have dinner with me. After work? Bridges?

I've heard it's nice and I've got some theater tickets for the Arts Centre."

"What's the play?"

"Sex and the Single Celibate."

It sounded dubious. But then it had been a long time since I'd had a night at the theater. Even a ticket for a dubious play was beyond my means. "Terrific."

"That's a yes? That means you'll come. Say you'll come."

I didn't have to say it. Coming with Ian Trutch was something I did really well.

I hesitated, then asked, "Ian, why me? Why am I getting all the attention? Why aren't you taking out someone glamorous? Like Cleo, for example."

He smiled. "Cleo doesn't look like a woman who'd be easily surprised and I like surprising the woman I'm with. Correct me if I'm wrong, but she talks and sounds like a lady who knows her way around."

But I felt guilty when Cleo came into my office later in the afternoon, shut the door, and said, "Ahhh, Dinah. I am *so* happy for you. You did it. You got it together with Ian Trutch. About time, too. I knew it was going to happen for you one of these days."

"Is it written all over my face? I was going to see what happened before I told everybody in the office about it. How did you find out?"

"Get this. Ian told me himself. Just casually let it drop that you and he were 'dating.'"

"He used the word *dating?* That's almost funny. Nobody *dates* anymore."

"I know, Dinah."

"People hang around together. They don't date."

"Very unromantic, hanging around."

"It's like he's come out in the open. I feel flattered."

"You ought to."

When Ian picked me up that night, I'd barely had time to

shower and cram myself into my white stretchy lace T-shirt and all-purpose long straight jeans skirt. He was wearing a high-collared black shirt and multi-pocketed beige safari pants. We were both the right degree of easy elegance but although we looked okay together, more or less, I still couldn't believe that I was with him, that I was his date. I couldn't help feeling as though I were the stand-in for some big star in the movie about somebody else's more impressive and glamorous life, and any minute, the real female lead, Catherine Zeta-Jones or Julianne Moore or Gwyneth Paltrow, would come along and take over from me, waving her hand and saying, "You, the stand-in, whatever your name is, you are dismissed."

Wednesday

My first private tango lesson with Hector Ferrer. It was almost a relief to have a night off from Ian although I was still thinking about him, still feeling him all over my body. We'd snuck out of the play (as dubious as I'd suspected) before the end and gone back to the hotel, and our performance was definitely superior.

And so Wednesday night, I was distracted and thinking about Tuesday night as I walked into the room at Los Tangueros and came face-to-face with Hector. He had his coat on and was on his way out.

"Where are you going, Mr. Ferrer? We have a lesson."

"So you have decided to show up after all," he accused.

"I have showed up. I'm here," I stammered. I looked at my watch. "And I'm on time."

"You forget the warm-up. You must arrive earlier to allow time to warm up. Dancing cold can cause strain to your muscles. It is your responsibility to arrive well before the lesson to warm up."

Fussy bugger, I thought. It wasn't as though it were a ballet class, for crying out loud. I said, "I'm sorry but you'll have to teach me. I came halfway across town for this lesson and I'm not leaving until I have it." Personally, I think he just didn't feel like it. He was probably on his way out for a drink.

He allowed a little smile to escape and then said, "Let me see what you can do."

He gave me a second to throw off my coat and drop my purse then he grasped my hand with his, put his other on my waist and ordered, "Just try to walk with me."

I walked.

Sort of.

"No," he snapped, "across the floor, not across my feet. I do not wish to teach tango to a *flanes*."

"What's a *flanes*?"

"A weakling, an insecure person who lets themselves be bent and swayed and thrown about like a rag on the wind. Even though the man is leading, the woman must still be strong within her moves."

"I'm sorry," I mumbled.

"Sorry does not help you learn the tango. Try again… now you are walking like a stevedore," said Hector, becoming suddenly light with laughter.

I was starting to get mad, all my feelings bubbling up in one mean brew. I'd give *him* stevedore.

He pulled back. "Ha-ha. You are showing your *bronca*. You are angry with me? Ha-ha. Good. Tell me something. Why are you taking these tango lessons? Do you think you will find a man this way?" he sneered.

"I have a man, thank you very much."

What a relief to be able to say that.

Finally.

It didn't matter that Ian wasn't technically mine, but the way we'd been going at each other, where was he going to find the time or energy to go at somebody else while we were together?

"Ah," said Hector. "This man. Why is he not here, this man of yours, dancing with you?"

"I wanted lessons with you personally. Rupert told me you were a good teacher. *The* tango teacher in these parts."

"Rupert?"

"Rupert Doyle."

Hector narrowed his eyes and shot a withering black look at me.

"Victoria didn't tell you that it was him who put me on to you?" I said.

"No." Hector had tilted his head sideways and was looking at me with greater curiosity. Reevaluating me. "You are Rupert Doyle's girl then?"

I laughed. "No, no. You've got the wrong idea. He's an old friend of the family…." And then I clammed up. I'd said too much.

He stared at me a little longer then said, "We will not talk about him. Now, the *paseo*."

Now even doing what he called a simple *caminata* was a task. For an expensive hour, sixty dollars worth, Hector was harsh, overbearing, and even, for a second, toward the end, wolfish.

Was it my imagination or was he flirting with me?

Incest, screamed my Inner Prude.

But I realized I wasn't as put off as I should be. On the contrary. I was strangely drawn into it all. How amused Thomas would be when I told him all about it.

What I really wanted, deep down, was to make Hector jealous, please him, make him fall a little in love with me then tell him I was his daughter, make him suffer the way I'd suffered, make him act like the father I'd never had, the one who was supposed to chase potential boyfriends off the front porch with a shotgun.

Well, hey, Oedipus, you had your turn. Everybody deserves the chance to make up for lost time and go through the screwy parent thing.

Hector Ferrer was a challenge. He was a talented, grizzled, alcoholic and bad-tempered conundrum. I needed to know everything about him, and I wasn't sure how to go about it. It wasn't going to be enough to read him during lessons, to grab quick glimpses of his face when he was looking away. I tried to scour those slate-black eyes and their opaqueness, a murky dark sour shade that reminded me of a well, of unhealthy stagnant impenetrable water one minute, and the next minute the clarity of fizzing Coca-Cola.

I was curious to the point of agitation. What was lurking down there?

We did the basic walking step over and over trying to get the feel of moving around the room, which, he told me, was to be done only in an anticlockwise motion. I stumbled constantly at first. He stopped and murmured gently, "Imagine that there is music, the tango rhythm," and then he did something complicated and rhythmic with his feet to keep the time for me.

"You must be proud," he said, "like a proud *portena*. You have sad shoulders. You are stooping like an old woman. Why are your shoulders like this? Have you had such a hard life?"

I shook my head and lied. "No, not at all."

"You must not let any of your defeats show in your body unless they are proud and stylized defeats. Not here and not in the *milonga*...when I finally let you dance there, which will not be soon, I can assure you. If and when you first start to dance with other people, it will be in a *practica*."

Tired and ticked off at his constant insults and nonstop brow-beating, I finally pulled myself together and began to do the step again to the beat of his pounding feet, letting the meanest, bitchiest part of me take over. Hector stopped in midstep, looked as though he had just heard a hundred bells ringing. He seemed jubilant. He let go of me, squeezed my face between his two hands and exclaimed, "You did it. For eight, or maybe nine seconds, you felt like a true *milon-*

guita in my arms. We must build on this sensation. Now tell me, what is your name, girl?"

"It's Dinah."

"Perhaps there is hope for you, Dinah."

That was when I first realized that there was no laxness in the tango. No loose ends. No wasted movement. It was thoroughly concentrated.

It was nothing like the kind of wild messy dancing Joey, Cleo and I did when we went out to the clubs. None of that shaking your limbs frenetically and carelessly all over the place and slamming into other bodies and getting generally sloppy and rowdy.

No.

The tango was completely energy efficient.

Only when your body had absorbed and memorized and synthesized all the tango steps to a point where they entered into your genetic imprint could you begin to relax.

"Thank you, Mr. Ferrer," I said, as I handed over my sixty dollars.

"You must call me Hector," he said, and brushed my elbow with his fingers. "Do you have a ride?"

"I have my car." I pulled on my coat.

"I will walk you to it." He lit up a cigarette and narrowed his eyes at me. "Tell me, Dinah, do you, possibly, have some Latin blood in your family?"

I hesitated then said, "Yes, as a matter of fact, I do."

"That is very interesting. I thought so. Your face is very much like the face of a *portena*."

I laughed.

"Why do you laugh like that?" he snapped.

"Some of my family are from Buenos Aires," I ventured.

His eyebrows shot up. "Really?"

I could tell he wanted to pursue the topic but by then we were nearing the bottom of the steps. I raced down the last ones to the ground.

As I hurried toward my car, I tossed a "Yes, really," over my shoulder. "Good night, Hector." I got in my car and turned the key in the ignition.

Hector stood on the bottom step, pulling hard on his cigarette, his black eyes scrutinizing me.

Chapter Nine

Thursday

Ian came into my office. He looked pensive, worried, and a little remorseful. Still gorgeous of course, but anxious and slightly charged, as menacing as a greenish-gray sky before a storm. He stayed near the door, keeping his distance, now very composed and professional. No rushing over to touch me, kiss me, or generally find out how I was.

No siree.

I was instantly terrified.

This is it, I thought, it's all over, after less than a week. The moment has arrived. He's going to tell me he's found a fabulously thin, tall, beautiful model to go out with. Somebody with no thigh issues.

"Dinah."

"Ian."

"What are you doing this weekend?"

What was I doing this weekend?

Was he out of his mind?

I was going to spend my weekend hovering around both my telephones, the regular and the cell, waiting for *him* to call me, the blockhead. Along with trying on every single outfit and set of seductive underwear I owned, and then when the definitely hostile and silent telephones still hadn't rung by Sunday night, I'd shed some tears. Not quite enough tears to fill Lake Michigan but enough to bring Joey running over to my place with the First Aid Kit (Moskovskaya vodka and the most lurid orange cheesies he could find— you'd be amazed at the healing powers of hydrogenated palm oil and artificial coloring). And then after the infusion of delicious toxins, we'd both go out clubbing.

Ian still hadn't considered smiling as an option that morning so I smiled first.

I tested the waters. "What am I doing? I thought I'd throw a party."

Accomplished man-eaters of the world, never let on that you are having anything but heaps of riotous fun. Capital *F.*

"Oh." He seemed disappointed.

I leapt in. "But I haven't actually made up my mind. I mean, I haven't invited anybody yet or anything like that...I mean, if you have a suggestion, I'm open to it."

"Then pack an overnight bag, casual clothes. We're going away for the weekend. We'll leave tomorrow after work." He raised his eyebrows to wait for my assent.

"Uh...yes, fine, great," I said.

He nodded, made the faintest attempt at a smile, and left.

I felt breathless.

Over the moon.

Stunned that he was still interested.

At the same time, a little more confident.

And malicious.

That evening just before going home, I waited for the right moment then followed Penelope to the ladies' room. Well, stalked her, really.

There she was in front of the mirror, adjusting her chastity belt and practicing her facial expressions for all those poor unsuspecting men out on the street who'd try to pick her up. You know the ones? Look all you want but touch me and I'll stick your goodies with a cattle prod expressions?

"Penelope, dahling. Just the person I was looking for," I sang out.

"What do you want, Dinah?"

"Well, I thought that since you're such an expert on my love life, you'd be pleased to hear that my diet of men has improved quite a lot recently. I've had a big man-eating week this week. And he's so good you wouldn't believe it. I started at the top of him and went right on from there, and I can't tell you how yummy he was. Sweet and salty and soft and crunchy and spicy and tart, all kind of mixed up together. Delicious. Just thinking about Ian Trutch makes me so hungry I can hardly stand it. In fact, I think I'm ready for dinner."

Penelope's expression went from irritation to pure undisguised jealousy. I would swear to this day that the green pulsating aura all around her was so real and solid I could have reached out, broken off a piece and taken it home as a souvenir.

I smiled at Penelope, gave her a big thumbs-up, and left the building.

Frantic, I called up Cleo as soon as I got home from work. "I need clothes. Casual clothes. Ian Trutch is taking me away for the weekend."

"Come on over. We're staying in tonight."

"You and...?"

"Simon. Who else? See you later."

Simon. Still parking himself and his stuff at Cleo's. I allowed myself a cynical little smile.

Cleo and I were definitely not the same size. She was two inches taller than me and almost skinny. But Cleo liked her casual clothes too big. What was fashionably baggy on her usually hugged my body perfectly.

Cleo's place was a suite in a big old house near the university. It was decorated in bordello chic, with an abundance of pink drapery, bloodred cushions, multicolored bead curtains, gauzy white mosquito nets, and cream-colored lace everywhere. The place felt like one big bedroom, which was possibly her intention.

She and Simon were looking very relaxed when I arrived. I'd probably come at the wrong moment, but then with Cleo, it was often the wrong moment.

"Hey Di," said Simon. He was wearing a brand-new enormous smoke-gray velour bathrobe and stretching himself out on the couch like a big lazy housecat. Probably hadn't bothered to get dressed that day either.

"So Simon, when are you heading out for the rock?" I asked.

"What rock?"

"Any rock will do."

He shrugged and grinned.

It was worse than I thought.

"C'mon in here," said Cleo, motioning toward the bedroom. She began to pull clothes out of drawers and closets. Designer woolens flew onto the bed along with fisherman knits, tweedy ensembles in autumn colors, capes and ski jackets. We wanted to cover every possibility.

"He hasn't told me where we're going. I hope we're not going skiing," I said. "I've never skied in my life, Cleo."

"Don't worry, if he does take you skiing, you just tell him you'll meet him out there on the slopes then hang around in the lounge drinking Irish coffees... Dinah, calm down. I'm sure everything's going to be fine."

Friday

The wind had blown all the rain south to Washington and a clear, star-cluttered night sky whizzed by above us as Ian lowered his foot on the accelerator. I couldn't believe I was letting him take my life in his hands like that, but then he'd had quite a lot of me in his hands recently, so I guess it made a perverse kind of sense. And the more I was with him, the more reckless I felt.

Until I was able to make out the bald mountainside dimly looming before us, and along the roadside, a row of newly-planted trees.

"Look at that? Did you see that? Did you see what they're going to do there?" I blurted out, pointing out the stand of Douglas firs and Sitka spruces that was vanishing quickly into the distance. "That is a perfect example of their cunning."

"What are you talking about, Dinah?" Ian drove even faster.

"The beauty strip," I grumbled.

"What's a beauty strip?"

"You're joking, I hope."

"A bunch of beautiful women doing a striptease?" he offered.

I shook my head, despairingly. "You're the CEO of the western branch of Green World International and you don't know what a beauty strip is."

"Something women use for depilation?"

I groaned.

"For removing their body hair. Like a wax strip. Am I close?"

I groaned louder.

He tried again. "It's a whole row of hairdressers' places in a strip mall."

"You're warmer but you flunk anyway. Go directly to the doghouse and do not collect your dog biscuits."

"So what's the beauty strip?"

"It's those few hundred feet of trees that the logging companies plant or leave along the side of the road so that the public won't see all the clear-cut logging, bald landscape and general devastation behind it. They figure what we don't see, we don't care about. And you know what?"

"What?"

"They're right."

'Dinah, it's dark. How do you know it's a devastated mountainside?"

"Do you want to go back? I'd put money on it."

"How much?" He looked sharper all of a sudden.

"You're joking."

"No."

"A hundred?" It was all I had in my purse.

"You're on," he said.

The tires squealed as he did a perilous U-turn and gunned the car back to the mountain. He slammed on the brakes with another squeal then said, "You have to do this with these cars. You have to use them to their full potential."

Sure. Just like your women.

I made him get out of the car and we wound and crunched our way in the dark through the narrow strip of new growth and out to the open area where the mountain was showing off its full baldness. The silvering wood of the slashed trunks made it possible to see the extent of the clear-cut.

"The whole mountain," I said, trying not to choke. "Look at this. It's criminal. Now do you get the picture? This is what the beauty strip is supposed to hide."

He pulled out his wallet, and offered the money.

"I wasn't serious," I said. "It's only a bet for the idea of a bet, not for actual money."

He quickly put the bills away and said, "I told you I needed you, Dinah, and this is just another example."

I didn't care if Ian needed me. I wanted to phone Thomas, rant and rave about forestry. It was a minor glitch in eco-crisis terms, but the shaved mountain had just dampened my mood. I struggled to come up with something else to distract me. Something that had nothing to do with ecology. Something that would make me laugh.

All that came to mind were Hector and the tango.

We pulled into our destination, Wickaninnish Inn. Even from the road, I could hear the roar of the surf from the beach.

Ian took a brochure from the glove compartment and read, "Chesterman's Beach, part of the Pacific Rim National Park."

I said, "Nothing between us and Japan but thousands of miles of Pacific Ocean."

He looked out into the darkness and said, "Let's go in."

We pulled out our overnight bags and walked into the lobby.

The hotel sat on a small point of rugged trees and rock jutting into the vast sweeping coastline. The building was a rustic designer orgy of wood, glass, furnishings in natural tones, beiges, browns, creams, and every shade of off-white imaginable.

"If my mother knew I was here she would tell me I was being wasteful."

"We won't tell your mother then," said Ian as he checked in and was handed the key card. A porter showed us through the comfortable corridors to our room, which was another smaller orgy of these soft warm noncolors.

"Rugged place," said Ian, "but they say this has one of the fifty best restaurants in the world. La Pointe restaurant. A great eating experience, so they say."

Rugged?

I tried not to giggle but it bubbled out of me anyway. "You think this is rugged?"

Ian nodded. "What's so funny?"

"You should have grown up with me. Then you would have seen rugged."

"Oh, really." He looked completely uninterested so I didn't launch into my tales from childhood, all about my mother's every-man-for-himself jaunts up the coast, digging our own latrines, fishing for supper, gathering berries for dessert and chasing off the wasps (which my mother always said were there to remind you that the West coast was not actually paradise).

As we unpacked, I couldn't stop myself from tripping and stumbling down my untamed memory lane. I'd spent most of my childhood grappling with solitude, my mother expecting me to simply grow up and if I couldn't do that, be a miniature adult. It had been easy to run wild with the family animals. And then when I was nine, Simon had come along. I think I was in love with him from the first day, by virtue of the fact that he was my only human playmate. Simon was always plotting. I loved to be part of his schemes, which could only be described as harebrained.

So, we'd been children together, comparing our mosquito bites, clambering up trees, building forts over anthills, jumping naked into the ocean, taking the ponies on day-long rides through the trails and then, suffering through homeschooling lessons during the long rainy winters.

Ian's voice broke in, "Dinah. A penny for your thoughts."

"Sorry?"

"You were far away. Where were you?"

"Back in my childhood."

He frowned.

"But I'd rather be here with you. Really." I put my arms around his neck.

He finally gave me a proper smile, the one that requires sunglasses with high UV protection. "You're sure about that now?"

"Absolutely."

"Then let's climb into that thing." Ian motioned toward the huge bathroom and the hot tub. It was located by a big picture window that looked out over the dark ocean swells.

"Phew, this is really roughing it," I said.

Ian pretended not to hear me. "And after we've had our bath, we should eat something."

"It's pretty late. The kitchen will be closed, won't it?" I pulled on the big plush complimentary bathrobe and went to turn on the taps to fill the hot tub.

"I hope you're hungry," he called. "I arranged for something to nibble on."

I nodded. I was beyond hungry.

We lowered ourselves into the tub. The sensation of pounding water was too pleasant to disturb with any movements other than breathing. We sat back, allowing the rush of water to pummel all our city tensions away. When we climbed out, we both felt blissful, our muscles like liquid.

When the food came, Ian picked at it methodically, while I had to fight myself not to shovel it in.

When we'd licked the last crumbs from our fingertips, Ian said to me, "Let's stretch out on the bed and you can tell me all about your rugged childhood."

So I told him, all about my great-grandparents and my mother and the homeschooling, the escape to Vancouver. Everything except Thomas and Hector and Mike.

And then I asked, "What about you?"

"Me?"

"Your childhood." I laughed. "And don't try and worm out of it."

He looked past me at the far wall and said, "There were those lonely summers in great rambling Cape Cod houses, the sailing and the fishing, unbearably cold and lonely Boston winters."

"So you're a lonely American?"

"No, a lonely Canadian. My mother...my family moved to the States when I was young. That was where I met Chaz."

"So then it was just you and good old Chaz Heffelfeffel, eh?"

"Vanpfeffer. We were friends. We grew up together and went to the same university."

"That would be Harvard again?"

"It would be...again..."

I was looking up at the ceiling. There was a long silence. When I turned to look at him, his eyes were closed. "Ian?"

"Uh...Dinah...you'll have to forgive me...but I must still be on Eastern time..." He'd barely finished the sentence before he was fast asleep.

Right. What does the accomplished man-eater do when the man she's come with doesn't come with her, so to speak?

She organizes a manicure, a massage in the spa, and maybe something on the DVD player, a good film in peaceful solitude, while she regroups and gathers her strength for the next victim.

I was out of my mind. This was a thousand-dollar-a-night hotel. It was no place to stay in and not have sex.

I got my cell phone out of my purse, snuck into the bathroom and called Joey.

"Home for strays and waifs," his voice answered. There was laughter in the background.

"Joey, it's me, Dinah. Where are you?"

"Dinah, you're the last person I expected to hear from. Shouldn't you be getting screwed silly right about now?"

"He's fallen asleep."

"He's what?"

"Fallen asleep."

"You must have bored him."

"I was just wondering the same thing myself. What's going on there? Where are you?"

"Over at Jon and Kev's. We're playing killer Scrabble."

"Big night on the town, eh?"

"Hey. Never underestimate the power of words."

"I'm bored, Joey," I whispered.

"You have every right to be. Is his snoring going to keep you awake? Pretend you're suddenly single again and you're treating yourself to this weekend…oh…Jon wants to talk to you."

Jon's voice said, "Hi there. Where are you? We could have used you here tonight for the Scrabble."

"My Savior."

"At your service. Where are you?"

"I'm at Long Beach. Wickaninnish Inn."

"Long Beach? How did you get there? It's one beautiful place."

"I guess so."

"You guess so?"

"It would be more beautiful if the man I came with hadn't just conked out for the night."

Jon laughed. "Never mind. Go down to the beach and run along it in the dark. It's a great sensation."

"It's almost pitch-black out there. I can hear the ocean but I can barely see it."

"That's the whole point. It's amazing."

"You mean run along the beach chanting 'The sea is my mother'?"

"Why not?"

"I'd kind of hoped that tonight all that outdoorsy nature stuff would be a distant cousin. It was supposed to be *human* nature tonight."

"Would that be the new man in your life, your boss?"

"The same."

"I'd do it with you if I were there, Dinah."

"Do what?"

"Go running in the dark."

"I wish you guys were *all* here. It would be so much more fun."

"Uhh, Joey wants the—"

The phone was grabbed back from Jon and Joey said, "Gotta hang up now. You're wearing down my battery and we're going out clubbing."

"Wait a minute, Joey, I thought you said it was Scrabble night…." But he'd already hung up.

I sighed. It was one of those moments. You're out on what is supposed to be the date of your life, and the party is somewhere else.

It was too dark to go running.

What a crazy idea.

I had another inspiration.

I dug my laptop out of my bag and started to surf the Net.

Okay, I know. Sad.

It was a last-ditch alternative.

Just in case things got boring.

Okay, I confess.

It was an addiction.

I liked to stay informed.

At least, that was my excuse.

To date, I'd not heard anything from Rupert. Still, my curiosity was piqued. I started to look up Hector Ferrer. Over and over the words *Scarlet Tango* came up. At first, it was hard to tell what the Scarlet Tango was exactly. I continued to surf. Up it came again between names like Chick Corea and Astor Piazzolla. It was appearing in anthologies everywhere, anthologies of tango music. There it was again and again, a piece of music composed by my father. "Scarlet Tango" by Hector Ferrer—8' 42".

I stared out at the beach again.

Jon's idea was crazy.

But there was no way I could fall asleep in my present condition, so I put away my laptop, got back into my heavier clothes, pulled on the knee-length red down jacket that Cleo had lent me, and headed out toward the booming Pacific.

I ran along the windy cold beach in the dark. It was strange. I kept expecting to bump into or trip over something. But I didn't because the beach was so vast and the tide was out. It was like being on another planet, or just floating free in some distant part of the universe. Or like running in a vacuum except for the waves breaking out in the distance. I enjoyed myself, running and jumping and spinning around until I lost all sense of direction.

Out on the sand, I leapt and howled at the dark sky and beating waves.

Ian Trutch be damned.

Jon was right. It felt good to run out there by myself. In no time I was thinking in tango rhythms. I remembered those weird, exciting, exotic strains I'd already heard and tried to imagine what kind of piece Scarlet Tango could be. I started to dance, improvising my own kind of tango on the beach. I did the *paseo* past the bright crashing breakers, did a grand *caminata* along the sand, and tried a few *giros* into an imaginary man. By the time I was tangoing my way back to the hotel, I was ready for anything.

When I got to the room, Ian was in exactly the same position.

I was woken by the sound of a door opening. The light from the hallway flooded the room. Ian was at the door with an enormous bouquet of pale roses. I switched on the bedside light. They were yellow roses and there must have been three dozen of them. How had he managed it at two in the morning? Driven like crazy down to some little mill town with an all-night grocery? Robbed a hothouse?

I got up and went over to him. He held the bouquet out to me. "Forgive me for falling asleep, Dinah." I took the bouquet and sniffed the roses. They had no scent. I'd never received three dozen yellow odorless roses from anyone. So I forgave him.

Twice.

Saturday

Ian's side of the bed was already empty. Apart from being a fur-buying hedonist, he was also turning out to be a person who never slept when other people were sleeping. It fit the profile of executive vampire quite well, really. But then when he came into the room and smiled, and said he was sorry again, and took me for a delicious breakfast in the restaurant, and under the table, kept my feet squeezed between his feet the whole time, I was able to overlook this defect.

The weather turned gray and cold by morning so the rest of the weekend was spent inside the hotel, Ian letting his body do the apologizing. And eloquently too. And when we weren't doing that, we toyed with crosswords and looked out at the foggy drizzle from various windows, the restaurant window, the lobby window, the bar window, the bedroom window, and the window by the hot tub.

Later, while we were having a hot stone massage in the Cedars Spa, and knobs of heat were radiating through my muscles and making me forget, finally, everything that was wrong with the world, Ian turned onto his side and said, "I've been meaning to ask you, Dinah. Why isn't a girl like you married?"

Ouch.

Searing pain.

Someone, somewhere, had a voodoo doll of me. Whenever that horrible marriage question was asked, my anonymous tormentor gleefully jabbed and pricked away at my poor little effigy. It was like a curse, that question. I glared at

Ian. Every muscle, nerve and fiber in my body had become rigid and inflamed within seconds.

"Why do I take two sugars in my coffee?" I asked, my voice oozing with boredom.

"You like it sweet, I imagine."

"Ditto for my private life, Ian. I like it sweet."

So stop asking stupid questions.

Sunday

On the drive back to Vancouver, a cloud of disappointment enveloped me and I couldn't shake it off. I'd hoped a weekend together would have helped me get to know him, but Ian seemed as much of a stranger as ever.

Chapter Ten

Ian dropped me off at my apartment with a peck on the cheek. I climbed the stairs slowly and when I dropped my bag in front of my door to put the key in the lock, there was an explosion of laughter from Joey's place. I opened my door, put my bag inside, and banged on Joey's door. When he opened it, I came at him like the bad cop. "Okay, what's going on here? You know laughter's forbidden in this building."

"Just a quiet little stuff-your-face-with-potluck among friends. Come on in."

I stepped inside.

Joey's place was furnished in early Salvation Army with brilliantly clever touches, such as vivid enamel paint on old wooden furniture. Bright blue chest of drawers with orange and yellow knobs and outlines. Pink-and-turquoise kitchen table and fuchsia and peppermint-green chairs. The art on the walls was classic movie posters. His living-dining room had terra-cotta walls, his kitchen was painted lemon-yellow and his bedroom a rich dark indigo with metallic silver stars on the ceiling. In the bedroom, he had hung large photographs, tributes to the glories of the male body. It was a bit like living inside a comic book.

Joey had invited everybody. Cleo, Fran, Simon, Kevin and Jon, Jake, Ash and Lisa. We'd all gotten on so well at the block party that Joey had decided to repeat the experience. Only Ida hadn't come. She had a busy social life elsewhere.

The voices in the room had risen to deaf-making. Everyone was talking at once about everything, and everyone seemed to be having a much better time than I'd had all weekend.

"Dinah," exclaimed Kevin, coming over and giving me a big hug. "You're back from the wilds. Tell us all about it."

"Not much to tell. It's a beautiful hotel."

"Were the clothes okay?" Cleo called across the din.

"They were perfect," I called back.

Simon asked, "Spot any whales?"

"No."

I wandered over to Jon's side of the room and sat down at the table next to him. A big sigh escaped from me.

"Did you do what I suggested up there at Long Beach?"

"Running in the dark?"

He nodded.

"That first night? I ended up tangoing on the beach. In the total darkness. By myself. It was the highlight of my weekend, I might add."

He shook his head, chuckled, then looked up. His eyes caught the light. He glanced over at Kevin, as if checking on him, then said to me, "Romantic weekend not too successful, eh?"

"He actually had the nerve to ask me why a girl like me wasn't married?"

"So?"

"So what?"

"So why aren't you?" He raised one eyebrow.

"No," I moaned. "Not you, too." I gave him a small shove.

"What did I do?"

"That question. It's taboo."

"It is?"

"It's like saying how come you're such a failure? How come you can't get a man and keep him?"

"Okay," he said, laughing. "So how come you're such a failure, Dinah?"

"I'm a free woman. That's what's wrong with me. Nobody makes me compromise. I like that. And I think I'm going to stay free as long as I can manage it. I don't see the glamor in that marriage stuff."

I was such a brazen liar it was all I could do not to choke on my own words. But I wanted to believe them. I really did.

"I'll buy that. Totally agree with you," he said.

"So how do people do it? I'd really like to know. How do people keep it alive?"

"Booze," said Jon, raising his glass with a smile.

"Right. That's about the same as the lobotomy effect. So how do they do it? Really."

"Uh…I, er…don't really know. I've never analyzed the successful couple." He raised his voice so that Kevin could hear. "A lot of couples fall in together by accident, because they are in a certain place at a certain time, and then they decide to keep on stumbling along together by accident." Kevin was watching us both and listening and when he caught my eye, he blew us both exaggerated kisses.

I blew one back.

"Now tell me about the tango." Jon smiled.

"It's a long story. But the short version is that I'm taking tango lessons."

"It must be fun."

"I'm not sure about that."

"Then why are you doing it?"

"Because my therapist thought it would help me learn to follow a man."

"He sees it as a problem? Not following a man?"

"My therapist seems to think so," I said glumly.

"Well, hell. Why?"

"Because of the way I broke up with my fiancé."

"How was that? Was it spectacular?"

"Not at all. I just realized that he was an academic climber, packed my stuff and came over here to Vancouver, without a word to him or anybody else. I didn't even give him a chance to defend himself or talk me out of leaving. My therapist thought I should have talked about it. But some things just can't be talked about because talking only makes it worse."

"It's a shame."

"What is?"

"That you didn't throw a big scene. I can just picture you doing it. I'll bet you can make sparks fly."

"I wish I had. But it wouldn't have helped. I had all my big scenes later, in private, by myself."

"So what was the situation with your ex then?"

"Maybe I'll tell you about it when I'm really, really drunk."

"Tell me now," he prompted.

"Well, you are my Savior," I said, "and I wouldn't even be around to tell it if you hadn't happened along when you did. So I do owe you."

"Yes, you do." He smiled.

"Well, it's just that Mike…"

"Your ex…"

"After we got together…got really interested in my past."

"Yes?"

"I thought it was a lover's thing, you know, wanting to know every single stupid little thing about the other person. So it was, show me where you cut your knee, show me where you rode horses, show me where you slept when you were a girl…"

"Hmmmm," said Jon, his eyes exceptionally bright.

"He was using me to get to my mother. We were always over there. Used to drive up from the university and spend the weekends... I should tell you, Jon, my mother is a very generous woman. She always helps students out."

"Ah."

"So when Mike started sucking up to her big-time, I got the sensation that he'd do anything, I mean anything at all to get in her good books. Because she's the big name marine mammal scientist and I'm just her daughter and that's his area of study."

"I'm getting the picture," said Jon. "So he was using you for eventual career reasons?"

I nodded. "She *has* been helping him all along. But then he really pushed it. He started giving her little gifts, tokens. My mother's very gracious about that kind of thing. A lot of people give her gifts. But *I* wasn't getting any gifts. It was absurd. I just felt so jealous. So left out. He'd bypassed me. So I left."

"Gotcha," said Jon. He massaged my shoulder and said, "Shall we get ourselves some of this great food?"

I nodded.

We stood up and went over to the table where it was all spread out.

Jon became like a mother hen. He got me a plate and began heaping things on and saying, "You have to try this and this and this. Kevin made them."

He seemed so proud of Kevin when he said it that I had another pang of envy.

"It's too much. I can't eat all of this," I blurted. "I have to consider my thighs."

"Real thighs are in this year," said Jon, through a mouthful. "Not those airbrushed and cyber-manipulated gams."

Later, after the dinner, and a taste of several of the liqueurs, I grabbed Joey and dragged him across the room in a messy *caminata* and then tried a few *giros*. Jake called across the room, teasing, "Hey, Dinah. We have programs for that kind of problem. Here's our one eight hundred number."

After that we divided into two teams and played charades. Lisa didn't want to play by the rules. None of that two words, first syllable, sign language stuff. She wanted to be a drama queen and act it all out.

Then Joey piped up, "Hey Di, show us again what you learned in tango class."

"I need a victim," I said.

Jon stood up. "Take me."

Liquid courage was surging through me, so I said, "Well now, the first thing you have to do…is…uh…plaster your body up against your partner's." Jon plastered himself against me. I looked right into his yellow eyes and suddenly felt as though I were looking into the cougar's eyes. I looked down at our feet. "And then just try to walk with me." And for a seamless few seconds we glided, glided across the room, bumped into the wall, stumbled over each other, fell on the floor and hooted.

That was when Kevin began to look unwell.

Jon stood up, dusted himself off, and said, "I think Kev and I had better be going."

Monday

Lisa grabbed me by the hand and pulled me into my office, then shut the door.

"I just did it, just now," she said, rolling her eyes and grimacing.

"What did you do?"

"I said I'd go out with him."

"With who, Lisa? I'm not following you."

"I said I'd go out with Roly, the yellow slicker guy."

I opened my eyes wide. "Well…uh…Lisa, you never

know. Maybe it'll be a fun date. You can't always judge a book by its cover."

Although in my humble opinion, the cover is always a good place to start.

Two fret lines appeared between Lisa's eyebrows. "Oh, gosh, I sure hope so. I sure hope I'm not making a huge mistake."

"Where are you going for lunch?"

"That Greek place on Broadway. His choice."

Greek?

A bit suspicious.

Now I had reason to worry about Lisa and her lost causes again. At GWI, Lisa's lost causes were our lost causes. There are those who try to save the world in a sweeping impersonal way and those, like Lisa, who were trying to do it with their own two hands.

I said, "You think he can be redeemed then? What's the story on him anyway?"

She grimaced. "He likes big blond women."

"Apart from that."

"He's very well-spoken. Have you ever talked to him? He's completely, totally a gentleman. If you close your eyes while he's talking, you imagine somebody who looks completely, totally different from him. And he doesn't smell like a street person. I think he actually washes. With soap."

"Well, that's definitely something."

"So I figure I can just about handle a lunch. That's forty minutes' worth, right? That won't kill me."

"How are you getting there?" I asked.

"Taxi?"

"Who's paying?"

"He said he'd take care of it all."

"You're a good woman, Lisa."

"That's what Roly always says."

Lisa left and I called Moira in Ottawa. "Extension twenty-two, please."

Moira's voice answered. "Dinah. I was hoping you'd get back to me. I never got to finish telling you about the union woman here. He pressured her, Dinah."

"What do you mean?"

"I mean if he hadn't pressured her so much, she wouldn't have had a heart attack…damn…I can't talk. He must have his goons monitoring everything. Call me again tomorrow."

Almost as soon as I'd put down the receiver, the phone rang. It was Rupert. He was calling from God knows where. The line crackled with static and all I heard was, "Got… messages…I promise I'll…" before the connection ended abruptly.

A "bling" told me I had new mail. I clicked on the icon.

From: Ian Trutch
To: Staff Members
Re: Vacation time: All vacations up to and including the month of December are cancelled in light of Space Centre fund-raiser event. New vacation time will be examined and allotted following results of Space Centre event.
Re: office stationery: Contract with recycled paper suppliers cancelled due to excessive cost. Find "normal" paper donors.
Re: employee donations: included file attachment A is the new employee donation module with suggested donation based on wages earned, and bank agreement form to have the sum taken off at source, a highly recommended time-saving action.
Re: Coffee: From today forward, only Kona coffee will be used in the machine in the coffee room. Everyone will be expected to contribute to the cost.
Re: PA: I am now accepting resumés for personal assistant.

I opened up the attachment for employee donations. It was one wild, official-looking document. I didn't bother with the fine print but I was sure it included something about first-born children.

I suddenly felt very uncharitable.

Jake poked his head around my office door. He looked nervous. "Dinah, your mother's here." He was already fiddling with the end of his mustache. A bad sign.

"Really? She told me she didn't have a lecture until next week."

"Trutch invited her."

"Really?" Everyone wanted my mother. "What for?"

"He'd like her to host a documentary on Green World and its pilot projects. His plan is to use the media to give GWI a higher, more commercial profile. He wants it to be this big PR thing."

"PR is *my* area. Why hasn't he spoken to me?"

"Well, frankly Dinah, he's been asking a lot of questions about you."

"He's calling my performance into question?"

"Not in so many words…"

And then my intuition made me say, "Jake, I have a confession to make."

"A confession?" He looked puzzled.

"Sit down."

He sat.

"You know that Tod Villiers, has left town?"

"Now that you mention it, I did hear some rumors. I didn't take them seriously."

"He told me to tear up the check."

"The check? Which check?"

"The one for Mudpuddle," I said, gathering all my courage. "Tod Villiers is bankrupt."

Jake slapped his forehead with his hand. "Christ, Dinah. How long have you known?"

"A few days."

"Why didn't you tell me as soon as you knew?"

"I was buying time. He told me that he had a replacement donor. That he'd spoken to the guy and that he was definitely coming on board."

"Who is it? What's his name?"

"Hamish Robertson."

Jake stared at me blankly for a second or two, then muttered, "Christ. Damn. Goddamn. Jesus, Dinah. I gotta get a chocolate bar."

I got up and followed him into his office where he was yanking open the bottom drawer and ripping the wrapper off a Jersey Milk. It disappeared into his mouth.

"Jake, if I can just get to Hamish Robertson, I'm sure we'll get our donation."

Jake shook his head. "Dinah, Dinah, Dinah. *Nobody's* been able to get to Hamish Robertson. Not for the last ten years. He's a recluse. The invisible man. You should have told me right away. We're up to our knees in it now."

When I got back to my office my mother was there, re-organizing Mr. Potato Head's body parts. "Isn't he lovely?" she said. "You're looking awfully glum, Di Di. Come along. We'll get a bite of lunch down the road."

In the restaurant, my stomach shut down completely. While my mother tackled her triple deluxe burger with fries and onion rings, I poked at my Caesar salad. I was dying to interrogate my mother on Hector Ferrer, but having been warned, I stayed off the topic.

"Well, lovey, it seems that this new boyfriend, this Trutch man of yours has rather extravagant plans for your organization."

"Mine? Did he say he was mine?"

"Well, he did mention you were 'seeing each other.'" She chuckled. "Quaint."

My stony look was eloquent.

My mother held up her hands. "You know I would never interfere in your private life. You're a grown person. I'm sure that when you made your choices you had your extremely good reasons, Di Di."

It was not quite what I wanted to hear. "Are you going to do it, Mom?"

"What, pumpkin?"

"The documentary."

She wiped her mouth neatly with the napkin. "Do you want me to do it, lovey?"

How could I tell her, "No. Once, just once in my life, let me do it on my own. Let me prove to myself that I can. That I don't need your help." A documentary hosted by my mother would be grand for the greater good of Green World but not the greater good of Dinah Nichols.

She looked at her watch and said, "Heavens. He's awfully late, isn't he?"

"Who, Mom?"

"Your Trutch man, dear. I invited him to join us to talk over the details."

The words "Don't do it, Mom," rushed out of me.

"Heavens, Dinah."

"Don't do it. Don't take this the wrong way but I don't want you to help Green World out."

She paused, fiddled with her gold earring, scrutinized me then smiled. "I thoroughly understand, pumpkin. I really do. This is your life and your job and you don't want me interfering in it. You need to test your capabilities."

Why did she have to be so damned understanding? "It's not that I don't think you'd be the best person to help us out…it's just that…you're my mother…and it's not always so easy…"

She laughed. "I know, I know. Dear, dear. I sense that this might upset your Trutch man. He did seem awfully adamant. What shall I tell him?"

"Anything you like. But not that I told you not to do it.

It might get me fired. That's what he's here for, Mom, to fire people."

"Lord. That does seem a trifle drastic. But just remember, Dinah. There are an infinite number of wonderful jobs out there for you. There's nothing you can't do if you set your mind to it. And if worse came to worst you could always give me a hand… Ah…here he is now. I think we won't commit to anything right at the moment. That strikes me as saner. I'll let him down gently when the right moment comes."

I laughed out loud. I don't think my mother had ever let a man down gently in her life. With her it was usually a fast clean cut. Snip, snip, snip.

Ian sat down at our table. It was the first time I'd seen them together. He'd bypassed me to meet her, but he also seemed wary of her, vaguely threatened.

My mother immediately broke the ice by saying, "Ian, I was just saying to Dinah, do you think your Trutch man would fancy a bit of sailing? Or is he the safe dry land type?"

I'd seen my mother throw down the gauntlet before, but never so blatantly.

"Ah… sailing? Yes. I've done a bit of crewing."

"Well, I know it's a working day for all of you, but town does give me such claustrophobia. What about this afternoon? I have a little time and the weather isn't too bad." It was a blustery day, with a mix of sun and cloud, a bit choppy, but nothing my mother wasn't used to.

"And we can talk about the documentary?" he said.

My mother's mouth was conveniently full as she nodded.

"What sort of craft is it?" he asked.

"A jolly sturdy reliable one," she answered, her eyes twinkling wickedly.

"I should change my clothes…" he said.

"Righto." She looked at her watch. "Will forty minutes be enough? What do you say, Di? We've got the extra kit if he needs it."

"Oh yes." I was enjoying this a little more than I ought to.

She gave him the details, the berth number and how to get there and we agreed to meet at the boat.

I raced back to the office to let them all know I would be out for the afternoon but when I arrived, everyone was up in the coffee room. Ash was at their center.

She was wearing a sea-green sari and her thick glasses. She looked like the Hindu deity, Shiva. A near-sighted Shiva. In Destruction Mode.

She stabbed the air as she spoke. "I do not drink coffee. I drink tea. I am not paying for Ian Trutch's fancy Hawaiian coffee. If he gets fancy coffee, I want fancy tea. I want Darjeeling. I want Ceylon. That man is not going to get an extra penny out of me. I know what kind of expense account he's given himself. The receipts go through *my* hands. It's GWI who services that car of his and pays for half his meals. Who does he think he is anyway?"

Ash was making progress. She was complaining to real live people for a change.

When Ian came striding along the dock, dressed in a navy blue yachting jacket over a cream fisherman knit sweater, white pants, and a captain's cap, my jaw sagged open. He was carrying a bottle. When he spotted me, he held it up. "Champagne. A nice boating vintage."

It all made me wonder what boat he'd crewed on. The *HMS DILETTANTE*?

When he came closer to my mother's boat his pace slowed. I struggled to keep a smile off my face.

"This is it?" he asked.

My mother's boat is an old twenty-eight-foot Bristol Channel Cutter, a floating laboratory, cluttered with equipment for tracking whales, dolphins and seals. Completely utilitarian.

My mother came up from below deck. "Welcome aboard,

Ian. Let me just make a space for you. Mind the wet spots. Oh, no, don't sit there, my student was taking apart the engine, a bit of grease there, I'm afraid. Wouldn't want to mark those lovely trousers. Just shove those ropes to one side. Yes, they are a little manky I'm afraid. Little fuel spill. Champagne? Di, take this bottle below and find a glass, would you, lovey? I won't have any myself just now but perhaps you'll pour some out for Ian."

My mother had always maintained a strict "No drinking aboard" rule, for the safety of her students.

Ian was squeezing himself into a tiny corner of the little available seating room and smearing suntan lotion on his face. My mother started up the motor. I went below deck with the bottle and hunted for a decent glass. There were some scratched plastic beach glasses, but they looked reasonably clean. I popped the cork and sloshed some in, then took it up to Ian. He took the glass and struck a fair-weather pose while around us the weather was quickly growing worse. We motored out along False Creek towards English Bay over water that was now turning from blue to gray. Small whitecaps were appearing and the boat began to lurch through the swells, rising then slapping down against the water.

When my mother and I were aboard there was no need to speak; we could read each other's minds. She turned off the motor, I raised the mainsail, she took the rudder and we were suddenly shooting through the water in a wind that was growing quickly fiercer. The boat was already keeling at a forty-five-degree angle. I yelled to Ian, "Get to starboard. We need your weight over there."

He looked bewildered.

"Over there. Your right-hand side."

He crawled and grappled his way over to the other side. His glass skittered along the deck and over the edge. I watched as his tan took on a greenish tinge. We were well out into the bay by now. The few sailboats that had been there earlier were heading for shore.

All of a sudden, a crosswind made the whole boat shudder. My mother let the sheets go slack and the sail flutter every which way. The boat had turned into a bucking bronco.

Ian was now on his feet, slipping and sliding. "Dinah, is there a bathroom on this thing?"

I pointed toward the hatch. He skidded backward, turned and caught himself against the edge of the boat, and retched violently over the side.

My mother was cheerful. "Di Di, we have to get the spinnaker up. Do lash the poor man to the mast before he goes overboard or something equally dreary."

I told Ian to go below and he gratefully clung to the fittings as he made his way to the hatch. My mother and I raised the spinnaker.

As soon as it was hoisted, the boat lifted up and glided above the chop. We turned about and headed back into the harbor, and when the boat was finally tied up in its berth, Ian climbed off and stood on the dock, trying to compose himself. "It's not like the Atlantic at all. I can handle the Atlantic."

Sure you can, Ian. Sure you can.

Tuesday

Word of Ian's little seafaring adventure had spread throughout the office. Lisa came into my office and began to sing under her breath, "I'm Popeye the sailor man, poop poop…I live in a garbage can, poop poop…"

There was a knock at my office door. Ian put his head in. "Am I interrupting?"

"Just leaving," said Lisa.

They exchanged places, Lisa going out with a little wave, and Ian coming in with a dark look in his eye.

He said, "Dinah, I have to step out for a bit. When the workmen come, would you deal with them for me?"

"Workmen? What workmen?"

"For the third floor. My new office."

"Your…office? Uh…"

"Come with me and I'll show you what you have to do."

I couldn't wait. I followed him out into the building's common hallway, and up another set of stairs, chattering all the way. When we reached the next floor, I realized that Caloo, the import-export offices that had occupied the other half of that floor, had vanished. "But where have they gone? They were doing a booming business last week…."

"Not anymore."

I followed Ian through the corridor, poking my nose into the tiny rabbit-warren rooms, all abandoned, the only things left behind being dust balls, scattered papers and in the big main office, a couch with a slightly moth-eaten green velveteen cover.

He adjusted his tie in the window-glass reflection. "They have instructions to knock down anything that isn't a supporting wall, more or less. You're to see that they don't stand around smoking and wasting my time."

His time? I doubted he was paying for this office out of his own pocket. It would most likely be the *company's* time. I said to him, "This whole half of the third floor is going to be *your* office?"

"GWI has an image problem and I intend to do something to fix it. See you tonight? For dinner?"

I shook my head. "Don't you want some time off?"

"I prefer dining with a pretty woman to dining alone."

Aha. I was getting the picture. I was a blow-up doll that sat with him at the dinner table and filled the empty space on the other side of the bed.

But he kissed both my hands so I said okay, I'd go to dinner on the condition that we should go to that really chic place that did nouvelle cuisine for the movie stars, gave you one carrot shred, one lettuce leaf, one endive, one asparagus tip, a sliver of duck breast and a sprinkling of truffle, then charged you enough to pay some kid's university tuition for a whole year. All this "dating" was making me put on weight.

He rushed away. I waited for a minute then went down to the second floor and knocked on Ash's door. She'd sent me an e-mail earlier telling me to come to her office. When I opened the door, she said unhappily, "Oh, it's you, Dinah." She searched through a pile of receipts. "Who went to the Urban Waste Congress in Seattle?"

"That was Cleo."

"And who went to the conference at Wickaninnish?"

"Uh…the…uh…conference…at…uh…Wickaninnish?"

"Long Beach. I have the receipts here but I can't find the names."

"Uh…I was there…and, uh…so was Ian Trutch…" I suppose we were *conferring,* in the broadest sense of the word.

"Okay. I've now been instructed by Ian Trutch to tell you all that the per diem for out-of-town conferences is now twenty dollars a day. Whoever goes over budget will have to take it out of their own pocket. That goes for all of you. And there's something else. We can only pay for a portion of the accommodations for the international visitors coming to the Space Centre for the fund-raising event."

"We *what?* But it's already been organized. What am I supposed to do?"

"Ian has suggested that the YM-YWCA has reasonably-priced accommodations."

"The Y…" I tried to picture it.

"Those are the directives," she said dryly. "Your Villiers donor didn't work out, I see."

She ought to have known better. The things that didn't work out for one of us were the things that didn't work out for the whole of Green World.

Wednesday

I was fifteen minutes early for my tango lesson. Los Tangueros was deserted. I stood on the small iron landing outside, banging, but nobody was there. Nobody answered. I sat down on the top step, deciding to give him five more minutes.

A blue Ford van pulled up and Victoria climbed out. She ran up the steps.

"I'm sorry," she said, "Hector's not coming tonight. He's…"

"Indisposed?"

She looked back toward the van and raised her eyebrows.

Incredulous, I went down the steps and up to the van. There was no one in the front. I opened up the back. Slumped across the carpeted floor was Hector, snoring loudly and reeking of alcohol. I was on the verge of waking him up and yanking him out but Victoria called, "Don't! He'll just have to sleep it off. I'm sorry."

"I came all the way down here for this lesson," I protested. "And my teacher gets pissed. Great."

"I can teach you if you want. And I'll make it half price for the inconvenience. We'll go over what he showed you if you like."

I thought about it. Victoria sounded so apologetic. I was already there and primed and it was better than nothing. "Okay," I nodded.

I was disappointed but in the long run, Victoria was a much easier male partner than Hector. Her teaching technique was the opposite of his. She told me right out that she believed we all have some talent and that the talent should be nurtured rather than bullied out into the open.

After the lesson, I said to Victoria, "Tell me something more about Hector."

"What would you like to know?" By her response, I guessed that everyone wanted to know more about Hector.

"Well…where he was born. A little something about his

life… I mean, it can't be simple being from Argentina, with all that's happened in that country. I mean, Hector was a popular figure. He wrote 'Scarlet Tango,' for crying out loud. It's famous in the tango repertoire. He's an artist. He must have been involved… I mean, I know that artists didn't have it easy during those years…"

She looked at me with suspicion. "Be careful."

I hesitated then said, "Listen, Victoria, when I'm handing sixty dollars an hour over to a person, I like to know something about them."

"Yes. But there are some things in his past he gets very upset about."

"Rupert was about to tell me but he never got the chance."

"I see." But as she put her tango shoes into her bag, I could tell that her attitude toward me was changing. She was closing up as tight as a clam. "Perhaps you should ask him yourself if you're so interested."

It sounded like a challenge. "I will," I said. "And thanks for the lesson."

Thursday

"Extension twenty-two, please."

A man's voice answered. "Who did you want to speak to?"

"Moira Kelly."

"Is this a business or personal call?" he asked, cattily.

"Business."

"That's a surprise."

"Why?"

"Moira's personal calls outnumbered her business calls. Which is why she doesn't work here anymore."

My mouth went dry. I hung up.

Jake was there at my door. He raised his eyebrows and said, "Notte's. After work."

★ ★ ★

At Notte's, I was definitely the center of attention.

Ida said, "You've got him in the perfect position, Dinah. You can help us all out. If you have to tie Ian Trutch to your bedposts and torture him to get the names of the redundancies, do it. I won't tell. I can lend you the whips."

Cleo opened her eyes wide. "Whips, Ida? I never would have pegged you for the type."

Ida plucked the maraschino off her cupcake and held it up. "Why is it you young people always think you're the ones who invented sex?"

Fran sighed. "'Cause when it's been so long you've forgotten what it's like, it *seems* like they invented it."

Jake was impatient. "Can we get to the business at hand? Dinah?"

"If I can just find this Robertson guy, I'm sure I can get his donation. You know my track record."

"Your methods are a little unorthodox…but you've hooked a few. No doubt about that."

"She has," said Lisa, "but this one's a real toughie."

I'd organized an Egyptian theme event when the Tut exhibit was in town, a city-wide treasure hunt with prizes, a sponsored Polar Bear Swim-a-thon at Jericho Beach one December, an Artists' Ball, an International Food Fest, and a mud-wrestling gala where local politicians got into the ring with several pairs of the most preposterous breasts anybody had ever seen. I had sniffed out, staked out, and stalked my donors. Nobody was exempt.

"I'm sure I can get to him," I said.

Jake sighed. "I've worked for GWI since the beginning. I hadn't really considered a career move."

Fran, who'd been looking pretty depressed lately, said, "Career move. That sounds so much prettier than the ugly thing it is. I can't get fired. Who'll hire me in this sexist, ageist society? I can't afford to get body work. And I've got my kid's braces to pay for, car payments, house payments, you name it, it never stops."

"There've been rumblings that the province is looking for advisors on sewage outfall…" said Jake.

"Naw, Jake. You'd hate it." Cleo shook her head. "But I guess it would be better than having to move to another town."

Jake grimaced. "Don't forget, I've got those alimony payments."

Fran patted Jake's shoulder. "You're one of the good guys, Jake. One who makes the payments. Not like somebody I know who's investing all his wages in silicon."

"What about you, Ida?" asked Jake. "What'll you do if you're made redundant?"

"Ah, hell. I'll go on a cruise. I'll find a wealthy husband. If there's one thing I've learned, axe or no axe, you gotta live for the moment."

"You, Lisa?" asked Jake.

She smiled. "I was thinking of maybe opening my own business."

We all stared at her.

"What kind of business?" Fran wanted to know.

"Not sure yet, Fran."

"You have the start-up capital?" asked Cleo.

Lisa was unfazed. "No. But I trust in the universe."

"That makes exactly one of us," muttered Fran.

Lisa went on, "But you know what, guys? I really don't want to quit the work we've been doing. I *love* the work we've been doing."

Everybody sighed in agreement.

"I'm sure I can get to that donor," I repeated.

Saturday

It was a wintry morning. I looked inside my closet; the moment of reckoning had arrived.

"Evil beast," I shouted into the dark hole. But there was no putting it off. I reached in and grabbed it.

The vacuum cleaner.

No ordinary vacuum cleaner but a Christmas present from my mother, state-of-the-art German technology with an unpronounceable name. I pulled it out of its cubbyhole.

Have I mentioned that I hate housework?

It didn't help matters that using my vacuum was like wrestling a bull elephant. It had a life of its own and one hell of a powerful suck. Barely would I spot one of my long-lost earrings in a dark corner at three feet than it had gobbled it up, forcing me to rummage for ages through the bag of disgusting dust to find it.

But there was no going back now. I'd invited Ian to dinner at my place and now I had to clean up. It was going to take me all day. It meant getting into all those telltale corners, the grouting in the bathroom, that place way back behind and under the sink, the dust along the skirting boards, the tiny cobwebs in the far corners of the ceiling. And then I had to think about clean sheets on the bed, the best towels on display, and room scent that would cover the smell of curry. If he happened to snoop in my drawers and cupboards when I wasn't looking, I had to show him what a meticulous orderly woman I was. I had to have every base covered. I had to keep him sweet.

The beast whined and roared as I lugged it around the tight corners. Under the roaring I could hear the sound of a ringing telephone.

Great.

Saved by the bell.

I switched it off and ran to answer. Any excuse not to vacuum. I was infinitely grateful to my caller as I picked up the phone and said, "Whoever you are, you just saved me from a fate worse than death."

"Your breasts are like two pert round mounds of spanakopita," hissed the caller.

"Listen, you Mr. Telephone Pervert. Don't you have something better to do than get your jollies with me and Greek food? Don't you have something to do? A job? A life?"

"You. I want to do it with you," he said.

"Listen. You could open one of those bakeries, a porn bakery maybe," I said, feeling inspired, "where all the goods are obscene, baked in the shape of body parts…"

"I want *your* body parts…"

I hung up. I hadn't been able to bring myself to use the whistle, even if I could find it. I felt sorry for the poor slob and his obsession with me.

I switched the beast on again and went back to work. As I cursed and untangled the vacuum cord from around my feet, Joey appeared outside on the little balcony. He knocked on the glass.

I switched the vacuum off again and opened up to Joey, armed with his habitual cup of coffee and copy of *Variety.* He pushed his way past me and into the center of the living room. "Is that what I think it is?"

I nodded fatalistically and stared at the malevolent hunk of stainless steel.

"My God, Dinah Nichols is vacuuming. Cleaning up. Alert the media. Somebody call CNN. It's that Ian Trutch hunk o' man, isn't it? You're having him to your dump. Just you and him? Or an intimate gathering of fifty or so?"

"Joey…"

"I know, I know. Go and weave baskets, Joey, is that what you're telling me? You can just say it to my face. I won't be offended."

But as he said it, I thought I'd never seen anyone look so hurt in all his life. Either that or he was a very good actor.

I whined, "Joeeeeey. It was supposed to be a two couple evening. Two *straight* couples."

Joey waved at the air with one finger and called to an imaginary person, "Waiter? Double lobotomy on the rocks, please?"

I continued to glare at him.

"I'll be as quiet as a mouse," he whispered. "You won't even know there's a faggot in the house."

I sighed in resignation. "Dinner's at eight."

"Now who's the other couple?"

"Cleo and Simon."

"Ooohoo. She didn't tell me about this din-dins either, the conniving harlot. This is a conspiracy."

"No, it's not. You have to bring wine then. Something white, chilled and fizzy that goes well with hors d'oeuvres. And you'll have to serve them because I'll be in the kitchen slaving, producing a masterpiece of a three-course dinner."

"Dinah, you're only supposed to be test-driving this man, not parking him forever in your two-car garage."

"But you never know in life, do you? You never know when man-eating might turn into that love thing. Call it practice. Anyway, I need an excuse to clean up my place."

"Gawd, well I can tell you, you don't Ell Oh Vee Ee him, believe me," Joey cringed as he spelled it out.

"Did you hear me say that? I didn't say that."

"So you're cooking, too, Di? Not picking up the phone and calling the nearest caterers?" He seemed worried.

"I know how to cook perfectly well. I had Mike and Dawn over for goulash the other week."

"Yes, well, Dinah sweetheart, we don't care if you poison *them*."

"I know how to cook."

"Of course you do, dear."

"All right, if you're going to be such a pain in the ass all day, the ingredients are in the kitchen. Get to work."

Joey looked gleeful. He put his coffee cup and copy of *Variety* on the dining room table, rolled up his sleeves and went to take inventory.

I'm not a bad cook. Really. But it just so happens that Joey is a better one. A first-class, almost gourmet chef. As he is always explaining to people, being an actor often means being unemployed, or being a waiter, a dog-walker, a dishwasher, a telegram delivery boy, a phone sex voice, a male stripper, and many other things that an actor has to work in around his real acting gigs. Including chef's assistant.

So I let him take over. I'd have been crazy not to.

He took my stuffy boring old cut of roast beef and made it Mediterranean by rubbing the outside of it in rosemary, sage, garlic, salt and pepper. Then he seared it in olive oil in a big pan on the stovetop. The salad got tossed with blood orange sections and paper-thin purple onion slices, the potatoes got mashed with sour cream and parmesan, and we both got silly on the wine he was supposed to be cooking with.

By the time Ian, Cleo and Simon turned up, everything was feeling better than good.

I grabbed Simon right away and dragged him into my bedroom.

He grinned. "Hey babe, I was wondering when this would happen. Cool."

I shook my head. "The same old Simon Larkin. It's nice to know some things never change. But that's not what I want you for."

"That's cool, too…"

"We need to do another infiltration."

"Oh, yeah? Right on. You say where and when and I'll be there with my stuff, babe."

I don't remember actually eating the dinner, or serving it for that matter. I do remember the after-dinner entertainment though. We all ended up playing poker for real money and Ian cleaned us all out. After the others left, he asked, "Are you going to let me stay the night?" He was already unbuttoning his shirt and heading for my bedroom.

Chapter Eleven

He crawled into the bed, pulled me close, stroked my hair for a few seconds and fell asleep.

I stared at him, fascinated, and wondered if I could ever learn to fall asleep as fast as he did.

I was just dropping off myself when I heard a rapping at my back door. I figured it would be Joey but when I opened up, there was Mike, minus Tinkerbell, so drunk that he had to prop himself up against the post where the steps met the porch.

"Di, you have no idea how glad I am to find you at home," he slurred and sputtered.

There was a world of expectation in those few words. "God, you look so great," he continued.

He didn't look so great. His three-day casual stubble effect just looked degenerate, as though he'd been out carousing for days and needed to go home.

"What are you doing here?" I spat. "You can't stay here."

I stepped out onto the porch and pulled the door shut behind me. "Go on home to your little wife right now."

"We made a mistake. We never should have broken up, you and I, and I never should have married…uh…Dawn." He was teetering dangerously.

Don't throw up on my porch, I prayed silently.

"But you *are* married, Mike. It's too late for second thoughts."

"We can still see each other, can't we? We just live around the corner from each other," he slurred.

"Sure, we can see each other. In passing at the supermarket. But our shopping carts are never going to bump again so you can forget about it. Go home to Dawn and don't tell her you were here. She must be wondering where the hell you are. It's after one."

"She doesn't care about me."

"No? I really can't believe that."

"It's the truth." By now he was trying to insinuate his way through my door. I continued to block the path while he swayed precariously close to me. "She has a problem."

"What sort of problem?"

"Some kind of female thing."

"Oh, that really explains it, Mike."

"She won't have sex with me."

My Inner Bitch rejoiced. "That sounds more like a male/female kind of problem. Not my territory. I'm only good at charities and you're not on my list."

"You're a hard woman, Di. But really, it's her. She has a lot of problems."

Which reminded me.

He always did blame problems on other people, never on himself.

I tried to sound wise and motherly. "The two of you will just have to work it out. Other people can't solve it for you."

"I want *you,* Di," he whined.

I said nothing.

"Remember that day last year when we made love in your old bedroom?"

I did remember the day but was going to be the last person on the planet to admit it. I'd hated myself afterward. "No, I don't, Mike. And you have to leave."

"Why? You expecting someone?"

"As a matter of fact I've got guests at my place."

"You're wearing your bathrobe. It's a guy. It's gotta be a guy. Is it a guy?"

"A girl, a guy, a goat. It's whatever I want it to be because it's none of your business, Mike. Now go." I tried to pull him toward the stairs but he was too heavy. And he was resisting.

"It's over," I said.

And then Mike lost his head. He lurched closer to me, wavering, and began to pull off his pullover. Then he took off his T-shirt. He was just unzipping his pants when a noise from inside my apartment made me bark, "What are you doing? You'll catch pneumonia. Do up your pants."

"I'm not budging," he said.

"You're just doing this to get to me," I hissed. "Now stop being such a baby."

"Who is he, Di? Tell me who he is?"

I was starting to get frantic. I yelled at him, "He's the new CEO for GWI. Satisfied?"

He began to swagger and mimic me in a high squeaky voice. "The CEO, it's the new CEO for GWI. Oh joy."

"I'm calling Dawn and telling her you're here," I said through gritted teeth.

Mike flung both arms around my neck. "No, don't." He was at least a head taller than me and sturdily built. "Dinah, we always had a good thing."

I eased him away. "How's it going at the university, Mike? I want to know about that."

"I don't want to talk about that. I want to talk about us."

"There is no us. There's you and Dawn and I'm going to go and phone her now and tell her to come and get you. I wouldn't want you to fall facedown in a ditch and drown in a half inch of water or anything like that. Does Dawn drive, by the way?"

What I really meant was, "Do her little fairy feet reach the pedals?"

Then came the click of my back door. I froze and watched as it opened and Ian appeared. He was dressed in my amber-and-burgundy silk Chinese dressing gown and wearing a pair of black socks that came to midcalf. A forest of black chest hair gaped at the front, and it struck me in that moment, in that outfit, that he was a bit on the weedy side, physically speaking. This was emphasized by the silly dressing gown.

I stared down at the porch floor. It was the one moment in my life when he needed to thunder onto the scene looking macho and heroic so I could inspire a little envy in Mike, and what did he do? He appeared in the doorway looking like a cross-dressing accountant. I wanted him to make Mike jealous, not make him roll in the aisles.

I did perfunctory introductions. "Ian, Mike, Mike, Ian."

The two of them sized each other up. A tiny smirk crept into the corner of Mike's mouth.

Ian said, "Ah. I see you have a visitor, Dinah. Does this happen often?"

I snapped, "He's not a visitor. He's my ex-fiancé and he's not staying."

Ian looked weary. "Well, I think I might as well go back to the hotel. I still have some work to finish up."

"Do you really have to go?" I asked feebly.

Ian nodded then said to Mike, "I'm sure Dinah wants to get some sleep. I can give you a ride on the way, if you like."

I winced quietly.

"S'okay," Mike bellowed into the night. "Dinah and I are old friends. And I can get home by myself. S'no problem."

"My Ferrari's just around the corner."

"Ferrari?" Mike was suddenly alert. Sober almost. "No kidding? How many cylinders?"

"Twelve cylinders, five hundred and eighteen pound unit with five point five liter capacity…"

"Love to see it," said Mike.

"If you want to take a look at it, it's parked around the corner. I'll just get dressed. Be down in a minute."

"Yeah, cool. Right on. See you round, Di," said Mike. He turned and started to walk down the stairs.

I sighed audibly.

I hoped it wasn't going to end up being the two of them comparing notes on my bad housekeeping habits or chunky thighs. Maybe it was just a case of boys being boys, wanting to show off their new toys, their motorized machismo.

But then Thomas's voice was there in my head, interrupting. "You're being simplistic, Dinah, trying to cram them into those boy boxes. You have to remember that you've been guilty of Ferrari-dreaming too."

I went back inside and watched in silence as Ian got dressed. Just what I needed. Ian and Mike, together. With no ethics committee to monitor from the sidelines.

I sat and pondered the situation while Ian made all his final adjustments. When he went into the bathroom to fix his hair, I slid my feet into my fluffy hound-dog slippers and pulled my old terry bathrobe tighter. I raced down the steps after Mike and managed to catch up before he turned the corner.

"Mike."

"You changed your mind, Dinah? Want me to come upstairs after he's left?" He started to come nearer but I backed away.

"I get the impression that your wife Dawn is pretty well-to-do."

There was a long silence. Mike kicked an imaginary clod of dirt. "Uh…yeah?"

"You talk her into making a nice fat donation to Green World International, and you both get an invitation to the big event at the Space Centre. It'll be a good party."

"Will you be there, Di?"

"I will. On the far side of the room."

He stared at me and said, "Jeez, Dinah, you have become one brutal woman."

"Night, Mike."

I climbed back up the stairs.

Maybe it was time for Dinah Nichols the man-eater to change partners and tango.

Sunday

Simon and Cleo were at my place.

"Here's the plan," I announced. "I've already been around to the place three times. You can't see into the property. I've knocked. I've rung the bell. I've tried the phone number they gave me. It's deserted as far as I can tell. We just want to get closer to the house. Leave a letter on the front porch. First we knock, ring the doorbell, or whatever there is that lets whoever inside know there's somebody at the door. Exhaustively. If nobody answers after fifteen minutes, we go over the wall."

"Are you sure about the address?" asked Cleo.

"A nice woman who works for the Census gave me the address and phone number. And she said I wasn't the first person to ask and she isn't supposed to give out any of that information. It's the one listed as residence, but he also has a bunch of rental units and other properties all over town. But when I told her what it was for, she was so amenable. It gives you faith to know that people really are interested in saving the world."

Simon checked over his gear. "Even if she's got it wrong, babe, you don't have to sweat it. It's no problem. It'll be a night out. We've been doing this since we were kids. Right, Di? And they only bagged us once."

I laughed.

"But it's breaking and entering if we get caught," cautioned Cleo.

Simon grinned. "Everybody should have one little B and E on their record."

Cleo shook her head in despair. "He's hopeless, Dinah. He has no sense of danger. He just runs head-on into it like a three-year-old. You know how he comes into our apartment? He scales the side wall to the top then drops down from the roof. I'm getting complaints from the neighbors."

Simon squeezed Cleo. "Your neighbors are cute old folks. I love to tease them. Just like I love to tease you."

"And I'd love you to grow up," she replied.

"I get such a great reaction out of her," he said to me. "Her face goes all red and her lower lip quivers."

"Because I'm mad, you idiot. One of these days you are going to tease them right into pressing charges," said Cleo.

While they were arguing, Joey appeared on my balcony.

"Uh-oh. Company," I warned.

Joey let himself in. He looked at our black clothes, flashlights and climbing gear, and said, "All right. I know when people are trying to sneak off and have an infiltration without me. I can smell it."

"This is serious, Joey," I said. "Several jobs and an important project are at stake. We can't afford to blow it. If you come along you have to shut up and do exactly as you're told."

Joey did a little shimmy and crooned, "Ooooo, Mommy, beat me again."

"Go get something black on," I ordered.

"Will you let me lick your shoe first?"

I scowled.

"Okay, okay, I'm going."

It was after midnight when we piled into my Mini and

headed for Southwest Marine Drive. When we reached our destination, we all got out and stood on the road, staring.

Cleo asked, "Is it legal to have walls that high? And made of stone?"

"I don't think so," I answered gloomily. "It's a bit of a fortress, isn't it?"

There was a central gate of iron, and it would have held off an invasion by the Huns.

Simon was impressed. "Heavy metal."

"That's one way of putting it," said Cleo.

"Mommy," whispered Joey, "I wanna go home."

"Let's get on with this." I stepped forward and leaned on the bell at the side of the gate. If it was ringing somewhere, we couldn't hear it. I tried again. No answer. "Let's make a lot of noise. Knock on the gate, everybody, just so we can say we tried."

We all started knocking on the gate. It was loud but not loud enough to wake the distant neighbors.

Joey called out, "Yoo-hoo, Mr. Robertson, it's Avon calling."

"Joeeeey," I snapped.

We all continued to ring and knock. I looked at my watch. "We've been at this long enough. Let's go over."

Simon was happy. "Right on, babe." He scaled the wall like a gecko, leapt over, secured the cords and sent them back over to us. We went over with the speed and agility of three baby elephants, but when we reached the other side, and flashed our torches around, we knew it had been worth it.

"Wow," gasped Cleo. "What is all this?"

"Eco-heaven," I said.

"Fucking amazing," said Joey.

"Suuuweeet," added Simon.

The Spanish-style mansion and vast grounds had been given over to renewable resource experiments. There were three windmills on the property, one antique Dutch style and two newer, innovative designs. A creek running through the grounds powered a large and small water mill. Solar panels covered stretches of lawn and the roof of the main house. There were hothouses too. I insisted on taking a look. Inside I found smaller, earlier versions of Mudpuddle.

All the vegetation on the property looked a little neglected. We tried ringing the front doorbell and knocking but there was no answer. It must have been dumb luck that Tod even knew Hamish Robertson, because, by the looks of things, the place had been deserted for a while.

I went up the front steps and left my presentation package and letter on the doorstep. We wandered the grounds in awe for an hour knowing that Hamish Robertson was the man for us. So, where was he?

Monday

At Notte's after work, it was just Cleo and me.

"So, Dinah. How's it going? With you and Ian."

I shrugged. "It's still going, I guess. I haven't seen a lot of him lately. He's been pretty busy with company business, and overseeing the construction of that new office."

"Yeah. The Garden of Eden. You going to apply for the job of Eve?"

I raised my eyebrows.

Cleo used a lecherous tone. "Personal Assistant?"

"You must be joking, Cleo. I really can't picture me as his personal slave. But I'm not so sure about Penelope. I've seen the way she sucks up to him. I'll bet she's applied."

"Well…I did happen to overhear her mention something about it to Lisa in the coffee room."

"Figures." I took a huge hard bite of my black forest cake.

Cleo became serious. "What are we going to do if we lose our jobs, Dinah? I don't want to move back to Montreal. I like it out here."

I licked the cream off my finger. "Lisa says she's going to open a business if she loses this job. Maybe she'll hire us."

"Just as well Lisa isn't here. She's been acting a little strangely. I'll bet she's started looking for another one."

"You think? I have to say, Lisa's head is definitely somewhere else. I almost get the feeling she doesn't want to be around us."

"Forget about her. The other thing I want to know is, what are we going to do without Hamish Robertson?"

"We could tell Jake we've found him and have his pledge. Just to buy time," I offered.

"How are we going to do that?" Cleo was looking intently at me now, worried.

I popped the last bite of cake into my mouth. "I have an idea."

Wednesday

Argentina was on my mind as I drove toward my tango lesson. Ian had come into my office and caught me with the *Buenos Aires Herald* up on my computer screen.

"Vacation, Dinah?"

"It's my new obsession, Ian."

"Is that right? Well, maybe you could spare some time to prepare the Space Centre's itinerary. I'd like it to be a special presentation, something that people will really remember."

"Sure thing." *If he only knew.*

When I entered Los Tangueros, piano music trickled into the hallway. I tiptoed toward the main room and stood silently in the doorway. Hector, seated at the piano with his back to me, was playing another of his improvisations. Rhythmic, melancholy, the coolest of jazz harmonies sparking into something bolder then retreating to coolness. It was spirited, even funny in moments. I felt a strange surge of pride. It was as if I had a little mental camera in that moment and was clicking a picture to remember it forever. Whatever else happened with Hector and me, this moment had to stay intact.

And then I interrupted it by allowing my purse to clatter to the floor. I took off my coat. He whirled around. "You are here then."

"Hello, Hector."

He reached out and took my hand. I tried to read its strength and direction and sensed that he was about to twirl me. When he did, I smiled.

He laughed. "I forgot to mention one little thing. It helps if you are telepathic with this dance."

"I noticed that."

He was already walking me across the floor, testing me.

"Last time. We didn't finish our conversation. You did not tell me your last name. I wondered. If your family is from Buenos Aires, it might be a name that I know."

"Just Dinah," I said.

"You are being mysterious."

"It suits the tango, I think."

"Perhaps. Shall we work now?" He brought us to a standstill and said. "Show me now if you have learned this *caminata* in your bones."

"Will you let me have some music to dance to this time? Maybe the 'Scarlet Tango'?"

"You know my piece?"

I nodded.

"Not many know it."

"It's a classic."

"Ha," he said, disbelieving. "If it is, then this is news to me."

Like aiming a gun in the dark, I said, "You must have been away from your country for a very long time."

"A lifetime. Maybe two."

"Do you miss Buenos Aires?"

"It is dangerous to miss it. Now I think after this we will try an *ocho,* a figure eight. Without music." Then he added playfully, "If you learn it properly, the music will be your reward at the end of the lesson. Or your punishment." His eyes were shining.

I tried hard. Hector seemed less bullying with me. Toward the end of the lesson, he said, almost gently, "You are not doing so badly. There are some people who choose to remain beginners forever. They do not dare try even a *milonga,* but they refuse to give up. You…you are a natural…."

My heart beat a little faster when he said it.

"One day you will decide if you want to do *milongueros* style tango or *fantasia.* The first is one that you feel for yourself, for the pleasure of the dance. *Fantasia* is for show."

"Is that what you danced?"

"I have danced every kind of tango. The tango is my language. And it was my family's language. My sister…" But the sentence vanished in midair and he said nothing else.

"Your sister?"

He had difficulty speaking. His throat had tightened and he made a slightly strangled sound. "My sister Alicia was a famous tango dancer. Fantasia. You remind me of her. I wanted to say this to you. There is something in your eyes, in your expressions that is just like her. It has been…haunting me."

"Where is your sister? Is she here in Vancouver?"

I wanted to meet her, too. My aunt Alicia.

Hector leaned in close and said in a voice that chilled me to the bone, "You cannot meet her. She is gone."

For the rest of the lesson, we were contained and mostly silent, concentrating on the dance to keep our other worries at bay.

Before going to bed that night, I called the Eldorado Hotel and left a message for Rupert Doyle. They told me he was still out of the country. Which was a pity because I badly needed to talk to him.

Thursday

Ian's face looked a little twitchy. "I'm calling this meeting to order. I want to address the volunteer situation today."

There had been a few groups of occasional volunteers but lately, our steadiest had been Roly, the most obedient dogs-body our office had ever seen. And the Helium Sisters were in training, having pledged their services for the Space Centre event. Some people will do anything for a party.

"We want to discourage street people from donating their time. It's detrimental to Green World's image to have shaggy, unwashed derelicts wandering through our hallways." Ian was looking directly at Lisa.

She looked daggers back at him. "If you're talking about Roly, he's not unwashed and he's a good volunteer. He's reliable and doesn't talk our ears off like some people I won't mention."

"The girls are fine. The girls can stay," said Ian.

I'll bet they can.

Jake suddenly spoke up. "Sorry, Ian. I'm not with you on this one. Volunteers are the backbone of Green World. You wouldn't remember this, because it was before your time, but I've worked for GWI for nineteen years, since its beginning. You know it was founded here in Vancouver, eh? You didn't? The Eastern branches opened later. Well, I can assure you that GWI was conceived and floated entirely by volunteers, people who *looked* like shaggy, unwashed derelicts."

Ian shook his head. "Times have changed. This is the twenty-first century. Image is tantamount to success."

"Whoa," whispered Cleo, nudging me hard.

"Well, Lisa's our volunteer coordinator. What do you think, Lisa?" asked Jake. "You think we might be able to talk Roly into leaving his slicker at home and maybe getting…a trim?"

Lisa's face was pinched, like that of an indignant child. She nodded slowly. "I'll talk to him about it but I'm not promising anything."

A cruel smile caught one side of Ian's mouth. "Perhaps if the volunteer co-ordinator had a better sense of style herself, the level of volunteer staff might improve…which brings me to another point. I will be accepting new applications from other Green World branches. Some of you might want to consider a transfer. Another city can be a positive change. A little reshuffling allows for some fresh blood, fresh ideas."

He was looking between Jake who began to twist the end of his mustache, and Cleo, who was making a low growling sound that only I could hear.

Ian hadn't finished. "Now, another matter. I notice some employees have not yet filled out their donation module. I'm expecting that to be done by next week. It will reflect poorly on any employee who decides to withhold their contribution. We are trying to set an example here. I've received Penelope's…oh, and Penelope, I want to take this opportunity to compliment you on the excellent job you've been doing in communications with the GWI Moscow office." He addressed all of us now. "Apparently, Penelope's Russian is nearly flawless. Head office says everybody's very excited about the Space Centre event and they're very enthusiastic about you in particular, Penelope."

And they weren't the only ones, I thought with panic. Ian was definitely trying it with her. He beamed like a schoolboy at Penelope and she basked in it.

By then, I was getting so many nudges from Cleo, I was going to have bruises on that side.

Was I rotten? We'll never know for sure.

When I asked Ian if he wanted to go over to the Island on the weekend and see where my mother lived, he answered, "Yes, it would be a good opportunity to talk about the documentary."

Thomas would say that we know everything instinctively, if we care to, but we spend most of our lives denying our instincts for the sake of getting along with people.

Or getting laid.

Or trying to hang on to our jobs.

Saturday

We pulled into the wooded drive to the Nichols family estate. The house dated back to 1850 and was a big run-down clapboard mansion on a granite foundation, wide porch all around, a part of which was a closed-in sunporch. The sunporch was never intended as a sunporch. It was an accident. One of the earlier Nichols, a great-great grandfather, had been a doctor, and one of the first men to experiment with X-ray. The porch had been his laboratory and the porch panes had been the glass X-ray plates of his patients' innards and skeletons. Later, the plates were scrubbed clean of all the old bones to allow for a clear view out to the ocean.

A fruit orchard, its tree trunks and limbs now gnarled and mossy with age, stretched up to the forest that separated the property from the road. Outbuildings had grown up like mushrooms since then, closing in and cluttering up what must have once been elegant grounds, well before my life-time. Now there was a riding ring and stable to house the ponies, a dog kennel and run, an aviary where proud but wounded eagles looked cowed by their new situation, and many stray cats prowling about. Also scurrying around the grounds were a few stray young men and one young woman, students of marine biology, intent on pleasing Marjory Nichols and doing her every bidding, including all the me-nial labor that a spread like my mother's requires.

That day I was seeing the house through Ian's eyes, and I noticed how badly it could have used a coat of paint. It was weathered and gray, its bare boards showing through the scabby remains of the white paint. Tiles were missing from the roof. Any attempt at a proper garden had been abandoned years ago so that the things that thrived on neglect, like the forest of rhododendrons, gorse, and arbutus trees, flourished and grew jungly. Thorny stretches of blackberry had taken over what had once been a green velvet lawn tennis court reaching to the ocean bank.

As we stepped out of the car, six dogs—two golden retrievers, a wire-haired dachshund, a Norwegian elkhound, a Scottish terrier, and a Rhodesian Ridgeback bounded up the drive, yelping and leaping all over us.

"Jesus, would you call off these dogs, Dinah?" yelled Ian, brushing at the muddy paw marks on his clean black pants.

I paid no attention. I was momentarily swallowed up in a nostalgic reunion. After all, given my relationship with the dogs and cats of my childhood, these dogs still held a place as my "great nieces and nephews." I couldn't help myself. It was stronger than me.

I called out, "Goldie, Spritzer, Timmy, Budi, Luna, Jock." I ruffled the fur and rumpled the ears on each and every dog and they greeted me back, a mess of long pink slavering tongues lapping around me, and slapping tails sending mud flying everywhere. I nodded at Ian to follow me. We went into the house, leaving the yelping entourage, except for Spritzer the dachshund and Jock the Scottie, behind us.

I took Ian by the hand and led him through the grand entrance of carved oak doors, the wood-paneled hallway with the fireplace, vaulted ceiling, and wide staircase, through the dark hallway to the living room. It was warm inside. A big fire had just been lit in the stone fireplace, and more wood paneling fluttered orange with the glowing light. It was in that room that I always had the strongest sense of my family's history, our own peculiar colonial aristocracy, made up of those wild-eyed Scottish and English remittance men and black sheep who, landed with a modest piece of frontier property, were able to tame their wildest instincts long enough to coax the land into some kind of civilized shape and eventually squeeze money out of it.

In our living room were all the family prizes—the chintzes, the Persian carpets, the Queen Anne side tables, Sheffield Sterling silver samovars and tea services, the ebony and ivory sewing boxes, and mahjong sets, Chinoiserie of the late British Empire. I could tell right away that Ian approved of that room.

Until one of the rugs began to move.

It was Fishbreath, our twenty-four-year-old arthritic cat, sleeping as close as he could to the heat without actually catching fire. "Fishbreath," I crooned. "Come here, honey pie." The old cat stretched slowly, creaked to his feet and tried to walk over to me. I scooped him up to spare him the trouble, and a fine web of ginger cat hair immediately covered the front of my periwinkle blue cashmere sweater. Ian drew back as though Fishbreath had visibly contracted something horrible and contagious.

"He's just old, Ian. In cat years, he's about a hundred years old. He's the most ancient cat I've ever known. He's been around since I was seven. He ought to get a prize for being so old."

Judging from Ian's expression, he must have had a sudden vision of *me* when I got to be that old.

"We can't stay long," he said, looking anxiously at his gold Rolex then at me.

"Don't we have to talk to my mother? Have tea? We always have tea at four when she's at home. It's a ritual."

Ian shrugged.

"Take off your coat and relax." I went over to him and helped him out of his brown suede, sheepskin-lined coat, which I laid on the couch. I led him over to one of the two big armchairs near the fire and said, "Poke it if it gets low."

He raised his eyebrows.

"The fire. I'll get my mother. She's probably in the kitchen."

I went along the woody-smelling corridor. There was something wrong with me. It actually felt good to be on home turf. My mother was there in the pale green kitchen preparing tea for her army of students, clattering around with dishes that were all antiques. Her back was to me.

"Hi, Mom."

She turned to face me. "Di Di. Lovely to see you. Are you staying?"

"I brought Ian. He's in the living room."

"Lovely. We'll have the smaller pot in there. I'll just take the big one out to the kids. Darjeeling all right?"

"Fine."

My mother piled cookie tins, milk and sugar onto an enormous tray and disappeared out the back door to call the "kids."

She reappeared and began to prepare the four-tiered antique cake tray for us. "Let me see, there's a little of that short-bread, some very nice carrot cake, and how about some crumpets?"

"Crumpets? I haven't had crumpets in over a year. Oh, wait. I bought some organic grape jelly at the Barking Dog vineyard. We stopped along the way." I dug in my pocket, found the little jar and gave it to her.

"Lovely," she said.

Since my meetings with my father, I had been bursting to tell her all about Rupert Doyle and Hector but I knew that it was impossible. I knew what her reaction would be. Rare incandescent fury. So again, I kept the conversation safe. "And we could use some extra butter and plum walnut jam, too," I said.

"Righto."

We toasted the crumpets, set everything out on the plates and onto the cake dolly, and took it into the living room.

Ian stood up slowly when my mother came in. "Nice to see you again…Marjory."

"You too, Ian. I see your color has returned."

He gave her a dark glare.

"Ian. Now. Have a crumpet while they're hot. Milk? Sugar? No? I'll have some. Three teaspoons. So kind. Like it good and sweet. Do believe it comes from all that boarding-school deprivation I suffered as a child. Left me with the most dreadful sweet tooth." Then she laughed melodically, and something in that laugh, so self-assured and ringingly happy, made me feel that there couldn't possibly be anything wrong with the world. And in that same moment, I wondered what my problem was, why I had ever paid over a cent to Thomas. My mother was perfect.

And then she picked up her binoculars and went over to the big picture window with its ocean view. "Got a limp dorsal out there, Di Di."

"Uh-oh, somebody's not happy."

"No, she's not happy at all. Not much light left now. Won't spot them today. Grays. This one lost her calf to the nets. We've called her Mara. Awfully worried about her."

I winked at Ian and said, "Whales. It's one of my mother's projects."

He looked bored. "Uh-huh."

My mother spoke from behind her binoculars. "Which reminds me, Ian. I'm terribly afraid I shan't be able to free myself up for your little documentary. Can't possibly leave when there's a limp dorsal. Could be months before it's erect again, if ever."

Ian was speechless. He made some strange huffing sounds and ran his hand through his hair, which didn't budge.

I ate my crumpet and licked my wrist when a dribble of butter rolled onto it. For several minutes there was a warm lazy quiet, the only sound in the room the crackle of the flames. It was broken by a quiet scuffling sound and Ian's voice. "Oh, Jeeezus, would you call off your bloody dog, Dinah." Ian sounded as though he were in pain. Spritzer, the dachshund, had singled out Ian and was having a passionate love affair with his leg.

My mother grabbed him by the collar. "Spritzer, do stop humping the poor man's foot. It's very uncivilized of you." But Spritzer leapt back again and wouldn't stop. I let him go on just a little too long.

As Ian unsuccessfully tried to get the dog off, Spritzer started to make little grunting noises. Finally, my mother went over again, yanked him off, gave Ian a little smile and carried Spritzer outside.

"I was counting on your mother to do the documentary."

"Well, uh…"

"This would never happen on the East Coast," ranted Ian. "People on the East Coast take things seriously."

My mother had just come back in. "You're from the East then, Ian?"

"Grew up there. I went to Harvard. I was very good friends with the Vanpfeffer family," he said testily.

"Harvard, you say. Well, yes, I know some of the Vanpfeffer family. They're very involved with ecology and the arts on the East Coast."

Ian frowned. He'd suddenly lost the urge to talk.

Another quiet moment of munching cookies and sipping tea took over. My mother picked up the poker and gave the fire a prod. Flames leapt and sparks shot out. And then there was another silence.

Until out of nowhere, a high-pitched blood-chilling howl, like a child screaming, cut into the peace. Something small and brown shot through the air across the room and landed on Ian's head. He jumped to his feet with a squawk. His teacup and plate crashed to the floor and shattered. His clothes were soaked with scalding tea. He clutched at the brown thing, screaming.

It took me a minute to get my bearings. And then I laughed. "Bomba."

I'd forgotten all about her.

Bomba, the gibbon, and the latest addition to my mother's menagerie, was shrieking and showing her teeth and attempting to chew off Ian's ear. His arms flailed and grabbed at the gibbon. He shouted, "Ow, ow. It's biting me. Get the fucking monkey off me. Get it off me."

"It's not a monkey, it's a gibbon," I said. "The gibbon is a member of the ape family."

"Just fucking get it off me," he yelled.

My mother stood up and calmly plucked Bomba off Ian's head, then cradled the gibbon in her arms like a baby. Bomba was contrite. Ian was white and trembling.

In a soothing tone, my mother said, "Bomba, aren't you a bad girl? Leave the poor man alone. Take the cookie. Go on. Take it. There's the girl. I think she likes you, Ian."

Ian had a bad case of *bronca*. He stood up and vainly swatted at all the wet spots on his clothes. "A bathroom. I need a bathroom."

"Come with me." I led him along the hall to the small downstairs sink.

He didn't look at me as he said, "I want to get going. I think we better get back on the road. It's nearly dark."

Dinah Nichols had satisfied her maniacal need to give Ian Trutch the inevitable and defining Nichols experience. When Ian came back into the living room, as damp and furious as ever, he retrieved his coat, pulled it on, quickly pulled it off again, grimaced and said in a quiet, incredulous voice. "One of your fucking animals has just peed on my coat."

Fishbreath lay nearby on the couch, looking quite helpless. I crooned to him, "There, there. It's okay, Fishie. You couldn't help it."

On the ferry crossing back to Vancouver, and the drive

home, Ian didn't say a word to me. Four hours of total silence that I couldn't be bothered to break. What was there
to say?

Had I done it on purpose?

Hmmmm.

Ian let me off at my place, let me open my own door
and get my own bags, impatient to see the back of me. He
did a wheelie as he drove away. I mean, a *wheelie*. How ju-
venile is that?

December

Chapter Twelve

Monday

On Monday morning in the boardroom, Ian looked past me, then nearly walked through me, forcing me to step aside. He went straight on over to the chair next to Penelope. He touched her back lightly, and smiled brilliantly.

Cleo swooped into the seat next to me. "What is going on over there with Little Miss Muffet and the Spider?" she whispered.

"Reorganization of priorities. Me out, Penelope in."

"Penelope in for some in out, in out?"

"Depends. He's very smooth, you know."

"Just like that?"

"It can be explained by animal behavior, I think."

"What?" Cleo was fascinated. "Would you look at that? She's trying to be so cool and aloof but her nipples are standing at attention under that schoolgirl blouse of hers."

"Cleo," I protested.

"What?"

"Your talking is keeping me awake."

"He's going to be having hot sex with his right hand as long as he's with Penelope."

"I'm not sure. Could be that I'm going to be the Office Virgin while Penelope becomes the man-eater. How's it going with Simon?"

"Simon's beautiful."

"Good, I'm glad."

"This meeting is called to order," interrupted Ian's voice. "I want to address the problem of office Internet time and computers being put to personal use. Anyone found surfing the Net, checking personal e-mails, or using the office computers for anything other than GWI business, will be risking redundancy. Part of the new zero tolerance policy. Coffee breaks will be exactly fifteen minutes long and must be taken at eleven o'clock. Break time cannot be hoarded and added on to the lunch break. You are to be accountable at all times for your whereabouts. I would prefer not to have you all punch a time clock, but if it turns out to be necessary, I'll have one installed. After the Space Centre event, I'll be holding personal interviews with each of you to review your performances in detail."

Cleo whispered, "We need to find a nice high bridge to push him off."

I picked up the phone and punched the number. "Hal Ridley, please. It's Dinah Nichols."

"Dinahhh," yelled Hal down the line. "What can I do to you?"

"Hal. I'm still waiting for your answer on our big December Space Centre event. What do you say? If you come with your news team, I can promise you guys a great party."

"Oh yeah? What's the wine?"

"A nice little California Frizzantino."

"Uh-huh? What are you serving for food? You know I don't eat red meat."

"You'll like this, Hal. There's going to be finger food—crab cakes, chicken satay skewers with peanut sauce and crossover sushi designed to look like the stars, nebulae, and galaxies in the Hubble space photos. Very sophisticated stuff. So what do you say, Hal?"

I'd been working on Hal (The Groper) Ridley for months to inveigle him into doing the news story; GWI Vancouver and GWI Moscow Working Together to Make a Better World was already a headline. He would give us our PR sound bite, and in return, Hal would get to reap his reward for this charitable act by sneakily fondling his way around every female buttock in the crowded room.

He thought we didn't know about it.

Forewarned is forearmed.

"I'm in," he said.

Wednesday (the following week)

Penny and Ian hadn't been sighted for days. I knew that they were out there exploring. It got to the point where Jake, who was not happy at all about the new development, was considering having serious words with Penelope.

I resumed my tango lessons that week. Hector sensed that something was up. He was surprisingly sensitive to my state of being. He looked right into my face and said, "You are unhappy tonight. You are having problems with your man?"

"Problems at work. And the lack of a man."

"That is the main reason people are unhappy. The man. The woman."

"Then this is probably a good place to be. I'm in exactly the right mood for the tango," I said.

He studied me wordlessly, strolled over to turn on the music and said, "Tonight we try to dance a little. No rules."

Then he did something I absolutely did not expect and it was so comforting. He pressed his forehead against mine in true *milonguero* style. It was the kind of dancing I'd seen in the lesson tapes I'd taken out of the library, to try to get on top of things, something peculiar to the dance halls of Buenos Aires. I let myself be led and forgot about my brain, let it slide into my legs, let the movements be my only thoughts. It calmed me. The music and dancing did all my feeling and thinking for me. *Caminata, salida, risolucion, zarandeo, cruzada, ocho, entrada, giro* were no longer a foreign language but a language I was now speaking with my body.

We danced in the dimly lit hall with a strange new spirit. Both of us were silent for the whole lesson, just anticipating the other's movements. We were aware that the mood was different, intensified by my list of disappointments and the things we'd said to each other. All my troubles were coming out of me, taking shape, dancing between us, throwing a shadow, like a third *milonguero*.

When I got home, I put "Scarlet Tango" on the CD player and stood at my window in the dark. Jon was working out. My sighs and the music kept rhythm with his movements. My mind whirled out of control and ended up tangoing in a bed with all those muscles. When I realized what I was doing, I reprimanded myself, "Forget it, Dinah. Just forget it. He's not *available.*"

I wanted to run down and knock on their door, but Jon had started clearing up and setting out candles. They were probably going to have one of their heart-to-heart nights, and it would have been selfish of me to intrude.

Thursday

I made phone calls. Everything was in place for our big Space Centre Donor Event. Except for Hamish Robertson. But I was still hopeful. And I had a plan.

Our donor events were the moments in which we did a little fund-raising and rounded up all the donors who'd given more than five hundred dollars and invited them out to say thank you to them in a big way.

Of course, our own Ian Trutch of the thousand-dollar-a-night hotel suites had not made one single personal donation. I'd checked with Ash who'd checked with the bank. No employee donation module coming from Ian Trutch. So I sent him an e-mail.

Dear Mr. Trutch,
As previously mentioned, all GWI employees give as generously as they are able. I would ask you to consider doing the same, if only for the sake of form. Many of our employees have opted to bring a bag lunch rather than lunching out. They then donate the daily difference. Even that seemingly minimal difference, Mr. Trutch, makes a difference. We encourage you to cut back on those fancy restaurants, five-star hotels, and exclusive weekend getaways you've been writing off as Green World business expenses (read: Wickaninnish). We are counting on you to set an example to all the GWI employees throughout the lower mainland and make your gift a substantial one.
Thank you in advance,
Dinah Nichols, Communications and PR Associate

I was just doing my job.

Which was more than I could say for Ian Trutch.

I could see exactly what he was doing.

He was laying out the red carpet for himself and his buddies. All that stuff about transfers and applications from

other GWI branches meant he was planning to get his cronies beside him.

The Dark Side was building his empire.

I mentally shoved Ian Trutch aside and went back to the
business at hand.

A second later, Lisa popped her head into my office and
said. "I've been meaning to tell you about this for ages but
with everything that's been going on lately, I just forgot."

"Oh, yeah, what was that?"

"I had another lunch date."

"Oh right. With the yellow slicker guy?"

Lisa corrected me. "Roly."

"Right. Roly. How did it go? Was he wearing the rain gear
this time?"

"As a matter of fact, he was not. It was pretty interesting."
She seemed excited.

"So what was it like?"

"Well, at the first meal, he paid for everything. And he
didn't talk with his mouth full. And I also noticed he had all
his own teeth and they weren't bad."

"That's nice. So he paid for the meal. There went his wel-
fare check, I expect."

"Maybe. And he was dressed okay. He was clean. He
looked nice. His hair was washed and his beard was combed."

"No kidding. That's a major heartbreaking effort for some
of those types."

"Yeah, but that's not the best part."

"No?"

"Uh-uh."

"So what was the best part?"

"The second meal. What we talked about."

"What did you talk about?"

"Everything."

"How everything?"

"We talked about everything. Oh…life, love, the oceans,

forestry, whales, seals, cougars, coyotes, oil, the recycling program, sustainable development, Red Cross, Green World International and Mudpuddle. We even talked about money. I mean, gosh, Dinah, money. I've never talked about that with any man."

No. The men in Lisa's life usually just took her money and ran without talking about it. Or thanking her for it.

She went on, "He is the most amazing guy. Very, very smart."

"That's quite…interesting." I really didn't want to encourage her. After all, she'd already been the supplier of free lunches for so many lame ducks and hash pipe technicians. Poor Lisa. She just didn't know how to say no.

"I thought it was pretty interesting myself. Not what I expected at all," said Lisa, grinning, "so I invited him to the Space Centre event tomorrow."

I had been working for more than a year to get the Space Centre to donate their venue. Now my big Planetarium soiree was finally about to happen. The speeches and Mudpuddle presentation were going to take place right there in the H.R. MacMillan Star Theatre with its wraparound panoramic screen and its circular seating with room for two hundred and thirty people. The reception was going to be held in the Star Deck, which had great views of English Bay and downtown Vancouver.

There were problems though. Jake practically had to kidnap Penelope to get her to do her job. She'd been flouting her duties so badly lately that Jake had to take her aside and remind her of her job description, because she was never at her desk to answer the phone when the Moscow GWI people called, and the rest of us, even when we pooled our linguistic resources, had a joint Russian vocabulary that amounted to the words *vodka martini*.

The Moscow people were arriving that afternoon and

no one in our office except her spoke Russian. Penelope had been sneaking out the door, on her way to lunch with Ian without a word to any of us. As far as we could tell, and from what she'd let slip to Lisa, she was falling, her whole life precipitating toward Ian's. She took every opportunity to be with him and go as far as possible without actually letting Ian take out his rod and do a little ice fishing in her pond. All her responsibilities were going to the dogs. It would have been easier for us if she were a drug addict. We could have given her a good knuckle-rapping, then forced her into a rehab program. Unfortunately, as far as we knew, no programs for sex-crazed virgins existed. Yet.

Jake nabbed a pouting Penelope at the front door and dragged her off to the airport. It was the fact that the Moscow people had decided to attend our event and have a first face-to-face meeting that had turned the Space Centre people around and convinced them to donate their venues and their staff. I'd promised them excellent press coverage and a certain amount of prestige, given the stature of our guests. They were even willing to let me do a little decorating in the Star Deck. I'd had the idea of putting up gold-and-silver helium-filled Mylar stars and moons, hitched to the tables and floating upward in long strings.

It was about to happen and it was looking good.

Friday

The Star Theatre was packed by 7:00 p.m. Jake was a basket case. He'd made the mistake of wearing a dark shirt and the sweat patches were louder than his tie, which was very loud indeed. "I can't believe you've found Hamish Robertson, Dinah. You've achieved the impossible." The sweat came more profusely as we approached the moment of his speech and he continued to mop his beaded brow with an enormous white handkerchief. He was standing at the vending machine, about to plug in his coins.

I sighed. "It's too bad he can't be here tonight in person. Business in Tokyo. But we have the next best thing. A conference call. Just hope the technology doesn't go on the fritz."

"I'm sure everything will be great, just great. Great." The chocolate bar dropped to the bottom and Jake reached in and grabbed it.

"How do the guests like their accommodation?" I asked him.

"You'd think they were staying at the Pan Pacific and not the Y. They love it. It makes me think things must be pretty harsh for them at home."

Cleo approached us, looking splendid in a moss-green raw silk minidress.

"Where's Simon? Didn't you bring him?" I asked her.

"No. He's staying and helping Joey with you-know-what." She seemed as tense as I was. As soon as Jake was gone, she whispered, "It's a crazy idea. It's never going to work."

"It's just to buy time. When you have a clear idea of what you want, it eventually happens. So Simon's not coming at all. Not even after?"

She shook her head.

"I see."

Cleo raised her eyebrows. "Is that 'I see' supposed to mean something, Dinah?"

I beat a fast retreat. "No, no. Just making conversation."

She was smiling, but she was definitely tense.

Penelope, dressed in a very skimpy strapless fire-engine-red dress, looked like somebody else. Certainly not herself. Ian hovered nearby, chic and brooding, not quite hanging upside down like a vampire bat but nearly. Okay, I'm exaggerating. But it did feel as though he were just lurking around waiting for us to put a foot wrong. He still hadn't spoken to me since the visit to my mother's.

Penelope was suffering. She wanted to be with Ian but had to stay with the GWI Moscow people's people, to translate. The word was that the people themselves couldn't make it but had found a competent subcommittee to send in their place. They were a group of three, a stern looking middle-aged woman named Olga with a bad haircut, a tall young blond man named Vassily, and an elderly stout bald red-faced man named Dimitri. Their last names could not be pronounced, except by Penelope.

Mike and Fairy Girl were there, too, which meant that my little moment of extortion had worked. I had managed to turn them into GWI donors against their will. Mike kept trying to catch my eye and send secret signals to me from the other side of the room when Dawn wasn't looking.

I hoped and prayed the PowerPoint and the rest of our technology were going to perform the way they were supposed to. For most of our technical and computer services we were at the mercy of The Vulcan, a gangly, spotty, pale young geek with Spock ears in his pocket ready to be donned at a moment's notice. He donated his time to GWI by fixing our computers and in return, we endured his enthusiasm over the upcoming *Star Trek* conventions and the Kirk/Picard/Who was Hotter Debate.

Tonight, The Vulcan was as wired as the rest of us. I'd been over the routine with him. Jake would speak first, with no soundtrack and on the screen, just Green World International's logo; a hand that looked like a tree, white with a black outline, and five green leaves, one shooting up above each finger. There was also going to be the honor roll of donors read off while photographs from the Hubble Space telescope were projected all around us, the donors' names appearing at the centers of the various galaxies and nebulae. But before that would come Mudpuddle and my surprise presentation.

So when Jake stepped up to the microphone and there

were ten seconds of dead screen and dead silence, I felt my heart stop. But then after a lot of frantic fiddling on the part of The Vulcan, and an electronic squeal, the microphone was working.

Jake loosened his tie and launched into the opening speech. "It's great to see you all here tonight. When we talk about Green World International, we are talking about community, our community, and lately, this community has also extended to include the global community. I want to give a special thanks and a special welcome to our three guests from the Moscow Green World International office. Their presence here announces a new phase in the life of the not-for-profit organization.

"Many people's response to organizations such as ours is 'Why should I give? What does this have to do with me?'"

Here Jake paused. You could have heard a pin drop.

"If you think hard, you will probably realize that you are all touched by Green World International's programs and the issues it is addressing. Who of us doesn't use water? Okay, my teenage son doesn't count…"

There was a ripple of laughter. "We haven't yet begun to solve the world's problems, but we are addressing them, not ignoring them. So I want to thank you all very much for your donations and would like you to consider increasing the size of your gift as the scope of our programs increases. Think of it as a kind of financial Feng Shui. It's your world. Why would you not want to save it?"

There was scattered applause. In many ways, he was preaching to the converted. But if there was the chance of seducing one new person into helping us with our causes then the speeches were justified.

"Now I'd like to call on Dinah Nichols for our next presentation. Dinah, over to you."

I stepped up to the lectern. My throat was dryer than the Sahara.

"Our involvement in biomimicry has just begun, but we are confident that with the co-operation of donors with vision, we can start a trend, a 'business model' that will not exhaust the world's natural capital, but provide a cradle-to-cradle model for handling our resources. What knows better how to convert solar energy than a leaf? Then we must take our lessons from a leaf. What knows better how to convert toxic material in water than wetlands and their complex systems? Then we must learn from these systems to create the Living Machine. Our latest pilot project, the aquatic waste-treatment pond system, also known as Mudpuddle, is our most ambitious to date. It requires huge resources in terms of time and financing, but we are certain that the final product will not disappoint. We are proud to have the support of a first-class donor. A first-class donor, as you all know, is someone who contributed over three hundred thousand dollars. He will be making out a check for just under five hundred thousand dollars, a sum the government has promised to match. The aquatic pond model and explanation are on display in the lobby. But now I would like to pass the word over to our donor himself, Hamish Robertson. He cannot be here in person tonight, but we've managed to get him online from Tokyo."

I signaled to the Vulcan. He fiddled for a few seconds until a window popped onto the screen and at the centre of it, a peculiar looking man wearing a wide-brimmed black hat and dark glasses. His nose was an odd puttyish creation and his five-o'clock shadow was very pronounced, a little too blue.

In the distant background were a Japanese screen and some wall fans. A figure passed behind the man in the hat and I swore it looked exactly like the Mikado from a recent production in which Joey had been an extra. The man in the hat did quite a bit of middle-aged harrumphing and throat-clearing and then he spoke.

"Good evenun' ta ye all, laddies and lassies aback there in wee Vancooovurrr. I regrut that aye cannae be there meself, but aye'll be writin' oot me wee check as soon as aye'm back in Vancoooovurrr. So enjoy yeselves. I used ta love a wee dram as much as anyone, da ye ken? Dinna fesh yeselves...."

I stopped myself from groaning out loud, but I wished that Joey had left the ham in the fridge.

He "occch–ed" and "aye–ed" and brogued on and on in an incomprehensible stream of Scottish-like gibberish. I caught the Vulcan's eye and surreptitiously ran my finger across my throat. He was on my wavelength that night. There was another electronic squeal and the image on the screen froze, then disappeared.

The Vulcan turned, grinned sheepishly at the audience and stammered, "Lost our connection. Must be too much t-traffic..."

The audience was silent and bewildered.

I smiled at the Vulcan, looked back at Jake and said, "I'll turn the honors back over to Jake Ramsey." I slunk away from the podium.

Jake said, "Now, our new CEO, Ian Trutch, will say a few words."

Ian moved up to the podium and adjusted his tie. "First of all, I want to say a special hello to our colleagues from the Soviet Union."

Jake was beside me. "Did he just say what I think he said?"

The evening was shaping up. "Yeah," I answered. "There is no Soviet Union. Not anymore."

Ian made an attempt at welcoming the visitors by name but stumbled and quit when he got to the "skis" in the men's last names. He tried a jovial chuckle. "...I hope this will be the beginning of a long and fruitful collaboration with the Moscow office..." He went on for a bit with some "bureauspeak" and just when I was feeling a big yawn coming on, I heard him say, like a stand-up comedian giving an aside,"…and I'm sure we all want to know if it's true what they say about Moscow girls…" then winked.

I winced. Jake wiped his brow, then hurried up to the podium and grabbed the mike. He said hastily,"Thank you very much, Ian. And now it's time for the donor awards." Ian looked a bit confused. Jake gave him a pointed look and finally, he sauntered off the stage.

Jake then read out the honor roll, naming all the donors and the size of their gifts. I maintain that the important thing is always use people's sense of keeping up with the Joneses against them, and get them to outpotlatch each other.

I went off to find Cleo. She was outside in the lobby, sniggering into her wineglass."That Hamish Robertson act was godawful. No wonder Joey never gets work. He looked like a has-been rock star and he sounded like the Highlanders' arterial sclerotic mother."

I sighed."It's a popular look these days. That Mikado costume fitted Simon perfectly…oh well. We tried, is all I can say. Nobody's seen the man. He could be anything."

"But Ian Trutch…has he been drinking?"

"It sure sounded like it."

I went up to the Star Deck to make sure everything was flowing.

Lisa was herding the volunteers around and giving them instructions, as well as keeping them away from the helium tanks. Roly was standing in a corner looking unusually trimmed and tidy in a normal dark herringbone jacket, and watching Lisa with an expression that verged on devotion. She came up to me and stared, a strange smile on her face. "I think it's wonderful that you were able to track down Hamish Robertson. He was off in Japan. That's just amazing." She started to laugh and shake her head, then went over to Roly and put her hand on his shoulder."Isn't it amazing, Roly?" A new fit of laughter overtook her. The sound was so contagious that he started laughing, too.

A few other people were milling about, having skipped the ceremonies. That was when I spotted Ian. He was standing in a corner near a food and drinks table talking to an uninvited guest, a notorious politically incorrect local politician, the last person I would have put on my guest list. I couldn't believe it. Ian had bypassed me again. As soon as their backs were to me, I dropped to the floor and crawled under the table near them.

Ian's voice was intense and hushed. "…a shoo-in. Once Mudpuddle is functional, we'll have an abundant supply. We can set the price."

The politically incorrect politician was enthusiastic. "I've been trying to get our water south of the border for years. If we can get past the obstacles, they'll be willing to pay. I've got an old friend on the water board down there who has a friend with a connection who'll give us a hand…"

The Dark Side was revealing his true self.

Thinking they'd left, I crawled out from under the table. Ian stared down at me.

I patted the ground. "Contact lens. Can't find it anywhere."

"But you don't wear them," said Ian.

"That just shows you how good they are. Didn't even know I had them," I replied.

And it got worse. Penelope came in looking for him. I got up off the ground and dusted myself off. Penelope took Ian by the elbow and steered him into a far corner where they started up their own Mucous Exchange Program.

But I was obsessed with water. Water that would be exploited if somebody didn't stop these guys.

I desperately needed to call Thomas. I tried my cell phone but there was no signal. I ran outside to try it again, but stopped myself from calling in the end. I'd started to cry. I couldn't speak. I needed air. It was crazy.

I ran outside and into the shadows, leaning against the wall where nobody could see me exploding with *bronca*.

"Dinah?" said a familiar voice.

I stopped and peered.

It was Jonathan Ballam, dressed up in casual black. My Savior. Looking great.

"Dinah?" he asked again. "What are you doing out here? It's freezing. You're not leaving, I hope."

"Jon. What are you doing here?"

"I'm late. I donate. Hey, that rhymes. Are you…uh…are you okay?"

I tried to put on my best hostess voice. "You good man. I'm very happy to see you."

He grabbed my hand and twirled me in a boogie spin.

I laughed. "Whoa. So where's Kevin?"

Jonathan frowned. "He's out of town at the moment."

Again I had to wonder if there was trouble between them.

I linked my arm through his. "Shall we go inside and get a drink?"

Inside, we got glasses and filled up plates at the buffet. The decibel level was getting higher and higher. Jon asked, "Is there somewhere quieter where we can talk?"

"Let's go into the theater. We can talk there."

I had arranged things so that the theater would be a chill-out zone after the presentations.

We settled into some theater seats and Jon said, "Now what exactly were you doing out there? You looked really pissed off."

I whispered, "Remember I was seeing that guy, the new CEO? We passed him on the way in. He was the one hanging upside down by his claws and baring his fangs."

He nodded.

"I'm not seeing him anymore. He's seeing the Office Virgin. The one person in GWI that I really don't get along with. And he's evil. He's planning things for Green World that really stretch its original concept."

"Dinah…"

"What?"

"You're not jealous, I hope."

"Not in the least…I don't think…oh, I don't know. Maybe there is a little…residual jealousy."

"Because it sounded as though…I mean, when you mentioned it before…that you…"

"What?"

"That you weren't really that sure about him. That the two of you were polar opposites, way too different. You said it yourself."

"Is that what I said?"

"It was what you were saying with the words and between the words."

"Maybe I did."

He shook his head a little wearily and smiled. "I know. You make an emotional investment in a person, and then when it's over, you feel like you've lost something no matter what. Even if they were more like a sparring partner than a lover."

"That's it," I said. "But listen. If he wasn't history before, he really is now."

We both paused and looked up at the wraparound screen, the universe unfolding all around us in images that looked more like gems and precious stones than planets and suns.

"These pictures are outstanding," said Jon. "This universe of ours is one great painter. Look at those colors."

The rich marble swirls of coral, red, amber and brown of the Keyhole Nebula rose before us, then faded into another image, rosy pink cometary knots against turquoise blue in the Helix Nebula.

Jon looked at me. He was smiling at me so happily with those easy amber eyes, that when Penelope and Ian walked into the theater, I almost didn't notice them.

"I have an inspiration," Jon said.

"Oh?"

"I'll pretend to be your new boyfriend."

"Boy what?"

"Boyfriend," he mouthed.

I stared at him. It was a classic situation. Good-looking intelligent gay man out to torture straight woman. A simple case of misogyny.

"Naw," I laughed.

"Oh come on, Dinah. Don't let them get the upper hand."

I had a long Einstein-like moment of contemplation then said, "Well, I'll put aside my religious beliefs if you put aside yours but it's just this once."

"My religious beliefs? Uh…okay, sure. Good."

He made a sporty limbering-up movement with both arms then put one arm around my shoulders. I thought that was going to be the end of it but when Ian and Penelope were looking our way, he took my chin in his hand and planted a long, sweet, exaggerated kiss on my lips. It seemed to go on forever and neither of us wanted to pull away. When we finally did, I sat there, just staring at him, immobile with surprise.

Penelope and Ian hadn't moved. They were both gawking in our direction.

Jon frowned and said, "Now you're going to tell me I shouldn't have done that."

I whispered, "I…I wasn't. Really… It was…"

Fantastic.

"Yep?" He was waiting.

"I, uh…I guess I should be getting back to my job, mixing and mingling."

Jon seemed unfazed. "Uh-huh."

"I don't want to get fired for acting like Penelope and getting all sloppy while I'm supposed to be working…."

"No?"

"No. But that was a…"

"Yes?"

"That was a…"

"Yes, it was, wasn't it?"

"I think you shocked those two." I flicked my head toward Penny and Ian.

He whispered, "No problem. These little things in life can sometimes make a big difference."

"That sounds like one of my campaigns."

"Any time I can be of service."

"I really should be getting back to work." But for some reason, my body didn't want to budge.

"Sure you should."

"I'm the PR and communications associate."

"And I'll bet you communicate really well."

Jon ran his hand up the back of my neck and began to play with my hair.

It felt good.

Too good.

I wondered what Penelope was thinking now.

That the Man-eater had found herself some fresh game?

I hoped so. I hoped our little act served some purpose because it was futile and a bit risky to be flirting with Jonathan Ballam.

And most of all, it was a mean thing to do to Kevin.

Jake's voice from a distance cut into my little moment. And just in time. "Penelope," he called out. "Oh, you're here, too, Dinah. I need you both in the reception area. The Russians want you."

"Ooops. Duty calls," I said to Jon.

"Sure." He slowly moved his arm off my shoulders. "I'll be around if you need me again." He smiled and breathed deeply.

As Penelope and I met up at the doorway, she said quietly, "It's so pathetic to see the way sad, desperate women behave," then pushed ahead of me.

I did feel sad, but not for any of the reasons that Penelope might have expected. I felt sad, first of all, for the fate of GWI. And I felt sad for *her,* for Penelope, sad that she was such a smug little priss who had blown her chances by not being nice to most of us in the office and especially, to me, when she could have behaved like a normal girl and had lots and lots of friends at GWI and gone to lots and lots of parties with all of us, and sat around stuffing her face with lots and lots of pastries, again, like the rest of us and trying to save the world. And it was sad that if, one day, *she* happened to be attacked by a cougar, before Ian married her, the stuff that flashed before her eyes would lack a climax, so to speak.

Chapter Thirteen

Saturday

The telephone screamed at me. I put a hand to my pounding head and stumbled out to the hall to pick it up.

"You're the walnuts in my baklava," hissed the voice.

"Oh, God, no I'm not, you silly pervert. Why don't you pick on somebody else. Listen, it's the *morning*. You bloody well woke me up. Get yourself some help and when you do, don't tell me about it, okay?" I slammed down the phone.

The room was reeling.

Black whirlies appeared in my peripheral vision.

I stumbled back into the bedroom, threw myself down on the bed, and closed my eyes.

How had I come home last night?

I'd worn my underwear to bed but I couldn't remember even getting into my bed.

And what about my car?

I lay there while my bed rocked and bucked like a fun fair ride.

It was slowly coming back to me.

The hangover wasn't my fault.

It was those Russians.

It was their fault. They were the ones who had produced the unlabelled bottles of vodka, finest product of their motherland, and begun to proudly pour it into everybody's wineglasses. Well, we couldn't say no, could we? They wanted us to drink with them, taste their national product. They were practically forcing it down our throats and we absolutely could not offend them by refusing their vodka. Refusing their vodka could have started an international incident. As it was, the event night was already a bit of an international incident in the eyes of the Space Centre people.

I had to hand it to them though.

The Moscow branch of Green World sure knew how to party. Not only were they good at making toasts and smashing glasses but they were also very good at delivering messages. Even though I don't speak a word of Russian, I recall each of them having a very animated, passionate even, conversation with me over the course of the evening. I swear we were communicating. Either they were speaking English or I was speaking Russian. I don't know which. They each said the same thing, that we needed to create a World Fund for developing alternative renewable energies, and that if a nation could find one hundred billion smackers overnight for going into war, surely they could find fifty billion smackers over the next ten years for researching and developing renewable energy sources. Olga, Vassily, and Dimitri really knew their business.

As for the rest of the evening…

Hmmm.

I'd gone to sleep in my bra and panties.

Where was my dress?

And how had I gotten home?

Had I driven?

I couldn't remember?

And if I hadn't driven, would I still find my car where I'd left it?

I crawled out of my bed again and navigated my way to the closet. The black dress was there, hung neatly in its garment bag. Had I done that? It didn't seem like the work of a drunken Dinah Nichols. Whenever I'd had a big night on the town, I usually found my clothes hung neatly on the floor the next morning.

So how had I come home? I staggered down to the kitchen and looked out through the window. No sign of my car in the little back alley space where I usually parked it.

I turned on the tap and filled a Nutella jar with cold water, then I stopped in the bathroom for two Tylenol and knocked them back with the water, then went back into the bedroom, lay down on the bed and tried to remember. A blurry tableau of last night's bacchanalia danced before me. It started to get clearer as I concentrated.

While we had still been at the Space Centre, we'd been relatively well behaved, with a sober Jake hovering like an expert but anxious diplomat making sure everything went off the way it was supposed to.

And then?

I badly needed a coffee.

I pulled my silk Chinese dressing gown around me, went into the kitchen, filled up the espresso maker, and put it on the gas.

So what had come after the Space Centre?

A great big bell pepper.

The dance floor at the Eldorado Hotel!

That's where we'd gone.

Olga and Dimitri had asked me if I knew of a club or night spot where they could let down their hair (the little that they had) and dance. They'd both spent a few years in Cuba on a professional exchange program and loved Latin music. That was when I'd suggested the Eldorado Hotel. I remembered a fleet of taxis arriving, and piling into one with the three Russians. And Penelope following along behind us and being petulant, because we'd all found out that we didn't really need her translation skills after all. We were doing just fine.

First I'd gone to leave a message at the front desk for Rupert Doyle to call me the minute he came back to town. Then we all went to the lounge with the dance floor. The tall blond younger Vassily had sat on the sidelines like a watchdog while Olga and Dimitri danced the mambo and the samba and the rumba and the Lambada and the Macarena, and I think I danced, too.

Was that possible?

Yes.

I went up to the orchestra and asked them to play a tango and then I danced with Dimitri. He was a very good dancer, just like an old *milonguero.*

And then?

Somebody else asked me to dance and I did and I remember thinking that it was the greatest feeling, that we were perfectly synchronized with each other and I'm sure it wasn't just the vodka.

But his face wouldn't come to me.

Why was that?

By the time I had made my caffe latte with lots of sugar, and taken a few sips, I could remember every detail of the evening.

Except for my last tango partner.

And where I'd left my car.

★ ★ ★

I needed to talk to somebody. There was only one thing to do. I got dressed quickly, went down to my living room, out through the French doors, along the balcony, in through Joey's French doors and down to his bedroom. The door was ajar. I was about to go in, but pulled back quickly when I saw who was in the bed with Joey.

God, what a mistake.

I tiptoed out soundlessly and back to my place.

I needed to think.

I'd been so caught up in the vodka-sodden comings and goings of the night before that I hadn't bothered to think that Joey might not be alone.

What I'd just seen was none of my business.

Or was it?

I was up against that age-old problem of Finking Etiquette.

Are you supposed to tell the offended party, or does that make you sound like some bitter loser whose flash boyfriend has just dumped you for a younger, purer woman?

Or are you supposed to tell the offending parties that you know about it? And that they better not try it again?

I didn't want to act like the Sex Police.

It was a dilemma.

I had to find my car.

I put on a warm sweater and hurried out down the back steps, along the side path and up to Jon and Kevin's front door. I leaned on the doorbell and hoped Jon didn't have telepathic powers.

Jonathan opened up. He was wearing a dark green parka with a hood and carrying an overnight bag. "I was wondering when you'd get here. I have something of yours."

"You do?"

Uh-oh. What had I done? I didn't remember doing a striptease but anything was possible. It was very high-quality vodka we'd been drinking. I tried to buy some time before Jon produced the mysterious and offensive object.

"I was just on my way out. If you hadn't dropped by, I would have brought them to you."

"What would you have brought?"

He held up my car keys and dangled them in front of me. "These."

I took them, ecstatic. "Thank you. Now. You wouldn't happen to know where my car is, would you?"

"Exactly where you left it. There was an exuberant moment last night when you thought you would drive so I relieved you of your keys."

"That was very thoughtful of you. My Savior."

"I've got to go, Dinah, I'm on my way out of town. There's a little longhorn cattle situation that I've been called in for."

"Oh, okay. Well, you drive safely, too."

"Come around tonight anyway. If you feel like it. When Kevin gets back. He'll be bringing back some decent California wine. I'm not sure if he's staying or going, but if he does stay, come over and have a drink with him. He's been upset lately. He shouldn't be alone."

And you shouldn't be alone with me.

"Maybe. But I doubt if I can handle a single drop of wine for the next week. I sort of overdid it yesterday."

Jonathan just smiled.

"So. I'll see you when you get back then, Jon."

I was disappointed. It was Jon I wanted to drink wine with, not Kevin. I needed to give myself a good talking-to. I needed to repeat over and over, "Dinah, you shall not lust after your gay neighbor, Dinah, you shall not lust after your gay neighbor, Dinah, you shall not…"

One good thing that came from my evening out at the Eldorado was that I was inspired to go online and order my tango shoes. First they would send me their fitting device, free of charge, I'd measure my foot, then send them the numbers which would then be sent to Buenos Aires, where they were made by hand by Argentine cobblers.

It was the Valentina model, eighty-nine dollars worth of slim high heel, red suede, black patent leather, and open toe. Money-back guarantee if they didn't fit. After that I turned on a tango video and practiced. It was just as well that nobody could see me.

Sunday

I should have known that it was going to be one of those days. It got off to a bad start with yet another phone call from the Telephone Pervert. I was much too blasé on the phone with him.

"So," I said. "You seem to know what I look like. Now tell me what you look like."

Where had my sense of self-preservation gone? Was I nuts? This guy could find me at the drop of a hat.

"I'm your perfect match," he whispered. "We were made to drink retsina together."

"Gag. I can't stand retsina. It tastes like turpentine."

"Ouzo?" he tried.

I hung up.

As soon as I'd put down the receiver, the phone rang again. I picked up.

"Di?"

"Simon? What's up?"

"I've been feeling lately…"

"I know, I know. You need a smaller world."

"No."

"A larger world."

"There's an ashram in Tibet…"

"And while you're there, you might get a little windsurfing done out of base camp Everest?"

Simon didn't find it funny. He let out a huge sigh.

"Have you said anything about this to Cleo?"

"No. Not yet. It's still early. Not the season for going there." His voice was full of remorse. "Don't say anything to her, will you?"

"No, I won't, but you'd better tell her soon."

"Yeah. Bye."

I said goodbye and hung up.

My dear, beautiful, fickle, seed-in-the-wind childhood friend.

My nerves were all over the place. I badly needed to talk to somebody.

I couldn't talk to Joey. For obvious reasons.

I couldn't talk to Cleo. I might accidentally spill the beans.

I couldn't talk to Jon. Not only was he out of town but there was a serious kissing hazard there.

I couldn't talk to Kevin. I might accidentally slip up and tell him how much I liked kissing Jon.

I couldn't talk to Lisa. She was there but her mind was clearly on the Yellow Slicker Guy.

I couldn't talk to Thomas. He'd want me to make more appointments and then that would cost me the next few tango lessons.

And finally, I couldn't talk to my mother. Because what I really wanted to do was talk to her about Hector.

It was time to chill out and talk to myself. Try to sort things out between me and me. With the phone off the hook and the crisis skin treatment. It was a drastic measure for those very bad days when the only thing left to do was pamper yourself. When there was no one else left in your life to pamper you.

The treatment consists of taking a few pieces of the mushier fruit in the house and putting it in the food pro-cessor with a bit of olive oil. I like the less acidic fruits like peaches and bananas. Once whipped up you apply the mush all over your body, not leaving out a single square inch. It's wonderful. It moisturizes brilliantly and you feel like you're swimming around on the inside of a gigantic fruit cocktail. And if you happen to accidentally lick any part of your body, it tastes good, too.

I whizzed up the fruit mush, climbed into the bathtub and slapped it on everywhere. Then I pulled an old towel around me and sat in the bathroom singing along to the bluest of Billie Holiday songs. That woman sure could croon. When the CD was over, I rinsed myself off and pulled on my bathrobe.

Then I went to the phone and called the Eldorado Hotel to leave a message for Rupert Doyle. If he ever decided to show his face in Vancouver again, he was to call me ASAP.

Monday

Jake came into my office. "Just took Dimitri, Olga and Vassily to the ferry. They want to hop over and see the island. Those folks sure can walk. Have you ever tried to see all of Vancouver in two days? Well that's what we did. They've got ten days here and, no kidding, they're going to see all of B.C. and I wouldn't put it past them to try to see the rest of Canada, too. I'm exhausted."

"They seem like good people."

"Great people. We understand each other perfectly in terms of common goals, Green World issues. They've asked me to take a trip to Moscow, see how they're handling the program from there. I'm thinking about it and I'm pretty excited about the idea. As for prevention of liver disease, we're coming from different places."

"Don't remind me. Those people sure can drink."

"They say it's the cold there, eh? In Moscow. If you don't drink, you die of hypothermia."

"I've heard that, too. But you wouldn't let it be an excuse, would you now, Jake?"

"Hell no, I've invested too much hard time and effort in staying sober to blow it all away for a visit to a cold climate." He twisted the end of his mustache and said, "Well, gotta get back to the paperwork. You talk to Trutch yet?"

I lowered my voice. "Jake, Ian isn't talking to me. Not a word since we broke up two weeks ago. I don't know what to do."

"Jeez. I hate this kind of crap. We've got enough office crap of our own without adding the personal stuff. That's why they always tell you not to mix business with pleasure, not to sleep with your boss. Anyone can tell you. It always causes problems in the workplace. I sure wish you'd thought about that before you got involved, Dinah. I've seen it before. One half of the couple usually ends up leaving."

"You don't need to lecture me, Jake. I can beat myself up just fine on my own," I mumbled, staring at my desk.

"Yeah, I know, Dinah."

"But just for the record, Jake, I love my job here at Green World International. The pay is shit, the hours are shit, my office is made of cardboard, the CEO is shit, our international conference interpreter is super-shit but I have no intention of quitting just because I slept with the vampire in the fancy suit who is doing dick-all while the rest of us work our guts out."

Jake grinned and said, "That's why I hired you, Dinah. Your ability to pinpoint the situation."

"Listen, Jake. Are you up for an out-of-office coffee break? With everybody but Trutch? Ash, too."

"Important?"

"I think so."

"No problem. I'll let the others know."

Half an hour later, Cleo came into my office like a whirlwind. She ranted and railed and gesticulated while I grabbed at my toys, my ceramic mug, my Marge Simpson for President statuette, to keep them from getting knocked over by Cleo's flying hands.

"I can't believe it," she fumed. "They're reducing at the Recycling Depot. Cutbacks. Evidently, we're giving them less funding. Ian made a few calls."

"What?"

"It's going to set the whole process back. We had a lot of volunteers there and now where are they going to go? We're going to have to give it up to the landfill barons again. It stinks. Literally. If we don't get on top of recycling every last frigging pin, we're all going to drown in our own garbage within the decade. And that is not the death I pictured for myself."

"Oh yeah? What kind of death did you picture for yourself?"

"Me, age ninety-nine, swinging in a hammock on some tropical island, a clean energy-efficient tropical island where they all recycle and have up-to-date structures for dealing with urban waste. And I'll be surrounded by a lot of tight young male bodies waving those palm fronds and refilling my drink. Then in a moment of extreme beauty, the sun setting over the ocean and that sort of nonsense, I'll just pop off."

"That does sound like a happy death, Cleo."

"It does, doesn't it? I'm going out again. I need a hit of chocolate cream pastry."

"That ought to hasten your happy death," I said.

"Yes. And make a note. I want a takeout order in my coffin with me when I do pop off."

After Cleo had left, I picked up the phone and called the Eldorado Hotel for the umpteenth time.

"This is the television studio," I said authoritatively. "I'd like to speak to Rupert Doyle. It's urgent," I said.

The voice on the other end replied, "I'll try his room." There was a ringing and then the voice came back on and said, "He's not in his room."

"Can you leave a note to say…?"

"I know. Dinah Nichols called. I know who you are. I'll give him the message."

Okay. Okay.

I went back to my computer screen and the Mudpuddle project. I could feel it slipping out of reach. Although the Space Centre event had brought in some more substantial donations, it would never be enough for the startup. I wondered if Ian Trutch was building himself a new office because he thought Tod's money was still there.

As I was looking over the figures, I had a sudden irresistible impulse. I left my office, went out through the main room and down the stairs to the reception area where Ida worked.

She was flicking through *People* magazine as she listened to somebody else's conversation on the headset.

"Hey Ida, could you do me a favor?"

"Anything. Just name it."

"Could you call up to Ian Trutch's office and see if he's in?"

"He's out. Believe me, honey, I always know if that Trutch guy is in. Or out. Or on top. Or on the bottom. I don't miss a second of him. He's better than *Days of Our Lives.*"

"He's out, eh? When did he leave?"

"About forty minutes ago. Took Shirley Temple with him, too. Looks like they were going for an early lunch." She winked.

I raced up the stairs to the third floor and opened the door cautiously.

I called out his name five times but there was no answer. I went past the secretarial cubicles, positions still to be filled by a parade of anorexic dilettantes from wealthy families, no doubt, and into the huge main office. Although some of the cabinets still needed to be fitted and the room wasn't finished yet, I could see that it was a shrine to luxury. I wandered around, running my fingers over the expensive surfaces, the rich dark mahogany desk and shelves, the smooth pink marble bar and counters, the custom-crafted brass fittings in the private bathroom and shower, the deep green leather couches and chairs. I took off my shoes and walked across the luscious deep-gray carpet.

With what he was spending on this office, we could have been halfway to setting up Mudpuddle.

To one side of the desk was a tiny tape recorder. Without thinking, I picked it up and pushed the Play button.

It was Ian's voice making lists.

The sound of it did something eerie to me so I pushed the Rewind button.

I pushed Play again. His voice said, "Item. Redundancy. Under review. Ida Fairfax, Cleo Jardine, Lisa Karlovsky. Jake Ramsey. Penelope Longhurst."

I clicked it off.

Redundancy?

And "under review?"

Is that what they called it now?

Penelope was under review?

Hey, sailor, you wanna come home and put me under review?

What about me? Where did I figure in his schemes? Did he really think I was going to stay on and work under him (in a manner of speaking) while he axed the rest of the office?

I pushed the Play button again. Ian's voice went on, "Item. Policies stipulated. Alliance Health and Life. Jake Ramsey, Aishwarya Patel. Dinah Nichols, Fran Meyers..."

There were more names listed but I didn't recognize them.

I hurried out of Ian Trutch's office and downstairs to the safety of my own. Except that it wasn't very safe at all. The ship was taking on water. Going down. Sinking.

Lisa interrupted my revelation. She stepped into my office and said, "Bears."

"What about bears, Lisa?"

"There's a bear problem now. Up in Squamish area. Maybe heading toward North Van. They're wandering into those big forest gardens people have. They've treed a few already. Habitat, Dinah, habitat. There's nowhere to go."

I put my head in my hands.

She squeezed my shoulder. "But it's okay, Dinah. We're addressing the issues. Oh, and remember. Only ten shopping days until Christmas."

Ouch, Christmas.

My mother was going to be out of the country so I'd be spending it in town instead of on the island. She'd asked me if I wanted to go with her to Mexico on a manatee-chasing expedition but I'd said no, that I had to track down a certain donor.

I felt like doing something wild so I spent a good part of the afternoon chasing down Alliance Health and Life. By the time I'd finished talking to them, a crisis of the real kind was on its way.

Chapter Fourteen

"Bastard," said Fran. "And he *has* had work. That nose belongs to somebody else."

"Probably paid for by Green World Recycle-a-Face Fund," said Cleo.

It was the first time Ash had ever come to Notte's with us, and I could see she was bursting to have her say. "I've been getting receipts for restructuring, plumbing, Italian marble, brass fittings, leather furniture…and they amount to…a lot."

"Five figures?" ventured Jake.

She shook her head.

"Six?" yelled Ida. "Well, decorate my interior, big daddy."

"Italian marble imported from Carrara," said Ash. "I have the invoices."

"Shit," muttered Jake, and took a huge mouthful of his black forest cake.

I said, "I can tell you who's under consideration for redundancy. Ida, Cleo, Lisa. Jake…and Penelope."

Ida shook her head. "What a creep. Axing his squeeze."

I put down my éclair. "You guys haven't heard the worst of it yet. He's got insurance policies out on me, Ash, Jake, and Fran. And not just any old policy. It's called 'janitor's insurance.' If one of us kicks while we're working for the company, the management gets the money. We don't even have to know about it."

"Jesus." Jake rubbed his chin.

"The last place he was in, there was this union woman. Moira told me, before she was fired, that he pressured her. She had a heart attack…and *died.*"

Everyone stared at me, stunned.

"She was covered by Alliance Health and Life, too. But wait, I still haven't finished. At the Space Centre event, I overheard him talking to a certain politician, and you all know who I mean, the one who hates us, and Ian Trutch and him are planning on selling water to anyone who'll pay up…"

Everyone was frozen.

Except Lisa.

Lisa was smiling and serene. "You guys are getting all worked up over nothing. I'm sure everything's going to be all right. I'm sure it is."

Tuesday

After work, I went to see Thomas. I stretched out on his creaky leather couch and took a big breath.

"You look well, Dinah," said Thomas.

"I don't feel well."

"Why do you say that?"

"First of all, the man I was going out with dumped me and hasn't spoken to me since."

"In the Buddhist way of seeing things, pain is a given, Dinah. We've talked about this. It's all right to feel pain."

"Pain. Right. Feel it. Gotcha."

"Is that sarcasm I'm hearing?"

"I would never be sarcastic with you, Thomas," I lied.

He made a satisfied little snuffling noise.

I went on, "And second of all, I danced with somebody on Friday night and I can't remember who it was although I can remember everything else about the rest of the evening. I still can't picture his face. Could that be psychological?"

"You're answering your own questions."

"Okay. But could it?"

"Possibly."

"And the third thing is, I'm a dead peasant."

"Excuse me?"

"There are these things happening at work. I just found out that our new CEO, the same guy I just told you about who dumped me, has taken out life insurance policies on me and five other people."

"Oh, yes?"

"I spent the whole afternoon researching it. First, I called up the insurance company pretending I was his secretary and it turns out that he can do this. A lot of corporations do it, take out insurance policies on their employees without telling them, and if the employee dies suddenly before retirement age, the corporation gets the benefits. Nothing goes to the employee's family. They don't even know about it. Sometimes the corporation funnels the money back into their retirement fund, and sometimes they don't. Sometimes that money is buying a nice vacation home for the CEO in the Bahamas. It's called dead peasants insurance. Or janitor's insurance. The name dates back to the days when plantation owners took out insurance on their slaves."

"Are you sure about this?"

"Too sure. And do you know how this makes me feel?"

"That's...disturbing."

"You're telling me."

"How do you feel about it?"

"God, Thomas. Do you really need to ask? How do you think I feel?"

"Let's talk about it. "

"I feel like a nothing. Like dust. And why does he think I'm more likely to drop dead accidentally than some of those other people who he didn't take out policies on?"

"That's good. Keep going. Tell me about all your feelings."

"It makes me feel very, very angry."

"Let's talk about that anger…"

"*Bronca*. I'm full of *bronca*."

"You've lost me, Dinah."

"It's an Argentine word. It means full of anger to the point of exploding, but not actually exploding."

"It's all right to explode, Dinah."

"I don't like wasted energy."

"What do you mean by that?"

"I mean that when I explode, my anger's going to have a direction and a purpose."

"Oh."

"Oh what, Thomas?"

"I'm not sure that we're making progress here, Dinah."

Wednesday

I was early for my tango lesson. And so was Hector. There was a feeling growing between us and it was all wrong. Our wires were crossed and I had to uncross them.

"How are you tonight, Dinah?" he asked me.

He looked surprisingly good. Rested. Happy. Jeans and T-shirt casual. And he wasn't smoking. I didn't mind him being my father at all.

"I don't know."

He laughed. "I don't believe you." He went over to the stereo and put some music on it. "Astor Piazzolla. A master.

He tried to deny his tango heart but in the end it captured him. Now tell me how you are."

"I'm full of *bronca.*"

"Bronca?" He laughed again. "Why is that?"

"Everything. Everything in my life is a mess."

"Then you must come to the *milonga* this Friday."

"Can I?"

"First show me what you learned last time."

I repeated the steps with him.

"I think you will be all right, Dinah. You are a very fast learner. It is hard to believe that you have never danced the tango. You have a natural ability."

I didn't tell him about all those hours of practice, trying to follow the tapes from the library, and posturing and gesturing like a crackpot tango diva in front of the bathroom mirror, and the prancing and stumbling back and forth in my living room and along the hallway with imaginary partners. Inner tango, I called it.

He turned me in an elaborate figure. I let myself go and followed.

He said, "Tell me about your family in Buenos Aires."

"That's not so easy for me to do, Hector."

"No?"

"No."

"And why?"

"You were telling me about your sister?"

"Yes."

"When you mentioned your sister Alicia…"

"Yes, Alicia. She was older than me. It's hard to believe that in one night, my life was changed forever."

We moved faster around the dance floor, our figures growing more complex. And when the dance was over, neither of us wanted it to end. The two of us stood at the center of the floor, face-to-face.

Hector looked me in the eyes and said, "You must understand that my family was privileged. We grew up with nannies and tutors for French and English. We were members of the polo club. At the time, we believed we were some kind of royalty. This is a problem that some of us Argentines have, wishing we were European. And wishing we were royalty." He laughed bitterly.

"When the generals took over again, things became difficult. Artistic families like mine were a target. In a moment like that you realize that some artists, and I am talking about many of my friends who were writers and musicians, are more vulnerable than you believed. And my sister. She had such a spirit. We were very close, only a year apart. She was a famous dancer in Argentina. Very talented. She was an icon in Buenos Aires."

"What happened?"

"My family lost everything in the upheaval of the time. I wasn't there when it happened but they were left with nothing, and were unable to bear the strain, emotionally, physically. My mother, father and sister. I should have been there. I should not have left them alone. Argentina has always been a difficult and temperamental country. I was away at the time, in New York, playing with a group. There was no reason to go back. I would not have been able to bear it."

"You could go back now. Years have passed. Things have changed."

His voice became low and gravelly. "I don't think so. What would I find when I went back? Memories. There are so many ghosts. I'm afraid they would follow me."

I nodded.

For several minutes there was only the sound of the music, and our feet scraping and clattering across the wooden floorboards.

Hector murmured, "Now I would like to hear about *your* ghosts."

I swallowed. It was now or never. I jumped in. "I also have a father from Buenos Aires."

"You have not told me your family name. Who was your father? Perhaps I ran across him. You never know."

I hesitated. I was scared, a little sorry about my deceit, and ready for Hector's *bronca*.

I choked out the word. "You."

He hadn't heard me. "Pardon?"

"You."

I waited for the explosion.

Nothing.

"My father's name is Hector Ferrer," I said.

He stopped dancing and pushed me back. He shook his head. "What do you mean? What are you talking about?"

"You and Marjory Nichols."

"Marjory…?" He peered at me, searching my face for clues, struggling to grasp what I'd just told him.

I said, "Marjory Nichols is my mother. I'm your daughter."

In a split second, Hector Ferrer became another man. His expression closed down and became unreadable and formal. He was now an embarrassed stranger. He went over to the stereo, turned off the music and said politely, "I'm sorry. I can't teach you again. You must leave. This has all been a mistake." He became flustered and said, "Go, you must go. I can't see you. Please, don't come back. I'll make sure you have a refund for any other lessons."

"I don't want a refund. I haven't paid for any other lessons."

"Please, just go." He seemed disoriented and confused. He turned his back on me and walked toward the little room off the stage. He went through and shut the door. I followed him and tried the door, but he'd locked it. I thought about banging it down but I'd had enough rejection for one evening.

* * *

On the way home from Los Tangueros, I stopped at the Eldorado Hotel. Just on the off-chance. The same accordion-faced receptionist was on duty. Sort of. I had to yell at him to wake him up.

"Is Rupert Doyle here?" I asked.

"He is," said the man. "Room five-thirty-three. But he'll be sleeping. Still getting over all the travel and the change of climate. He's come in from…Brazil," whispered the man, as if he were Rupert's proud father and Brazil was at the end of the universe.

I headed for the elevator. It was a Claustrophobia Special and groaned and jerked in a way that did not inspire confidence. It took just a little too long to arrive on the fifth floor, but at least I did arrive.

I knocked hard on his door.

A whole two minutes passed. No answer.

I tried knocking again, and calling his name softly.

After a few minutes of this, there was a noise from within.

The door opened and Rupert Doyle filled the doorway wearing nothing but a pillow in front of himself.

"Oh Christ," he said when he realized who I was. He jumped back out of the doorway and half closed the door. "Just give me a minute, eh, Dinah. Just let me get something on here." The door opened up again. He was wearing pants and not much else. "Come in. This is an unexpected…uh…pleasure."

I stepped inside. The room was chaos, bachelor-style, wall-to-wall books and photographs. An unmade bed. Clothes heaped on the floor.

"Excuse the mess. They have maid service here but I don't like them cleaning. I can never find anything afterward. Can I offer you something to drink? I've got a bottle of Bahia…"

I shrugged.

"It's a Brazilian coffee liqueur."

"Sure, I guess," I said.

"I just got back a few days ago. I was down there doing a piece on the rain forests." He snorted. "Ha. What's left of them, I ought to say. I didn't say goodbye, did I? I'm sorry I left in such a hurry last time we met… I have a glass around here somewhere. Patience." He went into the bathroom and came out holding a tooth mug triumphantly. He poured some of the liqueur into the tooth mug and some into an old paper coffee cup for himself. He handed the glass to me and raised his. "Cheers."

"Your health," I said.

"Have a seat." He pulled a chair over near the bed. I sat down. He perched on the edge of the bed and then gazed at me. "Amazing. I saw a little of it before but now I can see it more and it's so remarkable."

"What is?"

"The resemblance."

"Who? What resemblance?"

"I should show you something, Dinah." He stood up and began to rummage through books and papers on the shelves above the desk. "I haven't been completely honest with you."

"It's okay, Rupert. November was National Dishonesty Month. We all get a second chance to come clean in December."

He chuckled. "Okay, I found it." He came over to me and held out a color photograph. A black-haired woman in a gorgeous tight red dress held a tango dancer's pose. I peered a little harder at the woman's profile.

It was almost like looking at myself.

"Who is this?" I asked.

"An old flame of mine." He spoke quietly. "Alicia Ferrer."

"Ferrer? Hector's sister. You were…"

"We had a little entanglement. That was in my younger,

more headstrong days. Yeah. I have to say, you gave me quite
a shock there, Dinah, that first time I saw you."

"She looks like me," I marveled.

"She does, doesn't she?"

I gazed for a long time. "Can I keep this?"

"Hell, yes. Sure. She's a member of your family."

I put the picture in my purse, then got to the point.
"I've been taking tango lessons with Hector while you've
been away."

"Aha. How's it going?"

"It's not going. It's all over, I think. It was going okay. He
must have seen the resemblance too. Maybe that was why
he was being nice to me. Then I had to go and ruin it by
telling him who I was. He doesn't want to know me, Rupert."

Rupert shook his head and said to the floor, "Well. He
didn't handle the thing with your mother very well."

"What happened?"

"Well now. From the start?"

"Might as well."

He poured another dose of Bahia into the paper cup and
sat back on the bed. "I met Hector and Alicia in the seventies in Buenos Aires. It was at the start of the protests and
I'd gone down there to see what I could make of it, in terms
of a film. I was just getting started back then. Alicia and I
met in a crowd of demonstrating students and got involved.
She was a very single-minded woman. But what a woman.
She had such spirit, never a doubt about anything. She was
the kind to wave a red flag at a bull. You couldn't stop her.
Then after Alicia and their parents lost everything…I still
miss her to this day… Hector was without a home really.
He'd been knocking around with some jazz musicians in
New York, and then he was stranded with no home to go
back to, no family. He came up here to Canada because he
knew me through his sister. When he asked for help to stay

in the country, I introduced him to your mother. Hell, she was single. Well, we were all pretty young then. Your mother…wait a second now…has she told you any of this stuff?"

"She refuses to."

"Then maybe I shouldn't…"

"No, you have to. I have to know."

"Yeah, well, she'd been seeing a professor of hers. But I think he must have ended it with her. So the next thing I know, Marjory is marrying Hector. Not just to help him stay in the country, but to get a little revenge on the professor, I think. Except that she didn't know Latin men."

"What happened?"

"Well, in Hector's culture, the man has the wife, and then he has all the other women. As many as he can cram into his schedule. It wasn't a very successful marriage. It lasted just under a year. They lived together over there in your great-grandparents' big house. Your mother was taking care of them a lot then, but I don't think they thought much of Hector. He was too foreign for them. For a few months, I think your mother and Hector were really crazy about each other. And then Hector started being Hector and they fought like hyenas after that, until the marriage fell apart. Finally, Hector left, and I confess that I helped Marjory get rid of him. She enlisted my help and I gave it, because hell, I would have done anything for your mother. Unfortunately, she didn't really want me. She had decided early on she was going to raise you without the help of any man. Emotionally speaking, I mean. She did have men around, does still I imagine, helping her with the heavy work, but they were never allowed to get too close."

"That's what she's like now. They all think they have a chance with her and she lets them think it, but they don't."

"I could well imagine. I think her pride was badly hurt by Hector and his…uh…women."

"What about Victoria?" I asked.

"She let him do whatever he wanted. She picked up the pieces. She gave him credibility and helped him build his credit rating. They were a dance team. And she put up with the affairs and his bad periods."

"The drinking."

Rupert swirled the liquid in his paper cup. "Uh…yeah."

There was a long silence. We both took a few sips of our Bahia.

I put my glass down. "So now what do I do?"

"That I can't answer."

And then Rupert Doyle began to gaze at me a little differently, as if he were daydreaming. With a longing look in his eye, I thought.

In a fluster, I said, "I've got to go." He began to protest but I hurried out of the room with just a hasty goodbye and a promise to get in touch soon.

I took the stairs two at a time, raced out to my car and drove through the Vancouver streets, the Christmas lights everywhere blurring and making haloes in my tear-stained vision.

I could write a self-help book for others in my situation.

How to Find a Long-Lost Father and Lose Him Again in Five Easy Lessons.

My phone was ringing as soon as I came through the door. I considered not answering but in the end, curiosity made me pick it up.

A harsh woman's voice bit into my eardrum. "What did you say to him?"

"Who is this?"

"It's Victoria. Hector's companion. What did you say to him?"

"I…nothing. It's private."

"What did you tell him?" she demanded.

"Why? What's happened?"

"He came back from your lesson and went right out again. I know this look. It's serious. And it's Christmas. When this happens at Christmas, it's worse."

"He told me he didn't want to see me again. And that he wouldn't teach me any more lessons. So you have nothing to worry about."

"It's just as well then. You've brought nothing but trouble."

"Is that so? I think I have every right to bring all the trouble I want as I happen to be Hector Ferrer's daughter."

There was a thudding silence at the other end. Maybe she was doing sums. With all of Hector's alleged womanizing, perhaps I was one of many daughters.

Her voice was calmer when she said, "I had no idea. Who's your mother, if you don't mind my asking?"

"Marjory Nichols."

"Marjory Nichols," she echoed, as if it were all making sense now.

"We have to find him," she said. "This isn't like the other times. I didn't like the way he looked and I really don't know where to start."

Chapter Fifteen

Thursday

Lisa's sing-song voice was at my office doorway. "Only seven more shopping days left till Christmas."

"Please don't remind me."

"Oh, Dinah. There you go again. Always looking at the can't, won't, don't side."

I could hardly remind Lisa she was maybe about to be made redundant along with quite a few other GWI staff members. How could she be so flippant about it? It was nearly Christmas, for crying out loud. In the last few days since discovering Ian's plot, I'd given Green World International a lot of thought. I was curious to know when exactly that bastard with the pretty face was going to bring down his streamlining axe. Although I assumed he would wait until his office was finished so that he could call people up to the brand-new chopping block, one by one, in private.

"How's it going with Roly?"

She blushed a little. "You know, I can hardly believe it. But Roly is really a very nice man. We had dinner together at Umberto's last night and it was so delicious. Gosh. I'd never been there before and all the food was just so yummy."

"Umberto's?" I squealed. "Umberto's? Are you having me on? That place is bloody expensive."

"Oh, I know," said Lisa, smiling. "I kept telling him we should have picked someplace else but he insisted. Gosh, it was just wonderful."

"He insisted? Who paid, Lisa?"

"Roly did. I can't afford a place like that. Are you kidding me?"

Something was very strange here. Perhaps the Yellow Slicker Guy was pulling bank jobs on the side. It wouldn't be the first time Lisa had innocently hooked up with criminal elements.

I said casually, "Ask him if he ever runs across a drunk named Hector Ferrer out there on the street." A bitter little laugh escaped me.

Lisa became confidential. "You know, I don't know. I've never seen where he lives. He's awfully secretive about that. But I will ask him when I see him tonight. I promise."

Tonight?

Lisa, Lisa, Lisa.

That was the start of my hunt for Hector. Where do you look for someone who has decided to go on a drinking binge in metropolitan Vancouver? If that's where he was going to do it. Maybe he wasn't even in town. Maybe he went somewhere else to do his misbehaving. So I called up every connection I had, everyone I knew, every donor and corporate donor that might be able to help, including the radio stations, TV stations and the police and fire departments. They were all very nice to me. I explained that they had to find him because he was a musician and the cold and drinking would ruin his health and his pianist's hands. I told them that he was my father, that I'd just recently found him and now I'd lost him again and really wanted to get him back. I repeated the name Hector Ferrer several times over the course of the conversation. Then I sent each of them a MP3 download of "Scarlet Tango" just to clutter up their already cluttered computers, and so they'd know what kind of musician I was talking about.

Everybody was very kind and said they'd do what they could and I have to say, the response was fantastic.

Friday

I got the call telling me where Hector was. Someone had found him trying to get close enough to hug the sulphur mounds on the North Shore waterfront. He'd been deliriously drunk and raving something about going home. They told me that they had been holding him at the closest police station but that he needed medical attention and had been transferred to St. Paul's Hospital. They said that when they'd found him, he looked and smelled like a cesspool.

I got to St. Paul's within the half hour.

When I finally found the room, a doctor with scruffy gray hair and a bloated raspberry bon vivant complexion said, "We'll keep him for twenty-four hours or so. He's suffering from dehydration and hypothermia. We don't think his system and, particularly, his liver are going to be able to take much more of this kind of abuse. His health is severely compromised by the drinking. We recommend that he refrain from all use of alcohol in the future."

Oh, easy for you to say, Doc.

I went into the room. Hector was dozing. I pulled up a chair and sat down by the edge of the bed, just watching him, thinking. Ten minutes of this watching had passed when he opened his eyes, looked up at me and said, "Dinah. I told you to go away. I can't see you." He closed his eyes again.

Something happened to me. Everything that had been piling up, the whole *bronca* bubble, burst apart.

I raised my voice. "I'm not going away so you can stop saying that. You're my father, goddammit. I've been wondering about you for years and years, all my life, and now that I've finally found you, do you really think I'm just going to let you off the hook like that? No. You can forget it. It's time for you to take a little fatherly responsibility. I don't care if you have a death wish. You can't kill yourself like this, mourning your family forever. What about me? I'm here. I'm alive, and I want my goddamn tango lessons, goddammit. I want to hear you make more of that fantastic music before the gig is all up. You're talented and you're wasting it and in my world, that's almost a criminal offence. And I'm not ever going to let you forget I'm your daughter."

Hector feigned mild shock. "I did not say that you were not my daughter. Not yet."

"And just to make a point," I ranted, "I'm going to change my name. I'm going to change it legally to Dinah Nichols-Ferrer. I think that sounds pretty good, don't you? Dinah Nichols-Ferrer. What do you think of that, Hector? I can do it, and I'm going to do it, and there's nothing you can do to stop me."

Hector was trying to see me with his squinting red watery eyes. In a weary voice, he said, "I think perhaps you may have inherited the same stubbornness my sister Alicia had."

A nurse marched into the room at that moment, and gave me a mean look. "I'm going to have to ask you to keep your voice down or leave. This is a hospital, in case you'd forgotten."

"I'm leaving," I said, putting up both hands in surrender.

Saturday

I didn't tell Victoria that I had found him. I wanted to keep it to myself for twenty-four hours. So the next day, it was me who drove him home to the little house he shared with her. When she heard my car door slam, she was outside and at Hector's side of the car practically before I could open it. She didn't want me near him, but she couldn't do without my help in getting him to walk as far as the front steps. He was still weak and depleted from his misadventures.

Their house couldn't have been more different than my mother's. It was near the border with Burnaby in a treeless and undistinguished neighborhood. The house itself was small, fussy, tidy, and stuffy, a minimuseum of glass and porcelain figurines, ducks flying north along the peach-colored walls, treacly landscape and religious theme prints, furniture burdened with doilies and antimacassars and crocheted throw rugs, a grass-green carpet for whose protection we all had to remove our shoes at the door. Once the front door was shut, the heat was overwhelming, cranked up high.

I could tell that Victoria felt even more threatened by me than before. For me, being in that house was like wearing a warm sweater that was so tight it was squeezing the life out of me. I helped Victoria get Hector to the couch and when she told me she could do the rest on her own, that she'd had to do this dozens of times before, I was only too happy to get out of there.

As I was about to leave, I turned to Hector there on the couch and said, "I suppose there isn't really any way to convince you that what you did the other night was just so incredibly stupid and futile. I was going to give you a speech about how I haven't finished with you, that I'm only just getting started so you better not try any more of these tricks, but I suppose with a man like you, the best thing to do is just let it go. I would like to have had the chance to be your daughter and I *am* going to change my name. I like the sound of Dinah Nichols-Ferrer. I think it will help me to feel a little differently about myself, and it fills in that missing piece.

"I would like to have gotten to know you. Learn more about your life, have you learn about mine, but I realize that I'm probably just dreaming a very old and tired dream. If you want to drink yourself into a coma, then be my guest. It won't change anything, except the fact that I won't be coming to your funeral. And by the way, Merry Christmas."

He reached over to the side table for a packet of cigarettes, knocked a cigarette out of the packet, lit it, and through the smoke genies, began to give me the shrewd up-and-down, assessing me and reassessing me, with a streetwise glint in his eye.

I was in a very strange mood after I left Victoria and Hector's house. I stopped at a phone store and bought myself a sleek white combination cordless call-checking phone and answering machine. It was so long overdue. I had it gift-wrapped too, just for the sake of having it gift-wrapped, in a beautiful aqua-blue metallic paper with a silver bow.

Then I wandered with my gift bag through to Robson Square. I bought myself a caffe latte and went down to watch the skaters on the little outdoor rink. The place was Christmas Deluxe, with hundreds of colored lights and decorations and everyone rushing around in the dusk to get their shopping done.

Only five more shopping days.

A wire of panic shot through me.

My mother was out of the country, her students in charge over on the island. Joey and I had tentatively been invited over to Cleo's. But how was I going to get through the day, looking Joey, Cleo and Simon in the eye?

I would feel like a spy, the Woman Who Knew Too Much.

Maybe I should cancel and spend Christmas alone?

What would Thomas say about that?

I knew what he'd say.

Dinah. There is self-reflection and then there is antisocial behavior. You are walking a fine line.

I finished my caffe latte and wandered up to the centre of town again to take a last look in the wide windows of Birks jewelers at all the expensive rocks.

That was when I spotted them.

Penelope and Ian. Standing in front of the window with the biggest rocks on display.

The diamond engagement rocks.

I ducked behind a lamppost.

Penelope was wearing a black coat with an astrakhan collar, the same black coat, I'm sure, because the sleeves were a little short on her.

Ian was making circles with his hand at the small of her back.

How about that?

Secondhand man and secondhand coat.

Penelope was under review and they were looking at rings?

Monday

At Notte's we all ordered more pastries than were good for us.

Jake had three cream-filled maritozzis and a chocolate slice on his plate. "So, Cleo, where do you think you'll start looking for work? If you have to, I mean."

"I dunno, Jake. A job change wasn't in the program. Maybe I'll try phone-sex operator."

"I did that once," piped up Ida. "Nice little filler job."

Fran was helpful. "I say we just march upstairs and trash that fancy office then cut his nuts off. Bastard."

"Here, here," Cleo agreed.

Jake chuckled and turned to me. "So Dinah, you heard any more from Hamish Robertson?"

I winced inwardly. "Uh…well, he's still in Japan but he said he'd contact us the minute he gets back to town."

"So where's Lisa today?"

"On a date."

We all looked at each other, skeptics.

Thursday

Christmas Day was unseasonably warm. On my way out to the car, I saw a red rose blooming over the back alley fence. I ran over and plucked it furtively, then raced to my car before the rose owner could spot me.

When I got to Cleo's, Joey was already there ahead of me. He must have taken a taxi because he usually rode with me.

"If you'd come earlier, you could have had a champagne breakfast with the three of us," he said, looking much too twinkly for my liking.

"I have bad news for you, Joey. For all of you," I said a little louder. "Dinah Nichols is considering going on the wagon. Solidarity with the paternal unit."

Cleo made an extravagant entrance in black low-riders and a slinky red silk chiffon T-shirt. I gave her the red rose. "This is for the hostess."

"Wha…wait now, Dinah…did I hear you correctly? Paternal unit? As in a father?"

"As in a father," I replied.

"My God, Dinah. You've been holding out on us. Who is he?"

"His name is Hector Ferrer. He's a tango teacher and composer of…jazz tango."

"This calls for a drink," said Cleo. She sang out toward the bedroom, "Simon, honey. Did you know about this?"

Simon sauntered out, wearing the same gray velour bathrobe I'd seen him in last time. It was if he hadn't bothered to get dressed since then.

"No, I don't. Not a thing. You finally found your father, Di? That's cool. More champagne. We need to toast that."

"Just a little one. I shouldn't really be drinking with you guys. I'm thinking of going on the wagon, to keep my father company."

There was a silence and then Joey, Cleo and Simon all said in unison, "More for us."

Then Cleo said, handing me a full champagne glass, "But while you're doing all that thinking, drink this and help us toast."

I'd never seen Cleo so domestic. That day she did battle in her tiny kitchen, armed with oven gloves, an apron, and a couple of forks. For a while it looked like the turkey was going to win, but then Joey stepped in and saved the day by changing into SuperChef. Apart from a few charred roast potatoes and some flying carrots, the dinner was a relative success. The wine kept pouring, but rarely into my glass. I watched as my friends got oblivious.

Later, after we'd all eaten, there was a general sagging of the atmosphere. Joey had brought over videos of some of the TV shows in which he'd appeared and forced us all to watch them. After that, Simon went off to read a mountaineering magazine and I, not knowing what to do with all my half-sober energy, decided to tackle the dishes. And then Cleo wanted to dance. She was cross-legged down on the floor going through her CD collection, discarding names. "Joe Cocker, no, Barry White, no, how about Johnny Clegg and Savuka?"

"You can't dance to Johnny Clegg," I said.

"Yes, you can. Simon and I have done it. Simon? Where is he? Simon? We want your expert opinion on something." Cleo got up and went to look for him. I sat back and listened to Morrissey.

Cleo's voice shrilled from the other room. "I can't believe you're doing this. How could you, Simon? With Joey? I don't believe it."

I heard the low rumble of male voices. Cleo's rose above theirs. "No. I don't care what you thought…. Get out. Both of you, get out of here."

The problem was that now, Simon had nowhere to go and Joey had no car, so they both had to come home with me, leaving Cleo to stew and be upset on her own. It wasn't fair. I would rather have stayed behind with her to bitch about men, but it was also important that I get the two of them out of her sight before she started throwing things. Cleo likes to throw things from time to time. Just to stay in shape.

But at least I no longer had the problem of Finking Etiquette. Not for personal issues, at any rate.

By five o'clock, I had all Simon's equipment and clothes and both Simon and Joey crammed into the back of my car looking like a pair of guilty schoolboys.

I said to Cleo, "I'll phone you. We need to talk anyway." But I knew her. She would smash a few plates, then take to the clubs. That was what she did when her pride was suffering.

I helped Simon carry all his things into Joey's place.

"Where would you like to sleep?" asked Joey. "Bedroom or living room couch."

Simon's bags and climbing equipment were piled all around Joey's living room. "Couch is great. I'm beat. I haven't been getting much sleep lately."

I'll bet you haven't.

Both of them seemed a little edgy.

Simon said, "I think I'll pack it in early, Di. Just drop down where I fall. See you tomorrow then, eh?"

"Yeah, me too," said Joey, looking a bit sheepish.

"Okay, good night then to the two of you."

Except that it was barely nighttime. What was I going to do? It was five-thirty and I was frighteningly sober. I went back to my place and opened my fridge. It was nearly empty except for some nacho chips and a bottle of Diet Pepsi. Maybe quitting drinking wasn't such a good idea after all. I took a bottle of Barking Dog wine from the case, popped the cork, and poured myself a slug. Then I went over to the stereo and put on a new tango CD that I'd given to myself as a Christmas present. I flopped down on the couch and listened, imagining myself in some crowded distant *milonga*.

I left the lights off and let the music slither under my skin. A few beams of streetlight lit the living room but it was dark. I closed my eyes and stood up. With my eyes shut, I danced around my living room and down to the kitchen, groped my way to the kitchen door, grabbed the bottle of wine and then went out onto the porch.

It was much too warm for Christmas. I sank down onto the top step of the stairs to enjoy the damp air and the city smell of exhaust, curries and fried food, smoke fires and evergreen. Colored house lights made cheerful suspended islands and miniature coastlines along the alley and into the distance. And just when I was thinking that my Christmas Day had been a bit of a downer but could have been worse, Jonathan Ballam's brown Honda SUV pulled into the garage at the back of his house.

Chapter Sixteen

I watched him from above as he hauled his bag out of the back of the vehicle and walked confidently up to the kitchen door of his house. Just before he got his key into the lock, I called down to him, "Merry Christmas, Jon."

He looked up and squinted. "Dinah, is that you? It *is* you. What are you doing out there all by yourself? It's Christmas. Come down and have a drink."

I raised the bottle and grinned.

"Well then come down and have another…in a proper glass."

"But you haven't even arrived. You probably have a lot to do. You'll want to unpack and shower…"

"Dinah Nichols, come down here this minute."

"Right away." I tucked the wine bottle aside and raced down the stairs.

He met me at the back gate, not quite smiling, his wide face perturbed. He looked me in the eye and then interrogated me. "Why aren't you somewhere else? With your family? At your ancestral castle? Christmas is when you're supposed to get together with people."

"My mother's in Mexico. And you're a fine one to talk, Jon. What are you doing here? Coming back on Christmas Day? Don't you have people to be with? Where's Kevin?"

"Kevin had other plans. He won't be back tonight. And in case you haven't forgotten, cows don't respect statutory holidays and neither do vets."

"I haven't forgotten."

"After you." He ushered me inside and began to switch on the kitchen lights.

"I'm really glad you're here," I said. "I badly need someone to talk to."

"Well then, I'm glad I found you perishing on your steps."

"I wasn't perishing. I was listening to tango music."

"Aha."

"Aha?"

"Yes, aha. I'll pour the drinks. How about something fancy?"

"Absolutely."

"Good."

Soon he was pouring various kinds of high-octane alcohol into a stainless steel shaker.

"A good shake." He poured the liquid into two martini glasses and handed me one. "Hang on a sec. Low blood sugar. Need a fix. Let me throw some stuff onto a tray. Now how about some music?"

"Sure."

"Then take these and follow me, miss."

He held up the tray with bread, honey, and the cocktail shaker and went into the living room. I followed.

He set the tray down on the long low coffee table. "Now, don't argue. I'm the doctor around here and I know what's good for you."

"Yes, sir. But you're an animal doctor, sir. But I guess the big question is, are you an animal of a doctor?"

Jon grinned sadistically. "Fortunately, my patients can't talk so we'll never know, will we? Now come and sit down and tell the nice animal doctor all about whatever it was that so badly needed talking about."

He patted the brown leather couch cushion next to him. I sat down, sighed heavily and said, "A bunch of people at Green World International are about to become redundant. But it's okay because we're studying up on how to turn his hair green and ruin the leather seats in his Ferrari."

He laughed. "Nice practical solution."

"Yep. It's the same guy who's about to do it. It's his fault. The CEO. The one who dumped me. Or did I dump him? I can't remember."

"That's good. We could make a country-and-western refrain out of that. The One Who Dumped Me," he twanged.

"Are you making fun of my failed love life?"

"Sorry. That's rough, Dinah. Are you looking for another job?"

That's when I told Jon all about the dead peasants insurance. He stayed silent, straight-faced, and poured out the drinks. By the time I got to the bottom of the glass, I felt very relaxed. It was no ordinary cocktail I was drinking. It was a bomb. I couldn't stop myself from babbling on and on. It all came out, the whole messy package, everything that had happened in the last month including Hector Ferrer and the "Scarlet Tango."

When my litany of woe finally wound to a close, he said, "You know, Dinah, there are a lot of things in this world that are out of our control and all our worrying and fretting isn't going to make an ounce of difference." He put his hand on one of my shoulders and squeezed it gently.

"That feels quite nice, Jon. Please don't do it again. And don't make me beg."

"I won't. Here now. I'll stop doing it right away. But keep those black eyes of yours turned away from me so we won't have any trouble."

"I won't look at you." I had my back to him.

He did what I hoped he would do, put both his hands on my shoulders and began to massage.

"My God, that feels good. You better stop doing it right away. Where did you learn that?"

"Animal doctorin', Miss Dinah. We work out. We need big strong hands fer all that wrestlin' livestock to the ground."

"Like I said, you better stop while we're ahead."

He took his hands away.

"What are you doing?" I laughed.

His voice was straight again. "I could bounce a tennis ball off your back. I think what we need here is some serious massage. Stretch out a little more on the couch."

"I think this is a bad idea." I giggled again.

"Sure it is. It's a terrible idea, but stretch out anyway."

I did as I was told because I just had a taste of paradise and now I wanted the whole meal.

Kneeling beside the couch, Jon began to do the full screaming deluxe massage. At first I thought I was going to die, I was so knotted up and resistant, but then my muscles started to soften and turn to liquid. It went on and on, for much longer than I would ever want to work on someone else's back. I wanted him to do it forever, never stop.

But he did stop.

When I was in a luscious semi-unconscious place, almost on the verge of sleep, Jonathan's hands slowed down then rested gently on my back. I could feel him shift position and the sudden shock of the sandpapery touch of his face and lips grating on the place above my neckline where my sweater dipped into a V at the back.

I absolutely did and did not want him to stop.

And then I came to in a blinding flash and jumped up to

a sitting position. I was about to say, "Get your gay hands off me," but there was something in his amber stare that stopped me.

"I see something pretty good in there," he said.

"Your own reflection?" I ventured.

"How do I get inside?" he asked.

He moved his head forward to try to kiss me. I moved sideways and he banged his mouth against my injured cheekbone.

"Ow," I screamed. But I was pretty anesthetized. I was really screaming for how I thought it ought to feel.

"Oh, jeez, sorry." He took my face in his hands and examined it. That was when the real kissing started. It went on for an infinity. Then he stopped and pulled away again to look at me and I had a second of thinking, "Oh good, now we won't have to do this to Kevin."

"We better not do this, Jon," I rasped and laughed and pushed his hands away.

He was laughing, too. He pushed me back down on the couch and said, "No…uh…and we better not do *this* either." He was unbuttoning the front of my sweater. I was fascinated. I did nothing to stop him. He pulled it off in one smooth slow move.

"Or this." He eased my bra off.

"Or this." He reached across to the coffee table, grasped the plastic honey bear and squeezed the gold liquid in thin swirling lines around my nipples. I gave a little squeal but didn't move. I was having too much fun. With an artistic flourish, he turned the honey bear upright, put it back on the coffee table and bent over me to taste, moving his tongue everywhere.

Giggling with the sensation, I made a feeble try. "That… is…so…we…should…really…stop."

"Don't move, Dinah. I didn't get that last little bit." He put his head up and licked his lips, taunting.

"Jonathan Ballam, I'll bet you never ever did what your mother asked."

He nailed me with those eyes again and whispered, "No, I never did. I'm bad." Then he took a long time finishing the last sticky spots and raised his head.

Everything snowballed. We somehow ended up on the floor, rolling and laughing into the middle of the carpet. It was my turn now. I pinned him down and worked off his bulky sweater and then his shirt and then his Fruit of the Loom T-shirt and then the thermal underwear under that.

Boy, he had a lot of clothes on and they all smelled a little of cow and horse.

It was like undressing an onion. I thought I would never get to the bottom of them. But when I did, what an onion.

Sitting on top of him, I ran my hands over his washboard stomach and muscular shoulders. "I'm going to stop all of this in just a minute. I am. Really."

He pulled me into him and held me tight, not moving, just pressing me into his hard chest. "We're not actually doing anything. This is just a fantasy. Pure imagination. And in my fantasy, I haven't finished with you. Relax."

He made me roll back onto the floor on my stomach and started up the slow massage treatment again. This time my arms and legs got to take a turn, and somehow all the rest of our clothes ended up in a pile on the floor.

In a voice drunk with new sensations, I said, "Shouldn't I be taking a turn and doing this to you? It's not fair that I get all the good stuff."

He stretched out, pressed his body flat on mine and said quietly into my ear, "Whatever it is that we're not doing, we've only just started. Come with me."

I'd never had treatment like this before. Jon stood up and pulled me to my feet then led me up the stairs. At the top was a big bathroom, cream tiles with black trim, which had connecting doors to two bedrooms.

Jon turned on the shower, adjusted the temperature and gestured for me to come in. The jets of water gushed over both of us. Neither of us touched.

He turned off the water, stepped out of the shower, and dried himself off quickly with a forest-green towel. He handed a dry towel to me and watched as I rubbed it over my body. Then he took a small bottle from the bathroom counter and said, "Come with me, little girl."

He led me into one of the bedrooms—terra-cotta walls, a sparse Japanese feel to the furnishings—pulled back the jade-green bedding and patted the center of the bed. "Now just lie down here, and let the nice doctor have his evil way with you." I did as I was told.

He lit three fat scented candles. They smelled of laurel and tangerines. After pouring oil scented with cinnamon and other spices from the bottle, he warmed it in his palms and then rubbed it into my skin. Every part of my body was given close attention.

Except for the war zone between my legs.

If he touched that, it was guaranteed. All hell would break loose.

But Jon was keeping the peace. He went on keeping the peace for the next fifteen minutes. Touching every other part of my body, oiling it, working the joints, fingers, toes.

Then he took a little break and sat for a minute at the edge of the bed.

I reached out and stroked his arm. "Jon?"

He turned. His eyes were like the cougar's.

I said, "I absolutely do not, in any and every way, want you to touch me ever again. Everywhere."

And then, with his whole, slow, hard body, he had his evil way with me.

Except that it wasn't evil at all.

It was fantastic.

* * *

I slept until dawn in the embrace of those well-pumped shoulders. When I woke up feeling like another person, then realized where I was and what I'd done, I panicked.

My Inner Sex Police Patrol Woman screamed at me. "Dinah Nichols, do you have no self-control at all? You're in big shit now. You've gone and fallen in lust, no, something more, with your neighbor and he's gay and partnered. What the fuck do you think you're doing? Couldn't you have thought beforehand about how complicated your life was going to get now?"

Obviously not.

And even though I was quite sure that Jon was a thinking person too, thinking had not been on the agenda last night for either of us.

The guilt that had been brewing inside me bubbled up to the surface. Kevin would never find out about this and it would never happen again. I tiptoed downstairs, yanked on my clothes, and snuck out of Jonathan and Kevin's house.

Later that morning, on St. Stephen's Day, it was unusually warm again and the clouds were giving way to blue sunny patches of sky.

I would never be able to look Jon in the eye again. I would need to be out of the house for long periods of time. What if he came around looking for me? What if he knocked on my door? How long could I pretend I wasn't home?

That afternoon, I went for a run under steely gray skies. When I was still half an hour from home, the clouds burst apart and slushy rain pelted down, soaking and freezing me to the bone. I had thought that I could stay out there, away from my place just to avoid Jonathan Ballam. I wanted to. In one night, Jon had taken me apart and put me back together in a way that Ian Trutch hadn't been able to in a whole month.

I would have to stay out of sight.

Come and go at odd times.

Move out of the neighborhood.

I allowed myself the luxury of a small crying session, right out there in the middle of the park. And it's not true what Joey says, that the water level was two inches higher that night.

Monday

My weeping in the sleet storm was a bad idea. I picked up the flu and a bad cold and my Christmas holiday turned into sick leave. Somehow, I couldn't get worked up about the fact that I was using up all my sick days. I was not going to give Ian Trutch the satisfaction of my accidentally dying of the common cold and having the dead peasants insurance pay out. I was going to look after myself.

When I felt well enough to put on a dressing gown, I straggled over to Joey's by way of the balcony and knocked on the French doors. Simon opened them.

"Dinah, you look like shit."

"You don't look so hot yourself."

"Haven't been getting much sleep lately."

I gave him a twisted look.

"I don't know what I'm going to do. Cleo and I are in negotiations right now. We might be getting back together."

"You are?"

"Well, I think…I think…I want to be with her, Dinah."

"You do?" I was stunned. "Enough to give up fluttering around the world like a hundred-and-eighty-pound butterfly?"

He ran a hand through his messy blond locks. "Yeah."

"Well, you know, Simon, Cleo's my friend. She doesn't fall in love. Or so she would like to have us believe. But she's really hooked on you. I've never seen her so possessive."

"She is? You haven't?"

"Yeah. So don't blow it again. Don't cheat on her and don't abandon her."

Simon seemed more cheerful. "Did you need something, Di?"

"Joey must have some flu drugs around here."

"Oh, he does, and then some."

Simon sent me away with a nice supply. I took everything I was allowed to mix together then went back to bed.

I think Jon may have come to my door several times. In a high-fever dream, I remembered hearing knocking and his voice calling my name. But even if I'd had the strength to get up and answer the door, I wouldn't have had the strength to think up something to say to him. Because I didn't know what to say to him. I was afraid to look at him.

Monday (of the following week)

By the end of the first round of sniffles and coughing, I was perky enough to stay propped up on the couch to watch daytime TV and listen to music. But I still wasn't in the mood for visits. I had a hard enough time just reaching for a box of Kleenex.

Ida, my second pair of eyes, called me to keep me filled in. "We are missing you something awful. Ian didn't realize how much you do till you're not here. That'll teach him. Ha! And you should see that office of his. Got the cleaners to let me in. Gonna throw my grandson's bar mitzvah in there. No axings yet. Oh, and I should mention, your best pal Penelope? She is not a happy little girl."

I had just put on "Scarlet Tango." I'd been finding more and more of Hector's music from his young New York jazz days. I was settling back to listen when somebody knocked on my door. I decided to give in and answer because you never know when there could be a gas leak in the building. Or a fire.

"Yes?" I croaked.

A girl's voice asked, "Dinah Nichols? Are you in there?"

"Yes. Who is it?"

"It's Penelope."

I would have happily opted for the gas leak. It would have been more fun.

"Penelope who?"

"Longhurst. Penelope Longhurst. Stop pretending you don't know me."

"Surely not the same Penelope who works at Green World International?"

"Please, can I come in?"

"The same Penelope who doesn't know what she's talking about half the time?"

"I'm sorry if I hurt your feelings with that man-eater comment. I apologize."

"My feelings? I have no feelings."

"Please, Dinah, let me come in. I have to talk to you."

"I can't. I'm a sad, pathetic, desperate woman."

"I said I was sorry."

"Only if you crawl on all fours and lick the porch floor all the way."

Through a faint, wet, wobbly voice, I heard her say, "I'm already down on my knees and I'm really, really sorry. Your porch floor tastes disgusting."

"What? What was that I heard? Irony? Humility? From Penelope Longhurst?"

That was enough for me.

"C'mon in," I said.

I opened the door to find Penelope looking humble, ugly almost. Her face was flushed, and her eyes were red and swollen.

We were like a set of matching bookends.

"Penelope." I sniffed.

"Ask me in," she said.

"Okay." I stepped aside and let her pass.

She went straight to the front of my apartment and my

dining room table and slumped down into one of the chairs. She wouldn't look up at me but started digging in her purse and bringing out ugly little balled-up Kleenexes, wiping her running nose, which was already giving Rudolph's famous reindeer nose some hot competition.

I was afraid to ask, but took the plunge anyway. "What's wrong, Penelope?"

A low wail came from her and then the tearful words, "I've been so stupid."

I wasn't about to contradict her.

"What's happened?"

"I'm hoping you can help me, Dinah."

"Go cry on Lisa's shoulder. She's good with charity cases."

"Lisa said I should come to you."

I stared at Penelope for a long time. I knew what Lisa was doing. She was trying to make peace on earth. With her own two hands. By getting Penelope and me to talk.

I continued to stare and wipe my own dribbling nose.

She said, "I know nothing about these kinds of things."

"Help you with what?"

"I'm…oh, God…I feel so stupid having to say this to you. I just didn't know who to turn to. You see, I don't really know anyone here…."

"What's the problem?"

"I'm…pregnant."

She'd stopped crying but this was worse. She seemed small and pinched as if she were about to retreat into herself and then disappear forever.

"Why are you calling on me? I didn't get you knocked up."

She started to snivel, her shoulders heaving uncontrollably.

Guilt. In case you didn't know, it works on me every time.

"Sorry, Penelope."

"I just thought…"

"What?"

"I thought you might have more experience in this kind of thing."

"This kind of thing? What kind of thing? Making babies?"

"Things to do with…sex."

It was time to pull out my *bronca* and give it a good buffing up. "Well, why would you think that?"

"Just that your…reputation…"

I exploded. "Jesus, Penelope, what is with you? What is all this bullshit about my reputation? Where is all this coming from?"

"Well…" she sniffed, "I was at an ice-breaker just after I arrived. It was for the Young Entrepreneurs…"

"Aaaagh. The Young Entrepreneurs always say they're going to give and then don't. We lost money on them. I want nothing more to do with the Young Entrepreneurs."

"Anyway… I met this man who said he knew you. Really well. He knew all about you and the different men in your life."

"The different what in my what?"

"Men in your life."

"Oh," I said, coolly, "There are so many of them. Hundreds and hundreds. What was this guy's name?"

"Michael something."

The penny dropped after a second of flu-fogged consideration.

Mike.

My ex-Mike.

I am not a violent person.

But Mike was D-E-A-D.

I went over and sat down at the dining room table beside her. "Who's the father?"

She looked at me aghast. "You *know* who the father is. How could you?"

"It was a joke…sort of."

"Ha-ha," she wailed through fresh tears.

"Ian, eh?"

She nodded.

"He nailed you. He seduced you. You gave in. All your great moral principles went out the window. That's the thing I've wanted to tell you all this time. Life is unpredictable."

She nodded, wracked by a new bout of sobbing.

"The thing that I have been trying to get through to you, Penelope, is that sex is one of those big unpredictable things. It could happen to anyone. Absolutely anyone. It's an atavistic impulse. It grabs us when we least expect it. That's why we have prevention."

Full-scale bawling now.

"Have you told him?"

She nodded. Her voice became tiny again. "He doesn't want to know anything about it. When I told him, he gave me this." She reached into her purse and pulled out a wad of bills then threw it at the wall. "I don't need his freaking money."

"You can swear all you like, Penelope. It's okay. I won't tell."

"No, I can't."

"That's okay. I'll do it for you."

I then called Ian Trutch every name I could think of, shouting them at the walls and ceiling, for Penelope's sake, because I'm sure it would have killed her to say them herself. I won't repeat them here. The printers would have to use blue ink to render them justice.

"What am I going to do?" she sniffed.

"Jeez, well, the options are limited." There was a long silence. "Can I ask you an indiscreet question?"

"I suppose…"

"What kind of birth control were you using?"

"The rhythm method."

I shook my head. "Penelope. There are funded programs for this. It's basic stuff. Sex education, we call it. The earlier you tell people, the better. The rhythm method isn't a method. They call it 'unplanned parenthood.' They're finding that women can be fertile in any moment. The most unlikely moment. Not to mention the other risks that go with unprotected sex."

"He told me he loved me. I thought he was the man I was going to marry. I'm stupid, stupid, stupid."

I felt stupid for both of us. And a little sad. He'd never told me that he loved *me*.

There was a long silence. I said softly, "What do you want to do? How far along are you?"

"I took the test as soon as I realized I hadn't had my period. They figure six weeks. I got the results yesterday morning. I told Ian yesterday afternoon, and that was his answer. I was awake all night thinking about what to do."

"Do you want to keep it?"

"I'm too much of a coward."

"I had to ask you that. You have to know that it's one of the options. Lots of people keep their babies and things work out all right."

She shook her head and began to sniff again.

I grabbed the box of Kleenex and offered it to her. "I almost envy you, Penelope. No matter which way you turn it, a baby is life. It's an optimistic thing. A fresh start."

"That's a nice thing to say, Dinah, and I know you think you're helping. But you're wrong. It's not a fresh start. Really. You think it is but it's tied up to all the problems right from the start. That's what makes it all so hard. It's a life. But the baby is *his*. And I'll always know that it's his. And he'd know it, too. And it would make me his prisoner, or him mine. I couldn't live with that. I couldn't live with knowing it was his and that he was out there knowing it was his. And who knows? Maybe one day he'd decide he wanted to spend time with his child and start fighting me for it. It hurts too much. I want an abortion and I don't want my parents to know. They'd die of disappointment."

"No, they might not. They might like the idea of a grandchild."

Penelope became stern. "Well, I don't and I don't want anybody to talk me out of this. It's my own fault and I have to deal with it by myself."

"You're not by yourself. We'll get you through this thing."

"Thanks, Dinah." She sat staring into space and listening to the music in the background, then murmured, "Scarlet Tango. Hector Ferrer. I love this piece."

Who was this Penelope Longhurst? I didn't know her at all.

"You know this piece?"

"Yes. It's a shame he hasn't written anything lately."

"Hector Ferrer is my father."

"He's not."

Penelope came to, alive, interested.

"He is. Wait." I went into the bedroom and found my photo of Alicia Ferrer. "This is his sister, Alicia."

"She looks like you. Exactly like you. It's uncanny."

"So how…why?"

Penelope said, "I did part of my thesis in Argentine Spanish. Español Rioplatense. I know Buenos Aires. I've been there. I went with my parents. Everybody knows who the Ferrers are there. I came across their names in my studies. Alicia and Hector were part of a founding family, noble Spanish descent."

"Listen, Penelope, first we'll get this problem of yours

sorted out, and then…when you feel like it, I'll introduce you to Hector Ferrer."

But Penelope was still a beat behind. "I can't believe it. You're Hector Ferrer's daughter."

January

Chapter Seventeen

Sunday

I made battle plans for my return to work. Occasionally, I interrupted my scheming to go over to the side window and look for signs of life. But Kevin and Jon's place had been dark for a few days and there were no cars in the drive.

Monday

Before anyone else arrived, I closed my office door and pulled out the piece of paper with the number on it, then dialed.

"Vanpfeffer residence," said a woman's voice.

Bingo. On the first try too. I had the private number thanks to The Vulcan and a few limp promises and cyber-shenanigans. Would have to find a way to wriggle out of that *Star Trek* reunion in Bellingham though.

"Chaz Vanpfeffer, please," I said.

"One moment please. I'll see if he's in. Who shall I say is calling?"

"Ian Trutch's office."

"Will you hold the line please?"

I heard footsteps echo and recede and then more foot-steps advance. The phone was picked up. A woman's voice, irate, said, "I told you not to call here."

"Excuse me?" I said.

"Excuse me?" replied the other voice.

"Pardon me. My name is Dinah Nichols. We're trying to arrange a surprise birthday party for Ian Trutch here in March, and we would like to have Mr. Vanpfeffer come if he could possibly find time in his busy schedule to fly out for the party. It will be just fifty or so of Mr. Trutch's clos-est friends."

The woman practically cackled. "I'm Mr. Vanpfeffer's wife. And you're really pushing your luck if you can find *three* of his closest friends."

"Does that mean that Mr. Vanpfeffer will not be attending?"

"Mr. Vanpfeffer would be happy never to set eyes on Mr. Trutch again. Have I made my point?"

I decided it was safe to bring out the biggest weapon in my arsenal.

Honesty.

"Mrs. Vanpfeffer, I want to be perfectly frank with you."

"Please do."

"I work at the Green World International office in Vancouver, B.C., and we are looking into Mr. Trutch's past. He's the CEO here at the moment but we're not convinced he's entirely on the up-and-up."

Mrs. Vanpfeffer cackled again. "I can help you, Dinah. You're speaking to the right person. I never liked that man.

Let me tell you why. His mother was the maid in my husband's household. No father in the picture that anyone knew of. Not that any of that's a problem. Chaz and Ian did grow up together though. They were playmates. But when it came to money, there was a huge rift. Would you like to know how Ian Trutch put himself through Harvard?"

"Yes?"

"Paid escort. Male companion. Gigolo. Whatever you want to call it."

"Ahhh."

"He worked his way through my husband's social circles and I believe there was even an incident of blackmail, but it was never pursued officially. Why? What's going on at your office?"

"Have you ever heard of dead peasants insurance?"

"Oh. Oh dear, he's doing that again, is he?"

"He's done it before?"

"When he worked for Chaz. Needless to say, he isn't working for him anymore. When a company takes out those policies, it's supposed to reinvest them in employee benefits. That's the fair way. We did have two deaths that the company should have received funds from, but when we looked into it, we were unable to trace the money. Didn't anybody check Ian Trutch's references?"

"He was appointed by the higher-ups, so we never questioned it. Ian has already been at our branch in the east. He downsized it. And there was a death."

"What happened?"

"The woman was the type who got stressed out easily. They think she may have had a weak heart. Ian got on her case and wouldn't leave her alone. He kept pressuring her, calling her up on the carpet for her performance. I would say harassing her. She had a heart attack, went into a coma and a week later she had passed away. That's what I've heard, anyway."

"All I can say is, be very careful. Ian Trutch is legally astute. We couldn't get anything on him but he's not to be trusted."

"Thank you, Mrs. Vanpfeffer. Thank you very much."

I hung up and did a few minutes of deep and panicked thinking. Then I went from Ash's office to Lisa's desk to Cleo's desk to Penelope's desk and finally, down to Ida at the switchboard. I asked them all to meet me after work at Notte's Bon Ton.

Everybody except Jake and Ian, that is.

We were all assembled, armed with our coffees and cream pastries.

Lisa said, "Before Dinah depresses us completely with one of her miscellaneous news bulletins, I have an announcement to make." She thrust out her hand and wiggled it. A trinity of diamonds glittered on her ring finger. "I'm engaged. And you're all invited to the wedding."

We stared at her.

"Who's the lucky man?" asked Ida.

"Roly," beamed Lisa.

"The Yellow Slicker Guy?" I asked.

"Yes."

"That's…uh…it's…uh…pretty interesting…" I said. Everyone offered hesitant congratulations.

Lisa, Lisa, Lisa.

Lisa became solemn. "I know what you're thinking. You're thinking I'm nuts. You're saying, Lisa's about to marry a bag man. But you don't know him. He's got money coming from somewhere and to be honest, I don't care where. I don't want my bubble burst. I'm just going to live this thing for as long as it lasts. I love being with him. You haven't talked to him. He's wonderful and he treats me like nobody else has ever treated me. Nobody else has ever asked me to marry them, you know. Men don't exactly pop out of the woodwork every day. Not men who like big blond women over thirty-four. Why shouldn't I be married?"

"Yeah," said Fran, "why shouldn't she be married, too?

Why shouldn't she suffer just like all the other poor slobs who are stupid enough to get married?"

"Cynic," muttered Ida.

Cleo was looking at her watch. "I've got to go soon. I want to hear what Dinah has to say."

"I'm going to be the first to get fired."

"You what?" Penny looked puzzled. Since it was Penny's first real company meeting, she'd sprung for the goodies.

"I couldn't find Hamish Robertson."

"He's in Japan. We all saw him."

"You saw Joey Sessna in makeup on the *Mikado* set. I lent him my laptop."

Cleo said, "It's true. I helped."

Penny said, "When they find out, you're gone."

"It was just to buy time."

Ash said, "The project is supposed to start in the spring. There is no time."

"I'm sure I can still get to him."

Penny warned, "Dinah, Ian's going to find out about this."

"I want him to. But could I ask you a favor. Could you wait till next week to let the information leak?"

"You want us to leak it?"

"Thanks, guys. Oh, don't look at me like that. I haven't actually murdered anybody..."

Tuesday

It was surreal. And it couldn't have been better timing. Jake was off sick with what I had likely given him. Step One: everybody made a point of finding Ian and stopping him to ask useless questions and offer him misleading information, including me. I hadn't spoken to him since our breakup and I prattled on about Hamish Robertson and how thrilled I was with the donation he was soon to make. Ian was cool but polite.

I still got a little knot of regret in my stomach when I looked at him. It was such a waste. If I had been another type of woman, I might have tried to save him, make him repent. A quizzical look stayed on his face all day. He wasn't completely without instinct. He sensed something was going on but couldn't figure out what it was. Meanwhile, we were all working around the clock to distract him at one end of the office while at the other end (Step Two), we hurried to download every last GWI file to personal laptops and home computers.

Monday

Penelope and I sat in the waiting room of the Vancouver General Hospital.

"Have you ever had one of these?" she asked.

I kept my voice down. "An abortion? No. But a good friend of mine has. She said she kept a copy of *The Talented Mr. Ripley* with her the whole time and it helped her a lot."

"How was that?"

"The main character's problems seemed so much bigger than hers. He was forever having to dispose of the corpse of somebody he'd just killed, or untangle his web of lies, or be somebody he wasn't."

"I guess."

"Murder mysteries with serial killers work well, too."

"Dinah?"

"Yes?"

"Do you really have to? It's bad enough already."

"Sorry, Penelope."

That was when the nurse called her. Penny gave me a look but there was nothing I could say to make it easier.

Two hours later, I accompanied her back to her apartment. It was impressive. Like a turn-of-the-century European salon. Prints everywhere; impressionists, futurists, pointillists. Lace tablecloth, ornamental washstand and jug, fresh, fresh flowers, and when I went into her kitchen to make coffee and get her some water, I found an actual silver tea service.

I brought her some painkillers and the glass of water, and tucked her into her romantic lacy bed.

She looked like a ten-year-old kid. She burst into tears and said, "I feel like I've just murdered God."

"It's okay, Penny."

"No, it's not."

"It'll be okay. Really, it will. Trust me. Some things just take time. You're young. This will make you wiser. What else can it be good for? Nothing else. It's a trial by fire. And if there's anything you need, you know you're not alone. I'll be right here, rummaging through your drawers, eating you out of house and home, and reading your diary."

Penelope cracked a smile.

I added, "You know…"

"What?"

"About murdering God? I'm no expert in religious matters but there's one thing I'm fairly sure of."

Penelope said wearily, "What's that, Dinah?"

"One of the things God does best… I mean, one of his very best vaudeville numbers from a way way back…is getting himself resurrected. The circle of life and all that."

"Hmm. I suppose."

I stayed at Penny's place for three days, sleeping on the bed of nails she called her sofa. The hard thing gave me ardent dreams about Jonathan Ballam's magic hands working me over and over again.

Penny went into a deep depression the day after the abortion. One of those messy-haired, unwashed, undressed, nobody loves me and pass the donuts depressions.

"You're too young to get down like this," I told her. "At least wait until you're my age. Then you'll really have something to be depressed about." But there was no talking her out of it. My presence there was important, nevertheless. I had to stay on the premises to make sure she didn't put her head in the donut box and try to suffocate herself with the little cellophane window.

Thursday

The moment I had been waiting for had arrived. It was bad enough that I had taken off more sick days to stay with Penny, and now word of my little Hamish Robertson scenario had reached Ian. He paused in my office doorway and said, "Dinah, in my office. Ten minutes."

I looked around me. I was going to miss the cramped and tacky dive.

Lisa came by after him and in a hushed voice, said, "I just sent a little peace offering I baked up to Ian. It's a cake with a very special filling. I asked him to taste it right away and tell me what he thought because I was going to include it in a vegetarian cookbook and I valued his opinion."

Her eyes were like two bright blue buttons.

She waited another beat then said, "I iced it with chocolate Ex-Lax."

"Thanks, Lise. You're a pal."

As I walked through the main room, Fran sang "The Funeral March." I was cheerful, carefree almost. There was nowhere to go but up.

Without knocking, I walked into the Shah of Green World's palatial retreat. Ian was behind his enormous desk, looking meaner than I'd ever seen him. Lisa's cake, minus a large slice, sat near his elbow.

It came fast, almost out of the blue. "You're fired. Get your stuff and get out of here."

"What? No speech? No fancy excuses. No insults couched in metaphor. I'm very disappointed, Ian."

"Not half as much as I am."

I was calm although my *bronca* was trying to fight its way to the surface. "You haven't heard the last of me. I know what you're doing."

"Get out of my—" He looked startled, made a little moaning noise, and without another word, hurried out of the office in the direction of the en suite bathroom.

On my way back through to pack up my things, I gave the thumbs-up to Lisa. "He *was* full of shit, but he'll be better now."

Penny was still at home, depressed.

I was there when Jake called her with the news. "He's fired Cleo and you, Dinah and Lisa. The rest of us still have our jobs."

When she told me what Jake had said, I ranted, "That's not fair. He can't do that. You guys are the best."

Tuesday

I enlisted the help of Simon and Joey. I needed fit, young—well, relatively young—bodies.

This morning, I had to order Penny to get out of bed. "You have to help me with this. I can't do these banners by myself." I had commandeered her nice kitchen table. On pieces of old white bedsheet, sewn together to extend to a length of three meters, I painted, in huge carefully measured and stenciled dark green letters, the words Eco Girls Are Mad. Penny mooned around like an untidy phantom sleepwalker, getting high on the smell of paint and solvent.

Later, we told Penny to stop being depressed because we needed her. The way we needed her gave her a strong sense of mission. She was supposed to distract Ian Trutch. And there was no way he could refuse to meet her. Not after what he'd done.

She washed her hair, put on makeup and a new navy-blue pinstripe suit that I'd chosen for her. The skirt was short and the blouse showed a hint of cleavage. "This fits your new fallen woman image," I said.

"Don't remind me. I feel like a total fool." She was on the edge of tears.

I touched her shoulder. "C'mon now, Penny. Feeling like a fool is part of every woman's emotional repertoire. Don't worry about it. Now are you sure you can do this?"

"Of course I can do it. It's only a lunch."

"Okay. Keep him away for an hour if you can. And don't scare him off."

While Penny was out entertaining Ian Trutch and pretending there were no hard feelings, Simon and I were infiltrating his suite on the Gold Floor. There was just enough window space to stretch the banner across the outside wall and secure it by tying it to rock-climbing spikes. On my way out, I helped myself to his complimentary bathrobe. Okay, well maybe it wasn't complimentary.

The first Eco Girls Are Mad report got a two-minute slot on the six-o'clock news that night.

"Who are the Eco Girls?" asked the newsman, "and what are they mad about?"

We struck with the second banner at five o'clock the following morning. It was a fast operation. Simon had to perform some quick and agile acrobatics to secure the banner over the side of the Burrard Street Bridge without being seen. He dangled, almost invisibly, for at least three minutes on each end of the banner, over the black water, as he secured the spikes.

That day, on the noon news report, the newsgirl said, "And it looks as though those mysterious Eco Girls have struck again. This time on the Burrard Bridge. And people are asking, 'What are they mad about?' Could there be a new terrorist movement behind this?"

As Joey, Cleo, Simon, Penelope and I watched our banner star on Penelope's TV screen, Simon said, "Let's do the tower next, eh, Di?"

I felt giddy. "You think?"

"Yeah, why not? Let's do it tonight."

"We're going to be arrested anyway," I agreed.

"Might as well be hung for an elephant as a sheep," said Simon.

"You two are wacko," said Joey.

"Publicity, Joey," I retorted. "A little of it wouldn't hurt you or your so-called career."

But the weather outside turned wicked and by afternoon we were all sprawled out across Penelope's throw cushions and plush cream-colored living room carpet, discussing alternatives. Out of the corner of my eye, I saw Cleo slide over to Simon and pull him soundlessly toward Penelope's empty bedroom. "Hey," I hissed in their direction. "Don't tire yourselves out. I need you both in shape for this."

But that night we had to pass on the tower. A storm blew up with icy rain and sixty-mile-an-hour winds. Simon and Cleo went back to Cleo's place, and Joey went out clubbing. At least somebody was happy.

I went home for the first time in a week. The mail that should have been piled up on the porch had flown about in the storm and was plastered up and down the back yard and alley. I was dashing around in the slanted rain, making an attempt to gather it up when I saw Jon, standing at his back gate, trying to keep a battered umbrella over his head.

"Uh…hi…Jon."

"Dinah? Where have you been? I've been looking for you. You disappeared without a word. I thought something had happened to you. Is that the way you usually treat the men you sleep with?"

He seemed very pissed off.

"I don't know. How do *you* usually treat the men you sleep with?"

"Don't be facetious, Dinah."

"There haven't been that many men in my life."

And there are going to be fewer, starting from today.

"Well, I'm glad to see you're back. And I'm here. Whenever you want to talk."

I winced. "How's Kevin?"

"He's fine. He'll be around tonight. Come over for a drink. He'd like to see you too."

"I'm cutting back on the drinking."

Look what happened last time.

"Well then. Come over anyway, for a chat. A cup of tea."

And we'll both sit there and pretend nothing happened? Or perhaps Kevin would like to join us in a menage à trois?

"I've got to wash my hair."

Jon laughed, then dug the toe of his boot hard into the ground. "Well, some other time then." He turned and walked back to his house, closed the crooked umbrella and went inside.

I took my handful of soggy mail and walked carefully up the slippery steps to my place. I'd only been inside for a minute when the phone rang.

I ran to pick it up. "Where have you been?" said the Telephone Pervert voice.

"Out," I said, as I grabbed a pencil and scribbled down the number on the call display. "And you're going to be out soon, too." I hung up.

I knew this number.

I quickly dialed it back.

When they picked up on the other end, I said, "You are a sick man, Mike."

"Dinah."

"You just called me."

"I did not."

"I've got call display, you doughhead. It's your number."

"It was a joke."

"Pick up a pen, Mike."

"What?"

"Now, write down this number. It's the number of Thomas, my therapist. He's pretty good. Then when you've had some treatment, a lot of it, maybe we can talk. Bye, Mike."

Thursday

The good weather returned. Our last banner was destined for the Capilano Suspension Bridge, in broad daylight. Joey had changed his mind and decided to join us. In drag. My only stipulation was that we all wear green. We were Eco Girls after all. It was down to Simon, Cleo, Joey, Penny and me. Lisa was planning her wedding.

Joey minced back and forth nervously, in a tight stretchy emerald-green Catwoman meets the Green Hornet body-suit with high sparkly lime colored boots, green nail polish and heavy black eyeliner.

Nobody else was around which meant it was time. The banner was easy and went up quickly. Then Simon slung and tied all the cords over the bridge. We hitched the cords through our harnesses and got ready to dangle. Joey used his cell phone to call up the TV station and in an excited jock voice yelled, "You gotta get down here to the Capilano bridge. There's some green people dangling. It looks like the Eco Girls."

Simon helped us lower ourselves, then came down after us.

We swung back and forth like four pendulums, the deep wild forested ravine below us making the adrenaline pump.

"I hope somebody comes soon," yelled Joey.

"They'll be here," I said.

"Do I look okay?" called Joey.

"Why am I doing this? Oh why?" wailed Cleo.

"Because you love me, babe," said Simon.

"While we're waiting, let me tell you about the Whale Rub, Cleo."

"Okay, Dinah," she said meekly.

"When Simon and I were kids, there was this place down on the shore, a cleft in the rock where the gray whales used to come in and try to rub all the barnacles and parasites off their bodies. We were always warned never to go down to the Whale Rub. So Simon gets this idea…"

"Uh-oh," said Cleo.

"We get a couple of ropes and tie them to the tree near the rocks. When the whales came into the cleft, we ran down and along them, kicking at the barnacles to help them get them off…of course, when those huge tails came up, we scrambled…"

"Oh, Jesus," wailed Cleo.

"Just so you know what you're getting with a guy like Simon. He has no barriers and no rational sense of danger," I said.

"Forgotten about that." Simon grinned. "Fun."

"They're coming," I said, "Can you hear that? Sirens. That's good. It means we'll be arrested. Just as long as we're arrested."

Penny looked down at us from the bridge. A small crowd of spectators had gathered.

There was a flurry of noise that came all at once with the arrival of police cars and a TV helicopter. We let the police talk us into hauling ourselves back up and as they were trying to unwind us from all our cords, I gasped my prepared speech at the TV camera.

"Eco Girls are mad? Yes, we're mad about the way Green World International's management has decided to run the organization. We are convinced that there has been a mishandling of funds by the same management, the new CEO to be precise. Ian Trutch's recent decisions represent the usual insular indifference of those management elements who do not believe they will ever have to face serious water issues on a daily basis. Instead of bringing good news to the poor, we're bringing bad news to the rich. Water is everyone's concern. And I think we should all be very worried about Ian Trutch's plans to sell water, and who knows what other resources, abroad and for profit.

"We intend to restore Green World International's priorities by starting up our own not-for-profit with just such a focus. The new organization, Outreach United, will now be stepping up to the plate, not just on local issues, but on those global issues that are close to our hearts. I, Dinah Nichols-Ferrer, personally intend to—" And then a huge hand stuffed my head into the back of the squad car and we drove away.

At least they had the decency to put the four of us in the same cell.

Simon was calm. He kept saying, "Stop pacing, Di, and don't sweat it. They'll be here. They'll bail us out."

"It flopped. We flopped. And we'll probably have to spend the night in here." I slumped down onto the cell bench.

"The TV people were there, babe. They got it on tape," said Simon.

"I wonder how I looked on screen," mused Joey.

"Like a gay aphid," said Cleo.

Figuring we were going to be there for a while, I said to Simon, "So Si, tell me where you've been and what you've been doing for the last couple of years."

Late in the evening, a police officer came down and called out, "Dinah Nichols?"

"Ferrer," I corrected him. "Dinah Nichols-Ferrer."

I'd started the paperwork for the legal name change the day before.

"They've paid your bail."

"What about me?" called Joey, grasping the bars dramatically.

"Oh, sit down," said Cleo, sulking.

The officer unlocked the cell door. I turned back to my glum friends. "I'll get you guys sorted out ASAP."

Simon gave me a thumbs-up. "My lawyer, Di. Call him."

"I will."

I followed the officer out to the front desk, dying to know who'd decided to spring me. The little clump of people blocking my vision finally parted and when I saw who had come for me, I wanted to shout with happiness.

Chapter Eighteen

My mother, Hector Ferrer, Rupert Doyle and Penelope Longhurst were all there, having a heated discussion. They spoke rapidly, a machine-gun fire of sound that switched back and forth between Spanish and English. I was seeing my mother in another life. As the person she'd been before I came into the picture. She moved her hands in an unfamiliar way. I couldn't believe it. She and my father, the man she never wanted to see again as long as she lived, were talking. Or were they talking? Perhaps they were arguing. It was hard to tell. The main thing was that she actually had red blood running through her veins.

She turned and saw me. "Di Di, you had me terribly worried. Whatever were you doing up there?"

I was excited. "Did they get it? Could you see it okay? Could you see that it was us?"

Rupert laughed. "We could see it was you. You made the

six-o'clock news. So I called your mother and father. They paid your bail."

Penny just shrugged. "I came down to bail you all out, but they said they'd taken care of it." She leaned in to me and spoke softly. "I met him. I met your father. I met Hector Ferrer."

"So what are we going to do about the others? Let them rot in jail for a few nights." I reminded her.

"No, no. I'm dealing with it right now. Everybody pitched in." She went off to take care of the others.

Hector moved in on me, dragging on a cigarette. "Dinah," he said through squinting eyes and a veil of smoke, "That was a foolish and dangerous little stunt."

"Are you telling me you care?"

"I cared long before I knew your last name."

It was the nicest thing anybody had said to me in a real long time.

Tuesday

Unemployment was hard work. My wrist was tired from circling ads in the paper. My eyes were tired from peering through my side window at my neighbor, Jon, as he lifted weights and looked angry, all by himself. I fantasized about putting aside my common sense and running over to his house, sharing a cup of tea, wine, forty proof alcohol, anything, and ending the peace. Again and again.

The new not-for-profit, Outreach United for the time being, was nothing more than an idea and a few cardboard boxes full of files and data on CD. I must have been crazy to believe that I could subtract the whole of Green World International from Green World International, and start the whole thing up, under another name, and right away. I knew that the good projects take time.

Friday

Home alone. Still unemployed and manless. Freezing January was about to turn into cold February. And then I got a phone call.

It was Jake. "Quick, Dinah, turn on your TV. Channel Two."

"Okay, Jake. Oh my God. Am I seeing what I think I'm seeing?"

"It does the heart good, doesn't it, Dinah?"

"Does it ever."

We were watching Ian Trutch being attacked by the media. They wanted to know why he'd been fired and about the alleged charges of mismanagement of Green World International funds. He repeated over and over, "No comment," and kept trying to cover his face with his briefcase.

I felt so good there was only one thing to do.

Milonga!

With money I didn't have, I'd bought myself the tango shoes and now I had a dress just like the one that Alicia Ferrer wore in her photo. I had found it in a secondhand store and had a seamstress make a few adjustments. It was tight and scarlet, made of silk crepe, with a diagonal twenties fringe hem, tiny spaghetti straps, and a plunging back and neckline.

And even though I knew that it takes years to learn how to tango, and that you mustn't think, except with your legs, and that it's a subtle conversation between two bodies plastered against each other and traveling to Latin blues, and that I was really quite hopeless, a perennial beginner—I put on black fishnet stockings, pulled my black hair into a tight bun and drove across town to the *milonga*.

There was a party atmosphere and a mix of people. Absolute beginners, motley middle-aged men, overweight housewives and professional dancers.

When I came through the door, Victoria rushed up to

meet me. "Hector's beside himself. They've been playing 'Scarlet Tango' on the radio. Now that they know he lives in Vancouver, they want to interview him. They want him to play. Thank you, Dinah."

I looked over at him.

He was wearing his gangster outfit.

He came over to me slowly and raised one eyebrow. It was an invitation to dance. He took my hand and pressed my head to his shoulder. "You are just like Alicia. Don't try to dance. Walk and follow me."

I stayed the whole night and danced with whoever asked me. I was waiting for that magic to happen. Hector's eyes didn't leave me all night.

Sunday

There was a thudding at my door. An aggravated thudding, actually. Not a normal knock. It was very late, after one in the morning. I struggled up from dark green dreams to drag myself out of bed.

"Who is it?"

When Joey's strangled voice answered, "The fucking Red Queen, who do you think?" then hiccupped, I opened the door, quickly.

Joey was weeping copiously. At first I thought he was holding a patchy old bundled up fur coat in his arms, one of those things you might find at a secondhand store, but when I looked more closely I realized it was a dog, a male with some wolf judging by the long pointed muzzle and pale yellow eyes. The animal was in very bad shape. And Joey wasn't doing much better.

"My God. Come in," I said. I ran to find an old towel, threw it onto the couch, and motioned to Joey. "Put him down there, Joey. My God, the poor thing. Where did you find him?"

"I was coming out of Anastasia's and he was there on the street. At first I thought I was having a coyote encounter and I told him to get lost but he wouldn't. He was standing, but barely. I started walking thinking I'd lose him, but he followed me, Dinah, he followed me across the bridge and all the way home, then he collapsed. I couldn't just leave him outside our place."

"No, you couldn't." I shook my head. I was afraid I might start crying, too. Whoever had gone to work on the dog had done a thorough job.

"We need to get Jon," he said.

I panicked. But Joey was right. The dog was all bones. He appeared to have been starved and badly beaten. He needed attention.

"Who gets to go and wake him up?" asked Joey.

"You go."

"I don't know why, but for some reason it's always me that has to go."

"All right already. I'll go."

Like jumping into cold water, I told myself. Like pulling off a Band-Aid. Just do it really fast and it won't be painful. I raced down the stairs, out along the side path and up to their front door. I rang the bell. After a full minute the upstairs window opened and a groggy Jonathan stuck his head out.

"Dinah. What is it? What's wrong?" There was a huge stab of longing as soon as he said my name. More than a month had passed since our wonderful, ruinous St. Stephen's Day celebration.

"I'm really sorry to wake you up. I didn't want to but Joey told me to and I wouldn't do it normally if I didn't think it was absolutely necessary but it is. I mean, I know it's really late and you were probably sleeping, but we really need you to come…."

"Would you get to the point, Dinah?"

"It's an animal emergency."

"I'm coming," he said. "Just let me throw something on."

He appeared at his front door, wonderfully disheveled in a fisherman knit sweater and jeans and carrying his big black bag.

"Nice to see you, Dinah," he said brusquely.

"I'm sorry."

"Sure."

I started back up the path. "He's up here at my place. Follow me."

Joey was frantic by the time we got to my apartment.

"I think we need some sedative here," said Jon.

Joey was wild-eyed. "Really? But he's having trouble breathing."

"Not for the dog. For you," he said, and grinned. "Let's take a look here." He knelt down and began to look the animal over. He was grim and silent as his fingers moved carefully over the dog's mangy fur. There was a long silence and then he gave his diagnosis. "Canine abuse. I'd like to take these bastards and do unto them as they've done unto their dogs. Jeezus."

"Amen," said Joey and I.

Jonathan took his time, cleaning and medicating the dog's wounds and scrapes, checking over every inch of his body, looking into his ears, eyes, jaws, between his claws. A little sigh of envy escaped from me. Jon heard it and turned around.

"So," he said.

"So."

"Was it something I said?"

"No, Jon."

"Something I did?"

"What we both did."

Joey turned his attention to the dog but he was all ears.

"We did it well. We should try doing it again."

Amber eyes. Strong arms. Perfect touch. Who wouldn't want to try doing it again?

"You know we can't," I said through my teeth.

"Why can't we?"

"There's Kevin."

Jon laughed. "Yes, there's Kevin. What about Kevin? What does he have to do with any of this?"

Joey watched the two of us like a referee watching the star players at Wimbledon.

"You're gay, Jon. You live with a man and you're trying to hit on me."

Joey's eyes got wider. Suddenly, he looked very, very sheepish.

Jon poked himself in the chest. "I'm gay? Since when am I gay? Who told you I was gay? If I am, that's the first I've heard of it. Okay, if you want me gay, I can be gay."

"Uh… Joey told me you were." I pointed to Joey who was suddenly trying to become invisible.

Jon stared at Joey, his mouth open, then said, "You told her I was gay? Why did you do that?"

The words tumbled out of Joey's mouth. "Well, at first, I kept seeing you around in all the clubs, you know, with Kevin. I saw you with your arms around him one night, and well, after that, I just thought, I assumed you were and then later, I didn't want Dinah to…spend all her time with you guys… I mean, we were friends first, Dinah and I, before you moved in…best friends…it's not fair."

"But you knew," accused Jon. "Why didn't you tell her?"

"Tell me what?"

Jon screwed up his face and shook his head. "Kevin's my brother, Dinah."

"Your brother?"

"My half brother really. We don't have the same last name. Joey knew that."

"I feel an exit coming on," said Joey. He rushed to the door, wiggled his hand and said, "Byeee. I'll be back to check on the doggie when you don't hate me anymore." He shut the door.

Jon muttered, more to himself than me, "All this time, and you thought I was gay."

"But Jon, I've seen the two of you, you and Kevin, holding on to each other. Tight."

"So? Big deal. He's my brother. I can't hug my own brother?"

"Uh…"

Jon rubbed his eyes. "When Kevin's lover died, he was in pieces, completely broken up over it. My wife had just left me…"

"Whoa…wait a minute. Your wife? You have a wife?"

"Not anymore."

"Why did she leave you? Your wife."

"She didn't like animals in the bedroom." He grinned. "Anyway, Kevin and I decided to make the move back up here. The scene wasn't too good for him down in San Francisco. I could see that Kevin wasn't going to do anything but mourn, so I had to drag him out to the clubs. Obviously, dragging him out to the straight clubs wasn't going to be any use, so we kind of got into a routine of doing the rounds of the other places."

"And Joey saw you and then just never bothered setting the record straight."

"Yeah. I was really worried about my brother for a while there. He was out of the woods, physically speaking, but not so good emotionally. He's doing better now. I couldn't leave him alone. We had lousy parents, a lousy childhood. We only have each other."

He looked at me wistfully. "Except that I was starting to think it was pretty nice having you around, sort of one of the family, and a bit more…" He cocked his head to one side and shrugged.

I looked down at the dog, who was now dozing, then back

at Jon. I put my hand on my chest and said, "Doctor, I have this pain…right here…in my heart."

"So do I." He came over, put his arms around me and pressed himself hard against me. "But it's not all in my heart. Didn't you once tell me you were a man-eater, Dinah?"

I nodded and swallowed hard.

"So you better get started. Because contrary to what you've been hearing about me around here lately, I'm a woman-eater." His magic hands were on my skin now. "And I don't mind saying I've enjoyed every single bite." He kissed me, stepped back, took up a tango position then danced me across the room.

"It was you, Jon, wasn't it? That night with the Russians. You were doing the tango with me that night. Weren't you?"

"Lousy childhood. Parents who wanted to lease us to Hollywood as child stars. Ballroom dancing lessons. It's a wonder I didn't turn out like my brother."

I gave him a worried look.

"Scared you there, did I? Well, it's just as well you're going to be cutting back on the drinking and increasing the dance practice," he said, *giro*-ing me into the bedroom.

February

Epilogue

Lisa's wedding was held outside in Stanley Park by special permission. It featured white canvas pavilions, a trendy curly cabbage bridal bouquet, garlands of dried flowers, leaves, gourds and berries, small white fairy lights, a transexual justice of the peace, and a distinguished mix of all Vancouver's social classes, from top to bottom. The homeless people who were also Roly's guests felt right at home there in the park.

Lisa was dressed in a long trailing mock Renaissance cream velvet gown with moss-green embroidery everywhere and her long blond hair braided with green ribbons. She looked like an oversize wood nymph. We, her bridesmaids, Cleo, Penny, I and Ida the matron of honor, were dressed in similar gowns of rusts and greens.

Ash had deserted us all. She was off to New Delhi to get married in suitable style.

The groom was wearing a full frock coat, top hat and spats. Jake was there, too, having quite a good time picking my mother's brains.

Since Ian's firing, Green World was doing very well under Jake's leadership, but Cleo, Penny and I decided to go ahead with our new tiny, not-for-profit, Outreach United, although we planned to collaborate with GWI.

Because the wedding was outdoors, Joey's dog, Errol Flynn, was able to attend too. He'd made an excellent recovery after that night he'd followed Joey home and attached himself to him. Errol Flynn's wolfish qualities, as it turned out, were much in demand by the big studios in Brollywood. Joey, after years of hustling his butt as a two-bit actor, had finally found his lucrative niche as Errol Flynn's manager and trainer. Errol, according to the Brollywood voices, was destined for stardom.

A small orchestra of jazz musicians was brought together to perch on chairs on the cold dried-up grass, cold blue winter sky glowing through the bare winter trees, and play "The Wedding March." Lisa looked radiant and not cold at all (it goes without saying that winter is her favorite season), and her groom looked…well…like a normal man, classy almost. But it was when the justice of the peace, in his/her deep and ringing voice, asked, "Do you, Hamish Robertson, take Lisa Karlovsky to be your lawful wedded wife?" that I nearly keeled over.

Shortly after the ceremony, and the big kiss between the two, Jon came over to me and asked, "Are you all right, Dinah? You look a little pale."

It must have seemed pretty rude, the way I was staring at the newlyweds. And then Roly, aka Hamish Robertson, came strolling over to me and said with the slightest Scottish burr, "I've had my eye on you for quite a while. Lisa tells me we need to talk about your new not-for-profit, Outreach

United. The tough thing about having money is finding the best way to spend it."

Lisa interrupted. "I'm really sorry I had to keep it a secret. Roly wouldn't let me tell. He's such a kid sometimes. He loves amateur theatrics and all that spy stuff." Roly smiled at her adoringly.

So as you can probably imagine, no expense was spared to make the reception a success. Outdoor propane heaters had been planted all around the provisional dance floor in another part of the park near Second Beach. Colored lanterns had been strung up and lit the night like the fairyland that Lisa had hoped for. Tables had been laden with food, and while my father's latest orchestra, Hector Ferrer and the New Milongueros, stirred up the cold air, set it on fire, made it sizzle, Jon and I danced.

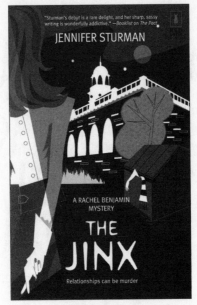

Lucy's Launderette

Betsy Burke

Ever had the feeling that your life is spinning
out of control? Lucy has! Despite her degree in
fine arts, she is working as a professional gofer
for an intolerable art gallery owner, her
free-spirited grandfather has just passed away,
leaving behind his pregnant girlfriend, and she is
the only sane member in her eccentric family.
Read LUCY'S LAUNDERETTE to find out what
finally puts Lucy back on the road to happiness.